DOWN IN THE ATTIC

DARYL NILBETT

For Mum and Dad,

for their love, support and guidance.

PROLOGUE

There were two images from the day of the house raid, deep in the forest, that Dane Cristian would never forget:

What walked out of the cellar and what he found in the attic.

Whenever he caught up with his fellow retired coppers at the local pub and they'd ask about that day, when he had joined up with the local Firearms Unit out of Southampton to help co-ordinate a raid on a large house hidden away in the New Forest, he would wave them away, change the subject, say nothing.

He'd never forget, but he hated remembering.

There was only one time when he had ever recounted the story.

One day his son asked, 'What's the worst thing you've ever seen, Dad?'

His son was in his mid-twenties at the time and had just graduated into the Hampshire and Isle of Wight Constabulary. He was taking a Constable position, working the streets of Southampton. Wet behind the ears, full of energy and enthusiasm. Raw, unprepared, vulnerable.

Dane understood the question. His son was enthusiastic, keen, but he was uncertain of what to expect. As a copper in a big city, what would he come across, what would he see?

What's the worst thing he could expect?

Dane had paused before answering, considering the question. How could he prepare his son for life in the police? What could he tell this young man to prepare him for what he would encounter, what he could experience on his worst days on the job?

He could repeat stories of car accidents, bar brawls, stabbings; go into the bloody details of what it was like to see human behaviour at its worst. Not a lot could prepare you for the experience of actual violence, during or after the event. The stark reality of violent acts was always diluted through the retelling of an incident, no matter how detailed the story.

After a moment's thought, he knew what he needed to say.

It was what both permeated his dreams and kept him up at night, what caused him to shiver and feel ill and what still nagged at the back of his mind to this day. It wasn't the experiences and images of violence. It wasn't human behaviour at its worst.

It was the presence of evil.

Over a dram of whiskey, over the sound of crackling fire coming from the hearth in the front room of their home, he began the story of Cheryl

1

Davies and her son, William. About what happened to them and the women and children before them.

About what walked out of the cellar and what he found in the attic.

His eyes were wet when he finished retelling the story, the bottle of Auchentoshan whiskey half drunk. They sat in silence, father and son, the fire crackling before them, warming their bodies but not their hearts.

Dane was glad he'd shared the story. It felt cathartic for him and useful for his son. His son, Arne, learned, albeit in only a small way, what to expect as a copper and how to deal with it, what may happen one day, what may not, but what he should prepare himself for. To a small degree at least, it had been worth dredging up the old memories.

That was the only time Dane had spoken of the events on that day up in the forest. He swore not to repeat the story again, not to the retired coppers at the pub, not even to his son.

That was the last time.

Until now.

CHAPTER 1

The door closes behind him and he leans against it. Shuts his eyes. Breathes out. Stands like that, held in the darkness behind his eye lids, until a memory flashes and he bolts upright.

He stops and listens.

The flat is quiet, like it always is. He lives alone. There is no one else here. There never has been. Still, he stops and listens.

The refrigerator hums. A distant siren. A flap of a bird's wings.

Nothing else.

The sounds of screaming. His own hoarse voice amongst endless tears. The pleading.

No, none of that. All in his mind.

The flat is quiet, and he must do what he has come to do. He is not looking forward to it, dreading it, scared by the process, but it must be done.

His home is a one-bedroom flat on the top floor of a converted school. Knebworth Road, Winklebury. From his bedroom window, he can look out over the train tracks towards the local golf course and shopping centre. Two miles to the east is the middle of Basingstoke. He's lived here for almost fifteen years now. It had taken months, but when he had found the rental in the paper, he knew it was perfect:

One bedroom, entrance hall, living room, bathroom, kitchen, loft storage. Converted school, quiet neighbourhood, car space, close to amenities. Perfect for single or couple.

The rent had been a little steep, but he made some lifestyle changes so he could afford it. The description had been too perfect and when he attended a viewing, he was convinced this was the place.

Loft storage.

He looks up from where he stands at the front door and sees the access point to the loft, a square door cut out of the ceiling. Entrance to the interior of the roof.

The loft: spacious, wooden ceiling beams, signs of previous insulation efforts. A barren floor that extends the length of the flat, the roof tall enough to allow anyone under six foot to stand, albeit uncomfortably hunched over.

Loft storage.

He prefers the term "attic" over the cited "loft". Loft suggests something cosy, appealing, functional. That isn't what he needs. The rest of the

3

description was accurate enough though. The attic is spacious but not enough for comfortable living, only big enough for storage.

He keeps it empty, save for a few essential items.

Looking up at the access point now, he feels his anxiety rising. The attic is big enough to create its own dark spaces up there.

He doesn't like the dark spaces.

In addition to the attic, the rest of the flat is perfect for a single man in his late thirties. Even one, if he had to admit, with simple needs.

As per the original listing, there are four rooms plus the entrance hall. A bedroom, a bathroom, a kitchen, and a main room where the television and sofa are. In a city, say like London, it would be out of his price range entirely, but here, in the outskirts of Basingstoke, he can afford it.

The bedroom and main room are south facing, looking down from the sixth floor towards the greater area of Basingstoke. The windows are large, almost floor to ceiling, and the natural light floods the flat throughout the day, removing all shadows and dark spaces. Another reason why the flat is perfect.

Kitchen and bathroom are small, but he doesn't mind. He cooks a lot for himself, but only simple meals: eggs on toast, spaghetti from a tin, sometimes he'll go upscale at Tesco and cook one of the oven ready dishes. Cooks it up and sits on the sofa, eating it in front of the television, watching documentaries, true crime and nature shows, predator versus prey, that type of thing.

A lovely flat in a nice part of Basingstoke. With an attic.

He knows he can't delay any longer. Time is important. He must start now.

He walks from his front door into the main room. The curtains are open, and the late afternoon light feels warm on his face. He closes his eyes for a moment, then opens them wide.

Time is important and should not be wasted.

Placing his keys and wallet in the basket on a side table behind the sofa, he walks into the kitchen, turns on the light, and takes a tall glass from the cupboard. He fills it up with tap water. The familiar sound of the pipes groaning as he turns the tap off comforts him.

He takes his time drinking the water. It is one distraction he allows. No point dying of thirst up there, even though he had been close to it many times before. Not here, not in this flat. Back then, in the old house, when it had happened for real.

He shivers, knowing that the time is near. He finishes off the glass of water and rinses it. Places it neatly back in the cupboard above the sink.

Returning to the main room, he stands by the window and looks down at Basingstoke. It is mid-afternoon and the town is busy. Cars on the roads, pedestrians on the pavement, golfers on the course. They all look like ants, crawling around inside a nest.

He draws the curtains, cutting out the light. The dark spaces move in towards him.

Walking swiftly now, he enters his bedroom, just off the main room. The bedroom windows afford him the same view, but this time he does not linger to take it in.

He takes his clothes off, carefully, slowly, one by one, folding them and placing them on his bed. He will wear them when it's all over.

Naked, he closes the bedroom curtains, bringing in the shadows again. Stepping out of the room quickly, he enters the main room, illuminated dully by the light coming in from the small kitchen. He will leave that as it is, allow a thin shaft of light to come into the main area of the flat, to allow him to move around without injuring himself. The light helps but it isn't strong enough to reach up towards the darkness of the attic. It will not impact what he hopes to achieve.

Up there, in the attic.

He walks swiftly across the cool floorboards, past the sofa and back into the entrance hall. Along the wall of the hallway there is a cupboard filled with brooms, boxes, and other household items. Stacked to the top with no room for even a small child to hide. He walks over to the cupboard and opens it. He manoeuvres several items around so he can access the step ladder and pulls it out into the middle of the hall, directly below the attic access door.

The step ladder is only three steps high, but it is tall enough for him to reach the ceiling and the access door. Rummaging back inside the cupboard, he retrieves a small plastic bag. Inside are several keys. He opens the bag and rummages around before fingering out a long key, cylindrical and smooth.

He grips the key in his fist, clasps the top of the step ladder and takes the first step. The metal is cool on his bare foot and he shivers. Another step and he looks up at the access door and shivers again. Reaching up, he slips the key into the small dark hole in the door and turns it. There is a click and he pushes the door in, taking another step up to give himself leverage. The door opens inwards and clangs against the attic floor.

Dust drifts down into his face and he wipes his eyes with his free hand. A cool gust of wind plays over his hair, the attic exhaling. The square of darkness above is complete. What it contains within those deep, impenetrable shadows scares him.

It needs to scare him. For the process to work, he must be scared. He will have the key, so he can leave the attic at any time, for practical reasons. It will take willpower to remain in the darkness, even when he cannot take it anymore.

He must take the fear, embrace it, for the process to work.

The process is important.

Taking one last step on the ladder, he uses his hands and arms to lift himself through the opening, the darkness swallowing his naked body whole.

Up here is the attic.

Up here are the dark spaces.

Up here, he will find the boy again.

The boy.

CHAPTER 2

Six Days Earlier

Roark checked her watch. It was close to three in the morning. They'd interviewed the bouncer at the Cross Bar, a new sports venue set under the arches between Vauxhall Pleasure Gardens and the Thames river, taken his account of the brawl that had put one guy in a coma and the other on an aggravated assault charge, and were due to head back to The Tank, as they liked to call the station in Camberwell, to write it up.

Roark wasn't planning on doing that.

Detective Constable Florence Knight, riding shotgun in the unmarked car checked out from the station, was keen though. She wanted to get back to her desk in The Tank and log onto the Wi-Fi, connect to her social media or dating apps or whatever, see what had updated in her life while she'd been subjected to the crappy 4G Network for the past few hours out on the street; cheap coverage that wasn't worth shit out in the field.

Roark liked DC Knight, really liked her, so Roark sympathised with her First World problems, but that didn't mean she was going to rush back to the station just to connect to the WiFi and refresh Knight's online feed. The fact of the matter was, Roark didn't want to give up the car for the rest of the shift. It was the only one she could fit in. The fleet was full of compact cars, and at six foot four, she was too tall for most of them to be comfortable enough to travel in, as driver or passenger. So whenever possible, she held onto this beautiful spacious four-door Hyundai as long as she could.

There was also something about driving around London at three in the morning that she looked forward to. She enjoyed rolling through the quiet streets late at night, traffic existent but not noticeable, a discreet lack of noise feeling like a captured moment of peace in the otherwise hectic and tragic life of living in a big city.

It was this love of night driving and her reluctance to return the vehicle that found Detective Inspector Krystal Roark and her partner, Detective Constable Florence Knight, pulling up at the crime scene on Bishops Street in Peckham only moments after the on-scene coppers had called it in.

'There they are,' Roark said, and stopped parallel to the panda car that was parked perpendicular to the street, blocking off the access. The two policemen present had not yet taped off the road, having only arrived minutes ago, so the parked car was the best alternative to controlling the crime scene.

Roark turned off the engine and stepped out onto the road. Over the wet roof of the Hyundai, she could see one of the policemen standing on the pavement, about five houses down, staring into the front yard of one of the two-story terraced houses. Further down the street, another policeman was knocking on doors. Beyond them, the street was dark and quiet. Closer to where Roark stood, house lights were on, inhabitants peeking out behind curtains to see what was going on in their usually uneventful residential street.

Roark knocked on Knight's window as she passed. Knight looked up from her phone, took her time unlatching her seatbelt.

'Anything exciting happening in the Twitterverse?' Roark said when Knight eventually opened the passenger side door.

'It's not called that anymore,' Knight said and pocketed her phone.

'I must have missed that headline,' Roark said as Knight stepped out of the car, her coat sweeping aside.

Roark coveted that coat. Long, dark, double-breasted, wool. Expensive. A gift from her mum. Roark couldn't remember the last time she had received a gift. Probably from her ex, in that early honeymoon period of their relationship before she married him and found out he was a complete and utter fuckwit. Nothing as nice as this coat though.

She immediately felt a little shameful. Knight's mother had gone through a tough time recently. Ovarian cancer. She'd gone through chemotherapy, a rough ride. Roark's mind flashed to the letter stuck on her fridge back home and she quickly turned to Knight.

'How's your Mum?' Roark asked.

'Better,' Knight said. She closed the car door, and they walked down the street, towards the crime scene. 'She went for her first morning walk in months since she finished chemo. She said she felt pretty good.'

'Glad to hear.'

'She's cooking up a storm most days too. She can't eat all the food yet, but she enjoys the process.'

'I still think about that pork belly she made when I met her. And those relishes, amazing.'

'You'll have to come see her again. She can have visitors.'

'I'd love that.'

8

They reached the policeman standing at the entrance to the front yard of one of the flats and Knight flicked her coat back to pull out her warrant card.

It was the length of the coat that Roark admired. Her own coat was almost long enough but a bit of a squeeze around the midriff. It was the best she could do, sacrificing length over a tighter fit, but it was old and fraying a little. She was due a new one; not just now though.

'Sergeant,' Roark said, not bothering with her warrant card.

'Ma'am,' the sergeant said, nodding.

They'd met numerous times before and could dispense with the pleasantries.

'Stay back,' he said. He pointed down at the footpath in front of him. 'Quite a bit of blood here.'

Roark looked down at the path. There was a wide smear of blood leading from near the curb and in through the front gate of the property. She followed it with her eyes, past planted shrubs lining the fence and in between two large trees obscuring the front of the terraced house, until she reached a large body laid on its back, hands and legs splayed like an overweight starfish, feet pointed towards them. The man was dressed in sweatpants and a T-shirt, the latter too short to cover the bottom of his large stomach. The T-shirt was drenched in blood, the source, and therefore, the cause of death, not readily visible. He had no shoes on.

'Who do I owe the pleasure?' Roark said.

'Male, mid-thirties, Caucasian.'

'Dead?'

'Hundred percent,' the Sergeant said. 'I've had a quick look, checked his vitals, but I didn't hang about, keen not to step all over the scene. Front door is unlocked, but nobody home. Blood on the road here suggests he was dragged from the curb.'

'That would've taken some doing, from the looks of him,' Roark said.

DC Knight leaned in for a look and Roark caught the scent of her perfume. She'd topped it up before stepping out of the car. Roark understood that. It wasn't an attempt to impress the uniforms. Some bodies were ripe from the get-go and a bit of fragrance dabbed under the nose helped keep the stomach settled. Knight had on occasion dry retched at a scene; a while back now, but she could still be a bit shaky. Roark was certain she'd get her cast iron stomach soon enough.

'Not dressed for this weather,' Knight said. 'And no shoes.'

'No,' the uniform said. 'From the looks of it, he wasn't heading out for a walk. Television's on inside. Looked like he was eating pot noodles and watching Netflix.'

'Living the dream,' Roark said.

'Can't see his house keys anywhere though. Haven't done a proper search, mind you. Of him or his home.'

'Looks like someone interrupted his night, gave him a nasty surprise,' Roark said.

'My thinking is he was cut over here by the curb and dragged up into his front yard, out of sight. No blood up by his door there, so it had to have happened back here.'

'We're certain this is his house?' Roark said.

'Not for certain, no. Educated guess.'

'Who called it in?' Knight asked.

'Someone across the way on the top floor spotted him.'

'They see it happen?'

'No such luck.'

'Gate was propped open like this when you arrived?' Roark said.

'No, closed. I did that so we could stand back from the scene but still see.'

'Interesting,' Roark said. 'Someone took the time and effort to hide him. From the casual passer-by at least.'

'Not many passers-by at this time of night, on this street. One of the quieter ones.'

'Any ID?'

'Not on him. We haven't checked inside yet.'

'Known to you?'

The Sergeant shook his head.

'You said he was cut,' Knight said.

'That's right. Well, cleaved is probably a better word for it. Took one to the shoulder, possibly the head too. My guess is an axe or a small machete.'

Roark heard Knight suck in her breath.

'I'd say we can rule out self-defence,' Roark said.

'SOCOs are on the way, ME too,' the police officer said. 'Excuse me. I've got to tape this one up before the locals start sniffing around.'

'Go for it,' Roark said.

'I don't envy your job on this one, Kris,' the sergeant said and headed back up the street to his car.

Knight was looking the other way towards the another policeman who was standing talking to a resident at his open door. She sniffed once, testing the air, seeing if she could smell the body. She looked past Roark into the yard, before turning away.

DC Knight was twenty-eight years old, smart, insightful, kind-hearted, addicted to her phone, loved her mum, stressed over her noisy neighbours, desk a mess, flat a tip, took pride in her appearance, wore an expensive coat and tasteless shoes, liked to date older men, annoyingly kept talking about having a family, a laugh both at the pub and on the job, cool in a crisis, professional, did the job right, good police.

Still, she was young and inexperienced. Detective Constable Florence Knight, affectionately nicknamed Gale, by Roark and no one else, joined the team six months ago. She was cautious to begin with but mixed in quickly, a valued member. She'd seen enough already, dead bodies, the lot, but still needed to harden up. Some things she saw on the job affected her, which was understandable. Roark would admit she was still affected sometimes too. The trick was not to show it.

'Gale, go help with the canvassing, could you? See what he's found out so far.'

Knight hesitated and looked back at the crime scene.

'Just until the SOCOs arrive, okay? It would be good to hear if anyone saw anything.'

'Will do,' she said, and walked down the street, pulling out her phone and checking the screen.

Roark watched her for a moment, then squatted on the pavement, a few feet from the smeared blood, a few metres from the body. She looked from the blood to the body, then back to the quiet residential street.

'An axe,' she said to herself. 'No one's subtle anymore.'

CHAPTER 3

Aaron Sparger woke with a start, a sharp intake of breath, a thumping of his heart, his eyes flashing open. He groaned, feeling like he was in the middle of a severe hangover, pain behind the eyes, his head pounding. He closed his eyes tight, and after a moment, reluctantly opened them again.

He stared into darkness, no sense of place, depth perception off kilter, the black mass both close to his face and far away. He slowed his breathing and tried to compose himself. Thoughts took time to form, his mind collecting itself, adjusting to the shock of waking, trying to deal with the throbbing in the back of his head.

He'd awoken suddenly. A bad dream maybe, or a sudden loud noise startling him out of a deep sleep. Or it was the powerful headache that had pulled him out of his slumber.

Aaron tried to remember what had happened last night, what he had been doing, what after-work drinks he'd attended and whether he'd made a fool of himself again.

He closed his eyes against the pain in his skull and winced at the thought that he'd gone ahead and done something *really* stupid. He tried to remember who was there tonight and hoped none of the partners had attended.

The thing was, he couldn't even remember what pub they'd gone to.

He groaned as his neck suddenly protested in pain. He tried to move, and his head rubbed against a metallic surface, hard and cold. A floor, but not the one in his flat.

Christ, what kind of night had he had? Where was he and how did he get here? Not only was his head pounding, his arms and back ached as if he'd been in a fight. What the fuck had he done this time?

Aaron felt the cold surface on his cheek and knew something was wrong.

He tried to move his right arm and something taut pinched at his wrist, rough, hard. He tried again and his arm would not budge. He felt new pain in his shoulder and Aaron realised that his arms, both arms, were behind his back. He couldn't move them. He turned his head to look, his right temple hard against the cold surface, but the darkness around him was thick, his eyes not yet adjusted.

Aaron pulled his left arm again, the tightness around his wrist biting.

Sudden realisation: he was tied up. Lying on his right side, both arms immovable behind his back, cinched with rope. His legs were pulled up halfway to his chest, and Aaron could not separate them. Moving his feet around, he felt the tightness around his ankles.

Aaron shook his body, ignoring the pain in his shoulders, his neck, his head, shaking both arms left and right, the binds around his wrists tightening with each struggle. He straightened his feet out, rolled onto his stomach and tried to pull his legs apart, but the rope did not budge.

He stopped struggling, face down on the cold floor. He breathed slowly and tried to think.

He hadn't been drinking tonight, he was certain of this now. He'd been working at the office, working late on the Reece & Co. acquisition. Working on his own, the other team members escaping early in the evening. On his own, in the office. No pub, no drinking.

The room lurched to the right and Aaron rolled onto his shoulder. A sharp stab of pain. He yelled out. The room steadied and he was back onto his stomach.

An engine revved, the sound of acceleration, and the floor rumbled and jumped.

Aaron's eyes went wide. A sharp intake of breath. A thumping of his heart.

He shifted his head to his left and stared out into darkness. There was nothing he could see. All he could hear were the sounds of a vehicle. All he could feel was the uneasy sense of motion.

Aaron moved so that his forehead was flat on the cold surface and closed his eyes.

Calm down, he told himself. It's a bad dream, this is not happening. This is not real.

Think.

He tried to recall what happened at the office, pushing past the pain barrier that clouded his mind. It had been late; he had been alone. He'd left around half past eleven, walking home as he always did, only living twenty minutes from the office. Remembered saying goodnight to Julian at the security desk, remembered walking under the trainlines, through the shortcut, under the arches.

Then nothing. He couldn't remember anything after that.

The floor jumped at him again and his head hit the hard surface, colours dancing behind his closed eyes. Something rattled elsewhere in the confined space, rolled, then settled in silence.

The engine revved.

Aaron's heart fluttered in his throat. He focused on keeping his breathing calm, but he was starting to panic.

This wasn't a dream.

The vehicle slowed, then stopped. The engine cut off. Aaron strained, trying to hear, but there was nothing. He opened his eyes and the darkness around him was pure. He closed his eyes and suddenly he felt like he was floating.

A door slammed, rocking the vehicle, and Aaron's eyes flashed open, and his breathing quickened.

He didn't know whether to yell or not. He didn't know if that would give him away or alert someone to where he was, someone who could help.

He felt panic reach up from his chest, around his neck.

There was a click, then a rumble, and Aaron instinctively shifted his head around, straining his neck muscles to see through the open side door of the vehicle. There was nothing, just a dark, formless night. Something swayed in the middle distance, and he could just make out tall trees moving in a silent breeze.

A shadow moved into view and Aaron screamed.

***

It was early morning by the time the Medical Examiner ordered the body to be taken away. Crime Scene Officers had finished cataloguing, collecting, and vacuuming up evidence in the front yard and the ME had finished her initial assessment of the body. She was pulling off her gloves as she walked across the road to where Roark and Knight stood, a team of white-clad men, the body collectors, disembarking a white van behind her.

The streetlights were still on along both sides of the street, houselights burning bright in the homes where the inhabitants had not returned to sleep. Birdsong could be heard a block over and the sounds of nearby traffic were picking up, but it was still dark.

'Carol,' Roark said, addressing the diminutive figure of the local Medical Examiner.

'Kris,' she said shaking Roark's hand, a strong grip despite her small frame.

'You remember DC Knight,' Roark said, gesturing to her partner.

'Of course,' ME Carol Xavier said with a smile.

Knight's face went red and Roark remembered it was Carol's crime scene that she'd recently dry-retched at.

'What have you got?' Roark said, moving on quickly.

'One dead male,' Carol said. 'Correction: one *large* dead male. Severely overweight. Obese. You should see his pantry. I can't believe people do that to their bodies.'

'How did he die?' Roark asked.

'Heart attack. Not due to the industrial sized bag of crisps he was mowing into along with a large bowl of curry noodles and a litre of Coke, but from shock and blood loss from two blows, one to the left shoulder, the other to the head.'

'Guesses on the weapon?'

'The cuts are short in length but deep. I'm guessing an axe or hatchet.'

'Okay, great, thanks Carol.'

'Better get back to the office,' Carol said, 'I've got one hell of an autopsy to do.'

'Ah, you love it, Carol,' Roark said.

Carol shrugged her shoulders with an impish smile.

'I'll send you a report later,' she said and walked back to her car parked up behind the police tape at the top of the street.

'Nasty,' Knight said. 'Sounds like we're looking for something like this.'

She turned her phone around, displayed an image of a short-handled axe.

'Okay, let the officers know. We'll need them to do a search up and down here.'

'What's next after that?' Knight said.

Roark scanned the scene, watched the numerous police officers standing around or conducting new interviews with the residents. Nothing had come from the initial canvas, other than the person who'd spotted the body from her second-storey bedroom window, so Roark had asked for the officers to do a second round.

Scene of Crime Officers were working hard in the deceased's flat after finishing off around the body. They would pull fingerprints, DNA, and fibres. Might tell them something, might not. The one thing they did confirm, after finding the man's driver's licence in his wallet on the kitchen table, was that the man's name was Corey Whitman, and the flat was where he lived. Roark had called in the name and gave it over to the team at the station to pull all they could on the victim.

She had also called her contact at Southwark council to see what CCTV cameras were in the vicinity. There was nothing obvious on this street or the surrounding residential area, but she had to check. Her contact would get back to her later in the day.

Until any new information came in, there wasn't much more to do.

'Tell the Sarge about the axe and then we'll head back to The Tank,' Roark said to Knight.

Knight nodded and pocketed her phone. She spotted the senior policeman halfway down the street and walked over to him.

Roark watched her for a moment, then turned back towards the flat. She sighed audibly. She'd led a hundred cases in her time as a Detective, had seen it all, and sometimes she got a feeling in the pit of her stomach that told her that a case was not going to be straight forward. Sometimes she was wrong, most of the time she was right. She had that feeling now.

The front door of the flat opened and a SOCO clad from head to toe in white waved a clear plastic bag in her hand. Roark walked over and as she approached, she swore she could hear the first verse of *Sabotage* by the Beastie Boys blaring out.

As she neared, she could make out what was in the baggie the SOCO was holding up, an iPhone, its screen flashing bright, the ringtone repeating itself.

'Someone's calling the fat man,' the SOCO said.

CHAPTER 4

A freight train with an endless trail of low blue carriages trundled along the bridge overhead, the sun peeking through the gaps, sharp and bright. A rare sight in central London, a reminder of a slower, gentler pace outside of the capital.

Roark pulled in behind a large white van, muddy around the wheels, just before the side road joined the main and continued through a high arch under the bridge. The narrow pavement was crowded in on one side by a high brick fence with peeling posters for obscure albums plastered over it. Graffiti made the album covers even more obscure. Roark parked the Hyundai and checked her notepad. Knight had her phone out, zooming in on a virtual map.

'Just up there, before the bridge,' Knight said, and exited the car.

The carriages were still rumbling by when Roark closed the Hyundai and clicked it locked. The sun flickered on her face. A cool morning, the hint of warmth from the sunlight, the smell of diesel in the air.

Head down, Knight led the way until they reached a long fence on rollers, open halfway, and a sign, dull white letters on a blue background splattered with pigeon shit.

'Peckham Van Hire,' Knight announced.

It was over four hours since they'd arrived at the crime scene in Peckham. Now, about half a mile south from there, they were just east of Peckham main road, in a side street, about to interview the owner of a delivery van hire business situated parallel to the overground train line.

The phone call had led them here. A call to the victim's mobile phone. The large man face-up in front of his house, Corey Whitman of 10 Bishops Street, Peckham, had received the call a few minutes past seven. The caller was in Corey's contact list, so Roark decided to let it go through to voicemail and noted down the number.

The SOCO holding the plastic bag containing the phone expertly accessed the voicemail without smudging any possible fingerprints on the screen and played it back for Roark:

'Corey, where the fuck are you? You said six o'clock, you fat fuck, and it's past seven and I don't see your fat arse over here. You better be on your way, motherfucker.'

Roark had called the number back and it was answered on the second ring.

'Hello?'

The caller was male, and his voice was rough, a heavy smoker or drinker. Or both.

'This is Detective Inspector Roark of the Metropolitan Police. Before you hang up, I need to speak to you about Corey Whitman.'

There was a long sigh at the end of the line.

'What's he done now?'

'Can I ask for your name, please?'

There was a brief hesitation and then, 'Warren.'

'Warren?'

'Campbell.'

'Thank you, Mr Campbell.'

'What's this about?'

'Mr Corey Whitman has been involved in an accident,' Roark said, keeping it vague.

'Ah, shit,' he said. 'I knew it. He's totalled my van, hasn't he?'

'Not exactly. Did he borrow your van recently, Mr Campbell?'

'Not borrowed, hired. I hire out vans and he's had mine for one week more than he paid for.'

'You were expecting him this morning? To return the van?'

'Yeah,' Campbell said, cautiously.

'As a matter of urgency, I need the details of the van you hired to him.'

Knight had appeared beside Roark after talking to the police officers about the axe. Roark motioned for her to take notes.

'Why?'

'We believe it may have been used in the commissioning of a crime.'

'That motherfucker,' Campbell said under his breath.

'We need to locate your van, Mr Campbell.'

'Yes, yes,' he said, annoyed.

He passed over the details, van type, registration. Roark repeated them out loud and Knight typed them into her phone.

'Where are you right now, Mr Campbell?'

'At work,' he said.

'We're coming to see you.'

Roark had taken down the address for *Peckham Van Hire* and finished the call on a gobsmacked Warren Campbell.

'Call it in,' Roark said to Knight. 'We need an APB on that van. Whitman was overdue returning it. My guess is the van was taken from him this morning.'

'And he was killed for it?' Knight asked, raising an eyebrow.

'Let's not get ahead of ourselves worrying about motive.'

'Okay, okay,' Knight said good naturedly.

Roark nodded. It was one of the lessons she banged on about all the time to Knight. Forget about the why until you arrest the guy, Roark would tell her on repeat, much to Knight's annoyance.

'Good morning, Mr Campbell,' DC Knight announced as she stepped up to the partially opened gate of *Peckham Van Hire*.

Mr Warren Campbell stood outside a small ageing modular building, hands in the back pockets of his oil-stained jeans. Dark chest hairs poked out from under a dirty white short-sleeved shirt, opened one button too many at the neck. He stood and stared, and Roark could see him sizing them up, her in particular. She was used to it, expected it, but it immediately told her a lot about Campbell: lad's lad, good old boy, father of a few and a wandering eye.

'Ladies,' he finally said, his voice grating from his morning cigarettes.

'Detective Inspector Roark and Detective Constable Knight,' Roark said, stepping up next to her partner, raising her warrant card. Knight did the same, her coat swishing. 'Can we speak with you?'

'I said so on the phone, didn't I?'

'That you did,' Roark said, and they both stepped over the threshold.

The yard was about two blocks in length, with a small office and a long shed running along the back. The shed was open with three filthy white vans inside, one up on a surface mounted lift with a man in blue overalls tinkering underneath, trying to look like he was not interested in the two women who had walked onto the lot. Several other vans were parked nearby in no particular organised fashion. The ground of the lot was overgrown with weeds and puddles, uneven and unkempt.

Campbell didn't move to meet them. Instead, he waited until the two detectives walked up to him on the other side of the property.

'Find my van yet?' he said.

'Not yet.'

'What did he do with it?'

'How well do you know Corey Whitman, Mr Campbell?'

'He's a customer. Not a very reliable one. To be honest, after this latest fuck up, I'm not going to deal with him anymore.'

Roark bit her tongue.

'How long as he hired vans from you?' Knight asked.

'Past few years or so,' he said. 'On and off. I only rent out vans for a week, tops. He always wanted them for longer, so he rarely returned the van on time. He's got a backlog of late fees to pay too, but I'm happy to write them off just to see the back of him.'

'Do you know why he needed the vans, Mr Campbell?' Roark said.

Campbell looked across at the parked vehicles in his lot and said, 'I think he was doing some delivery jobs. One of those freelance delivery type deals, you know, use your own private vehicle to deliver shit to other people's homes. Of course, he didn't have his own van, so he rented one of mine. That's fine, I have other customers that do the same, but they return the vans on time.'

'Not like Mr Whitman.'

'Nah. He had to pay up front, like everyone else, but rarely did I get the van back on time.'

'And on this occasion, it's been how many days?'

'A week overdue. Today. Not the longest time he's been late on it, but I'm at the end of my tether with that useless twat.'

Roark shoved her hands in her jacket pockets. The sun had disappeared behind a cloud and the slight wind was biting.

'How much does he owe you, Mr Campbell? Overall,' she asked.

'I'd have to check, but after this current fuck up, I'm guessing around a couple of hundred.'

'Could you confirm that for us?'

'I guess,' Campbell said. He turned, then looked back. 'What happened to my van?'

'We are in the process of locating your van, Mr Campbell.'

Campbell paused waiting for more, then walked inside the portable office.

'Two hundred's hardly a sizeable debt worth killing over,' Knight said.

'Maybe this guy's not the only one Whitman owed money to.'

The background check on Corey Whitman had come back on the short drive over from the crime scene. Corey was a colourful character, not unfamiliar with illicit behaviour. He'd been charged with a few minor offences, drunk and disorderly, an assault charge outside a Peckham pub a while back that was dropped by the victim. Was cautioned but not arrested for distribution having been present at a drug deal out the back of the local Primark. He pleaded he was taking a leak and had nothing to do with it and got off with a reprimand. He was small fry but would be the type to have dealings with dodgy characters, dealings he could have reneged on, dealings he could've got killed for.

Forget the why until you arrest the guy, Roark reminded herself.

'Two hundred and sixty quid,' Campbell said, handing over a thick notebook with coloured tags. Roark took the book, scanned the page it was opened at, noted the dates of overdue payments dating back almost a year.

'Here's a copy of the van details you asked for on the phone,' he added, passing over a photocopy of the van's V5C logbook to Knight. 'One of my older vans. Reliable, but old. Didn't trust Corey with anything else. But I've got other customers who need it.'

'Thank you, Mr Campbell,' Knight said, folding the page and tucking it away in her jacket. 'Can we come back to you if we have any other questions?'

'Yeah,' Campbell said, his brow furrowing, 'but what about my van? What's he done with it?'

'We'll keep you informed, Mr Campbell, but, as we said on the phone, it's likely your van was used in the commission of a crime. As soon as we locate it, we'll let you know.'

Campbell shook his head.

'I knew something like this was going to happen. You tell that prick to bring my van back and that we're done. I can't deal with dickheads like him anymore.'

'Thank you for your time, Mr Campbell,' DC Knight said.

Walking back to the car, Knight was on her phone, checking messages and emails. Nothing new from The Tank or the crime scene. No axe found yet. No bites on the APB for the missing van.

'What now?' she said.

'Back to The Tank,' Roark said.

'To do what?'

'Preliminary SOCO findings, CCTV footage, location of that van. Plenty to get on with. And you can start the case file.'

'Okay,' Knight said, looking down at her phone as they reached the car. 'You good?'

Knight looked up, nodded, and opened her car door.

Roark sensed something else.

'Something on your mind?' she asked when they were both seated in the car.

'I'm okay, Kris,' Knight said, head down, looking at her phone. 'Just worried about my mum.'

'Call her,' Roark said as she inserted the key into the ignition.

'It's okay,' Knight said. She put her phone away. 'I'll call her later.'

Roark looked at her own phone sitting in the well between the seats: just past eight in the morning. It was the end of their eight-hour shift. Technically, they were off the clock, but a murder investigation took precedence, and there was still work to be done. Concepts such as shifts went out the window. That said, Roark preferred to be flexible and knew Knight's mother was the most important thing in her life right now.

Knight had come so close to losing her mother, how it was only through quick action that they caught the cancer before it spread. There was a lesson there, Roark told herself, and shook the thought away.

'Find a quiet place back at the station, call her, okay?'

'Okay,' Knight said.

'And if nothing breaks on the case, you can go see her this afternoon. Take extra time. Our shifts are going to be all over the place for a while anyway.'

Knight turned to Roark, a thin smile on her face, and said, 'Thank you.'

'My pleasure.'

The Hyundai roared to life.

'I've got a feeling that this one might be complicated,' Knight said.

'Yeah?' Roark said, thinking the same. 'Could be. Let's see. No need to get ahead of ourselves.'

Knight put on her seatbelt as they pulled out from the curb, heading east towards Camberwell and the station.

'Who knows though,' Roark added, 'we could find the van, find the perp and sweat it out of him in the box by lunchtime.'

'As simple as that,' Knight said.

'As simple as that.'

They both gave a quiet laugh, knowing that it rarely was ever that simple.

CHAPTER 5

When the police arrive and buzz the intercom system outside the main entrance to the converted school of flats, he is in the attic, in the darkness, sweating and shivering, whimpering and crying, alone in the dark, alone and afraid.

It must have taken several attempts for the sound of the buzzer to reach him. By the time he flicks his eyes open and realises what is happening, the buzzing is incessant, urgent, aggressive.

Stumbling around, his knees scraping on the wooden floorboards of the attic, he reaches towards where he knows the access door is and fumbles around for the metallic key. His fingers find nothing, then his left hand knocks the cool metal of the key further out of reach. The buzzing continues, someone leaning in hard on the button outside. He grasps around desperately and eventually finds the key. In a swift motion, he inserts the key into the hole and yanks open the access door, the sound of it clanging against the attic floor deafening to his ears.

The step ladder is still there where he left it and he slowly reaches for the top step with his right foot. The metal of the step ladder is still cool to the touch. He gains balance and makes his way, naked, down the ladder.

At the front door, he pushes the intercom button.

'Hello?'

'Mr Howard Bloch?' says a gravelly voice over the speaker.

'Yes.'

'This is Basingstoke police. My name is Constable Montgomery. Can we come up?'

His heart is hammering in his chest. He has goose pimples along his bare arms. Remnants of newly awakened memories shift behind his eyes.

He buzzes the door, lets them up. He rushes to his bedroom, dresses in the day's clothes, the ones that hold a human stench, mild but present. He doesn't have time to choose anything else. When the knock comes from the front door, he opens it quickly.

They speak for about ten minutes, Constable Montgomery talking in a rough voice that is both clear and intimidating. The constable asks him a few questions and his voice wavers with each reply. The constable requests that he help their detectives with enquiries on an ongoing case. The constable does not go into too much detail about what the enquiries relate to, but they believe that he could be of some help, and his tone suggests that is enough reason for compliance. Eventually, he agrees that he will go with them to the police station.

The drive in the back of the police car is not what he expected. It is stuffy and smells of fried onions. The floor is sticky. The Constable and the driver don't speak to him. He had thought that maybe it would be a little bit exciting, driving in the back of a police car, but it isn't. Five minutes into the journey, he starts to feel claustrophobic, like he's back in the attic. The stuffiness is oppressive, the smell of the fried onions making him feel ill.

'How much further?' he asks.

Constable Montgomery cocks a finger and fires it through the windscreen at a five-storey flat blue and white building behind a small car park. A blue sign states in white letters: *Police Investigation Centre.*

The driver parks the car in front of a ramp that leads to sliding doors. Montgomery steps out and opens the rear door.

'Mr Bloch?'

He takes a deep breath and shuffles across the seat and out of the car. It is night out, cool and breezy. The constable walks him towards the station, a hand lightly on his back, imperceptibly guiding him. In the main reception, a uniformed officer stands behind a high desk, glasses down on his nose. Another man in uniform, taller, older, stands in front of a closed door to the left of the main desk.

They sign him in as Mr Howard Bloch.

In front of the desk, a third man, wearing shabby civilian clothes, trousers, shirt, jacket, and an unkempt moustache, slouches on one of the nearby chairs, seemingly asleep. He isn't though. There is a glint in each eye, a reflection of the dull interior lights.

'This way, Mr Bloch,' Constable Montgomery says, gesturing towards the tall officer blocking the doorway.

In the corner of his eye, he sees the slouching man sit up in his chair, stand up and disappear through a second door to the right of the desk.

'I'll take him from here,' the taller police officer says and pushes open the door behind him.

He is lead through the door and down a corridor with squeaky floors and blank walls. There is no one else around and all the doors they pass are closed. Near the end of the corridor, the tall officer stops at a brown door with a small window in it, crisscrossed with mesh.

'Through here, Mr Bloch.'

The room is small and dark. Too small, too dark. The dark spaces slither up towards him and he takes a step back.

The police officer flicks a switch, and the overhead light illuminates the room and sends the dark spaces into the corners. The bulb is dirty and the window at the rear of the room frames a scene of dense foliage, blocking out most of the artificial light from nearby streetlights outside. The dark spaces recede but do not disappear completely.

'Mr Bloch, please take the seat over there and the detectives will be with you shortly.'

He is left alone, the door closed behind him. He walks slowly, tentatively, around the table in the middle of the room and pulls a chair out from under it. He stares at the seat of the chair. It is dirty, black marks spotting orange plastic.

Before sitting down, he slowly looks around the room, taking it all in. There is not much too it. Four walls, one with a door, another with a window. Dirt, stains, pockmarks across all surfaces. Two orange chairs on either side of the wooden table, another chair in the corner.

Nothing to it except the dark spaces.

The foliage outside the window shifts in a noiseless wind. The darkness in the corners of the room swells.

The room is too small. The walls too close. He does not feel comfortable.

He jumps at the sound of the door opening and grips the back of the chair. The dishevelled looking man who had been slouching on a chair in the reception area of the station walks in, wiping his nose above his moustache. He looks at nothing but the chair in the corner and walks towards it, almost nonchalantly. He drops down in it, slouches, crosses his hands on his bulky chest and stares across the room at him, eyes lidded, pinpricks of light, reflections from the dirty bulb. His hands and chest rise as he sighs deeply.

'Mr Bloch?' comes a female voice and he jumps again. The voice is clear and startles him, but it dies before it reaches him across the table, as if the close confinement of the room soaks up the noise.

'Yes,' he says tentatively, as a tall woman in a dark coat closes the door to the room.

'Please,' she says, gesturing towards the chair next to him, 'take a seat.'

He does as he is told, the chair screeching on the floor as he pulls it out.

The woman places a pile of manila folders filled with paper on the table, takes off her coat and folds it over the back of her chair. She pulls out the chair and sits down. She watches him across the table for what seems like an eternity before reaching into her jacket. Her fingers are long and slender and move efficiently, pulling out a small notepad and pen.

She is intimidating. Sharp features, clear skin, a hint of wrinkles around the eyes. Striking eyes that are hard to hold, easy to look away from. Short blond hair, broad shoulders, and tall. Over six foot. Taller than he is. Her voice is clear and resonating before it dies on the table between them. Clear, but not harsh, soft but not quiet. If she was to shout, it would have an impact.

In that clear, commanding voice, she introduces herself and the man next to her, who still slouches in his seat. He doesn't catch the names but hears the word "detective" and accepts that these are the people that Constable Montgomery had requested he come down to the station to help. He is willing to help, but despite the calmness of the female and the disinterest of the male, he feels intimidated and entrapped, under pressure.

The male continues to stare at him from his slouched position. The female looks directly at him, takes a sharp intake of breath, as if to begin speaking.

She places a small device on the table, just at the top of his eyeline and says, 'Thank you for coming to the station tonight. I know it is late, so I hope this will not take too long.'

He doesn't know how to respond so he just nods his head.

'We are in the middle of a criminal investigation and your name has come up,' she continues. 'I would like to clarify a few things with you if I may. Your assistance in our investigation would be greatly appreciated.'

He swallows and the word 'okay' stumbles out of his mouth.

'I would like to inform you that I am recording this interview. The red light on this device,' she says, giving the small machine on the table a tap with a long index finger, 'will indicate that the audio of this interview is being recorded. Do you understand? As you have come to us voluntarily, I request your permission to record this interview.'

He stares at his hands clasped on the table and notices the knuckles turning white. He relaxes, unclenches his hands, and places them in his lap, out of sight.

'Can you please confirm your permission to record this interview?' she says, her voice slightly harder, slightly louder.

'I'm sorry, yes.'

'Thank you.'

The red light blinks on.

CHAPTER 6

For the second time in what felt like only hours, Aaron woke up in the dark. His reaction time was quick, yanking his arms up, shuffling his body back, anticipating danger, a threat, the trauma he'd gone through still raw and alive. He wasn't tied up this time, his arms and legs moving freely, but the ground he sat on and the wall he leaned up against was cold and damp, and it was pitch black, all around him, wherever he looked, jerking his head left and right.

He instinctively raised his arms in front of his face and turned his head, waiting for the impact of an attack. The image of the shadowy figure striking him was fresh in his mind, his throbbing face a reminder that it really happened, that the violence was not a nightmare. It had been real.

After a few moments, flinching and cowering, Aaron slowly dropped his arms and turned his head. The darkness around him was pure and perfect. He could not see anything. Pitch black, intruding, tangible in front of his face. Panic set in again, feeling the darkness grab at him, clenching his arms, around his throat, seeping into his eyes. He shivered, not just from the cold surroundings.

The darkness was the same, but he knew he was in a different place. There was no metallic floor, no sense of movement, no sound of an engine idling. This was different.

Shifting, he felt the hard damp concrete beneath him and a cold hard surface against his back through his thin work shirt. He was sitting up against a wall, knees up to his chest, and he could feel another surface to his immediate left, another wall he may have been leaning against while unconscious from the blows to his head. He gave a quick shiver, his bare feet on the ground cold and numb.

Disorientation remained, but he imagined he was in a corner of a room, a cold damp room with concrete walls and floor. A garage, possibly. The darkness remained deep around him, his eyes not adjusting or finding any light to adjust to. Maybe a warehouse, but he felt claustrophobic, as if he was in a confined space, the air stale and unmoving, the ceiling low and descending, a sense of water in the air.

And there was a smell. Food long gone off in a fridge, rotten fruit maybe, a putrid stench that took a moment for Aaron to notice but when he did, he could smell nothing else. With the lack of light, the smell made him feel a little dizzy.

A scattering sound moved from his right to his left, ahead of him, the sound of a mouse or rat. Aaron pulled his knees up closer. It wasn't the sound of a rodent. It was the sound of the man who had attacked him, kidnapped him and brought him here to this godforsaken place.

Aaron scrambled up against the wall, flinched, raised his arms again, let out a muffled shriek, not wanting to be hurt again, not wanting to die.

Nothing. No attack. No movement. No noise.

Not the man who attacked him, the shadow that had appeared in the open door of the van and struck him hard over the head.

Not the man. Just a mouse. Or a rat. Whatever it was, it scurried back, from left to right.

Silence, for what felt like hours. Aaron took a deep breath, felt pain in his nose. He reached up and felt it. He winced. It was wet, throbbing, possibly broken. He could barely breathe through it.

He needed medical attention. He needed something to eat. He needed to get home and safe and away from whoever had brought him into this deep, dark hole in the middle of nowhere.

Aaron moved from a sitting position onto his hands and knees, feeling the dampness seep through his thin work trousers. He felt around with his hands, touching cold damp concrete and nothing else. Head down in a crawling position, he felt his nose drip with snot or blood or both. He made to wipe it away with the back of his hand but stopped, knowing it would hurt and he didn't dare make a loud noise in reaction to the pain.

Aaron considered standing up, aware that he was in a most vulnerable position on his hands and knees, but the darkness around him was so deep. Unless he had something to guide him, he'd fall over. At that moment, he remembered the wall to his left, the wall that had propped him up when he was unconscious. He searched around for it, his fingernails scraping its hard surface. Flat hand on the wall, he lifted himself up into a standing position.

He felt dizzy again, unbalanced. The smell was stronger when he was in a standing position for some reason and it made him gag. His legs felt stiff as if they'd been forced into an unnatural position for some time. He wiped his mouth and took a deep breath to compose himself.

Walking slowly, his left hand guiding him, Aaron moved about fifteen small, stilted steps until he came to another wall, another corner of the room. It gave him some sense of scale but in his muddled mind and dulled senses, he couldn't compute the exact size of the room. Fifteen steps.

Maybe five metres. He couldn't think straight. One thing he hadn't done was bump into anything, as if the room itself was devoid of furniture or any equipment you'd find in a garage or warehouse. If that's where he was, of course.

It suddenly came to him. A damp, claustrophobic room with concrete floors and zero light ingress. A basement or cellar, that's where he was.

He couldn't recall any flats in London having a cellar, but he'd only lived in three places since moving to London when he was young, so it didn't mean that there weren't any. He didn't think it was common though. Maybe more common outside of London. He didn't know, but maybe that would explain the travel, in the back of the vehicle, the van.

A cellar, in an old house in the middle of the British countryside, with no one near him for miles.

That sparked Aaron into action.

The dark was suffocating but he was certain there was no one else in here. He'd have heard them by now. It was time to find an exit out of this hell hole.

Continuing to use the wall as a guide, Aaron padded with a little more urgency, his bare feet finding small pools of water and the occasional rough surface, but he didn't falter, didn't pause, until his left big toe kicked something bulky on the floor.

He stopped, pulled his foot back. Listened and heard nothing. He poked the object with his foot again, a rough surface, like material, soft in some places, hard in others. He tried to move it with his foot, but the object was long and heavy and would only move a little, lifting and then settling back in its place. When Aaron removed his foot, the scurrying sound was closer.

Aaron's first thought was he should just move around the object, step out into the middle of the room without the support of the wall and make his way past, continue towards where he hoped the exit would be, or at least a switch to light up the room. There was something about the feel of the shape on the floor that made him think again. Possibly it was a sack, filled with useful tools, a torch, something he could use as a weapon. Maybe it was a pile of clothes, a jacket to put over his work shirt, socks and shoes to cover his feet. It would be stupid just to leave that all behind.

He crouched down, leaning against the wall for balance, and felt around in front of him, searching out the object again. His hands felt something round and hard and cold, a rough surface with what felt like short fluffy material around the edges. He decided to lift it, to sense its weight, try and make out what it was. He lifted it a few inches off the floor, but it wouldn't budge further and it felt like it was attached to something much heavier, keeping it down.

His fingers repositioned on both sides of the object when his right hand flickered something light and malleable and he dropped the heavy object. It fell with a thud and a crack and Aaron stepped back.

His mind raced, thinking through the possibilities, wondering what it was, hoping it wasn't what he thought it was, deciding he'd have to try again, he was being such an idiot, panicking, letting the situation get to him. He reached out again and touched the ear, the eyes, a nose, a mouth, a chin and a thick, congealed substance around a cool, rigid throat.

Aaron yelled out, fell backwards, wiping the substance on his trousers, scrambling away from the body, hearing scurrying from all corners of the room, bursting forth in unison.

Sitting down on the ground, leaning back, his hands supporting him, he felt light claws run across his right hand and he screamed the loudest he'd ever screamed before.

CHAPTER 7

The Detective Inspector rattles off information – dates, times, places, names – in quick succession, for the recording she says, and he can hardly keep up. He thinks she asks a question, but the pace and tone of her voice hasn't changed, so he isn't sure. The red light from the audio recorder stares at him, makes him feel nervous.

'Can you please state your name and address for the record?' she says again, sterner, harder.

He starts to talk, his voice catching. He clears his throat and starts again.

'Howard Bloch.'

'Do you have a middle name, Mr Bloch?'

'No.'

'Address, please.'

'Flat 23, 17 Knebworth Road, Winklebury, Basingstoke.'

'Postcode?'

'Ah, RG22 2TR.'

'Thank you, Mr Bloch. May I address you as Howard?'

'Yes.'

'Thank you, Howard. Do you need a glass of water?'

'No, I don't think so.'

'Are you comfortable? Warm enough?'

The room is stifling, claustrophobic.

'Yes, I think so.'

He glances up at her and she checks her notepad. When she looks up again, he drops his gaze.

'Just for our records,' she says, 'have you, at any time, gone by any other name or names?'

The boy.

'Howard?'

'Yes. I have, I mean, I did.'

'And that name, please? Just for our records.'

He hesitates. Saying the name out loud makes him pause. It feels blasphemous to speak it aloud, as if it is a call to something evil that may answer, something evil long hidden, suppressed.

He glances at the red blinking light on the recording device on the table.

'Mr Bloch?'

'Yes, I am sorry. It was, ah, James William Stern.'

'This is the name on your birth certificate? Your birth name?'

'That's right, yes.'

There is a brief pause in the room that is almost tangible. He glances up again and the two detectives are looking at each other, the female with her head turned, the male, still slouched, with twin pinpricks of light shifting to her. They both turn to him and he stares back down at the table.

'Can you please confirm when you changed your name?'

The boy.

'I, ah,' he stammers. 'I'm not sure.'

'An approximate year is sufficient.'

'Um, I guess, I was ten or eleven. Yes, I was eleven, so that was in 1995.'

Her next question is delivered slowly.

'Can you please confirm your address at this time? In 1995.'

He feels confused. He can't think straight. The questions she asks battle with memories brimming in his mind, threatening to overflow, brought to the surface by his time in the darkness.

Time in the darkness. Searching in the attic. Searching and finding.

The boy. In the attic.

'Howard?'

'I – I can't remember exactly.'

The boy. In the attic. In the darkness.

'Take your time.'

'Yes, I remember. New Forest. Yes, Ravenscourt Road. New Forest.'

The boy. In the attic. In the darkness.

In the dark spaces.

'14 Ravenscourt Road, Newtown, New Forest?' she asks.

He takes a deep breath, his broad chest rising. He puts a hand on it until it lowers, and he breathes out.

The dark spaces where the pain hides. Physical pain, hunger, weakness. And neglect.

He clears his throat once, then again more forcibly.

'Yes,' he manages.

'Do you recall the duration of time when you resided at this address?'

Eight years old: a quiet family, a happy family, a home of light and warmth.

Eleven years old: pain, hunger, weakness. Neglect.

'I was eleven years old. When I left.'

'Okay, please listen carefully to me Howard. For the record, can you please confirm once again that your name was once James William Stern and that you lived at 14 Ravenscourt Road, Newtown, New Forest for the years 1984 to 1995?'

He nods his head quickly, glances at the closed door behind the female detective. He feels hot. Sweat forms on his brow. He does not like these questions.

'I'll need you to respond please, Howard. For the audio.'

'Sorry, yes, I lived there, until I was eleven, yes,' he says, the words tumbling out.

The female detective takes another deep breath.

'At this point in the interview, I would like to caution you, Mr Bloch. You are not under arrest, but you are under caution.'

'Okay,' he says tentatively, confused. 'I'm not sure what that means.'

'Please listen carefully and I will explain. Under caution, you do not have to say anything, you do not have to agree to continuing this interview, but I must say that if you say nothing, it may harm your defence if you do not mention when questioned something which you later rely on in court. Anything you do say may be given in evidence. Do you understand?'

He stares at his hands in his lap. He frowns. He feels sweat making its way down from his forehead. He is confused. Her words invoke a sense of significance, but they are difficult to understand.

He forces himself to look up at the female detective and says, 'What is this about?'

She cocks her head in response.

'Howard, please confirm your understanding that you are under caution for the audio recording of this interview, as I have explained it to you. If you wish that I repeat the caution, I am happy to do so.'

'No, I understand what you are saying,' he starts, meaning to ask again for clarification about what she is talking about, but the female detective quickly moves on.

'You may terminate this interview at any time under caution. You can leave the station at any time under caution. Do you understand?'

'I guess,' he says, looking back down at his hands.

'That said,' she goes on, 'I'd rather you stay for the interview. I have some questions for you that should clear up the matter at hand, and answer your own queries, so we would appreciate your assistance. However, for legal reasons, I need to put you under caution as I have just done so. Please confirm again that you understand your rights under caution.'

'Yes.'

'If you request legal advice or representation, this can be arranged for you. Would you like us to arrange legal representation?'

Again, he raises his head and this time, he pleads, 'Please tell me what this is about. I – I don't know how to answer your questions if I don't know what we are talking about.'

She taps her pen on her notepad three times, gives him a reproachful look, and he immediately feels like he has overstepped the line, said something he shouldn't have.

'Of course, Mr Bloch,' she says. 'This discussion is in relation to the disappearance, six days ago, of Aaron Sparger, resident of Elephant and Castle, London.'

'Oh,' he says, still confused. 'I don't think I can help you with that. I don't know anything about that.'

He glances quickly to the man dumped in the chair in the corner of the room. The man doesn't move.

'Well, that will make this quick then,' the female detective says. 'Please can you confirm whether you need legal advice?'

'I don't think so,' he says, genuinely uncertain as to the what the correct answer is. 'Do I?'

'That is a decision only you can make,' she says, a note of impatience in her voice. 'You may have legal advice if you like. This is your right under caution.'

He shakes his head, looks at the floor on either side of his chair as if he has misplaced something, looking for an answer to the question put to him. He just wants this to be over.

'No, it's okay, I guess,' he says, eyes moving quickly around the surface of the table. 'If this will be quick, I don't need anyone.'

'Okay, therefore, would you please confirm that you would like to continue this interview? Again, I will reiterate that you are under caution, not under arrest at this point.'

He stammers his reply but eventually agrees.

'Thank you. Please note for the record that Mr Howard Bloch of Flat 23, 17 Knebworth Road, Winklebury, Basingstoke, has agreed to continue the interview under caution and does not request legal advice at this time.'

She writes in her notepad and places the pen on the table. Looking up, she smiles at him.

'Thank you again, Howard. I apologise for that, but we needed to get that legal process out of the way before we can talk.'

'That is okay,' he says, feeling a need to please her.

'I will try and make this as quick as possible, but we need your assistance, Howard, so your time is much appreciated.'

'That's okay,' he says, with a little smile of his own, feeling a little more relaxed. 'I'm not sure how much I can help you, but I will do my best.'

'Thank you, Howard.'

She moves the recording device so that the speaker end points directly across the table at him. He feels his smile dissipating, the muscles in his neck tensing.

'While under caution,' she says, 'can you please repeat your name and address, including your previous name and the address of your first home?'

He does this.

'Okay, thank you. Now that's all out of the way, let me start with some questions.'

She picks up her pen again and flips over a page in her notepad. He can see words scrawled on the new page but cannot make out what they say.

'Can you please confirm your whereabouts last Wednesday between the hours of ten p.m. and two a.m.? That is Wednesday night, Thursday morning.'

The question stuns him. He feels hampered by what should be a straightforward answer. He can't remember what had happened last week, not now, with the two detectives staring at him in this small room with the dark spaces, not now with the memories so fresh in his mind, the memories of, of—

The boy.

'I – I'm not sure. Last Wednesday? Um, midnight, I would be in bed, I guess.'

'In your flat in Basingstoke?'

He stops and thinks again. Another simple question, but that short-term memory is fuzzy.

'Yes,' he finally says.

'Do you have anyone that could confirm that, please?'

'Um, no, I don't think so. I live by myself.'

He watches as she picks up her pen and, barely glancing down, writes something in her notepad. He doesn't think that this is a good sign; he thinks he has said something that is incorrect.

'Did you call anyone during that time,' she says, still writing, 'someone who may be able to corroborate your whereabouts? Was someone in the flat with you that night?'

'No, no,' he stammers, 'I was alone.'

She raises the pen off the paper.

'And did you call anyone, or did they call you?'

'No,' he says, positive that this is true. He never calls anyone. No one calls him.

'Did you accept any deliveries, order takeaway, anything like that, during this time?'

'I don't order takeaway. I cook my own meals. I go to Tesco to buy my meals. Sometimes those Tesco Finest meals. I never order anything.'

He frowns, wondering why he mentioned the Tesco meals. That's not important, she doesn't want to hear about that, does she?

'That's fine, thank you, Howard.'

As if on impulse, he places his hands flat on the table and pushes up to stand.

'Please sit, Howard. I have a few more questions.'

'Oh, sorry.'

He sits back down.

'Have you travelled to London at any time during the past month?'

He stares at the table, thinks.

'No.'

'Any time before that?'

'No. I don't like travelling to London.'

'Oh,' she says, 'why is that?'

'I don't like big cities. All those people. All that noise.'

'But you have been to London before?'

'Yes,' he says, 'I guess so.'

'And for what reasons?'

He frowns.

'I'm not sure what –'

'What was the purpose of your visits to London in the past?' she cuts in.

'I don't remember,' he says, searching for answers. 'I have only been once or twice.'

'Do you know anyone in London? To visit?'

'No,' he says, shaking his head.

'Were you in London last Wednesday? Six days ago.'

He thinks, pauses, confused.

'Didn't we talk about that already?' he says, frowning.

'Answer the question please, Howard.'

'No, I was not.'

The female detective opens one of the manila folders on the desk and slides across two black and white photos:

A mugshot of a white male with fat cheeks and thin hair.

A side-on view of a white van parked near a row of trees.

He holds his face still, looks at the photos, forces himself to think about–

The boy. In the attic. In the darkness. The dark spaces.

And the light. The small beam of light, pointing upwards through the floor. The light he crawls to, along the floorboards of the attic, crawling towards the light, the light that lets him see down into the house that used to be his home.

The boy crawls towards the light and peers through the gap and sees his father. His father, lying on the floor, on his side, a red pool of blood around his head, growing, expanding, covering the kitchen floor.

'Howard, tell me what you see?'

The blood.

'Howard?'

He jerks his head up, stares at her for a moment, shakes his head.

'I'm sorry?'

'Tell me what you see, Howard?'

'The photos?' he says, gesturing to the table.

'Yes, Howard, the photos.'

He looks at the photos again, sees only –

The blood pooling on the kitchen floor.

'I don't know what to say.'

'Do you recognise them? The man? The van?'

He looks at the photos again.

His father lies on his side, blood pooling around his head, his rifle just out of reach. His father, shot. His father, dead.

The boy leans forward so he can see past his father's head, and he sees the stairs leading down to the cellar through the open trapdoor.

'No, I do not,' he says.

'Pick them up if you need to. Have a closer look.'

He looks at the photos again but doesn't pick them up.

The boy stares down into the light, holds his breath, focuses in on the dark square of the open cellar.

There is a creak, pressure on a floorboard, on a step.

They are coming. They are coming out of the cellar.

CHAPTER 8

The rats scurried. It sounded like there was a legion of them, as if they'd crawled out of the dark corners all around him, newfound confidence fuelled by Aaron's primal fear. Little feet scuttled from his right, rushing towards where the body was, the rodents driven into a frenzy by the fresh smells released into the dank air from the corpse's disturbance.

Aaron backed up, shuffling along, pushing away with his feet. It wasn't just the rats that were horrifying him. The body, the one he'd felt with his own two hands, had sent him into a panic.

A dead person. A cut throat. The smell suggesting it had been down here for some time, at least a day or two before he'd found himself in the dark cellar with it. A day or two, but what did he know; it could be fresh, it could be weeks old.

The person could still be alive.

The scurrying of feet gave way to the sound of rustling and Aaron pictured in the blank slate across his vision large rats finding ways underneath the clothes of the corpse, searching out the putrid meat.

He turned away and dry retched, his stomach muscles contracting but nothing coming out. It had been a while since he had last eaten, a snack late at night in his office in Waterloo, an hour or so before he finally gave up on the work and left for home.

The walk under the arches around Waterloo station came back to him. The dark recesses. The van parked up on the side of the curb. The hand around his mouth. The clobber to the back of his head.

Why was that so clear now? Why was he remembering the detail so vividly?

Adrenaline. Pumping through him. The pain in his nose and head, the cold floor on his feet, the body metres from him.

He had to get out and he had to get out now.

The darkness was still impenetrable but there was only one corner he hadn't investigated. He'd been in the room long enough to have some sort of bearing, despite the panic he felt, so he knew which way to go. He took a step to his right, away from the body and the rats, and after about a dozen steps, he found another wall. Using the hard surface as a crutch, he stepped slowly along its length, heading for the final corner.

Each step was difficult, his foot almost quivering before being placed in front of the other, anticipating the feeling of something heinous: rats, skin and bones, blood. After about ten careful paces, he slowed, sensing the dimensions of the room, expecting he'd reach the corner imminently, the corner and whatever may be lurking there.

Raising his left foot, he brought it down slowly, holding his breath. His bare toes brushed rough, splinter filled wood, about three inches from the floor. A step, a wooden step. Aaron gasped, an intake of breath that was loud in the confines of the cellar.

The rats paused in their work, silent.

Aaron held his breath. Waited. The last thing he wanted to do was bring attention to himself, alert whoever it was that put him here to his revelation, his discovery, his plan to get away. If this was a flight of steps heading up, he'd found his way out.

Aaron realised it was already too late. His screaming, only moments ago, from the rat running across his fingers. His scream which was deafening to his own ears. His revival from unconsciousness had already been announced. The murderer already knew he was awake. The murderer was already waiting for him.

Aaron took his foot off the bottom step and it creaked.

A heavy lock thudded above Aaron's head, a bolt slid back with a loud clack and the cellar door yawned open into the light.

***

On the way back to The Tank from *Peckham Van Hire*, Roark pulled the car onto a spot on Peckham Road and ducked into the nearest Costa to get two coffees and two pastries, leaving Knight in the car. Their shift was over already, but it was still a long day ahead, so they needed a jolt of caffeine and some breakfast. There was coffee at the station, but it was so bad, she only drank it in emergencies. Better to fill up at a more reputable establishment.

When Roark returned and passed over one coffee, Knight gave her an update. She'd been working while Roark was in Costa. She had checked the police alerts on the APB they had issued, using real-time updates on the Met app that Roark had never got around to downloading. So far, there was nothing. She had also called Roark's contact in Southwark council to see whether they had the requested CCTV footage yet. Not far off, Knight was told. They'd send it through within the hour. They could confirm, Knight said, that, as expected, they had no CCTV footage of the incident in Peckham itself, the residential street was devoid of security cameras, and a quick call to the police at the scene confirmed that none of the residents had door cameras either.

'Is it too much to ask for a full, widescreen, 4K recording of the crime?' Knight said, taking a sip from her flat white.

'Apparently it is. Croissant or Pain aux Raisin?'

'Croissant, thanks,' Knight said, and took the offered bag.

'Let's take a moment to wolf these down before we go in.'

'Do you mind if I call my Mum?'

'Go for it,' Roark said. 'I'll step out.'

'It's okay, Kris. You don't have to do that.'

Knight placed her pastry bag on the dashboard and pulled out her phone. Her mum answered on the third ring and Knight spent ten minutes speaking with her, talking in quiet tones, reassuring, concerned.

The cancer had really knocked the confidence out of them both and Roark had been generous in giving Knight time off when she needed it, and she would continue to do so. She also tried her best to take Knight's mind off it, taking her out to dinner on occasion, drinks with the team, and anything else that would bring out the happy-go-lucky version of DC Knight she had found infectious over the past six months. She knew it was only a temporary measure, but Knight always thanked her for the distraction.

'Take care, Mum,' Knight said and pocketed her phone.

'She doing okay?'

'Yeah, she's taking it easy. Almost took a tumble down the stairs a few days ago, gave her a bit of a fright.'

'If you need time,' Roark said, 'just take it. Whenever you want.'

'Thanks, Kris. I'll get started on this case file first.'

'Of course.'

They gave small talk while tucking into their pastries and warming up with their coffees. The case would get enough of their attention once they entered the station, but for now, they took a break. As the chatter went on, Knight's usual playful demeanour started to re-emerge, the call with her mother obviously doing her some good.

'How's the love life?' Knight said as she finished off her croissant.

Roark let out a laugh.

'That bad, is it?' Knight said, smiling, crumbs on her chin.

'It's fine, thank you very much.'

'You know, you still haven't shown me your *Tinder* profile, have you? Maybe it needs some work.'

'Shut it,' Roark said, tossing across a serviette. 'Last time I tell you anything.'

Knight screwed her pastry bag into a ball and wound down her window. There was a rubbish bin near the parked car and she tossed it in. She downed her cooling coffee and threw that in too.

'This case,' she said, 'looks straightforward, right? Someone attacked Whitman for his van, made off with it, killed him in the process. So why does that not sit right? Seems too simple.'

'We're both feeling it.'

'I guess you don't tend to see victims hacked to death over a van. Could be something more to it.'

'I've seen worse done for less,' Roark said, finishing her coffee and handing it across so Knight could pop it into the bin. 'And it's not *Tinder*, you crass wench. I've got more class than that.'

'Yes, very classy.'

'You should talk. How do you find all those over forties you keep dating? At the local meat market?'

'Why? You worried I'm taking all your toy boys?'

'Shut it, cow. I'm not that old.'

'We should double date sometime,' Knight said, smiling. 'Maybe find some twins.'

'Okay,' Roark said, stuffing the bag with her half-eaten pastry in it into the well between the seats, 'it's time we went back to work before I knock you out. We need to find this fucking guy.'

'Yeah, you know I hate to keep men waiting, particularly those with a fetish for sharp bladed instruments.'

'You're such a kinky bitch, you know that, don't you?'

'That's what my profile says.'

Roark laughed and started the car.

'Let's get back to work,' she said, and she pulled out and directed the car towards The Tank.

As soon as Roark stepped into station after parking the car, the officer on the front desk waved her over. Rawlins wanted to see her, pronto.

Detective Chief Inspector Rawlins, a gaunt faced man who looked a hundred and spoke as if he smoked the same number of cigarettes a day, was Roark's boss. He was one of the senior policemen of the Southwark

Basic Command Unit run from Camberwell station, an old general driving a battered war machine through the detritus of south London.

Roark knew Rawlins wasn't a hundred. He was in his late fifties, was a health nut, and had lost two daughters to teen suicide only ten years ago. He maintained his professionalism, worked hard and earned his epaulette with the crown and star, but he had lost a lot of weight since Roark remembered him as a Detective Inspector many years before the tragedy had changed his life, back when she was a young naïve Constable. Roark had always respected him. He'd been through a lot. He was old school but fair. He was proper Metropolitan police.

On the way up, DC Knight stepped off the elevator on the second floor, said she'd check up on the APB and chase the council for updates. Roark exited on the top floor, level four, and walked through the corridors holding the offices of the Chief Inspectors, Superintendents, and civilian officers.

These corridors always made her uneasy. The quiet was almost unbearable; quiet but with the hint of whispers behind closed doors. Roark preferred the outspoken wild noise of the open second floor over the stiff, conspiratorial labyrinth holding the seniority of BCU Southwark.

'Sir,' Roark said, popping her head through Rawlins's open door.

Rawlins looked up from his desk, shoulders hunched behind a computer screen and framed family photos. His mouth hung open for a second, cheeks drooping, chin protruding, and he motioned her in, pointing to the chair across from his desk.

Roark sat down and stretched her feet out in front of her, accidentally knocking into Rawlins legs under the desk.

'Sorry, sir,' she said, pulling her feet back under her seat.

'You'd think by now you'd realise how tall you are, Detective Inspector,' Rawlins said, his voice rumbling like thunder. The pleasant sound of thunder.

'I do forget myself sometimes, sir.'

Rawlins leaned back in his chair.

'What's going on in Bishop Street?'

'One male victim. Hacked with an axe or something similar.'

'Machete?'

'I don't think so, sir.'

'Drug related?'

'Not on the face of it, appears to have happened during the theft of a

43

vehicle, the victim's van. No other items appear to have been taken. We have the vehicle out on an APB.'

'Identification of the suspect?'

'Not yet, sir. The van is our only lead right now. Looking into security footage in the area.'

'I want a one-page summary on my desk. There may be media buzz around this one. I'll take the brunt, but I want you by my side at the press briefing at two o'clock this afternoon.'

'Yes, sir.'

She hated the press briefings, and for the majority of her time as a Detective Inspector she'd managed to avoid them, but about two years ago, she'd noticed Rawlins request her more often than not to attend the briefings. On one of the rare occasions Rawlins had joined the team for a drink, he'd told her that he thought she was a natural and that the press loved her, but she knew the recent push on diversity and was cynical enough to believe it was more a publicity play than anything else. Unfortunately, diversity didn't necessarily translate to promotion or salary increases to the same degree as her male counterparts.

'I'll have the page for you, sir.'

'Good,' Rawlins said, 'and keep it fresh for any updates.'

'Yes, sir.'

Roark stood up and stepped out of the office, knowing that the meeting was finished even though Rawlins showed no sign of dismissing her. She knew he gave as much respect to his unit as he expected from them, so rarely did he wave them off or return to his work until after they'd left his office.

Old school, but fair.

Knight frantically waved Roark over as soon as she stepped off the elevator on the second floor. She was holding a landline phone in her left hand, standing up over her cubicle.

'What is it?' Roark said when she reached Knight's desk.

'They've found the van.'

CHAPTER 9

'I'm sorry,' he says, blinking away his confusion. 'What did you say?'

The large man in the corner grumbles.

'The photos,' she says, pointing at the photos on the table. She is clearly annoyed.

'I'm sorry.'

He leans forward to take a closer look. He points to the photo of the man.

'Him. I don't know him.'

'And the van?' she says without missing a beat.

'I've seen vans like it,' he says.

'Have you *driven* a van like this before?'

'Yes,' he says without hesitation, 'I have. That's my job. I drive a van every day.'

The pen scratches on her notepad. He swallows, thinking he has said the wrong thing again.

'Do you own a van?'

'No, no, I use the company's van.'

'Is that van one of your company vans?'

He looks at the photo on the right, shakes his head. 'No.'

He raises his eyes from the photo and watches the female detective as she continues to write notes. She stops, stares down at her notepad. The male detective shuffles in his seat.

'Okay, thank you, Howard. Can you pass those photos back to me, please?'

He scrunches up his face, shakes his head.

'I don't think I want to touch them,' he says with disgust. 'I don't like the look of that man.'

The female detective looks over to her colleague with an expression that is hard to decipher. She leans forward across the table and retrieves the two photos.

'Do you know who that man is?' she says, putting the photos back in the folder.

'No, I don't.'

'His name is Corey Whitman.'

'Okay,' he says.

'He was found murdered last Wednesday night in London.'

'Oh,' he says, frowning.

'Do you know anything about that?'

'No, no,' he says, shaking his head quickly, leaning back. 'I don't know anything about that.'

She takes more notes, and he can't keep his eyes from flitting between her and the other detective. He feels his heart rate pick up, his breathing rise in his chest.

'I'm sorry, I thought this was about some disappearance, this guy that you mentioned, not someone dying.'

'Calm down, Howard,' she says, raising a hand. 'Why don't we talk about your father?'

The words smack him across the face, out of nowhere, a right hook across the table, and he blinks.

'I'm sorry, what did you say?'

'Your father, Howard,' she says. 'My understanding is that your father was killed by police in 1995, when you were eleven? At your home in New Forest. When you were James Stern.'

His father lies on his side, blood pooling around his head, his rifle just out of reach.

'That's – that's right, but what has that got to do with anything?'

'Why did the police shoot him, Howard? What did he do wrong?'

His breathing quickens. The dark spaces in the corners of the room reach out towards him. He sits up in his seat, looks to the door.

'I don't think I – I don't want to talk about this.'

A third photo slides across the table towards him, a colour photo, an identification photo for a passport or security card and he sees the face and closes his eyes.

'Do you know who that is, Howard?' the female detective says.

The door to the attic opens and the light from the stairway blinds the boy.

He rubs his eyes, focuses on the doorway, sees a silhouette of his father standing there.

'Come on, boy,' he says. 'Get these clothes on.'

His father throws rags at him and it takes him time to get dressed. He can't remember the last time he dressed himself, so he struggles in the dark, putting on the trousers backwards, the T-shirt inside out, but he wants to please his father. He doesn't know what this is about, his father hasn't spoken to him in months, but he wants to please him, so he doesn't ask questions, he just does what he says.

'Hurry up,' *his father growls and the boy panics, tries to put the socks on but he struggles, the socks bunching up and twisting around his feet.* 'Now.'

With socks hardly clinging to his feet, he stumbles forward, his weak legs betraying him, and he falls. He gets up again, hurries towards the stairwell, his arm raised against the bright light.

'Shoes,' his father points to a pair of old runners at the top of the stairs.

The boy puts them on, tight, two sizes too small, but he forces them on, feels a pinching sensation around his ankle and heel, his toes squashed.

'Tie them up.'

The boy grunts a question, looks at his father, pleading.

'Come here, then, you useless shit.'

His father crouches down by his feet and ties up his shoes. The boy starts to cry, seeing his father tying up his shoes.

'Shut up and get downstairs.'

'Howard? Can you please look at the photo?'

The boy follows his father through the house, and when he fails to keep up, his father comes back to him and grabs him by the arm, almost dragging him through the kitchen. His arm hurts, his father's fingers digging into his skin.

He is dragged through the kitchen, past the cellar with its trapdoor open, and out of the house. His father releases his arm. It is late afternoon, and the sky is dull outside. Still, the boy squints. He hasn't seen daylight for months. There is a wind whipping across the lawn and the trees lining the front near the driveway sway in unison.

He closes his eyes and feels the wind play with his hair, caress his face, stroke his skin.

The wind whips but otherwise, there is silence. Silence and solitude. He remembers the house is far from any neighbours, protected by the surrounding forests, the trees he used to play in when he was younger.

So long ago.

He opens his eyes. He hears crying.

'Mr Bloch? I must insist you open your eyes and look at this photo.'

'Stop daydreaming, you silly cunt. Get around the back.'

Confused, the boy opens his eyes, and the glare of the failing afternoon light makes it difficult for him to see clearly. He can just make out his father's pickup truck, which is parked near the house, in the driveway. There is something in the front passenger seat, but he can't tell what it is.

His father shoves him to the ground.

'Around the back.'

The boy scrambles to his feet and, still looking at his father, moves around to the rear of the pickup truck.

His father opens the passenger side door and leans in.

There is a whimper, and the boy jerks his head towards the back of the truck.

There is another boy there, sitting in the tray of the pickup truck, with his back up against the truck's cab, knees up to his chest, head down. He looks younger, small, frail, weak. His shoulders shudder as he sobs.

'Keep him there until I get back,' he hears his father say.

The sobbing boy raises his head at the voice, hair down over his face, tears on his cheeks, frightened eyes looking straight ahead.

At him.

'Mr Bloch?'

He opens his eyes, stares at the photo on the table.

'No,' he says. 'I don't recognise him.'

He takes his eyes off the crying boy and looks away, towards the front of the truck, and sees his father carrying a woman over his shoulder, a woman who is not moving.

'Are you sure you have never met him?'

The boy watches as his father takes the woman into the house and down the cellar steps, all the while the sound of wind whipping through the trees and the tears of a frightened boy fill his ears.

'I've never seen him before in my life.'

CHAPTER 10

Aaron didn't know he was holding his breath until he let it out in a short, shuddered gasp. He clasped his hand over his mouth but knew he was too late. Whoever opened the trap door above would've heard him.

When the door at the top of the stairs had banged open, Aaron had shuffled back quickly as if the sunlight beaming in was toxic, as if any part of his skin was illuminated, it would burn. He'd moved into the shadows, out of sight as much as he thought he could hide, knowing full well it was a fool's errand. Whoever was up there, whoever had taken him hostage, knew he was down here. There was no point hiding.

Aaron had covered his eyes, momentarily blinded, anxiety rising in him as he couldn't see any attack that may reign down from above. He had sucked in his breath and listened, trying to ignore the thumping of blood in his ears and head, waiting to hear the wood creak as someone descended into the cellar.

A few moments later, Aaron was able to drop his hand and squint. There was no noise, no voice or sound. It was dead quiet but the door to the cellar remained open and the sun shined. The steps leading out to freedom glowed with false promise. Dust lifted from the wood. No one came for him. No one called out. A floorboard above his head had creaked and he held completely still, willed himself to be invisible and silent.

Now, what seemed like forever since the door had opened, Aaron took in another deep breath, measured this time, and listened. No matter how hard he strained, there were no sounds, no indication of anyone in the house above him. Even the rats had kept a silent vigil, waiting for the light to be extinguished even though their corner of the room, with the body, was still, thankfully, enveloped in darkness.

Another five or so minutes passed, and Aaron decided he had to try. It was no doubt a trap, set up to lure him out into the light, but he was already in a trap and another moment in this darkened room with vermin and a corpse seemed impossible to endure. Sitting in the dark and awaiting his fate felt worse than what may await him outside.

Shuddering at the thought, losing his resolve for a split second, then recovering it, Aaron moved towards the bottom of the stairs.

The first step creaked louder than he had expected, the wood bending slightly in the middle.

Aaron stopped, waited. His eyes were adjusted to the light, and he could now bear looking directly up into the opening without being blinded by the sun. He could see a white ceiling but nothing else.

Another step, this time he positioned his foot at the far right of the step and there was no creak, no giveaway. If this was a trap, his best bet was to do this as stealthily and quickly as he could. Get two or three steps away from the opening and launch himself, take his abductor by surprise. If only he had some type of weapon, he might stand a chance.

Sweat trickled down his left temple and he wiped it away. The next step sent a splinter into the padding of his foot, but he gritted his teeth and kept quiet. As he moved up, breathing shallow, trying to keep his heart from thumping so loud it would give his position away, he could see more of the white ceiling, and then the top of a wall, painted egg-shell blue.

Another step and the wall gave way to a frame of a door, a white door with four panes of glass through which he could see the tops of trees, a patchy sky and a black bird flitting past, high in the clouds.

Outside, escape, freedom.

A trap.

Aaron didn't care. He had a chance out there. He had no chance back inside the cellar.

Three steps from the widening exit, Aaron could reach up and touch the corners if he wanted to, the opening within arm's length. He could also see almost two-thirds of the door in front of him, a framed picture of an elderly couple on the wall next to it, smiling back at him with nothing but warmth and kindness, and an old radiator below that next to the corner of a kitchen bench. To his right, the tops of chairs around a table, a bench and sink under a large window. To his left, a high bookcase filled with cookbooks, travel books, fiction hardcovers. Behind him, where the hinged cellar door rested on the floor, he could see the top of a wooden cupboard lined with crockery. Everything looked clean, tidy, cared for. There was a faint musty smell in the air mixed in with the tangy sweet scent of oranges or some other fruit. The air was clean and welcoming.

Scenarios ran through his head, explanations that tried to piece together the predicament he was in against this backdrop of a homely life, a house, a home, that he could easily imagine growing up in. A place for a loving family, not a homicidal maniac.

Aaron's thoughts drifted to the body in the cellar, and he snapped to. He couldn't see anyone from his vantage point, but it didn't mean he was alone, and the only element he had was surprise. He had to move.

Without further thought, he tensed his muscles, ignored the thumping in his chest and the anxiety in his throat, and launched himself out of the cellar, scrambling up the last three steps and onto the kitchen floor, up off his hands and knees and grasping for the bronze door handle of the four pane door, bracing his neck and back, expecting a blow from behind, preparing his hand and wrist for resistance against a locked door.

The handle turned in his sweaty, slippery hand and he was outside, running across a narrow cobblestoned pathway and onto a large low-cut lawn that stretched left and right and ahead of him, bathed in mid-afternoon sunlight. The grass was wet between his toes, as he kept running, not looking behind him to see if he was being chased, not daring to turn back to see the house he'd just escaped from, just running and hoping, whispering please, please, please, as he pumped his legs as hard as he could.

Ahead, there were several rows of high trees, dense but not impenetrable, glimpses of open field between thin trunks, as if a section of a forest had been lifted up and replanted. Not impenetrable but difficult to access, not a fast route through, made even more difficult due to Aaron's bare feet.

A frantic look to his right and he could see the lawn and trees gave way to a view of hills rolling away and to the horizon, trees and forests and fauna brought together in a picture postcard that he knew he'd never forget. Hard to see from his position, but it appeared the lawn dropped sharply down to the landscape, a long section of difficult terrain.

On his left was a dirt driveway that led back past him to the house and ahead of him around the side of the rows of trees. He dared a glance back to the house and saw the driveway led to a large garage, the shutter down. He thought he saw movement closer to the house and he turned back around, ran harder, deciding in that second that the route to escape was along the driveway.

Aaron kept running, two-thirds across the expansive lawn, making a beeline for the point where the edge of the lawn met the end of the row of trees, the point where he could dart around that corner and sprint for his life.

Closer, closer, he could see the trees thinning out as they met the driveway, less long barked trunks and wider gaps in between. It was still difficult to see clearly through the trees, but through a series of gaps, something winked at him, something shiny, sun bouncing off glass, a sharp bright glare off white painted metal.

A car, a vehicle, a means to escape.

The muscles in his legs screaming at him to stop, Aaron stretched forward, sprinting as fast as he could.

CHAPTER 11

On the second floor of The Tank, there were not many options for a private call, but they had to find somewhere quiet. The noise in the open plan was louder than usual and Roark was finding it hard to hear the police officers on the other end of the phone. They found a place at the back of the floor, a small meeting room for two, which was empty other than a left behind Costa cardboard coffee cup.

They patched through the call to the speakerphone on the small desk and crowded round it.

'We can hear you now,' Roark said. 'Can you repeat what you told DC Knight for me please?'

The voice on the other end of the call was distant and distorted but much clearer in the quiet room. The speaker was a Police Constable Bolton for Thames Valley police out of High Wycombe. Him and his partner had been driving out around Chiltern Hills area and up a country lane, a road rising up a hill with tall trees on both sides, when they had passed a white van parked up on the embankment. As they drove on, Bolton's partner took down the licence plate and matched it up to the APB that Knight had issued.

'*It definitely checks out. No driver in there, but it's your van,*' Bolton said over the loudspeaker.

'Where are you now?'

'*We drove past again and have parked off the lane down the bottom of the hill, about fifty metres away. We can see the van.*'

'Does it appear to be dumped? Left there?'

'*Yes and no, Ma'am,*' Bolton said. '*It's parked at a severe angle, up on the embankment, but there is a property nearby. Just beyond the van, there's a dirt driveway heading into the trees. We glimpsed a house back there.*'

Knight leaned towards Roark and whispered: 'I don't think he'd be stupid enough to park outside his own house, do you?'

'You never know,' Roark replied. 'Bolton?'

'*Yes, Ma'am.*'

'We're a bit cautious of this guy doing a runner. Is there any way you could approach and get a better view of the property without being seen or drawing attention to yourself?'

'*One moment, Ma'am,*' Bolton said and there was a moment when he switched his phone to mute, the background noise of the surrounding forests cutting out. A few seconds later, Bolton was back on.

'There's another property closer to where we are now at the bottom of the hill, on the other side of the road. We can access the property and approach further up through the trees. We won't be directly opposite, but we will have a better view than from down here.'

'Do it, Constable, but I want you to take us with you. We may need you to act fast.'

'No problem, Ma'am. I'll keep you on the phone. We're heading to the property now.'

Roark and Knight leaned back in their chairs around the desk. Bolton gave them updates as him and his partner drove onto the neighbouring property, spoke to the residents, and made their way on foot through the forest from the opposite side of the road to the van. They informed Roark and Knight that they had put on their overcoats, a darker blue that kept them obscured in the forest.

'I don't think he's there,' Knight said.

'I agree, it would be odd to dump the van right in front of his own home, unless he's planning on a siege situation.'

Knight had her phone out, looking at Google maps.

'I grant you,' she said, 'it's a perfect place to bunker down, secluded, difficult to approach from most sides of the property. Strange then to announce where he is by parking the stolen vehicle out front.'

'We'll just have to see,' Roark said.

There was a crackle over the phone.

'We're in position,' Bolton said.

'Excellent.'

'We've found a good spot. We can see down the driveway to the property, part of it anyway, but we are far enough back that no one should be able to see us unless they come out onto the road.'

'That's great, Bolton. Tell us what you see.'

'Wait,' Bolton said, and his phone went quiet. 'I think there's someone coming.'

Roark looked at Knight.

'Yes, Ma'am, there is someone approaching, running up the driveway towards the road and the van. Stand by.'

***

The loose stones cut into his bare feet and constantly moved under the pressure of his running, almost sending Aaron to the ground on several occasions. His breathing was quickening as he approached the point where the forest met the driveway, anxious to get behind the trees and to the vehicle he could see through the gaps in the thin trunks. Anxious that he'd be struck from behind just as he reached his escape vehicle.

His focus was fixed on the vehicle, not a car, but something bigger, maybe a van or other commercial vehicle, flashes of white between the trunks higher than what he'd expect from a normal sized car. It didn't matter. Whatever it was, even if it was the vehicle he'd been kidnapped in, there was a glimmer of hope that he'd be able get in it and drive away from the madman who had kidnapped him and left him to die in a dark damp cellar.

Aaron pumped his arms and legs quickly, adrenaline overtaking his senses, seeing with blurred, sweat-streaked eyes the last few trees receding as he pushed forward, catching sun winking off a set of headlights, desperate to see whether this was indeed his salvation, a way out of the hell of the last few hours.

When the vehicle came into view, Aaron slowed down.

***

'He's slowing down. I think he's spotted the van.'

'Can you give us a description, Bolton?'

'Yes, he's Caucasian, about average height. He's stopped next to the van, hang on.'

Bolton's voice quietened, followed by a muffled conversation, hand over the receiver.

'Constable?' Roark said, a note of impatience creeping into her voice. 'Bolton?'

'Sorry Ma'am, just checking with my partner. It's not a male, it's a female, Ma'am, in her mid to late fifties, in running gear. I guess this isn't the person you're looking for, right?'

'Fuck,' Knight whispered.

***

Stones dug into his knees and hands as he fell to the ground. On all fours, breathing heavily, he stared at the vehicle tucked behind the line of trees, parked up close to the driveway. He could hear a whimpering from deep down in his chest.

The vehicle was a pure white campervan, a Volkswagen with an upright grill and a raised roof, a big ungainly motorhome with chipped paint and cobwebbed side mirrors. No number plates. And no wheels. It sat up on blocks, dirty black blocks underneath the chassis, holding it above the wet ground. The front mirror was cracked, and the side door hung open, lopsided off one hinge.

It wasn't going anywhere.

Aaron momentarily dropped his head and let the sweat drip onto the dirt.

A crow cawed above his head and Aaron scrambled to his feet, kicking up dust, spurred into action. He would run, fast as he could, not looking back. Fuck the campervan, he would escape on his own two feet.

Ahead of him, the driveway continued across an open field, another forest spreading out to the left and right, the road curving down a hill, through the trees and out of sight.

The forest ahead blocked any signs of civilisation. There was no sign of any other houses, no roads, nothing, but Aaron found his feet, a new spurt of energy, one that would carry him far away from the nightmare he'd just escaped. He would run until his feet bled and then would run further until he found help.

As he rushed past the front of the dilapidated campervan, a shadow stepped out from around the bonnet, and there was a flash of movement and a large black shape collected Aaron across the face.

In the bright blue sky, Aaron saw stars and fireworks as he fell backwards. His head hit the ground but the pain across his face dwarfed the impact. In the dirt, he stared up and gulped, struggling to breathe, liquid filling his throat. A ringing noise filled his left ear. The sun beat down on his face as he choked. His nose sat flat across his cheek.

The sun flickered and Aaron strained his head to the right, tried to swallow, tried to spit. The sun flashed and disappeared, and a tall dark shadow stood there, at Aaron's bare feet, face darkened in silhouette.

It held a spade by the handle, the blade rested on the ground.

Aaron raised a hand towards it.

'Please,' he gurgled.

The spade dropped to the ground with a thud. A hand disappeared into the swirling darkness and returned, holding a short-handled axe.

'No,' Aaron tried to say but instead choked on blood filling his throat. Aaron raised his other arm in front of him, reaching out.

The shadow moved closer, kneeled at Aaron's side, so close that Aaron could smell its breath, rotten and putrid, and the shadow knocked his arms away and brought the axe down.

CHAPTER 12

The dark spaces grow. They extend a foot closer from every direction, every corner. The shoulder of the male detective is encased in shadow as he leans back on his chair, pushed up into the corner.

Does he not feel it? Does he not feel the darkness seeping into his shoulder, his muscles and bone? Spreading through his tendons and veins, making its way along his back, up his neck and into his skull, to take over his brain?

'Howard,' the female detective says and snaps her fingers. 'I need you to concentrate.'

He was staring without realising it. Staring at the male detective and the darkness only he could see.

'I'm sorry,' he says, returning his attention to her.

She sits forward on her chair, elbow on the table, picks up the photo and holds it, facing him.

'So, you don't recognise this man?'

'N-no, I don't,' he says, shaking his head. 'Who is he?'

She places the photo face down in her file and says, 'For the record, the photo shown to Mr Bloch is a recent photo of Aaron Sparger, the victim who was abducted last Wednesday around eleven-thirty p.m. in a van rented by Corey Whitman. Howard, please explain to me what you know about any of these details regarding the abduction of Aaron Sparger.'

He stutters before he can get the words out coherently.

'I – I don't know anything about what happened. I told you that.'

She checks her file notes, looks up at him again, stern eyes, clear voice.

'Tell me about the night of 16 August 1993.'

'1993?' he blurts out.

The boy. The woman. The child.

'Yes, 1993. If it helps, it was the day Wendy Cooper and her son disappeared from the Yorkshire Dales. They were on holiday and did not return. Their car was found near Hawes, no trace of them.'

He stares down at his hands on the table, notices they are clenched, and the knuckles are white again. He flattens them, palms down, feeling the cool surface underneath. Out of the corner of his left eye, something moves in the room, something dark and slippery.

'I don't think I want to talk about that,' he manages.

'It would help us greatly if you did.'

'I don't understand,' he says, his voice raised. 'How does this help you?'

'Please,' she says, 'calm down, Howard.'

'I'm sorry,' he says, eyes back down on his hands, hoping against hope that she will now drop this topic. 'I don't know what to say.'

'Tell me,' she says, leaning back in her chair, 'where were you when your father abducted Wendy Cooper and her son?'

He looks across the table at her, into those cold eyes, for once trying to challenge her. Speaking in that insinuating way about his father riles him. She has no right. She never knew his father.

'Does it upset you to talk about your father and what he did?' she says, sensing his sensitivity, digging into the old wounds further.

He shakes his head but means to say yes. He doesn't know what to say.

'It is a fact that your father kidnapped Wendy and her son on 16 August 1993. They weren't seen again until...' she pauses and checks her notes before continuing, 'a month later, left, relatively unhurt, physically anyway, somewhere in Wales.'

He focuses on his hands on the table. He can feel his biceps trembling and realises he is pushing down on the table with increasing force. He takes a deep breath, tries to relax.

'What happened in that month, Howard? What did your father do to them?'

The boy watches, staring into the light, staring down through the gap in the attic floor.

'He did nothing to them,' he hears himself say.

'Nothing? He abducted them, held them hostage.'

'He treated them well.'

'In what way?'

The boy watches as his father takes the stairs down into the cellar, holding plates of hot food. The boy hopes the woman and child do not eat everything on those plates. He hopes for scraps later, left in the kitchen, scraps he can take from the bench in the middle of the night, when his father is sleeping.

'He fed them,' he says, and he knows he is being defensive.

The boy watches as his father leads the child out of the cellar and closes the trapdoor. The six-year-old boy. The woman's son, who was left in the back of the truck, whimpering, crying. The boy watches as his father leaves the six-year-old in another room and waits outside, until the child emerges, dressed in clothes that are familiar.

His clothes. Clothes he hasn't worn for months. Years, maybe.

The boy looks down at his own naked body, ribs showing, sores across his arms and legs, bites from the critters that live up in the attic with him. He shivers.

'He held them as hostages, against their will,' she says.

'He looked after them, kept them warm, kept him fed and warm. He played with him.'

'Played?' she says quizzically. 'In a sexual way?'

'No,' he shouts across the table and the dark shadows in the corners flinch. 'I'm sorry,' he says in a quieter voice. 'No, he didn't play with him like that.'

The boy watches, staring into the light. Watches his father play with the other boy, the child. Playing with a deck of cards, playing with board games. One or two of the games he remembers, from what feels like a different life, remembers some of the rules but even though he can see the words on the board game boxes, he can't read them, not anymore.

The child sits there, stunned, not reacting, not enjoying the attention, not enjoying the delight of a father spending time with his son.

After a while, the boy watches as his father returns the child downstairs into the cellar. His father reappears in the kitchen, closes the cellar door, sits down at the kitchen table and cries with his head in his hands.

'How did he play with him?'

He picks at his finger, trying to remove a piece of dead skin. He pulls at it in the wrong direction and removes a long piece, revealing pink and wet flesh underneath.

The dark places pulsate.

'Like a father and son play.'

He sensed the female detective look across at her partner, then back again.

'And how did that make you feel, Howard?'

He rubs the exposed flesh on his finger, feels a slight pang of pain, says nothing.

'Where were you when this was happening, Howard? Were you with the child, playing together? Were you expected to treat him like a brother?'

He clasps his hands together on the table and looks at the female detective. His eyes feel wet.

'I wasn't expected to do anything.'

When he offers nothing more, she leans forward, arms on the table, and says, 'Why did he take them, Howard? Why did your father take the mother and child?'

He closes his eyes and shakes his head.

The boy watches his father crying at the kitchen table and begins to cry too.

He feels a trickle of warmth run from his eye, tracking down his cheek.

'Howard?'

He opens his eyes and states clearly, 'I don't know.'

'Did you ask him?'

He shakes his head.

'Okay,' she says, breathing out audibly. She refers to her file and without looking up at him, asks, 'Do you know why he let them go?'

Night after night the boy watches his father play with the child, watches the child sit there in shock or in tears or crying for his mummy, and he watches his father upset, then angry.

One time, the boy watches, through the gap in the floor, as his father takes them both out of the cellar, the woman over his shoulder, the boy at his side, and drives off into the night.

'Ryan wouldn't play,' he says without thinking.

'He wouldn't play the games?'

'No.'

'Is that all your father wanted? To play games with the boy?' She pauses. 'I don't understand. He had you for that, didn't he?'

'Ryan wouldn't play,' he repeats.

'And what about the woman? What did he do with her?'

'Nothing.'

'Where was she?'

'In the cellar. Always in the cellar.'

She takes this piece of information without comment and writes something down in her notebook.

'Tell me something, Howard?' she says, tapping her pen on the notepad. 'How did you know his name was Ryan? I never referred to his name. How did you know?'

The boy sneaks down from the attic in middle of the night, the steps creaking, even under the decimated weight of his starved frame. He sneaks down for food, for the leftovers or for anything unused in the fridge that he thinks his father will not miss. He finds scraps and swallows them quickly.

He finds a handbag on the kitchen bench, near the sink. Nothing he has seen before. Nothing his mother ever had. He looks through it and finds a card with the picture of a young woman on it. There is a name, and he can't say it, he can't read or understand, but he memorises the letters so he can practice it, learn it, and remember.

Wendy Cooper.

He hears a toilet flush elsewhere in the house, the one in the hallway near his father's bedroom, and he panics, dropping the card quickly into the handbag and rushing back upstairs, into the attic, through the door that is seldom locked, and collapses onto the thin mattress that is his bed.

He waits and listens, and the house settles. His father does not appear in the kitchen. His father does not appear at the top of the stairs to come beat him for leaving the attic.

The boy sits and waits and listens and thinks about the name of the woman in the cellar.

Wendy Cooper.

And after a while, he repeats the name he has heard his father say to the child so many times.

Ryan.

Ryan Cooper.

'Howard, how do you know his name?'

'My father used it. A lot of times, when he tried to play with Ryan.'

'His surname as well?'

He doesn't respond, pretends he doesn't realise that she has asked a question.

'Is it possible that you discovered the name later? Researched what happened perhaps? Attempted to understand what happened? Tried to contact Ryan possibly?'

He shakes his head and says nothing more.

'Okay, Howard, that is fine,' she says, a hint of annoyance in her voice that suggests it isn't fine at all. 'So, your father released Wendy and Ryan Cooper and then what happened?'

He says nothing, staring at his hands again, the tear from his right eye dripping onto his shirt.

'There was another one, wasn't there, Howard?'

'Yes,' he says, straightening. 'Yes, there was. There was a girl.'

CHAPTER 13

Teresa García decided one weekend, after listening to a podcast on the forgotten people of Manchester, to finally put herself out there and start doing some charity work in her neighbourhood of Eccles, a few miles west of Manchester city centre. She'd talked about charity work enough times, to her family, her friends, to one or two strangers she'd struck up conversations with who were doing similar work around the area, delivering food, volunteer work for local initiatives to help the poor or working in charity shops. She'd spoken about it too much and now it was time to act.

She worked in numerous jobs where she came across the homeless and vulnerable, a librarian at the Eccles library, part-time shop assistant in a worker's café on Liverpool Road and a member of the local drama group who performed at retirement homes and local halls, and although she always went out of her way to assist the elderly, impaired or down and out citizens of Eccles, she knew she could do more.

A week ago, she signed up with Home Assist, a charity that supported the blind and deaf elderly citizens of Manchester, providing them with support around the home, helping with cleaning, administrative tasks, and anything that they could not perform themselves. Overall, though, as the charity representative, a husky voiced woman in her fifties named Pam, had said, 'They just want to have a good old natter. They're on their own most of the time, so to have someone come around every few days for a good old chin wag really improves their quality of life.'

Teresa signed up immediately and within a week, after several forms were filled out and background checks conducted, Pam called her up again to offer her a regular home visit slot with a woman named Cheryl Palmer.

She was sixty-six years old, blind in both eyes, living with her son. Pam, with a conspiratorial note in her voice, which Teresa felt was slightly inappropriate, said that the son was a tricky one. They'd had Cheryl on the books for a while and she only qualified for the support because William, the thirty-nine-year-old son, had been diagnosed on the spectrum many years ago and was kind of a recluse, although he held down a job at the local hardware store, casual hours, with little responsibility.

'We had one of our people go out there for an assessment and the state of the place was enough for us to sign her up. It's a shame. Her son doesn't mistreat her at all, but he doesn't help around the house or talk to her much. I think Cheryl just needs a bit of company for the most part, you know what I'm saying?'

Teresa said she understood.

'William's totally harmless, so don't worry about that, you'll be fine. Just don't expect to see him or talk to him when you visit. It's probably better that way anyway. We'll send you around when he's at work.'

'Okay,' Teresa said. She felt it was better that way too. She thought she'd be fine with William, but she wanted to focus purely on Cheryl and her needs.

'She's a recluse herself,' Pam added, 'so you won't have to take her shopping or on walks or anything like that. Just sit with her, tidy up a little bit, give her a couple of hours attention.'

'I can do that,' Teresa said, and after Pam had given her the details and she hung up the phone, she had felt good and positive about herself and couldn't wait to see Cheryl for their first allotted time.

Now, as Teresa stepped off the number 67 bus from the city centre, she felt both nervous and excited about visiting Cheryl. It was the first time she'd done anything like this before. Sure, she'd worked in customer service for many years, but this was completely different. She just hoped that they'd connect and that she could make a positive difference in Cheryl's life.

Teresa had two grandparents, grandfathers, who she saw only on significant occasions like Christmas and birthdays. They resided in Spain, and they were both able bodied and healthy. She couldn't imagine what it would be like to be both blind and a recluse, locked up in your home, permanently in the dark, with a son who didn't or couldn't make the effort. Teresa thought she would go slightly mad if it was her.

Teresa walked a few blocks down from the bus stop to number forty-two, the home of Cheryl Palmer. The house was a two-storey terraced building on a long street lined on both sides with identical properties. A smattering of cars was parked on either side and two young boys were kicking an orange and black football back and forth across the road, stopping only for the bus to pass them, going onwards toward Cadishead. Somewhere nearby a dog barked without pause.

A small gate led onto Mrs Palmer's bricked front yard barely big enough to store the black rubbish bin and three coloured recycling bins, a short row of half-dead flowers in a terracotta pot and a clear walkway to the front door. Teresa opened the gate and closed it behind her.

Pam had informed Teresa that Cheryl would answer the door when she buzzed but it would take some time as she would have to find her way to the front door, using the handrails installed in the house. William wouldn't answer, even if he was inside. Pam said, just be patient, so Teresa buzzed the front door and waited.

About two to three minutes later, the door opened. Cheryl stood before her wearing a woollen shawl over her shoulders on top of a floral dress. She was diminutive, just over five feet tall if Teresa had to guess, and her hair was grey without a hint of colour, tied back in a ponytail. She smiled and wrinkles formed around her mouth. Her eyes, which were almost as grey as her hair, stared out over Cheryl's left shoulder. Several scars marred her skin, pink marks around each eye; burns sustained a while ago, probably the cause of her blindness. Teresa tried not to focus on them, even if Mrs Palmer could not see her doing so.

'Is that you Miss García?' Cheryl said, her voice smooth and velvety, in stark contrast to her ageing body and skin.

'Yes, it is,' Teresa said, with a note of surprise in her voice.

'You have lovely perfume,' Cheryl said.

'Thank you.'

'Please, come in, Miss García,' Cheryl said and stepped aside.

'Thank you, Mrs Palmer, and please, call me Teresa.'

'And you can call me Cheryl.'

The house was dark, curtains drawn in most of the rooms, and only the dullest of light bulbs hanging from the ceiling. Made sense, Teresa thought, although she had to remind herself that Cheryl's son also lived here. Teresa made a quick notion of looking around for him, but as Pam said, he would not be around when she visited, working normal daytime hours at the hardware store, and that appeared to be the case.

Cheryl led Teresa through a short hallway, guided by the installed handrails, and to a door to their left which took them into a front room with a two-seat settee with matching chairs. It was tidy enough, but simplistic, no books or television, as was to be expected, and very little furnishings or decorations. Before following Cheryl into the room, Teresa looked further down into the house, down the length of the hallway, where the shadows merged into darkness. She was unable to make out any other rooms to see what state they were in, but she'd have a look later, tidy up a bit, with Cheryl's permission.

'Please take a seat dear,' Cheryl said as she moved slowly towards one of the sofa chairs, which had been positioned to face the front window. The curtains were drawn, and faint light and warmth bathed her chair as she settled slowly into it. In front of the chair there was a low table with a plate of biscuits, two saucers and two glasses of water.

Teresa moved the other sofa chair so that it was positioned in the same manner and sat down.

'Please, have some biscuits, my dear,' Cheryl said, gesturing towards the table. 'I will make some tea for us later.'

'Thank you,' Teresa said, and even though she'd just eaten her lunch, she took a biscuit and placed it on the saucer. 'Would you like one?'

'Not just now, Teresa, thank you. I've been eating them all morning,' she said with a smile.

It was a lovely smile, thin, petite, but it lit up her face, despite the scarring around her eyes, and Teresa could not help but return it.

Teresa took a bite out of her biscuit, which was a little dry.

'I can see why you love them,' she said. 'Very nice.'

'Thank you, dear,' Cheryl said and shifted in her chair, so that she was facing, to some degree, in Teresa's direction. 'And thank you so much for coming to visit. I spoke to Pam on the phone, and she said lovely things about you.'

'That's very nice of her,' Teresa said.

'She's a funny duck, that one, but she is always so helpful.'

Teresa agreed and took another bite of her biscuit.

'García,' Cheryl said, her head titled upwards in Teresa's direction. 'Spanish?'

'That's right.'

'Where in Spain?'

'My grandparents live in Granada which is where my parents grew up. My family live here in Manchester, so I'm born and bred British.'

'Oh, how lovely,' Cheryl said, bringing her hands together. 'I can imagine your family get-togethers are full of love and delight.'

'Yes,' Teresa said, smiling. 'They are.'

'My husband, God rest his soul, used to travel to Spain a lot for business. Before we had Billy, he'd take me to the islands off the coast of Spain to wine and dine me. The food, the scenery, the sunsets, oh, it was so beautiful.'

'It is lovely,' Teresa agreed.

Teresa wondered at what point in her life Cheryl had suffered the injuries to her eyes, when the accident, that Pam from Home Assist had not elaborated on, had occurred. She hoped it had happened after that point in her life when she travelled to Spain with her husband, that she had been young and healthy and enjoyed the sights and sounds of Ibiza and the like.

'What did Pam tell you about your visits, Teresa?'

'Yes,' Teresa said, putting down her empty plate on the low table. 'Anything you need help with, Cheryl, I am happy to assist you.'

'Well,' she said, her hands steepled in her lap, 'I'm just grateful for the company if I was honest. Someone to talk to, to hear about what's happening out in the world. Billy doesn't talk much anymore. We used to be very close, but I think he just barely puts up with me these days.'

'I'm sure he loves you very much.'

'Oh, he does, he does indeed, and he would not be able to bear living on his own, but we're just like ships in the night, passing by occasionally, hardly speaking to each other. It's a shame, but he has his own life, and I know it's difficult for him. I don't want to talk out of turn, but he struggles with the pressures of the everyday. It's great he has a day job, but I know most of the time, he'd rather just stay in that room of his upstairs. He doesn't like socialising or confrontations. You'll hardly see him.'

'Anything I can do to help, Cheryl, I'll be glad to do, including having a good chat.'

'Oh, that's lovely, dear,' Cheryl said and leaned forward, her hand outstretched. Teresa took it and gave it a light squeeze.

'We won't have to worry about it today, but I'll have a few odds and sods for you to help me with, like reading the mail, organising my home delivery from Tesco, that type of thing.'

'I'll be happy to help.'

'Thank you, dear. Okay,' Cheryl suddenly said, both hands on the arms of the chair, pushing up. 'Let's make that tea.'

'Let me help you,' Teresa said, reaching forward.

'It's okay, dear, I can manage walking, but I would love you to help me make the tea, if that's okay?'

'Of course.'

Mrs Palmer stood and opened up her right arm. Teresa stood up and immediately hooked her own arm with Cheryl's and they started towards the hallway.

The front door of the flat rattled as a key was fitted in and turned. They heard the latch unlock and the door swing open.

'Oh,' Cheryl said, and Teresa turned to her, seeing the confusion across her face, the concern.

The door swung open and banged against the wall and Teresa immediately tensed. The hallway light went out and a shadow rushed down the hallway, an indistinguishable mass flashing past with an almost physical barrage of noise.

'Billy, is that you?' Cheryl said, her voice squeaking in what Teresa could only describe as fear.

Without pausing, William Palmer grunted a yes and continued through the house. Teresa heard him walking up the stairs situated further back in the house, thumping on each step.

Teresa looked to the ceiling as William dropped something heavy, an object, maybe his own body, onto the floor above them.

'Oh, it's only Billy,' Cheryl said, slightly out of breath. 'That's his domain, upstairs. I don't go up there, even if I could. That's his home up there. What he gets up to, I have no idea, but he's harmless and he won't come downstairs while you are here.' She gave a small nervous laugh. 'Funny, I thought he would be working today. Not to worry. Come through, my dear. Let's make that tea and get some more biscuits.'

Teresa said that was a good idea, breathlessly, having also held her breath during William's entire entrance. There was a thump above her head again and she looked up one more time, more than a little nervous about Cheryl's son being in the house with her. She shook her thoughts away and focussed on helping Cheryl to the kitchen.

'I only have cheap tea, I'm afraid.'

'That would be lovely,' Teresa said, and they walked down the hallway, arm in arm.

CHAPTER 14

Detective Inspector Graham "Darth" Lucas was an overweight, grumpy man in his mid-forties who was divorced, had three kids, wore suits that were one and a half sizes too small for him, had a bushy moustache fashionable many decades ago, and stared with eyes that suggested he was either bored out of his brain or was plotting your demise. He was good police and Roark, who was now officially Senior Investigating Officer on the Peckham homicide, was glad that Lucas had been assigned to be her second in command.

They sat in the same meeting room where Roark and Knight had taken the phone call with the constables from Thames Valley who had found the missing van. Lucas sat across from Roark, a note pad and file of papers in front of him, either staring, almost passively, at Roark as she first made small talk and then gave him an overview of the case, or tracing over the heading he'd scratched at the top of his note pad during awkward silences.

They were waiting for Knight to join them. She was picking up a few more updates from the crime scene in Peckham. While Roark had been at the press conference, sitting, for the most part, quietly next to Detective Chief Inspector Rawlins as he did most of the talking and answered most of the questions, DC Knight had been collecting updates on the Peckham murder and the discovery of the stolen van in the Chiltern Hills.

Both Roark and Knight had been on duty for over seventeen hours now (and awake for almost twenty) and as the Peckham case was to be Roark's main focus until it was solved, she and Knight had been switched to the day shift, instead of their usual midnight to eight. Even though they were in the heat of battle on this case, Rawlins had been insistent that the two of them got some sleep and that, as SIO, Roark should delegate the night watch on the case to a second in command. This was an important case, so the teams would work two shifts of twelve hours, solely focussed on the case, Roark during the day, DI Lucas the night.

It all made sense, although Roark wasn't sure how much sleep she'd get tonight. She was wired, running on adrenaline, and she didn't want to take her eye off this case; Knight would be the same, but orders were orders, and it made sense that they both rested.

The door to the meeting room swung open and Knight bustled in, face flushed, a stack of untidy papers in her arms.

'Sorry to keep you,' she said and dumped the papers on the table.

'That's fine, Knight. I was just giving DI Lucas a brief update on the background of this case.'

'Darth,' Knight said in DI Lucas's direction.

Lucas nodded and grumbled. His opinion on the nickname was still unknown.

'Thanks for coming in early, Lucas, we appreciate it,' Roark asked. 'Knight, what have you got for us? Why don't you start with the van.'

Knight laid out a few papers in front of her but did not refer to them throughout her update, having committed it all to memory. She confirmed that the van found by Thames Valley police in the Chiltern Hills was the same van hired by the late Corey Whitman.

'Warren Campbell will be happy,' Roark said.

'He won't be getting it for a while, obviously. SOCO are poring over it as we speak. Thames Valley police also confirmed that the middle-aged couple that lived at the property had nothing to do with the vehicle.'

'As we thought.'

'We've managed to reverse engineer the van's journey from London to Chiltern Hills by locating it as it entered the Hills area from High Wycombe. Not many roads going in, not many cars on the roads at that time, so it was easy to pick him up. From there, we backtracked to London, but only to the outskirts, in Hounslow. We haven't been able to locate it in Central London yet. The CCTV footage from Southwark Council didn't help, but we're still working on the surrounding areas, trying to track where it went after Bishop Street. It first appears in Hounslow, heading west on its way to Chiltern Hills, just after midnight.'

'Midnight?' Roark said, incredulously. 'Whitman's body was discovered around two-thirty, correct?'

'That's right.'

'So he'd been lying there for almost three hours before we found him.'

'At least. We don't know where the van went between Bishops Street and Hounslow. Whitman was murdered sometime before midnight is all we know at this stage.'

'Unbelievable.'

'They did say his gate was closed, residential street not busy, difficult to spot.'

Roark shook her head. Not often did luck come into solving a case, but it was still annoying that the body hadn't been reported sooner. The perpetrator was miles away by the time Roark and Knight had reached the scene.

'Anyway,' Knight said, 'from Hounslow we've tracked the van to High Wycombe but lose it as it enters the Hills area. That was about one in the morning.'

'Do we have any idea what happened after he dumped the van?'

'Well, if I had to guess, he switched to another car.'

Roark gave Knight a look. 'We're already resorting to guessing?' she said, raising her eyebrows.

'No,' Knight said with mocked annoyance. 'I'm in the process of confirming that. I have a couple detectives checking vehicles with what cameras we have in the area, which isn't a lot. There's not much traffic that late at night, so if he backtracked to High Wycombe, we'll spot him, but if he goes any other direction, we don't think we'll have much coverage until we reach more built-up areas such as Aylesbury.'

'That far out though, you've got a lot more roads, a lot more cars to check. Could be a problem,' Roark said, scribbling in her notepad. She glanced at Lucas. He was staring at the table, almost catatonic.

'I know,' Knight said. 'I'm not holding out much hope for anything to come out of that. His car may not have even been where he dumped the van. He may have walked, taken a bus, who knows. I have Thames Valley doing door-to-doors around the area just in case he was dumb enough to live nearby, but again, not hoping for much.'

'Anything in the van?'

'Empty, but there were traces of blood in the back of the van. That and fingerprint work still ongoing.'

'Any good look at the driver at any point on the CCTV route?' Roark asked.

'Nothing on the street cameras. Difficult to see into the van. Windscreen looks pretty filthy. We'll try businesses and other locations along the route but I'm not holding my breath for a clear ID on this guy.'

'Anything more from the door knocks on Bishop Street?'

'No, and the murder weapon is still missing. Not in the van either. I'd say our culprit took it with him.'

'Lucas,' Roark said, 'can you head back to Bishop Street tonight, find some more witnesses? Also, see if you can get anything on who Corey Whitman fraternises with. It's possible he knew his killer, if this is not a random van jacking.'

Lucas nodded but didn't write anything down.

'Tell me about the bloods,' Roark said, moving back to Knight.

'Like I said, nothing on the van samples yet, but the crime scene work on Bishop Street is pretty much done, except for DNA sampling which will take a bit longer.'

'What have we got?'

'Not a lot. Blood samples taken on the pavement match Corey Whitman. Fingerprints in his flat also match his. Other than the pending DNA, we have no evidence of anyone else on the scene.'

'Given we have no witnesses and not much evidence, this attack may have been over quite quickly. Leads me to believe that the murder wasn't planned. Whitman may have challenged the man stealing his van and suffered the consequences. Whitman may not have been the target.'

'Doesn't make sense to steal the van just to dump it an hour later though?'

'I'm guessing he panicked after the murder.'

'Guessing, Detective Inspector?'

'Can it, Knight,' Roark said, good-naturedly, knowing the young detective was right.

Forget about the why until you arrest the guy.

'No traces on the gate to the property?'

Knight shook her head.

'Interesting. Unless he kicked it closed, he may have been wearing gloves.'

'Fingers crossed for DNA samples and something on the van,' Knight concluded. 'Other than that, we're none the wiser.'

Roark looked down the table at Lucas, who had been listening intently but still had not written anything down in his note pad.

'Any thoughts or questions, Lucas?'

Lucas blinked twice as if waking himself up.

'No questions. Sounds like we're at a dead end.'

Roark gave a short laugh.

'Yes, you could put it that way. We've got leads to follow up, so keep on top of those, head out to Bishop Street to see if you can get anything more from the neighbours. Follow up on the SOCO reports on the van and the DNA samples, and we'll pick up in the morning.'

Lucas grunted, nodded, and picked up his papers and left, slightly disgruntled. Roark and Lucas were at the same level of authority,

Detective Inspector, but as Senior Investigating Officer on the case, Roark was the boss on this one.

'He's not wrong,' Knight said after the meeting room door closed behind Lucas. 'We haven't got much to go on.'

'Well, we'll just have to be patient. Something will shake loose. DNA results may give us an ID.'

Knight nodded and tidied up the papers on the table.

'Rawlins told us to end our shift,' Roark said.

'I heard. I'd rather not.'

'I know, but we've got Darth on the case, and we need to be fresh tomorrow.'

'I'm determined to make that man laugh somehow.'

'Maybe a strip tease?'

'Funny.' Knight stood up, papers under her arm. 'Well if we're closing for the day, how about a quick one at The Goat. I could do with a drink.'

'You're on. Give me a moment to pop in to see Rawlins and I'll meet you downstairs.'

CHAPTER 15

The Disgruntled Goat was just around the corner from The Tank, a five-minute walk, and at quarter past six, there were enough people inside to avoid it being called "dead". There were plenty of other pubs in Camberwell that they could've gone to, but they preferred this one: it was somewhere between a pub and a wine bar, not too scuzzy, not too pretentious, beer on tap and quality wine by the glass. The green tiling on the walls were an interesting touch and the seating, including a row of booths along the back near the kitchen, were comfortable and spread out enough so that it was unlikely that anyone would be eavesdropping on their conversations. The other plus side: not many other coppers drank here.

Roark and Knight sat in one of the booths, comfortable, close to slouching. It had been a long day, up since ten o'clock the previous night, solid twenty hours straight. Intense too. The adrenaline of a new murder case got them through it, but once they slowed down, the exhaustion took hold. The only saving grace of the day was that they'd been lucky enough to slip past the handful of media vultures hovering around the front door to The Tank. Having to deal with a barrage of questions on the Peckham case right now would be the last straw.

Roark had a large glass of white wine, Knight a Sailor Jerry's on ice. It was her third and Roark was halfway through her second. They'd been in the bar for just short of an hour and were still talking about the case.

'We agree it's murder, right?' Knight said.

'Sure,' Roark said, taking a sip of her wine. 'Possibly manslaughter.'

'Well, I'm glad. And we agree our killer took Whitman's van and ditched it.'

'Well,' Roark said, her face crumpling, 'the van could be irrelevant in a way. Anyone could've taken the van. The killing may not even be related to the stolen van. We must wait on the evidence from the crime scene and the van to make any type of conclusion.'

'I can't understand the holdup.'

'Matching DNA takes a while sometimes, and I hear there's a backlog.'

'Surely we take precedence,' Knight said, necking the rest of her rum.

'Don't worry, we're on the fast track.'

'So,' Knight said, slamming her glass on the table for emphasis, 'they lift DNA from the crime scene and we'll have our killer.'

'If he's in the database,' Roark said, leaning back.

'I knew you were going to say something like that,' Knight said, looking over her shoulder back to the bar.

Roark shifted her slacks, feeling them pinch a bit. She'd eaten like a rubbish bin today and was feeling it. She considered a quick swim at the local tonight but instead took a generous sip of wine.

'It's a start,' she said. 'If he's not in the database, we can hope that we can link him to the van and then, we track down the driver. Once we have him, the evidence will back us up.'

'And how do we arrest him if the evidence doesn't back us up?' Knight said.

'Good detective work?'

Knight gave a short laugh, then studied her drink.

There was a moment of pause between them, Roark watching a couple come through the door into the bar, Knight studying her empty glass, swirling what ice was left in it around and around.

'Sorry about this morning,' Knight said. 'With my mum.'

'It's fine, Gale, don't worry about it. You thinking of heading down to see her?'

'I think I'll wait until Friday. She seems okay now. Just tough when things like this happen, right? The cancer was one thing, now she's falling down stairs every other day.'

'I don't think it's that bad,' Roark said, shifting in her seat, 'but I get what you're saying.'

Knight leaned back against her plush leather seat.

'How you doing, anyway?' Knight said. 'I've been caught up in myself the last few weeks I haven't asked.'

'In general? I'm fine.'

Roark ran her finger around the rim of her wine glass. Her father used to do that all the time, wet his finger, run it along his glass until it made a lovely harmonic sound. Roark could never get it right.

'Something on your mind,' Knight pressed.

An imposition maybe, but even though they'd only known each other for six months, they were already comfortable enough together that Knight knew she could ask the question.

Roark saw the letter stuck to her fridge door, the one from the NHS.

'Older woman stuff,' Roark said.

'Oh dear. I think I need another drink.'

'Fuck off,' Roark said and laughed.

'It's not something to do with your sex life, is it?'

'Sex life, or life without sex?'

'Come on, get out. You've had more lays this year than a bag of crisps. What about that last one? The one with the crooked nose. That was only last week.'

'Last month, my love. Yeah, Nose Guy was a little weird. I ghosted him in the end.'

'Harsh. But last month was only two weeks ago. Hardly a drought.'

'A few decisions to make, that's all.'

'What, between dating and fucking?'

'The age-old dilemma. Yeah, a bit of that. How about you? Still seeing men twice your age?'

'Ha, yes, you know me, daddy issues and all that.'

A waiter in a white shirt, black trousers and what looked like second-hand runners walked by and Knight nabbed him for another round.

'Last one for me,' Roark said. 'Bed is calling me.'

'Got it. I think I'm finally winding down too.'

'So, what's your plan?' Roark said. 'Who's the latest? This Ronald chap?'

'No,' Knight said, moving further along on the plush bench seat so she could put her feet up and lean on the wall. 'Man-baby, that one. He's either booked up for the latest toy convention or catching up on episodes of *The Clone Wars*.'

'What's that?'

'I don't fucking know and I don't fucking care. I think I'm done with gentlemen of an elderly persuasion. Waste of time.'

'Well, this is a turn-up for the books. Why the change?'

'I don't know whether it was this latest fall or not, but Mum's been getting all nostalgic about my childhood, going through photos, recounting stories. We've hardly talked about that stuff since she left Dad, but I think since the cancer, and now that fall, she's reflecting a lot on her life, our lives.'

'Pressuring you to have kids?'

'No, nothing like that. Not directly anyway. It has me thinking though. I'm starting to think about it. Time is ticking away and all that.'

Roark scoffed.

'We've had this conversation before. You're in your thirties, hardly running out of time.'

'Sure, but I've still got to find someone to have the kid with, right?'

'Not necessarily. IVF, adoption, plenty of other options.'

'You ever think of it?'

The waiter arrived with their drinks and Knight sat up. Roark took the moment to think about a response. Did she ever think about it? Not until that fucking letter.

'I mean,' Knight said, not letting it go, 'you've been free of that fuckwit for how long now?'

'Ten years.'

'You must have thought about it after you ditched him, right? You were young enough.'

Roark shook her head.

'Not really. Brandon and I never really wanted kids from the start and once it came to light he was not exactly the man I thought I'd married, that wasn't on the cards.'

'He was a cunt.'

'Yeah, he was.'

'A complete cunt.'

'It wasn't just that though. It's a tough one. What we see every day, on the job, I mean, it's hard to think about bringing someone into this shit storm of a world. Hardly seems like a good idea. Hard to reconcile the worst of human behaviour we see with raising a child.'

'Yeah,' Knight said, looking back at her glass again, possibly thinking about the body at that morning's crime scene.

'I just decided it was not the right thing to do,' Roark said. 'Anyway, moot point for me now.'

'Bullshit. You just said it; adoption could be the way forward.'

'Nah. Doesn't change the fact that I think having kids in this world is the most stupid thing to do,' Roark said and took a sip.

'Wow, you're really selling it to me.'

'Hey,' Roark said, raising both hands up, 'that's just my opinion right.'

'I hear what you're saying.'

'You seriously thinking about it, though?'

'Yeah, it's possible, but I'd need help. I don't think raising a kid as a single parent should be a choice in my profession. Not just what you said, but the hours are not entirely flexible.'

'Does this mean you are thinking you might start dating men from your generation from now on?'

'Very funny. Possibly. Free some of the older folks for your Saturday Night Shag club.'

'It'd be appreciated,' Roark said, raising her glass to Knight before drinking the rest of her wine down.

'I used to find the men at my age so immature and reckless, but the last few of these old fellas have been the opposite in a bad way.'

'Boring and boring.'

'Right. No energy. Fan boys for Disney Plus. And all of them have baggage I could do without.'

'Here, here.'

They finished off their drinks, talked about family and friends, and ultimately, back to the murder on Bishop Street for another fifteen minutes. Roark found herself nodding off at one point, so they called it quits for the night. They left the bar as it began to fill up, nodding to one or two familiar faces as they exited. They hugged on the street and said they'd keep in touch if anything broke on the case overnight. Knight walked off towards Denmark Hill where she lived, and Roark jumped on the 36 bus to Vauxhall.

It was close to eight o'clock when Roark stepped off the bus. Vauxhall was busy. The national rail station was disgorging commuters and the tube was sucking in revellers and in between, people were drinking and eating at some of the restaurants and bars in the arches under the rail bridge. There was a nice vibe out, but Roark had to head home and rest. The case needed to keep moving and she had to be at her best tomorrow to make sure that happened.

A ten-minute walk down Kennington Lane and she turned off on to her street, a long line of three storey tenements on one side, council flats on the other surrounding a small park. Her salary as a Detective Inspector wasn't a lot but she'd done well out of her divorce settlement with Brandon, keeping the three-bedroom tenement that they'd bought together. It was still small, the rooms not that spacious and the stairway narrow, but she'd lived in it alone for ten years now and loved it. It was rare for her to look at the two spare bedrooms and think about the children they must have planned for when they bought the place. Rarely, but more often lately than she felt comfortable with.

The fucking letter. It was the letter's fault.

She loved her home, and it was days like the day she'd just had that she loved it even more. A place to herself. A kitchen with a fridge full of the food she enjoyed cooking from scratch or pre-prepared meals that she could bake in the oven for thirty minutes while she sipped a glass of wine.

There was a larger than normal bathroom separate to her ensuite, which she could run a hot bath in, fill up with candles and bath bombs and fragrance stuff that she absolutely adored and found essential for winding down. Occasionally, she'd drop a few rose petals in the bath, the hopeless romantic she knew she was but denied to anyone who pointed it out to her.

The meals, the bath, the home; it all came down to a functional process in the end. A way of regaining a sense of normality through a well-cooked meal, washing away the filth accumulated during the day, and closing the door on all the heinous shit she had seen. Cleansing her mind of the burden of work and the images of destruction she saw each day.

Tonight, the process didn't work so well. Sitting at the kitchen table, in her bathrobe after the bath, her short hair wet but drying fast, her legs crossed as she sipped the rest of her wine, she could only think of the dead body found in Peckham and the man who had killed him.

And of course, the letter.

She flapped the paper in her hand.

This stupid fucking NHS letter.

Before she could think logically about what she was doing, something she would later blame on the four glasses of wine, she was on her mobile.

'Julia speaking.'

'It's me.'

'Kris? Jesus.'

'Hey, nice to hear from you too.'

'You know it's not a good idea to call me.'

'I didn't know that.'

'Well, I'm telling you. It's not a good idea to call me.'

'I'm glad I called so you can tell me that.'

'What is it?'

Roark leaned back in her chair, a slight skip in her heart, a skip and a small stab of pain. She took another sip of wine. She flapped the letter again. Read the subject heading and immediately regretted making the call.

'Nothing. I just wanted to hear your voice.'

She cringed. That sounded bad. Needy. Should've just mentioned the letter.

'We spoke about this, Kris,' Julia said, her voice calm.

Roark wondered if she'd prefer it if Julia had been angry instead, not kind and understanding like she was all the damn time.

'You're right. I just miss our talks. You were always a good listener.'

There was silence on the other end of the line, then: 'This is unfair, Kris.'

'I know, I know. I've had a tough day today. I just . . . I know that's not a good enough excuse.'

Roark heard another voice down the line, just in ear shot, a male's voice, Julia's husband.

'I've gotta go, Kris.'

'I get it,' Roark said and was about to apologise but she knew Julia hated that. 'I'll let you go.'

'You take care.'

'Julia?'

'Yeah.'

'Do you think we could see each other again? As friends. We used to talk a lot, as friends, right?'

'We did,' Julia said, 'but I don't know, Kris. I don't know.'

Almost as punishment, something she'd later felt she deserved, the sound of a baby crying could be heard down the phone.

'I've gotta go, Kris, I really do.'

'Got it.'

Before she could say anything else, the call disconnected. Roark placed her mobile on the table and looked at it for a moment. Her eyes drifted to the letter lying next to it.

She'd have to make the decision herself. She knew that. Before she'd had her fourth wine and called Julia, she knew the decision was all hers to make. The fact that she didn't have anyone to talk it through with was by the by. She could feel sorry for herself about that particular topic another time. In the end, there was a decision to be made here and it was hers to make.

Roark finished off the glass of wine in one gulp, picked up her phone, and went up the stairs to bed, leaving the letter behind.

CHAPTER 16

Dull overcast day. The sky grey with a sea of clouds. The colours of London faded.

Roark felt tired, weary. The four glasses of wine last night were probably a bad idea, given she had to front up to a murder investigation this morning. The long first night of the case and the forced change in shifts were catching up with her. There was a fogginess behind her eyes that matched the weather, the threat of a headache looming.

At the corner, on the road leading to The Disgruntled Goat, she bumped into DC Knight.

'People will start talking,' Knight said with a smile.

'Let them,' Roark replied.

'Any news?'

'Nothing.'

'Looks like the media are still on it.'

They could see a few media vans parked on the road and a dozen reporters hovering around the steps leading up to The Tank's main reception. Cameras were set up at any available spare space to allow the reporters to provide live coverage. Even in London, the murder of an individual was news, but to have so many about suggested it had been a slow news week.

''Round the back,' Roark said.

The narrow alley at the back of the grey building was wet with rain from last night. Pieces of drowned rubbish stuck to the ground. A handful of reporters were in the alley, doing the occasional circuit around the building to catch coppers attempting to escape questions.

'No comment,' Roark said as they bustled their way inside.

Detective Inspector Lucas was at his desk eating a substantial pastry, half of it in his mouth, the other half disintegrated into crumbs on his desk. Roark and Knight hovered in his view, towering over him. He didn't rush himself, took precious moments to wipe sugar and pastry from his mouth and moustache.

'Nothing much happened overnight,' he grumbled.

Roark waited, thinking that there would be more but there wasn't.

'Interviews on Bishop Street?'

Lucas passed over a thin manila folder with a handful of handwritten sheets of paper in it.

'Check your email too,' he said, but nothing more.

'Thanks, Darth,' Knight said, unable to help herself.

Roark felt compelled to elbow her in the ribs.

They sat at Roark's desk, a cup of milky coffee each from the machine, and checked emails. There was a profile dump on Corey Whitman, some constable having consolidated the information that they had on him into a one-page report. There was the assault outside the Peckham pub and the unsubstantiated involvement in a drug deal. Nothing significant but both were worth checking out.

'Let's send an officer out to the assault victim,' Roark said to Lucas from her desk. 'Long shot, but maybe there was more to that altercation than a drunken brawl.'

'Already done,' Lucas said as he climbed into his jacket, crumbs dropping from his mouth as he spoke. 'Report's in your email.'

'And the drug deal?' Roark said as she scanned her computer screen for Lucas's email.

'Dead end,' he said. 'Dealer involved no longer with us.'

'Okay, thank you, Lucas,' Roark said. 'Thanks for covering us overnight too.'

Lucas grumbled something and left the office.

Roark opened Lucas's email and read out loud the report on the assault from the interviewing officer. There had been a fight in an alleyway outside the Peckham bar, a scrappy altercation over money, about ten pounds. Hardly cause for murder even if Corey did fracture the victim's cheekbone. The officer said that the victim didn't want to go into the details, was quite shy about it.

'Wonder why he was so shy. Maybe they knew each other.'

'Illicit behaviour?'

'Blow job in an alley?' Roark asked.

'Not right now,' Knight replied.

'Shut it. Anyway, the man retracted his complaint when he sobered up the next day. On record, but no charge on Corey.'

Knight swivelled in her seat next to Roark, stopped, tapped the desk with her fingernail.

'Probably worth me going back,' she said, 'pushing him a bit more on the reason for the fight. Might lead to others Corey has had similar altercations with. Over a greater amount of money. Enough to get him killed.'

'It's a stretch but could be something. Give him a few hours, then have a chat.' Roark scrolled down the short one-page report on Corey's priors. 'No known associates. I was hoping there might be some leads here.'

'Dead ends,' Knight said, blowing air and pulling out her phone.

Roark pushed the keyboard out of the way and opened the manila folder of witness statements taken by DI Lucas on Bishop Street. They were not memorable, from what Roark could decipher from Lucas's handwriting. Lazy bastard could've at least typed it up and stuck it on the online Case Database where all case reports, interviews and summaries were collated. Not that there was anything worthwhile in the pages she flicked through.

Another email pinged on her computer.

'SOCO report on the van has come in,' she said. She scanned the information quickly.

'Anything earth-shattering?'

'DNA matching is outstanding, but the trace blood samples found in the van's rear interior do not match Corey's taken at the crime scene.'

'Our man leaked some claret?'

'Possibly Corey fought back. Or it's unrelated.'

Knight was reading the same report on her phone when she said, 'No blood in the driver's seat. That's odd. If Corey bled this guy, why are there traces in the back and not in the front?'

'Not sure. The killer could've staunched the wound.'

'But he's bleeding in the rear of the van? Why is he back there?'

'Like I said, could be unrelated. Person who stole the van could be unrelated to the homicide, but note down the question in the case file anyway,' Roark said.

Knight rolled her chair over to her own computer and opened the Case Database and started typing.

'This could be payback for something Corey did. Or it could be a straightforward carjacking. Or,' Knight said, pausing her typing, 'it could be something else entirely.'

'Are you reaching for motive again, Detective Constable?'

Knight gave her the finger without turning around.

A figure appeared in Roark's periphery, and she looked up. Detective Sergeant Thompson was standing by her desk, one arm on the cubicle wall. She ignored him and returned to her screen.

'Hope I'm not interrupting anything, ladies,' he said with a smirk.

Knight didn't look around but said, 'What do you want, dumbass?'

'I found your van,' Thompson said, smiling.

Roark stopped, looked back up at him.

Thompson was a handsome lad, late thirties, short black hair, chiselled features, honed muscles under his short sleeved shirt, but a real full grade, full time dickhead. Knight kept her head down and Roark remembered he'd tried it on with her one crazy after-shift night in Brixton. She'd be in the unit for only a few weeks but hadn't needed Roark to tell her Thompson was a dick, didn't need her warning that sucking face with the asshole would be a mistake. All Thompson got that night from Knight was a glass of Rosé over his head.

'We've already got the van, you idiot,' Knight said.

Thompson ignored her, continued grinning.

'What is it, Detective Sergeant?' Roark said.

'This way, ladies,' he said, and beckoned them to follow.

Roark sighed and stood up. Knight remained seated, scrolling some app on her phone. Roark followed DS Thompson across the floor. He sat in a corner of the office that seemed to have been reserved for all the male fuckwits in the squad. A group of five of them, desks bunched together, the place a tip. It smelled like she'd stepped into a teenage boy's bedroom; sweat and spunk and beer farts.

'Make it quick, Thompson, I'm gagging here.'

Thompson dropped in his chair, stretched his legs out and crossed them at the ankles. He put his hands behind his head. One of the nearby Detective Constables joined him, sitting on the edge of the desk.

'We picked up a Misper early this morning,' Thompson said, grinning.

'And?'

'Suit in his mid-thirties, hasn't turned up to work for the second day in a row. No one can get hold of him. Last seen around his office on Wednesday night, working late. We did some searching around the Waterloo area and picked up this. Hit it, Johnny.'

The constable pressed the space bar on the computer behind Thompson and CCTV footage appeared on the monitor and started playing. Grainy, dark, but they had a clear view of a man walking down a quiet backstreet, the overhead streetlights illuminating his face.

'Who's that?' Roark said.

'Our Misper.'

'What time is this?'

'About eleven thirty.'

The camera switched to a view from further away and the opposite side of the street, capturing the man in the suit walking along the pedestrian pathway into a tunnel under one of the many train tracks in Waterloo. He disappeared into the darkness. The camera switched again, this time on the other side of the tunnel, a CCTV camera high up observing a one-way street. The narrow road leading out of the tunnel connected to the street at a stop sign.

Nothing happened for a few minutes and Roark took a breath, about to complain that she didn't have time to waste watching still life CCTV footage when Thompson anticipated her and raised a hand.

'Wait,' he said. 'Here it is.'

A white van slowly rolled out from the darkness within the tunnel, headlights off. As it moved towards the stop sign, it's high beams flashed on, momentarily dazzling the camera. The headlights switched down to normal and it turned into the one-way street. As it drove away from the camera, the constable reached over and tapped the space bar.

Thompson passed over an A4 page, a printout of a close-up of the back of the van. Slightly blurred, it was still possible to read the registration number on the plate.

'What you got?' DC Knight said, appearing beside Roark.

'That's your van, right? The one in your homicide?' Thompson said.

'It is,' Roark said, passing the page to Knight. 'And your Misper?'

'Never re-appeared from that tunnel. My guess, he's in your van.'

'Jesus,' Knight said.

'A thank-you will suffice,' Thompson said, the grin still spread across his face.

'Who's the suit?' Knight asked.

The Detective Constable, Johnny, picked up another piece of paper and passed it over. Roark looked down at an ID profile for a company security pass. Mid-thirties like Thompson had said, handsome, shock of brown hair, impeccable suit.

'Aaron Sparger,' Thompson said as Roark read it on the page. His smile, somehow, broadened. 'Looks to me like you've got a kidnapping on top of your murder, don't you think?'

'Shit,' Roark whispered.

'Well,' Knight said, passing back the page, 'looks like we're off the case then.'

'Come on,' Roark said to Knight and led her towards the stairwell, heading to the top floor and DCI Rawlins office.

'Our pleasure,' she heard Thompson shout out behind her and she swore under her breath again. Her headache was forming quickly behind her eyes.

Chapter 17

They leave him.

The female detective motions to the male and they both get up. She excuses herself, says they will only be a few minutes, offers a drink or something to eat. Howard says, no he is fine. They close the door and leave him alone.

He wipes sweat from his forehead. He doesn't feel warm, but he is perspiring just the same. He should've asked for water, he is thirsty, but he just wants this over and done with. He has nothing to give them. He can't help them with their enquiries, can't they see that? Can't they just leave him alone?

The boy.

The memories: he's used to them. Especially over the past month or so when he's made a conscious effort to drag them out of the back of his head. Sitting up in the attic in his flat, in the darkness, encouraging the dark spaces to envelop him, holding fast, trying to be brave, in the face of remembering everything that happened.

He can handle that. He controls the environment enough to know he can stop if he wants to.

But this, this consistent questioning, prying into his past, eliciting reactions from him that are private, that are only for him to experience, no one else.

It feels like rape, more than he ever thought it would.

He takes a deep breath and drums his fingers on the tabletop.

He must do it now that he agreed to help them. He must answer their questions, answer them quickly so he can leave.

When he decided that he would help the detectives out, he felt confident that he could keep himself together, keep a clear mind and provide concise answers. Help them out. Give them what they want and then they'd leave him alone.

That's all he had to do: answer their questions, short and sharp, and they would leave him alone.

It's the room that is making it hard. The small room with the windows blocked by foliage and trees, the dull lightbulb swinging above his head, the dark corners that move in and out, depending on how vulnerable he feels.

It's the room and the questioning and the memories.

There is a knock at the door and he jumps. The door opens and she walks in. She closes the door behind her and sits down.

'Sorry about that,' she says. 'I had to check something with my partner.'

He tilts his head slightly to look behind her at the closed door.

'Oh, he's gone to get us all a drink. I know you didn't want anything, but it's best to have some water. Just in case.'

'Okay,' he says.

He is relieved the male detective has not returned immediately. His gaze, both unrelenting and disinterested, is unsettling. More so than the female detective, who is also unsettling, but in a more direct, confrontational way. This, he prefers, if he had a choice.

He'd rather none of it. He'd rather be back at home. Safe and secure. He'd even prefer to be back up in the attic, reliving the memories, but on his own terms, not hers. In control. Not like this.

'We don't have to wait,' she says. 'Please, continue.'

His eyes go wide, questioning her, forgetting what they had been talking about.

'The girl,' she says, prompting him.

'Oh,' he says, scrunching up his face as if he has sucked on something sour, 'I don't want to talk about that.'

'Why not?'

'I – I just don't see the point.'

'Trust me,' she says, holding his gaze. 'It's important.'

He makes the face again. He doesn't trust her. Not at all.

'Okay, let me help,' she says, glancing briefly at her notes. 'It is March 1994, over six months since Wendy and Ryan Cooper were released by your father. Another mother and child go missing, this time in the Lake District. They are on holiday on their own and disappear. Your father took them, correct?'

The boy wakes up with a start. The attic around him is dark. No light shines through the gap in the floorboards. He stares into the darkness above him and hears his stomach rumbling. He is always hungry.

There's a sound from outside. Doors banging. Someone crying.

His father shouting.

She looks at him expectantly, but he drops his gaze, stares at the table. He is noticing all the imperfections in the table now, a typography of nervous scratchings, bored pen marks, dark spotted stains.

'The girl is four years old,' she says.

Father shouts and the crying gets louder. The boy hears anger in his father's voice and the crying stops.

Light shoots up from the gap in the floor and the boy scuttles over, looks down into the kitchen.

His father descends into the cellar, a woman over his shoulder, a small girl dragged behind him, noiselessly. She stares up and the boy flinches as if he has been seen, but the girl does not react, her eyes glazed over. So scared that she has slipped into a state of shock.

The boy wonders why his father did not ask for his help with the girl, like he had done with Ryan.

'Tell me what you remember, Howard?'

The door opens behind her and the large, grumpy detective with the dark moustache walks in, holding three mugs of various sizes and colours in his hands. He kicks the door closed behind him and places all three cups on the table. One of the mugs is filled with a dark liquid, a black coffee, one that fills his nostrils with an overwhelmingly pleasant aroma.

The male detective takes the mug of coffee for himself and sits back down in his chair in the corner, amongst the shadows. The female takes one of the mugs of water and pushes the other across. He doesn't touch it.

'Do you remember seeing the girl, Howard?'

'A little bit,' he says.

'What do you remember?'

'She cried a lot. All the time. If she wasn't crying, she was asleep, exhausted from crying.'

'How did that make you feel?'

The boy sees his father getting angrier and angrier every day. The girl cries non-stop, a high-pitched wailing followed by loud gulps for air, like a drowning fish. Every time she is taken from the cellar and placed at the kitchen table to eat or play games with his father, she cries. Unrelenting. And when his father slams the table in frustration, she cries even louder.

When his father gives up and returns her to her mother in the cellar, everyone breathes a sigh of relief and savours the quiet.

And in these moments of quiet, the boy tries to remember the last time he sat at the kitchen table to eat with his father. Tries to remember the last time he played with his toys and board games, wore his own clothes. Slept in his own bed.

Tries to remember the last time his father spoke to him, looked at him with love, registered his existence.

Tries to remember, fails and starts to cry. Not like the girl, but with silent, soft, private tears.

'Where were you when this was happening, Howard? Could you not have helped calm the girl down?'

'Nothing would stop her.'

'Nothing? Surely if you offered to play with her.'

'Nothing,' he says, forcefully.

'Did that annoy you?'

'No. It upset me. And it upset my father.'

'What did your father do, when he was upset?'

The boy stares through the gap in the attic floor and sees his father give up. Angry and then defeated. He wants to go downstairs and tell his father that everything will be alright, but he knows his father will beat him.

Or worse.

He could ignore him.

'I don't understand why I have to answer these questions.'

'Howard, indulge me.'

He makes to scoff but he splutters instead and spit dribbles down his chin. He wipes it away.

'Do you remember the girl's name?'

Another handbag. Another photo identification. His father's shouting at the crying girl, shouting at her to shut up.

'Yes.'

'Tell me.'

'Laura.'

'I see. Last name?'

He knows it but shakes his head.

'Laura Kilpatrick,' she says. 'The mother's name was Iona.'

'Okay.'

'Your father released them less than a fortnight after taking them, found alive and well in the Cotswolds. Laura was a mess but physically, they were both fine.'

She stops talking. He stares at the table but can see that she is studying him. Waiting for a reaction. She pulls out something from her file and places it on the table, face down.

'Tell me, Howard. Do you think you would recognise Laura Kilpatrick if I showed you a recent photo?'

He frowns, shakes his head slowly without looking up.

'Please Howard,' she says, and he sees a flash of light reflecting off the large photo she now displays in front of her. 'Take a look and tell me what you think.'

He stares at the table.

'Howard?'

He says nothing.

There is a screech of a chair and the male detective stands up.

Howard raises his head quickly, not looking at the male detective, but directly at the photo of the blond-haired woman, who stares back at him, her eyes intense, her smile warm.

One night the boy hears the crying stop abruptly and the sound of his father's truck driving away, down through the trees towards the main road and he thanks his father for getting rid of the crying brat, thankful that he will never see her face again, and he hopes that, finally, now that she has gone, everything will be back to normal again.

CHAPTER 18

Donald Pleasance walked towards the open window. He looked down onto the ground below. The Boogeyman had disappeared.

John Carpenter's score kicked off and Jaime's friends started whooping and hollering, jumping up and down on the sofa. Jericho started mewling like a ghost. Jaime had to start clapping. The screen flicked across images of the carnage left by the Boogeyman over the past ninety minutes, overlaid with Carpenter's music and deep rhythmic breathing.

'Ben, that sounds like you when you're sleeping,' Misaki said, elbowing Ben in the ribs, making him spill his espresso martini.

'More like when he's looking through bedroom windows,' Jericho laughed.

'That was fucking awesome,' Helen said.

With the credits on *Halloween* scrolling, Jaime jumped up in front of the television, spread her arms wide, losing most of her banana daiquiri in the process.

'What do you think of the best horror movie ever?' she shouted.

Her five friends yelled in unison, drinks spilling onto the sofa.

'And how about the best final girl in the history of horror and, of course, my namesake, Jaime Lee Fucking Curtis?' she shouted again.

The small group erupted.

'Okay, hand over your bingo cards and I'll tally them up, see how you guys went.'

Jaime leaned over and started taking the A4 pages she had printed up, seeing scribbles on all of them, excited that her friends were really getting into the movie night. The cards had been her idea, ticking off iconic moments in the film like bingo numbers, to keep the buzz going. She had considered drinking games, like a shot of tequila for every time you spotted The Shape in the background or a woman screamed, but she didn't want the night to end up in drunken debauchery one movie in.

'What's next?' Misaki yelled out.

'Alright, now, we're staying in the seventies,' she said, 'and moving onto another classic and what I think is the scariest horror movie of all time. Next on our Classic Horror Movie Night is, drum roll please... *The Exorcist.*'

Everyone cooed in awe.

'Isn't this the one U2 wrote a song about?' Ben said, getting up on his knees on the sofa.

'What song?'

"*Lady with the Spinning Head.*"

Misaki pushed him over.

'I don't get it,' Helen said.

'That's not a fucking U2 song, you idiot,' Jericho said.

'Yeah, it is. It's a B-side,' Ben said, picking himself up.

'Alright,' Jaime said, 'let's stay focused everyone. Now, who has seen the original *Exorcist*?'

Only Misaki raised her hand.

'Oh wow, this is going to be exciting. Okay, Ben, throw on some tunes and I'll hand the new Bingo cards out. We'll start up in twenty. I'll put more sausage rolls on too. Drink top-ups for everyone?'

She was met with a yell of positivity.

'Brilliant! Misaki come help me with the refills.'

Jaime and Misaki moved into the kitchen which was starting to look like a bomb had hit it. Used glasses and plates everywhere. Half-eaten food on the bench, crumbs covering the floor. A clean up job tomorrow for sure, but Jaime didn't care.

'It's going well, don't you think?' Jaime said, placing her daiquiri and *Halloween* Bingo cards down on the counter.

'Awesome, Jay. I love *Halloween*. One of my favourites too, but not my ultimate favourite.'

'I know, I know. *Scream* is your favourite.'

'Damn straight. Tell me it's movie number three, come on.'

'Sorry, love, nothing from the nineties,' Jaime said, pre-heating the oven. She moved over to the fridge and pulled out a packet of sausage rolls. 'I refuse to call *Scream* a classic horror movie because it makes me feel so old. I was six when that came out.'

'What's after *The Exorcist* then?' Misaki said, grabbing what clean glasses she could find out of the cupboard.

Music started up from the living room behind them, loud, but not too loud. It sounded like a U2 song, but not one she'd heard before. She could hear Ben telling everyone that he'd told them so.

'Don't tell anyone yet.'

'I won't.'

'*The Thing.*'

'Ooh, Carpenter again. I'm cool with that. I *think* I've seen it before but I'm not sure.'

'You'd know if you'd seen it. I hope you haven't. Nothing better than watching favourite movies with people who haven't seen them before. Another reason not to show *Scream*.'

'Okay,' Misaki said, 'you've made your point.'

There was a high-pitched ringing coming from the front door. Sharp and short, repeated seconds later.

'Doorbell,' Jaime said.

'Neighbours?'

'I doubt it. It's not that late and we're not that loud. It's someone downstairs trying to get in. Just ignore it.'

She hustled sausage rolls out onto a baking tray and popped them in the oven. She hit the timer for twenty minutes.

'I'll bake up another Camembert,' she said, heading back to the fridge. 'You've got the drinks?'

'I'm all over it.'

The door buzzed again.

'So,' Misaki said, 'I went out on another date with Gerry last night.'

'No way,' Jaime said, returning with the cheese. 'I thought the first night was a disaster.'

'It was, but he sweet-talked me into it,' Misaki said, throwing ice into a glass.

'How did it go?'

'Disaster.'

'Oh, Saki.'

'I'm seeing him again on Wednesday,' Misaki said, lifting a bottle of champagne and giving her hip a waggle.

'Glutton for punishment,' Jaime said. 'Prosecco, not champers, love.'

'Boo,' Ben said, jumping in between them.

'Don't be a fuckhead, Ben,' Misaki shouted. 'I've got fucking champagne all over the place.'

'Oh, the woes of the middle class. And it should be prosecco, not champagne.'

'No shit, dickhead.'

'There's someone buzzing the fuck out of your door, Jay,' Ben said.

'Just ignore it,' Jaime said, opening the oven door to put the camembert inside.

'Nah, I'll check on it,' Ben said. 'Whoever it is, he isn't going away and it's killing the vibe.'

'If it's the neighbours,' Jaime said, 'invite them in.'

'No problemo. Don't forget the orange slice, Saki,' Ben said, tapping Misaki on the shoulder.

'Fuck your orange slice,' she said.

Jaime laughed.

'So why are you persisting with this Gerry guy? You said he was boring. You said he smelled.'

'I said that?'

'And he keeps talking about how good the Tories are.'

'Yeah, he's still all that. Has a kid too.'

'Holy fuck, Saki, what are you doing? Why are you sticking with this guy?'

Masaki shrugged her shoulders as she topped up the prosecco with Aperol.

'What can I say, he makes me cum.'

Jaime slapped her on the shoulder.

'He does not.'

'Let's just say, he's on a hat-trick Wednesday night. The crowd's already doing the slow hand clap.'

'Stop it.'

'The bowler is running in.'

'Shut up, Saki. You know nothing about cricket.'

Ben emerged between them again and reached across for his Aperol Spritz. Masaki slapped his hand away.

'Fuck off. I haven't done your precious orange slice yet.'

'Please dear, let me,' Ben said, sidling up behind Masaki and wrapping his arms around her waist. Misaki didn't protest.

'Ben,' Jaime said, 'who was at the door?'

'Amazon guy. Said you had to go down and sign for it.'

'You go down, you big oaf,' Misaki said, reaching across and grabbing an orange from the fruit bowl.

'There's a half cut one just there, Saki,' Ben said, pointing further down the kitchen bench.

'Who's making this drink? Anyway, you need to go downstairs and deal with the delivery boy.'

'No can do,' Ben said, stepping away, already moving back towards the tablet that controlled the music. 'Has to be you, Jaime.'

'Really?' Jaime said, picking up a hand towel and wiping her hands.

'He said you had to sign for it. No one else,' Ben called as he disappeared back into the living room.

'That's bullshit,' Misaki said.

'Doesn't matter. I'll go.'

'I'll come with.'

'No,' Jaime said. 'Finish the drinks. I'll get it. It's probably not for me anyway. Can't remember ordering anything.'

'Secret admirer?'

'Sending me Amazon deliveries?'

'How romantic.'

Jaime laughed and walked through the living room to the front door. Ben had put on Tubular Bells. The vibe was excellent. She loved these nights. Friends, horror movies, cocktails; her favourite night in.

Jericho gave her a wink as she passed, and she gave him a warm smile.

Okay, some friends might end up being more than just friends. As she reached the front door and opened it, she couldn't help but smile, thinking about the night's possibilities.

The communal corridor outside her flat was empty, lights illuminating the carpeted floors and the other doors on either side. She didn't expect the Amazon guy to be here. There was no way to her front door unless someone had let him in the main security door downstairs. It did happen on occasion, but rarely, so Jaime had to make her way down the stairs and outside to sign for the parcel.

The music was loud coming through her open door, so Jaime closed it behind her and walked to the stairwell. She took the first flight of stairs down a little too quickly, almost tripping on the last step. She may have had more Daquiris than she had thought.

Her one-bedroom flat was on the fourth floor of a tenement block that held over thirty flats. It was her first home which she had owned, managing on her thirty-first birthday six months ago to put a deposit down and secure a mortgage. It had been a joyful moment in her life, buying property and leaving the frustrating rental game behind. Sure, her parents came to the party with the money, but she was proud of her purchase. She loved showing off her flat too, particularly to the people she cared about.

At the bottom of the stairs was the reception, bathed in overhead lights. There was a row of thirty mailboxes along the right-hand side wall, leading to the security door. The door was sturdy but had a glass

95

section which was opaque outside and only slightly blurred from the inside, so you could see who was buzzing the door, the outdoor security light sensor activating with movement. The solid security setup was one of the reasons she'd been attracted to the flat.

This part of Bristol, a few miles out from the city centre, was a reasonable neighbourhood with small pockets of troubled areas, but where Jaime lived, she felt safe and often walked home from her job managing a trendy bar near the university with no problems. It was currently late at night, around eleven-thirty, but she had no immediate concerns as she pressed the exit button on the left and pulled open the heavy door.

The security light switched on as she stepped out. Directly across the road, which was wet with a light mist of rain that had stopped moments ago, she spotted the Amazon delivery van, but no driver. The van was parked near the opposite curb, rear doors open, bathed in the yellow streetlights.

Jaime tilted her head, looking towards the front of the van. Its driver side door was closed, and there appeared to be no one sitting in the driver's seat.

'Hello?' she called.

No answer.

She looked up and down the road, thinking maybe the delivery man had moved on after she'd taken so long to come down from her flat, on to the next delivery down the street. There was no one though. To the left and right the pathway was wet and empty. Cars moved back and forth further up on the main street, but no one turned in, and there were no pedestrians that she could see. The other direction was a dead end, around the bend, so the delivery man may have wandered up there. It was unlikely. With the rear doors to the van wide open, no doubt full of undelivered brown cardboard boxes full of Amazon purchases, she doubted he'd have left the van unattended and out of sight.

There was a scuffling sound, a grunt, an exasperated sigh, all coming from the direction of the van.

'Hello?' Jaime said. 'Is anyone there?'

There was a faint reply, muffled, coming from the other side of the van.

'Over here,' someone called.

Jaime shook her head even though she knew no one could see her.

Hell no, she wasn't falling for that old trick.

'You buzzed,' she yelled out. 'A delivery for me?'

There was silence. Another scuffle. The van rocked, almost imperceptibly.

'Is everything okay?'

'I need some help. This is heavy.'

The voice was heavy set, deep, but clear.

Fuck that. She'd seen *Silence of the Lambs*. No way was she going to fall for that.

'I'll get my male friends to help,' she said, using the idle threat as something to put this guy off, whatever he might be planning, but as she said it, she thought it was probably a good idea anyway.

'Jaime?' the man said. 'Jaime Collander, right?'

'Yes, that's right,' she called back.

'Okay, I think I have it,' the man said from behind the van. 'It's just a bit tricky.'

Jaime stepped up onto the pavement, shouted okay, then stepped back down, turned to buzz her flat on the intercom.

She heard grunting and quiet swearing, heard the clanging of something metal near the front of the van, and turned away from the intercom. Another grunt, then a yell, swearing, echoing across the street. There was a loud crash. An Amazon box slid out from under the front driver's side wheel of the van, coming to rest in the middle of the street. A loud groan followed it.

'Are you okay?' she said.

She bent down slightly, squinting against the streetlights. There was an outstretched hand near the front tyre, palm up. Someone lying on the ground.

'Oh shit,' Jaime said.

She hesitated, thinking back to all the horror movies she'd watched where the characters investigated noises in the middle of the night only to be slaughtered by some raving lunatic in a mask.

The hand wasn't moving.

Jaime cursed herself for not reacting immediately, someone was in trouble, and this wasn't the damn movies. She made a direct line for the front of the van and the outstretched arm.

'Are you okay?' she said again. 'What happened?'

As she approached, she could see that the Amazon delivery man was lying flat on his stomach, head face down towards her, one arm stretched out. His Amazon cap was upside down nearby and as she rounded the front of the van, she could see a lifting trolley tipped over near the curb behind him, boxes scattered around it.

The delivery man didn't look good. Flat on his stomach and not moving. Jaime quickly squatted down near his head, not sure what to do. She'd done basic first-aid training for her management job at the university bar, but her mind was struggling to pull the information out, slightly blurred by the alcohol she'd had.

Check for pulse, she remembered. Check for breathing. Raise the head. Call a fucking ambulance.

She reached down, felt for a pulse in his neck. Immediately she pulled back, having touched something hot and wet. Raising her fingers up into the streetlight, she saw blood and gasped.

'Mister,' she said, and reached out and shook his left shoulder. He didn't respond. She pulled out her phone and quickly activated the torch on it. Shining it down on the man's face, she could see his eyes were closed, mouth partially open, blood specking his skin.

She leaned down, tried to listen for breathing. There may have been something there, something faint.

She stood up. Time to call triple nine. She scrolled her phone and tapped on the icon, bringing up the number pad to make a call.

She jumped at the sound of a car door slamming behind her and she almost dropped her phone. She turned around and stared down the length of the van, hoping it was someone who could help. She stopped, noticing that the rear door of the Amazon van closest to her was now closed.

A second delivery man?

'Hello?' she called. 'This man's fallen, he needs help.'

There was no response, no sound, nothing, and she immediately thought, no, she had never seen two delivery men deliver Amazon before, always a sole driver, not an assistant, that's not how they operated and that was not who closed the door. No, it was probably someone trying to steal the van and everything in it. Someone who had knocked out the driver, taken his keys, and was now about to steal the van.

She stood up and took a step back.

'I'm calling the police,' she said.

Head down, hitting nine three times on her phone, she saw the shadow rushing towards her too late. It leaped out from the front of the van, emerged out of the darkness behind the vehicle, jumping over the toppled trolley and the man on the ground, and rushed at her. She instinctively flinched and the large, heavy body smacked into her, sending her to the cold hard road. Her phone fell from her hand and the screen shattered, glass spidering across the emergency call she hadn't had a chance to make.

Flat on her back, she tried to get up, but the man was on top of her, heavy and unyielding, his body blocking out the streetlights behind him, his face in shadow. She tried to scream, and he gripped her head with both hands and smacked the back of it on the road. Then again. Then one more time.

Jaime blacked out, came to, looking up at the dark starless sky, blacked out again.

Her head bumping along the bitumen woke her again. She was dragged along by both arms, her clothes soaking in the fine mist of rain on the road. Her head was fuzzy, her sight blurred. There was liquid in her mouth, and she started to choke.

The shadow, over her again, lifted her up, strong hands under her arms, and she was flung with force into the back of the van. She landed roughly, her left side collecting a metal shelf bolted into the interior of the van, the pain sharp in her ribs. Numerous boxes fell around her, hitting her everywhere, something heavy landing on her legs.

Jaime choked again, spat out the hot liquid, tried to roll on her side, couldn't do it, no room to move. She took a deep breath, readying herself to scream at the top of her lungs, and the open door of the Amazon van closed with a thud, sending her into darkness, cutting her off before she'd had a chance to open her mouth.

Her breath cut short, and she held it, waiting, listening. The engine started up, loud in the confines of the rear of the van. The entire vehicle shuddered to life. Some more boxes fell off shelves. She tried to scream but her voice was hoarse, pitiful, ineffectual. The van rolled forward, bumped up and down again with a heavy clatter, driving over a bump in the road and Jaime realised it was the body of the man she'd tried to help, they'd just driven over the man on the road, and as the van accelerated, her scream found its volume.

CHAPTER 19

They continued to work the case.

DCI Rawlins took the news in his stride, that this was no longer just a homicide, but was now a manhunt for Aaron Sparger, the mid-thirties businessman who was abducted just outside of his place of work in Waterloo on the night of the murder. Abducted in the stolen van hired by Corey Whitman who had been found hacked to death on Bishop Street.

Rawlins not only accepted the new development with his usual calm demeanour, but he switched up a gear, contacting the National Crime Agency to request a team from the Anti Kidnap and Extortion Unit that worked on kidnappings of all kinds, to lead on the search for Aaron Sparger. He then organised a special press conference with his boss, Detective Superintendent Tully riding shotgun, to release the details of Aaron Sparger across the national news.

Despite Knight's prediction that they'd be dropped from the case, based on the fact that the homicide had turned into a time-sensitive kidnapping requiring national co-ordination, Rawlins insisted that Roark's team be kept on it, telling her that they needed to work closely with the AKEU team while they searched for Aaron Sparger, to stay on the case and continue focusing on identifying the killer who had murdered Corey Whitman.

'I want you working this alongside *and* independent of Anti-Kidnapping,' he'd explained to Roark in his office. 'They'll focus on finding Aaron and, with any luck, the bastard who kidnapped him, but you need to keep working the case so that when we do get this son of a bitch, we'll be able to put him away for the homicide too. You need to build up a solid case for the legal team, identify the killer through the case evidence. Obviously, any pertinent information needs to be passed on to our AKEU liaison, but I want you to be focussed on the homicide. Got it?'

Roark had nodded, agreed and thanked him. When Roark informed Knight they had not been kicked off the case, she was surprised. Roark explained that it made sense. They had a homicide charge to build that needed to hold up in court; the Anti-Kidnapping unit had a person to find. Independent investigations with a slightly different focus that would need to work together to achieve the goal: find Aaron Sparger alive and capture the man who had hacked Corey Whitman to death on Bishop Street.

'We're still an integral part of the investigation, Gale,' Roark said.

'Do you think? Feels like we're the B-team,' Knight said, scrolling down her phone.

Roark didn't agree, and to prove her point, she worked Knight hard all day, working every possible angle on the case with what little they had.

It was now close to midnight, and they were in The Disgruntled Goat. Knight was nursing her sixth rum on ice, and she looked exhausted.

'Still think we're a fifth wheel on this?' Roark said, more than a little tipsy halfway through her fourth large glass of white wine.

'How many times have you made that point today?' Knight said.

'Not enough.'

'I think we're *all* feeling like fifth wheels, Anti-Kidnapping and all.'

They'd been no news on Aaron Sparger throughout the day. No leads from the public that didn't end in a waste of time for the Anti-Kidnapping team. Roark and Knight and the rest of the detectives on the case did more door knocks around Bishop Street and tried to gain information from what little leads they had on Corey's regular hangouts.

So far: nothing. Not a single thread that they could pull. Vague recollections and incomplete descriptions. Red herrings and dead ends.

Knight sighed loudly and knocked back her drink.

'Fucking dead ends.'

Roark nodded silently.

'Does feel that way.'

'One for the road?' Knight said.

They'd been in the pub for a good couple of hours, secured the same booth as the previous night, had had dinner – burgers and chips – and the small crowds had come and gone.

Roark covered the top of her glass with an open palm, remembering how she'd felt this morning after their drinks last night.

'Not for me.'

The place closed in thirty minutes, so it was last drinks anyway.

Knight collared the waiter as he sped by and ordered another Sailor Jerry.

'You're right,' Roark said, looking into her glass.

'Of course, I am,' Knight said. 'What are you talking about?'

'Aaron Sparger. He's probably already dead.'

'Wow,' Knight replied, slouching back against the wall. 'Not like you to be pessimistic.'

'Not pessimistic. Realistic. He's been gone almost forty-eight hours and we've got nothing.'

'Doesn't mean he's dead.'

'It's likely, though, isn't it,' Roark said.

'Maybe,' Knight said, 'but we're close right? We have the evidence now.'

DNA samples taken from Whitman's body and the front yard of his flat on Bishop Street matched those found in the driver's seat of the van. They did not belong to Corey Whitman, those were tagged separately, so it was concluded they belonged to the killer.

Unfortunately, the DNA samples did not match anyone in the National DNA Database. There was hope that the killer had previous convictions, but that wasn't the case. They could not yet identify the man based on the evidence they had.

'We have the evidence, but not the perp.'

'Like you said, Kris, once we find him, we'll be able to charge him.'

'Tell that to Aaron Sparger.'

Knight spread her arms.

'Sorry, have we had a body swap? You keep banging on about evidence over motive and we have that. Granted, it's not getting us closer to finding who did this, but we have a clearer picture of what's going on, right? Much better than where we were yesterday.'

Knight was right, of course. The DNA matching proved beyond reasonable doubt that the killer had stolen the van for the purposes of kidnapping Aaron Sparger and that Corey Whitman had just gotten in the way. The blood samples in the back of the van, which had stumped them yesterday, matched Aaron Sparger, confirming what they suspected and seen on the CCTV outside of Waterloo: he'd been violently kidnapped.

What the evidence didn't tell them was who had taken Sparger and where he was. And, most importantly, whether he was still alive.

'I just don't want another homicide,' Roark said. 'Evidence supporting a case is fine when the victim is already dead. A kidnapping like this, where someone's life is on the line, we need evidence we can act on, and act on quickly, and we don't have that.'

'We'll keep working on it, Kris,' Knight said. 'Anti-Kidnapping will keep searching and we'll keep digging.'

Roark took a small sip of her wine. It didn't taste nice anymore.

'I like your enthusiasm,' she said solemnly, 'but I don't think that's going to work fast enough for Sparger.'

'Oh, you're really killing the mood now. I didn't take you to be a glass half-empty kind of girl.'

'My glass is never half-empty, darling. It's either full or drunk.'

'You're drunk.'

'Shut it.'

The waiter placed the bill on their table unsolicited. It was time to finish up.

'I'll get this,' Roark said.

'Don't be stupid. We'll go Dutch.'

Roark finished off her wine in one big gulp and immediately regretted it. She suddenly felt a little dizzy.

'You okay?'

'I'm fine. Relatively speaking.'

Roark picked up her jacket off the end of the bench seat and rummaged for her credit card. She found it next to her house keys, pulled it out with two fingers and dropped it near the bill. Knight was on her phone, the screen light illuminating her face. She looked tired in the stark light.

'How did your mum find out about her cancer?' Roark said.

Knight looked up from her screen. Roark immediately blamed the drink, again, for her not thinking before speaking. Knight, equally inebriated, could well take offense at the question, and it might just kick off, leaving a bad taste in the mouth for them both. Roark didn't think she could handle that right now.

Instead, Knight turned her screen off and placed the phone on the table.

'She had a lot of the symptoms, so went to her doctor. He referred her on to a specialist.'

'What symptoms?'

Knight hesitated.

'Sorry, Gale. Don't worry if you don't want to talk about it.'

'It's okay. Just, I almost lost her, you know? It wasn't looking good for a while there. Hard to think back to that time again.'

'I understand.'

'She was just feeling tired a lot, had pain in her hips. No appetite and needed to pee a lot. Sounds like old age but the specialist confirmed on the first visit. Ovarian cancer. Spread to other parts of her body too, but thankfully not too bad.'

'I'm sorry.'

'Hey, she's all good now. The treatment worked. She's still a little fragile, of course.'

'What treatment did she have?'

'I've committed this to memory, heard it so many times: bilateral salpingo-oophorectomy.'

Roark nodded and looked at her empty glass of wine.

'You know it?'

'I've heard it a few times too. Removal of ovaries and tubes.'

'Yeah. She had to have chemo as well, before and after, and that's what got her through in the end. Killed the cancer that had spread. She's totally clean now, but it still hangs over her, y'know?'

Roark raised her finger onto the lip of her wine glass and ran it around its surface. There was no sound. She wet her finger and tried again, and it still didn't work.

'I can never get it to sing.'

'You okay, Kris?'

Roark ran her finger once more around the glass and considered telling Knight all about the letter, thinking maybe she could be open with Gale, that maybe their friendship could handle the sharing of personal trauma and indecision, when the waiter appeared holding the portable card machine in his hand.

'Are we ready ladies?' he said.

'Sure,' Roark said, handing up her credit card.

'Fifty-fifty,' Knight informed him.

After the machine took Roark's payment, Knight hovered her phone over it and it pinged, also taking the payment. Roark told herself she should start using that on her phone too, but she didn't know the first bit about how to.

'Thank you, ladies. Have a good rest of the night,' the waiter said and left.

'You sure you're okay?' Knight said, leaning across and touching Roark's hand.

Roark smiled and nodded.

'I would love to see your mum again,' she said.

'Definitely,' Knight said, sitting up straight and then shifting along the seat. 'She wants to too.'

'Really?'

'I'm always talking about you to her. She asks about my day and I end up talking about you. Marginally better than talking about the blood and guts of a homicide.'

'Marginally,' Roark said and laughed.

They stood up and walked towards the exit. Knight hollered goodbye to the bartender who raised his hand in return.

'Cute boy, that one,' she whispered in Roark's ear.

'You know he's probably older than me,' Roark said.

'I wasn't talking about for me, you silly witch.'

Roark shoved her with a laugh.

'Right, off to bed. Another successful day awaits us tomorrow.'

'With any luck,' Roark said as they stepped outside into the cool night, 'Darth will solve the case overnight for us, but I doubt it.'

'I find your lack of faith a problem,' Knight said in a deep husky voice.

'What the fuck was that?'

'Darth Vader reference. I think. May have misquoted.'

'Oh, don't tell me you're talking to your ex again.'

'See ya,' Knight said without replying, walking off down the street.

'You're a maniac,' Roark shouted, and Knight gave her the finger.

Roark headed off to the bus stop, shaking her head and smiling.

CHAPTER 20

'Two loaves of bread, white bread, Billy likes his sandwiches,' Mrs Palmer said from her sofa chair by the window.

Teresa typed "bread" into her Tesco shopping app on her phone and scrolled down through the list that came up in the search results.

'Hovis?'

'Yes, please, dear. Some more digestives, there's a two-pack you can get.'

'Got it,' Teresa said, selecting the product and adding it to the basket.

'I think that is about it, oh, no, some milk, yes milk. Full cream for Billy, semi-skimmed for me please.'

Teresa tapped away and added both items.

'How much does that come to, dear?'

'Seventy-seven pounds, fifty-five.'

'Oh my,' Cheryl said, hand to her mouth. 'That wasn't a long list, was it? Seventy-seven pound?'

'I know,' Teresa said, 'prices have gone up a lot.'

Cheryl Palmer, hand still to her mouth, stared towards the window, not directly through it but slightly up and to her left, thinking. The late-morning sun brightened her face, reddening the scars around her eyes. She tapped her teeth with her fingers.

'How much was that tub of Celebrations?'

Teresa scrolled through the shopping list.

'Five pounds.'

'Okay, take that off, would you dear? I think that should be fine.'

Teresa removed the Celebrations and made a note to bring a tub with her when she next visited in a couple of days.

'All done?'

'All done,' Cheryl said.

Teresa checked out and using the details Cheryl had given her, paid for the groceries to be delivered the next time Teresa was visiting, so that she could help with the delivery.

'What time is it?' Cheryl asked.

Teresa checked her phone.

'Almost midday.'

'Okay, dear, you best be getting on. Thank you again for coming. I'm glad you came back.'

'Of course, Cheryl. I had a lovely time last time and today.'

'We had a good old natter, didn't we?'

'We did. I'd also love to hear more about your trips to Spain that you mentioned last time.'

'Yes,' Cheryl said, her voice dropping, 'yes, maybe next time.'

Teresa sensed Cheryl wasn't too keen to talk about that time in her life. Possibly it was to do with that period in her life when she had eyesight, possibly she was worried it would lead to questions about how she'd lost her sight, about the scars around her eyes. Either way, Teresa said nothing more and started to pick up her things.

'And next time, let's have lunch together,' Cheryl said.

'I would love that. I can bring something, if you like?'

'That is very kind of you. I do have a craving for Kentucky Fried Chicken.'

'Consider it done.'

They spent the next ten minutes writing up an order for KFC, ordering much more than what they should and laughing about it. After they settled, Cheryl said Teresa could remove most of it, that it cost too much, but Teresa would have none of that. They were going to have a fried chicken lunch that they'd never forget.

'Oh, speaking of forgetting,' Cheryl said. 'I just remembered I have some mail. Would you be a dear and read them to me?'

'Of course,' Teresa said.

'They are just in the kitchen.'

Teresa left Cheryl in the front living room and walked down the hallway. The kitchen, which she'd been in a few times already today, was lit bright with a series of long bulbs along the bottom of the wall cupboards. She'd tidied up the kitchen, as well as Cheryl's bedroom and bathroom, while Cheryl had taken a short nap about forty-five minutes ago, and it remained spotless and organised. Teresa had made sure she put everything back in its right place so that Cheryl could find them when Teresa wasn't there, but she still felt a sense of pride for helping Mrs Palmer out, making a difference by tidying up her home. Something Cheryl's son didn't seem to be bothered with.

Next to the kitchen, stairs led up to the first floor. William Palmer's domain. Billy, as Cheryl called him. The stairs were carpeted and ended in darkness after ten steps, no lights on anywhere on the first floor, all doors closed and curtains drawn. Cheryl had said that Billy was at work, but Teresa wasn't convinced. She'd heard creaking floorboards from upstairs on more than four occasions during the three hours she had been in the house. It gave her the creeps.

Not wanting to hang around too long, she grabbed the small pile of mail from the kitchen bench and took them back to Cheryl in the front room.

'Anything interesting?' Cheryl asked when Teresa sat down opposite her.

Teresa flicked through the pile.

'Looks like a gas bill from British Gas.'

'There will be electricity too.'

'Thames Water.'

'Oh, they're all sending out their bills this week.'

'A couple of flyers from property agents.'

'Bin, please.'

'This one looks like a handwritten letter, Cheryl,' Teresa said, turning over a small envelope in her hand. It had Cheryl's name and address scrawled on the front in black pen.

Cheryl sat up, hands on her knees.

'Well, that could be from my daughter. Pass it here, dear.'

Teresa stood up and handed the envelope over. Cheryl took it in her wrinkled hands and felt across the edges. She dropped one hand to the seat of the sofa, between her thigh and the armrest, and retrieved a silver letter opener.

'In case of emergencies,' she giggled.

She inserted the letter opener into the envelope and slit across in one swift motion. She returned the letter opener in the gap of the seat's cushion and pulled out the contents. Teresa could see that the envelope had held three stiff white pages of paper, but she could not see any writing on them. Cheryl ran her fingers along the top of the first page.

'Ah yes, my daughter,' Cheryl said, and her face broke out in a smile. 'She's such a lovely sort. Sends me letters in braille, can you believe that?'

'That's very thoughtful.'

'Yes, she is.'

Pam, the Home Assist liaison, hadn't mention anything about a daughter, and this was the first time Cheryl had said anything about it, but Teresa kept quiet. It wasn't her place to enquire; if Cheryl wanted to talk about it, she would.

Teresa wasn't lying though; sending letters in braille was very thoughtful and it made Teresa wonder if she could do something similar for Cheryl. Birthday card in braille or something like that.

'We were estranged up until a few years back,' Cheryl said. 'Entirely my fault. Still haven't met up, but we write a lot. One day I hope to meet her again.'

Teresa didn't know what to say, but Cheryl wasn't expecting a reply as she quickly said, 'I'll read that later,' and placed the pages back into the envelope, taking a few attempts to fit them in, and then put the letter next to her thigh alongside the letter opener.

'So, let's see if we can pay those blasted bills,' she said, clapping her hands together.

Teresa spent the last ten minutes of her second visit with Cheryl Palmer helping her pay her gas, electricity, and water bills online, trying her best not to look towards the letter from Cheryl's estranged daughter. When Teresa stood by the front door a few minutes later, ready to leave, Cheryl gave her a hug, which she returned with equal vigour.

'Two days' time?' Teresa said.

'Two days' time,' Cheryl agreed.

As Teresa walked down the steps that led to the street, Cheryl's front door closing behind her, she blinked tears from her eyes. She kept walking, noting to herself items that she'd remember for next time: a Celebrations box, the KFC order and a nice card in Braille. A few more steps and she thought better of the card. She didn't want to look like she was competing with Cheryl's daughter. Best to wait on that one.

As she passed the front fence of Cheryl's property, Teresa looked up at the second storey of the flat and quickly turned away and hurried along the road towards the bus stop, having seen the curtain to the upstairs window twitch closed, but not before she saw a long-drawn face staring down at her.

CHAPTER 21

Knight worked hard at her desk, perpendicular to Roark's main workstation. Roark was comforted that her partner was still working the case, but it had been touch and go for a moment there. DCI Rawlins had a quiet word with Roark earlier in the morning, part update, part pep talk, and suggested a Detective Sergeant she could use on the case.

'DC Knight is working out fine, sir,' Roark had said. 'She's a bright one and we've worked really well together these past six months. I know she's junior, but I'd like to keep her on this.'

'Your call, Inspector.'

Back at her desk, they turned their chairs in towards each other and gave updates. Due to work commitments, they had their lunch separately at different times and this was the first chance they had to see where the case was.

'I have something of a win,' Knight said, checking the notes on her phone via the Crime Database app.

'Pray tell.'

Knight looked at Roark funny, then referred to her phone as she spoke. Roark saw her switch apps on her phone and type something in.

'The team checking CCTV cameras around the Chiltern Hills area,' she said, 'where the van was dumped, have found a couple of possible leads so far. Ah,' she said, pointing at her screen. '"Pray tell". I get it.'

'What?'

'Nothing. Just trying to understand your medieval lingo. Google is such an amazing tool for conversing with old folks, right?'

'Detective?'

'Sorry,' Knight said and put the phone on her desk. 'There were two cars leaving the Chiltern Hills area that morning, the morning after the abduction, that had been recently reported stolen. Our theory is that he transferred Sparger from the van into one of these vehicles, having parked the car in the woods beforehand.'

'Or he may have used his own vehicle for the transfer.'

'Yes, that's a possibility, but we're working this angle right now.'

'Okay, go on.'

'One car was stolen near Basingstoke, about forty-five miles south from where the van was dumped. The other stolen from Wycombe.

All reported twenty-four hours before the murder and kidnapping. No footage of the theft, unfortunately.'

Roark leaned back in her chair and stretched her legs out past Knight.

'Christ, woman, I keep forgetting how long your legs are,' Knight said. 'Anyway, we managed to locate both cars leaving the Chiltern Hills area on CCTV but lost them again where the coverage dropped out.'

'I assume no camera coverage of the driver himself?'

'No.'

'Okay, well, I think it's unlikely the Wycombe car is him,' Roark said. 'It's unlikely he would steal a car so close to the van dumping site. Too easy to track back to him. That said, let's not rule it out.'

'Interestingly,' Knight added, 'we lost the Wycombe car on CCTV around Stadhampton, which is on the way to Oxford, going west. The other car we lost close to Donnington, Newbury, south.'

'Possibly heading back to Basingstoke where it was stolen. Interesting. These are all within the window of when we think he made the transfer?'

'Correct.'

'Okay, this is good news. We may have our thread to pull. APB out on both?'

'Already done. Team's scanning the CCTV network to see if we can pick the stolen cars up again, and we are checking to see if we can locate either of the cars entering Chiltern Hills after they were stolen. And AKEU has been informed as well. They are standing by for more information.'

Roark pulled her legs back under her chair, sitting up.

'Seems like that's all they've been doing. Standing by.'

'Fingers crossed this car identification takes us somewhere,' Knight said. 'You going to tell Rawlins?'

'Not yet,' Roark said, moving her mouse and activating her monitor. She'd been logged out of the Crime Database, as it liked to do after ten or so minutes, so she typed in her details and opened the case file again. 'Let's see if we can get something more concrete on those cars first. We haven't much else to go on.'

'No, we don't.'

'How about Corey Whitman?' Roark said, leaning back in her chair and turning to Knight. 'Anything more on where he fits into this?'

'No, nothing,' Knight said, picking up her phone and swiping. 'There's nothing to say Corey Whitman's involvement in this is anything more than a victim of a carjacking.'

'I agree. Let's look at Sparger more than Whitman. See why he'd be a target for a kidnapping.'

'Yes, there could be something there.'

'Check out who might know of his movements that night. What was he doing and who knew about it. Who knew he would be under those arches at that time of night?'

'Will do. Of course, there is also the possibility that the targeting of Sparger was totally random.'

'Ah,' Roark said, raising a finger and cutting her off. 'Let's not go there yet.'

A young Detective Constable hovered near their desks, a small slip of paper in her hand.

'Sorry to bother you, Ma'am,' she said to Roark.

Roark turned in her chair to face the young female detective.

'Go ahead, Detective.'

'We've had a call come through from Avon and Somerset. A DI out of Bristol. Says she has a case that might be of interest.'

'How so?'

'Sorry, Ma'am, she didn't say. Here's her number.'

The constable handed over the slip of paper and Roark took it.

'Detective Inspector Clarice Moody,' Roark read. 'Okay, thank you, Detective.'

The young detective nodded and retreated.

'What you got?' Knight said, hand out for the note.

'Call from Bristol,' Roark said, handing it over.

'Bristol? Wonder what it could be?'

'Give me the fucking note back and we'll find out,' Roark said and snatched the note from Knight's hands.

'Wow, you're so menopausal today,' Knight said, smirked and pushed her chair up to Roark's desk.

Roark punched in the number written on the note. She put the call on speaker.

'*Detective Inspector Moody.*'

Her voice was light and breezy, strong Bristolian accent; charming and approachable.

'Hello, Detective Inspector. I'm Detective Inspector Roark and with me is Detective Constable Knight.'

'*Alright there.*'

'You said you had a case that may interest us? By the way, I have you on speakerphone if that's okay.'

'No problems. And thanks for getting back to me. I saw your APB on your homicide earlier in the week, and I see you now have a Misper too.'

'That's right, just keeps getting better and better.'

'Don't I know it. I have one too. Not the same, mind, but similar enough that I thought it was worth calling you.'

'What have you got, Detective?'

'Got a call in around midnight last night for an ambulance. An Amazon delivery driver was found critically injured on a residential road just out of Bristol. Van stolen, looked like they'd driven over him after knocking him over the head. He's currently in a critical condition at Southmead.

'Thing is, another call came in not too soon after at the same street, same address. A woman in her early thirties had gone outside to accept a delivery from Amazon, from our injured delivery man we believe, but never came back. Just disappeared. We suspect she's been abducted.'

Roark looked across at Knight. Knight scribbled down on a piece of paper: "Same M.O."

'Definitely sounds similar to ours, Detective. The man we're looking for was abducted in a van too.'

'So I saw. Now, we've found the van, dumped not too far away. The Amazon vans have locators in them, so it was easy to find, but they must have been smarter than your average hoodlum. Parked and switched vehicles in a secluded place with no camera coverage. So we don't know where they went after dumping the van. I've got my team going through what CCTV footage we have.'

'We're just finishing up a similar exercise. If it is the same guy, which it sounds like it may be, the second vehicle will be stolen.'

'Got it. We'll look out for that.'

'Anything else?'

'We do have some footage, but nothing we can use to identify those involved, mind. Camera just outside the main entrance to the missing woman's block of flats picked up some type of scuffle, but all we can see are shadows and whatnot. Van is not in the shot and there's no sound. Our missing girl had left the building immediately before, so we're going on the pretty sound assumption that the stolen van and disappearance of the girl are related. Unfortunately, the van's cameras were damaged and give us nothing.'

'We are very interested in this,' Roark said, shifting closer to the phone. 'Like you said, there are similarities we can't ignore.'

'Agreed. Let's keep each other in the loop. I have my SOCO team working on the evidence from the van as we speak, so I'll pass that over.'

Knight leaned forward.

'We have a DNA sample from our main suspect which we will share with you, see if we can match it.'

'*Perfect. We haven't put out an APB as we have nothing to go on, right now, but we are drafting up a press release on the woman to go out in the next hour or so.*'

'Detective?' Roark said. 'I'd recommend contacting the Anti-Kidnapping and Extortion Unit to fill them in on this before you go to press. You'll get them mobilised on your case much quicker if there's even a hint of a link to the Sparger case. Inform them first, before the public.'

'*Got it, I appreciate that. I can feel it in my waters, this one doesn't look good.*'

'I'm with you on that. Here's the number.' Roark pulled up the AKEU team working the Sparger case and repeated their number over the line.

'*Thank you, Detective Inspector. I'm glad I made this call.*'

'We are too, and please, call me Kris. And this is Gale.'

'*Clarice. Very glad to be working with you on this.*'

'Thank you, Clarice. Please let us know when the delivery driver pulls through.'

'*Will do.*'

'Oh,' Knight said, 'can you let us know the name of the woman who is missing?'

'*Of course. Jaime Collander,*' DI Moody said, and spelled out the last name.

'Please send anything you have on her and we'll do the same with our Misper.'

'*You got it.*'

They exchanged email addresses, mobile numbers and said their goodbyes.

'Fuck,' Knight said, rolling her chair back to her desk. 'I feel both excited and sick. If this is the same guy. Jesus.'

Roark nodded, said nothing. London, now Bristol. Two different cities, miles apart. If this was the same guy, they'd have a multiple homicide on their hands, if the Amazon delivery driver didn't pull through.

And then there was Aaron Sparger and Jaime Collander. Possible victims already, numbers three and four.

But not yet. Not those two. Not yet.

Roark's computer pinged, an email from DI Clarice Moody, all the information she had on Jaime Collander.

'Right, let's get on this.'

CHAPTER 22

Jaime jumped awake, startled by a sound she only vaguely heard, and the pain in her head hit her. Dull pain, starting from the back of her head around to behind her eyes. Her vision was blurry, unfocused, but she could see a shaft of light ahead of her, darkness all around it. Where she was, she had no idea.

It was cold, that she could tell. Cold and damp. Her arms produced goosebumps immediately at the thought of it and she wrapped them around herself, wishing she wore something warmer than her white short-sleeved shirt. Only then did she realise she was sitting up against a brick wall, on a cold concrete floor.

The shaft of light gained focus and she could make out wooden steps leading up. The light was from above, dust mites floating and glinting in the sun. A square of light at the top of the stairs, too bright for her eyes.

Pain behind her eyes again. Throbbing pain, coming in waves. The back of her neck suddenly ached and she put a hand to it and rubbed. Her fingers felt something crusty back there, at the base of her skull, just at the hairline where she'd had it cut short only a few weeks ago. Something small came away and crumbled in her hand. She couldn't make it out in the darkness but knew it was dried blood.

She saw the shadow above her again, gripping her head, banging it onto the bitumen.

The steps leading up out of the darkness shined.

She remembered being dragged across the road and thrown into the back of a van. Remembered screaming as boxes fell around her. Remembered nothing after that.

Jaime shifted her body around and waited on her knees. Her head span, eyes blurred again. She waited as long as she dared. She didn't care how she got down here, didn't want to sit and contemplate the horror she was facing. She just wanted to get out.

She felt in her pockets for her phone but knew it wasn't there, the familiar weight of it in her jeans pocket absent like an amputated leg. It was gone, taken.

Fucking hell, she'd been abducted.

It didn't feel like it was happening to her. Like she was watching a horror movie, not living it.

You are living it, she thought. *This isn't a movie.*

Get up.

She leaned forward slowly and using the wall as support, stood up, feeling the cold, damp floor on her bare feet. Blood rushed from her head and she felt dizzy all over again. She leaned on the wall and waited.

A smell hit her nostrils, strong and putrid and she gagged, then to her surprise, doubled over and threw up. The sound of the vomit splattering on the floor, at least five banana daquiris worth, made her stomach let go again.

There was a brief whiff of the inside of her stomach, but it was quickly quenched by the rotten fruit smell coming from somewhere in the cellar. A smell like a garbage bag ripped open and left to bake in the sun.

This time, she dry-retched.

Her eyes blurred with involuntary tears from the vomiting, and she wiped them quickly.

She couldn't handle this anymore. Time to leave.

With purpose, a little unsteady but full of determination, Jaime walked over to the steps leading up out of the cellar. She shielded her eyes and stared up at the exit. She considered that the man who had assaulted and abducted her could be sitting up at the top of the stairs, waiting, but she didn't care. She wanted to confront that fucker, not sit down here in the darkness, amongst burst garbage bags and a pile of her own spew.

There was no bannister, so she had to take it slowly, hearing each step creak under her weight, feeling the wood bend and threaten to snap.

Her head reached the lip of the cellar exit, eyes level with the floor. She paused for a moment, blinking in the sun, and quickly looked around her.

An ordinary kitchen, tidy, functional, photos of an elderly couple on the walls, cookbooks and cupboards of China plates and cups.

She looked at the photos again. This didn't make sense. She'd been abducted by Granny and Grandpa?

Forget it, she said to herself, teeth gritted. Get out and worry about that later.

There was a kitchen door directly in front of her next to an old radiator and a clean kitchen bench and it led outside onto a clear, sunny day. Through the window in the door, past floral curtains drawn aside, she could see a green cut lawn stretching out to the edge of a forest, rows and rows of tall thin trees lining left to right.

Idyllic. Homely.

Jaime scanned around her again, making sure no one was going to jump out at her from behind. There was no one in the kitchen with her, but there was a closed door leading further into the house only metres away. Someone could be waiting behind it.

No time to waste. Jaime took the last few steps up out of the cellar, her knees groaning, her head pounding. She knew it was best that she get out as soon as she could, but there was a rack of knives on the bench only a few feet away and she took the time to lurch towards it and pull out the longest, sharpest knife. A Global Knife. Fine quality. A useful weapon.

She suddenly felt a clash of emotions: safe now that she was armed to defend herself, anxious to get out of the house before she had to use the weapon. Peering over the sink at the large window looking out onto the front yard, she could see a more widescreen version: finely cut lawn leading to a small forest, the ground giving way into a valley on her right, a dirt driveway leading out and around behind the forest on the left.

Not another house or car or person to be seen. The middle of nowhere.

She scanned the kitchen, looking for a landline phone, but there was none. Without her own phone or a landline, she had no option but to find help out there somewhere, hope upon hope that she wasn't too far from civilisation, that she could walk, or run, for assistance.

She forced herself to pause and consider her options. The driveway to her left would lead, eventually, to a road, which she could follow or, if she was lucky, have an opportunity to hail down a passing car that could drive her to the nearest police station. The only downside on taking that route was that she would be clearly visible to her abductor, wherever he was. Her escape would be known immediately and, assuming he still had the Amazon van, he'd be able to run her down quickly.

The slope down to the right into a valley, which she could see clearly from this angle, was the other choice. She wouldn't be found down there. She could hide in the undergrowth, behind bushes, or just run into territory covered by trees, which would be difficult for her abductor to one, spot her, and two, pursue her. Downside of that was, she didn't have a clue where she was and didn't have her phone to check her location, so she could be out there for days, lost in the countryside, found dead of starvation and exposure weeks later.

Come on, Jaime, she thought. I'm not in the Arctic. It's England for Christ's sake. There would be a town or village only a few miles away, tops. Scoot down into the valley and find help.

That was it. She'd take her chances down in the valley.

Jaime walked towards the kitchen door and gripped the handle. Turned it, expecting it to be locked, chastising herself that she should've checked that first before holding a strategy meeting by the drying rack, turned it all the way around and heard a satisfying click as the door released from its jamb and started to open inwards.

Jaime smiled, then stopped. Thinking, you idiot, this is a trap. Cellar door open. Kitchen door open. Just waiting for you to run across the open front yard so he could pick you off at fifty yards with a rifle on the roof.

Too many movies, she thought. *I've seen too many movies.*

Just go.

She pulled the door and stopped.

Through the curtained window of the kitchen door in front of her, she saw him. Or thought she saw him. Her heart skipped. She squinted against the sun.

Where the driveway passed the edge of the forest, where the trees thinned out and stopped, between two narrow trunks, he stood and stared at the house. A shadow amongst shadows, but a clear outline, tall, broad-shouldered, arms by his side, something in his right hand that she couldn't make out.

He stood amongst the trees and stared, not moving, a statue waiting for her next move.

'Fuck.'

No way she was going to fall for that trap. She might be quick, but she didn't want to take her chances, running down into the valley with this fucker on her heels, not if there was another way out.

Jaime turned back to the kitchen, saw another door just beyond the open cellar that led further into the house. There was the other door she'd first spotted at the end of the kitchen bench, which also led into the house. Two options. She hesitated, unsure. It crossed her mind that there could be another person in here, not just the maniac waiting for her in the trees across the way.

A double bluff. Another trap.

A glance out the kitchen door window. He was still there waiting, a shape in the trees, standing, staring.

Jaime moved, quickly, running the length of the kitchen bench to the door at the other end of the room. She grabbed the door handle, looked back through the double windows above the sink, and screamed. He was racing across the lawn, emerging from the tree line, running towards the house, the sun behind him, a short-handled axe swinging in his right hand. Running straight for her.

She pulled the door opened and ran down a hallway complete with photos on the walls and a side table with a vase of dead flowers. Two doors led off on either side and another heavyset door with a small, frosted window set in it was at the end of the hallway.

Her only hope was to get out of the house, so she ran towards the frosted glass door, hearing herself whimpering with panic, her breathing loud in her ears, her head pounding harder with every heartbeat. As she reached the door, the frosted window darkened as a shadow passed in front of it. The door handle turned before she could reach out for it.

She screamed and cut herself off with a hand to her open mouth and skidded to a halt.

She turned, ungainly, knocking the side table, sending the dead flowers to the ground, the vase breaking into large pieces. The knife she was holding nicked the hallway wall and Jaime's hand slid down the handle and hit the hilt, cutting into the skin between her thumb and forefinger. She yelled and dropped the knife. Blood spotted the wall.

The door creaked open behind her and she left the knife and scurried over the broken vase to the kitchen door, gasping for breath, struggling for breath. Banging through the kitchen door, she entered the bright, homely room and ran into the wooden table she'd barely registered before, the corner digging sharply into her hip. She winced, lost her footing for a moment, regained it, kept running, pain pounding behind her eyes relentlessly and rhythmically.

Her hand slipped on the kitchen door that led out into the front yard, slipped with the blood now running freely from the knife wound. She couldn't get a grip on the doorknob, the blood making purchase difficult and when she felt she had a strong hold of it and turned, it wouldn't budge. She tried again, and it didn't move, slipping in her grip, and she turned around and the other door to the kitchen opened and the man with the axe walked in.

She screamed again, spit flying from her mouth, as the man moved quickly around the table towards her. She turned away, too quick to see the man's face, too scared to see the monster that was chasing her, and she teetered on the lip of the open cellar. The man almost within arm's reach, she instinctively moved away, pushing off with one foot and jumping across the gap of the open cellar, and crashing into the cupboard, knocking a handful of hardback books onto the floor.

Without looking back, Jaime scrambled along the floor towards the second door leading out from the kitchen into the bowels of the house, not caring who or what was behind it, just wanting to get away from the axe-wielding maniac who loomed behind her.

The door swung inwards with her weight, already partially opened, not requiring the turn of a handle. She fell into the room beyond, feeling carpeted floor underneath her hands. She scampered forward, the door closing behind her, and ignoring the pain in her head and the cut on her hand, she sprung up like a runner at the sound of the start gun and sprinted along the carpeted hallway.

It ran parallel to the other hallway, but longer and wider. Doors to her right and what looked like an open entrance to another section of the house further along, which, possibly, she hoped, was a route to the back door of this fucking place. Beyond the corner, it appeared dark, but she had no choice. Choosing one of the doors would just lead to a dead-end room and already she could hear the man breathing hard behind her.

She ran towards the corner, slamming into the far wall before collecting herself and scampering into a larger, darker room. There were no windows in this section of the house, the light within weak, and she couldn't make out anything other than the faint outline of furniture, sofas, chairs, a low table, then another door to her immediate right and she fell through it, the force of her body almost breaking through the panelling, and she collapsed at the foot of a set of wooden steps, not going down, but going up.

Steps leading up, to an attic, or maybe, to the roof. She didn't have time to decide as the weak light in the room was blocked out by the large form that filled the doorway behind her. Jaime scrambled up, fell forward, her knees slamming into the edge of the third step. In her panic, knowing full well that in a matter of moments, her leg would be grabbed, and she would be pulled down towards the sharp blade of a rusted axe, she launched herself up the stairs as far as she could, her face hitting one of the steps hard across the bridge of her nose.

Blood gushed down over her mouth, the taste of it warm and coppery. Her vision blurred, she couldn't see ahead of her, how many steps to go and what lay at the top. There was a moment of silence, other than her haggard breathing, and a pause of resignation that quickly passed as she realised nothing had happened to her, no hand had grabbed her leg, no axe had lodged itself into her back, and she scrambled quickly, ignoring the pain she felt all over and reached the top of the stairs.

There was another door, wooden and splintered to touch, and she felt around for the handle, found it and turned it forcefully. The knob turned all the way around, but the door did not budge. In a state of panic, she rattled the door handle, moving it left and right, pulling on it but it would not open. There was a clanking sound, metal on metal, and she felt around the edge of the door near the handle and there was a cold, metal, rusted latch connected to the door jamb, secured in place by a heavy padlock.

Jaime screamed in pain and slid down the surface of the door to collapse at the top of the stairs. She yelled in frustration and slammed her fists on the bottom half of the door, hoping to smash through it, but she knew it was a waste of time. She knew that even beyond this locked door, there was no way out.

Crumpled in a heap, one foot down on the next step, she turned slowly to look down at her attacker, expecting him to be inches from her, ready to pounce.

He wasn't. He still stood in the doorway, legs apart, arms at his side, axe pointed downwards, blocking most of the little light that came from the outer room; a dark, deep shadow, just standing, staring, watching.

'Come on,' Jaime shouted, hysteria seeping in. 'What are you waiting for?'

The shadow took a tentative step forward, a foot inches from the first step on the wooden stairwell that led up to Jaime and the locked attic door. It stopped short, stepped back, uncertain.

'What are you waiting for?' Jaime screeched again, confused now, not understanding why this creature that had abducted her and pursued her was now hesitating.

Another attempt, a small step forward, and again, hesitation and retreat.

'What are you scared of? A fight? I'll give you a fucking fight. Come on, let's go.'

The man didn't move forward. Instead, he took another step back, filling more of the doorway now. Not leaving, not retreating, but not wanting to be in this room.

Not wanting to ascend the stairs to the attic.

Jaime laughed with delirium. Spat at the shadow.

'Is that what it is? You don't want to get me up here? You scared of what's up here? You keep your dead fucking mother up here, you psycho son of a bitch?'

She'd found his weakness; just like in all those horror movies she'd watched over the years. The monster scared of its past, unable to kill the final girl because of a memory, a bad experience, a trauma endured in its youth. And in that hesitation, in the monster's inability to make that final kill, the final girl turns the table and kills the villain, saving herself and ridding the world of the monster once and for all.

Jaime Lee Fucking Curtis. The best final girl ever. Until now.

She took a deep breath, about to yell an obscenity fitting for the heroine that she was, when the shadow shifted back and raised its right arm high and Jaime realised this wasn't the movies, that she wasn't the final girl and that she would not be saved, and she raised her hands as the man threw the axe, the blade somersaulting through the darkness towards her, the back of the head of the axe collecting her in the temple and sending her tumbling down the stairs to the feet of the monster.

CHAPTER 23

The girl does not stop crying. Over and over again, weeping, bawling, choking on air. She does not stop and the boy feels like he is in a new kind of hell. Only when his father gives up and takes her back down into the cellar can the boy lay back on his mattress and relax.

He lies there, arms straight down on either side, staring up at the small circle of light on the attic ceiling, the light from the gap in the floorboards, reflecting on the beams and rafters of the roof of the house.

The house, that used to be his home.

Not anymore. His home is the large expanse of the attic now, splinter-filled wood for a floor, cavernous arches for a ceiling. Darkness all around, the dark spaces constantly reaching out and engulfing him.

A thin mattress for a bed, no pillow. Broken toys long outgrown gathering cobwebs in the corner. No clothes, his nakedness open to the cold and damp, the rats and spiders.

Hair long and tangled, washed only briefly under the kitchen sink tap.

Sores and cuts and bruises across his body, some from the hand of his father, some self-inflicted, some through malnutrition and poor hygiene.

The boy stares at the light on the ceiling of the attic and ruminates with himself.

He wouldn't cry like that girl. He wouldn't shy away from his father's love. He wouldn't refuse to play games, read stories, be the son his father wanted.

If only he could show his father the type of son he could be. The type of son he used to be.

'Howard, do you recognise this woman?'

The photo stares at him, awaiting an answer.

'Any recognition?'

He stares at the photo, searching for an answer.

'Howard?'

'No,' he says, before the detective's voice raises in anger and frustration. 'I don't recognise her.'

'Is there not any resemblance to the four-year old girl Laura Kilpatrick who your father kidnapped?'

He wants to say something, just to get her off his back, but he doesn't know what it is.

'There is some, I guess,' he blurts out, nothing better to say. 'Blonde hair, mainly. I don't remember seeing her eyes or face that clearly from where I was.'

'Oh, and where was that? Did you not meet her, face to face?'

'No,' he says, again, searching for the right words, 'my father kept me away from the children.'

'I see,' the female detective says, and looks at the photo herself. 'So, same blonde hair, but nothing else.'

'No.'

'Makes sense. A lot changes in thirty years. Usually, you can still see the little girl in the grown woman, though, right? But, as you say, if you didn't see her face clearly, you wouldn't be able to see that, now would you?'

'No.'

'Do you recognise her in any other context? As someone else maybe?'

She turns the photo back to him.

The boy stares up at the circle of light on the ceiling, pondering, until it blinks out.

He waits for close to half an hour before going downstairs, searching for food, washing himself in the kitchen sink with a wet dish rag.

Keeping his ears open for sounds of his father waking.

'No.'

The detective stares at him, nodding slowly, as if she has come to an understanding. The male detective takes a large gulp of his coffee and places the mug on the floor with a clang. He wipes his nose and moustache with the back of his hand and sinks back into his chair.

The shadows from the dark place behind him rest on his shoulders.

The shadows in the other corner of the room, in front of the table, to the right of the female detective, creep forward.

'Her name is Jaime Collander,' she says, still holding up the photo. 'She was abducted from Bristol on Friday night, around 11.30pm or thereabouts. Taken from her home in an Amazon delivery van. Not unlike the van I showed you previously. Do you know anything about this, Howard?'

'No, I don't,' he says and immediately wonders if he'd spoken too quickly.

'Where were you on that night? Last Friday?'

'I don't know,' he says, looking around the room for an answer. 'At home, like I always am.'

'Unless you're working, right? What are your working hours?'

'Eight until four, but I have been off a bit lately. Sick with something, I don't know what. COVID maybe.'

She smiles and nods her head.

'That old chestnut.'

He thinks she is being sarcastic, as if he's making this up, as if she's heard these excuses before.

'Did you get tested?' she asks.

'No, I didn't. I just stayed in bed.'

'All the time?'

'Look, I didn't have anything to do with this,' he says.

'When did your mother die, Howard?'

'What?'

'Tell me about your mother.'

James lies in his bed, soft pillow behind his head, pyjamas warm around his body, his two teddy bears under the duvet next to him. His mother lies beside him, humming a lullaby, the one about the ducks that he likes so much. He turns towards her, sees her in the dull night light from the bedside table, lying there, eyes closed, mouth moving, long hair splayed out on the pillow.

'I love you, mummy,' James says.

She opens her eyes and turns to him.

'I love you too, James.'

'How did she die, Howard?'

He lets his head drop and he closes his eyes.

'During labour, wasn't it, Howard? Lost too much blood. Lost the baby. Lost your sister.'

He shakes his head.

'She was quite old to be carrying a child, wasn't she? Too old, it turned out. How old were you when it happened? Eight? That must have been tough on you. You and your father.'

He pinches the roof of his nose, wants to scream at her to shut up.

'Was it ever the same after that? Did your father act differently? Differently towards you?'

He grits his teeth down hard, hears the sound loud in his ears.

The boy lies on his thin mattress, in the dark spaces, hears the rats scurrying, hears the echoes of the girl crying. He turns his head and looks into the darkness, hoping to see his mother lying there, humming the lullaby about the ducks, but she isn't there and he can't remember what she looks like anymore and he cries.

Cries for his mother. Cries for his father. Cries for James.

'Did you disappoint your father, Howard? Did he ever look at you in the same way after that?'

He brings his hands down, clenches his fists under the table, his knuckles whitening.

'Were you enough for him, Howard?'

He opens his eyes, unclenches his fists and his teeth and stands up, the chair screeching back. The shadows lash out at him from all four corners of the room. He opens his mouth to say something, to possibly scream, but the female detective just looks at him and says,

'Or was your father looking for something else?'

The male detective stands up, stares him down.

'Please,' she says calmly, 'sit down, Howard. Sit down and tell me about the mother and the boy he abducted next. Tell me why he kept them and never let them go.'

CHAPTER 24

Teresa reached down to the low table near the window and picked up a chicken drumstick from the KFC tub. The greasy bird leg halfway to her mouth, she heard the thump again and stopped. Another thump like the last one: heavy, loud, above their heads.

'There it is again,' she said, looking across at Mrs Palmer. 'Did you hear it?'

Cheryl, who had been leaning back in her chair, head back on the headrest, savouring a mouthful of a chicken burger, suddenly sat up, her eyes flicking open.

'Yes, I did,' she said, staring off towards the door to her front room, eyes glazed, almost opaque. 'What is that?'

'Billy definitely left for work?' Teresa asked.

'Yes, yes, he did,' Cheryl said. 'I heard him leave this morning.'

'And he didn't come back?'

'No, no, I'm pretty sure he didn't.'

Teresa wondered. She recalled her last visit two days ago when Cheryl was also certain that Billy was at his normal day job at the local B&Q, but Teresa had been positive that she had heard noises upstairs on his floor. And then there was the figure at the window, peering down at her, from between the curtains, as she left.

Another thump, heavy, shaking the foundations, and a distant sound of something breaking, glass, ceramic possibly.

'Oh dear,' Cheryl said, her hand to her mouth.

Teresa put the chicken drumstick down on her plate and wiped her fingers on a paper towel. She was a little nervous, possibly even frightened, but she had to do something. Either Billy was up there and needed help or it was something else. Either way, she couldn't leave Cheryl alone in the flat like this. She had to go upstairs and see what it was all about before her time with Mrs Palmer was up.

'I'll go and have a look,' she said.

'Oh, I don't know if that is a good idea, love,' Cheryl said, shifting up to the edge of her chair, a small piece of burger still in her hand. 'That's Billy's floor.'

'I know, Cheryl, but I can't leave you alone not knowing what's happening up there.'

'It's probably a pigeon or something, came in through an open window.'

'Well, I can go up there and shoo it out, but I suspect Billy is home. I just need to make sure.'

Cheryl put her chicken burger down, shaking her head.

'I'm certain Billy is out, but if it is him, it really should be me who speaks to him.'

Mrs Palmer made to stand up, putting both hands on the arm rests of her chair and leaning forward.

'Cheryl, please,' Teresa said kindly, reaching over. 'I think its best you stay here, just in case. Look, I'll take up the Celebrations and see if he wants one.'

'Yes, yes, he'd like that,' Cheryl said, sitting back in her chair. She repositioned the walking cane next to her right hand.

'And if it's a bird or something else, I can entice it out with a chocolate treat.'

Cheryl gave a small laugh.

'That sounds like a good idea, love. Please be careful, though. Billy doesn't like being surprised. He's a bit jumpy, and he doesn't like the lights on that much. Always been more comfortable in the dark, from a young age.'

Cheryl said nothing more, just stared out towards the doorway, lost in thought.

'I'll be careful,' Teresa said, and she stood up and placed a hand on Cheryl's knee.

Cheryl jumped a little but pointed towards the open door at the same time, as if it wasn't Teresa's touch that startled her, but a revelation that had just come into her head.

'There's a flashlight in the kitchen, second drawer, I think. As long as you don't shine it directly at him, it won't startle him.'

'Okay,' Teresa said. She picked up the Celebrations tub and tucked it under her arm. 'I'll be back shortly. And it's best I take these chocolates with me anyway. I don't think I trust you, Mrs Palmer.'

Cheryl laughed nervously and waved her away.

Teresa walked the hallway down towards the back of the flat and the kitchen.

'Be careful,' she heard Cheryl call out and it gave her a shiver up her spine.

In the kitchen, once again immaculately cleaned earlier in the day, she found the small black flashlight in the drawer as Cheryl had said. She switched it on and off to see if it worked, but it didn't, and she found that there were no batteries in it. She located batteries in an unopened pack of six in the same drawer and put three in.

As she clicked the battery cover in place, there was another loud thump from upstairs, then what sounded like a curse, an unintelligible outburst muffled by closed doors.

Not a pigeon then.

It had to be Billy up there, having either never left today or snuck back in when Cheryl was busy doing something else this morning, napping maybe, before Teresa had arrived. Or possibly when Teresa had gone out for KFC. It had only taken her twenty minutes, but yes, that would be it, Billy had come back then.

Taking the first step on the carpeted stairs leading up to the top floor, Teresa didn't know whether she was more frightened at the possibility that it was a complete stranger, an intruder upstairs, or if it was indeed Billy, the son she'd never met.

William's totally harmless, so don't worry about that, you'll be fine.

Pam, the contact at Home Assist, trying to reassure Teresa but not entirely convincing. Not at all convincing right now.

The stairs from the kitchen led up to the first floor of the two-storey tenement, a dozen or so carpeted steps that ended at a wall and a window with its curtains drawn. A banister fixed to the stairwell on both sides aided her ascent.

Halfway up, she could tell that the only light illuminating the first floor was coming from the kitchen behind her. As she ascended, her body blocked more and more of the light and the first floor grew darker and darker. At the floor level, a balustrade emerged on her left, lining the top of the first floor hallway around the open space of the stairwell. As soon as her head was above the floor line, she gripped the wooden struts of the balustrade, Celebrations tub and flashlight in the other hand, and turned around on the stairs to look behind her.

Through the gaps in the balustrade that surrounded the stairwell, she could only see darkness and, at the far end of the hallway that stretched along the length of the flat, a very thin outline of a window. The window had its curtains drawn, the relatively clear day outside peeking through.

Nothing else. Pitch black.

'Billy?' she said, her voice only lightly above a whisper. She cleared her throat. 'Billy? It's Teresa, your mum's friend.'

The hallway remained dark and quiet.

'I have some Celebrations for you, if you'd like some. Chocolate.'

Still nothing. No reply. No thumping. Whoever was up there must have heard her and had stopped whatever they were doing.

Teresa swallowed. She now wasn't so sure it was Billy. If it was an intruder, she should really call the police.

'Billy?' she called. 'I'm coming up, so if it is you, please respond. If it's not, I have my phone and will call the police if you don't identify yourself.'

For a moment, she thought she'd left her phone downstairs, but taking her hand off the balustrade, she felt in her back pocket and it was there.

'Okay, I'm going to turn the light on now,' she said. 'Is that okay, Billy?'

A creaking sound reached her and sent another shiver up her back. A door, opening, somewhere down the hallway. She felt goosebumps rise on her arms. Teresa squinted but could see nothing.

'No light,' a deep voice said, rumbling in the darkness.

Teresa's heart jumped and she almost lost her footing on the stairs. She gripped the balustrade tighter and steadied herself. The Celebrations slipped from under her armpit, but she pulled her right arm in and held it against her body.

'Billy?' she called. 'Can I come up?'

A moment of silence, followed by: 'Yes.'

Teresa found herself letting out a short sigh. It was Billy, not an intruder, she was sure of that now. Her anxiety levels dropped but she could still feel it, buzzing around in her chest, quieter but still there.

'We thought you'd gone to work,' she said, taking a step up, four steps away from the top.

'Sick,' Billy said, his voice deep, but almost ethereal coming out of the dark hallway.

'I'm sorry to hear that, Billy,' Teresa said as she reached the top step. She turned around to face down the hallway of the first floor. 'Can you eat some chocolates?'

'Yes,' Billy replied in the dark.

'Can I turn on the flashlight if I promise not to shine it at you?'

A moment's pause, hesitation, and then: 'Yes.'

Teresa flicked on the flashlight in her hand and jumped, three faces staring back at her, eyes gleaming. The Celebrations tub fell to the carpeted floor and teetered on the edge of the top step, threatening to roll down the stairs to the kitchen below.

Teresa squatted to the floor, one hand on the metal container, the other shining the flashlight up at the faces in front of her. It was a photo portrait hanging on the wall, a family portrait, husband, wife, young boy. Teresa let out the breath she'd been holding and gripped the Celebrations tin, before standing up.

A closer look at the photo and she could tell that the young mother was Cheryl Palmer, the features of her face immediately recognisable. Her eyes shined and Teresa guessed it was taken before she was blind. She'd mentioned she hadn't always been blind, so this photo, which looked over thirty years old, was evidence of that. The husband was handsome enough, tidy haircut, business like. The boy, standing between them, his height almost the same as his mother, even at what appeared to be nine or ten, smiled warmly, a sunny demeanour. Billy, in happier times.

The door down the hallway creaked again and Teresa almost pointed the torch towards it, but she stopped herself, remembering not to startle Billy.

'I'm coming, Billy,' she said and shone the flashlight at her feet as she walked down the hallway.

The carpet was stained in parts, and it looked like it could do with a good vacuum. Cheryl would not be able to come up here to tidy the place and Teresa was certain Billy was not inclined to do his own housework. There was also a musty smell, almost tangible in the air.

She passed doors on her left and right and looking up, she could see, by the outline of the far window, that she was halfway down the hallway.

'Almost there, Billy,' she said, making sure he was aware of where she was. 'I think you'll like these chocolates. We have Snickers, Maltesers, Galaxy and lots more. Plenty for you to choose from.'

The beam of light crossed over the bottom of an open door and Teresa stopped. She raised the flashlight, keeping it pointed to the wall near the door, and it illuminated enough of the hallway for Teresa to see that Billy wasn't standing there.

'Are you there, Billy?' Teresa said.

There was a shuffling sound from within the room and something light fell to the floor with a small thud.

'Billy?'

Another shuffling sound from within, like covers moved across the surface of a bed.

Teresa took a deep breath and moved around the open door. She kept the flashlight low, just ahead of her, and she could see the door jamb built into the carpet. The carpet was darker in the room, almost brown, with small flecks of colour, rubbish, food, crumbs maybe, speckled throughout.

Beyond the light, it was impenetrable darkness. And it was silent. No more shuffling, no more thudding. Teresa held her breath to identify any signs of someone in the room.

'Billy, are you in here?' she said, softly.

There was no answer and, feeling suddenly exposed, she raised the flashlight, not caring if she would startle Billy or not, just wanting to see what was in front of her in the room.

Teresa gasped audibly.

Scanning the beam of light around the room, she could see that it was big enough to be a master bedroom and that there was a door to the left for the ensuite, but the setup of the room did not resemble a bedroom at all.

Furniture in the room, including two beds, was set up as what Teresa could only describe as a hidey hole or nook, but it was bigger than that, obviously designed for a full-grown adult. It was intricate, with a roof made from the two beds, forming a tepee type design that almost touched the tall ceiling. Boxes, some with B&Q stencilled on the side, propped up the beds at its base, creating enough space underneath. A full-size free-standing cupboard faced Teresa front and centre, one of the doors ajar. Teresa carefully shined her light inside, seeing that the backing had been removed and that there was a makeshift room beyond, a thin mattress, a side table with a small lamp and what looked like a serving tray with dirty dishes on it. She moved the beam a little to the left, catching a figure within, and said:

'Billy?'

Distantly, below her through the floor, she heard the front door chime, dull but recognisable.

'Billy?'

'Do you like my cellar?' Billy said from behind Teresa, and she yelled and jumped, dropping both the flashlight and the tub of Celebrations. The flashlight switched off and the tub opened and chocolates spilled out onto the carpet. She fell to all fours and reached around on the ground for the flashlight, frantically trying to find it.

A light beamed out past her bowed head, shining on all the chocolates on the floor. It settled on a small group of Bounty bars.

'I like Bounty,' Billy said. 'Here, let me help.'

Billy shone his flashlight just ahead of Teresa's outstretched hands, illuminating her own torch which was within reach. Teresa grabbed it and turned it on.

'I'm sorry, I startled you,' Billy said and Teresa detected a note of amusement in his deep voice.

'That's okay,' Teresa stammered breathlessly. 'Y – you just gave me a fright.'

'I'll shine the light and you can pick up the chocolates. You can leave the Bountys.'

'Oh, sure,' Teresa said, slightly confused. 'Of – of course.'

Before she began to pick up the chocolates, she briefly shone the torch back into the structure in the middle of the room, through the open cupboard door, and saw that the figure she'd thought she saw wasn't a figure at all but a free-standing tower heater, like the heaters she saw at alfresco restaurants. It was tall, like a person, and somehow fit underneath the two-bedded roof.

'It gets cold sometimes,' Billy said, having followed the trajectory of her torchlight with his own.

'Of course,' Teresa said and moved around on all fours so that she was facing Billy. Billy appeared not to be a threat but she didn't trust him at all. Frightening her like that, living in darkness, creating strange internal housing out of furniture; she'd rather have him in front of her, than behind.

Billy didn't help Teresa other than to move his flashlight around to assist in locating the escaped chocolates. Teresa picked them all up, save the Bounty bars, and put them all in the Celebrations tub. She stood up with it under her arm.

Billy shone his flashlight directly into Teresa's eyes. She raised her hand.

'Sorry, Billy, can you take that out of my eyes, please?'

He moved it away, pointing down. Teresa's light was also down and she could see, as the coloured glare on her retinas faded, that Billy was wearing red fluffy socks and light blue pyjama bottoms. He was a tall man and blocked the doorway out of the room.

Almost subconsciously, Teresa heard the doorbell ring again.

'I should get downstairs, help your mother with whoever that is.'

'I didn't hear anything,' Billy grumbled. 'You didn't answer my question.'

'Sorry,' Teresa said, 'what question was that, Billy?'

'About my cellar.'

Teresa was suddenly flustered, felt anxious to get downstairs, to get on the other side of Billy and out of this room. She briefly turned around to the structure behind her and flashed the beam across it.

'It's good, Billy, real good,' she said, facing him again, 'but I need to get downstairs.'

'Don't you think it's bizarre?'

'Sorry, what?'

'A cellar in the attic,' he said, and sniggered through his nose. 'Strange, right?'

'It's very good, Billy, but please, let me through,' Teresa said, and took a step forward, bracing herself for an altercation.

'I used to live in a cellar.'

'Billy, please.'

To her surprise, Billy stepped back and let her through. She moved past him, her shoulder brushing his chest, giving her the sense that he was a good foot taller than she was. Her heart was hammering in her own chest as she moved passed him into the hallway but all he did was say, 'I'll come down too.'

Teresa nodded even though she knew he couldn't see her.

'I'm sick,' Billy said.

Teresa's shadow jumped across the far wall, Billy shining his flashlight at the back of her head, and it moved and juttered around, making Teresa feel a little disorientated. She sensed Billy following her, just like he said he would do.

Teresa heard Cheryl talking downstairs.

'It might be my boss,' Billy said. 'I didn't work today.'

Teresa passed the family photo on the wall with barely a glance and gripped the balustrade as she reached the top of the stairwell. Turning back towards the first-floor hallway, already descending the stairs, the light from Billy's flashlight shone in her face.

She heard the front door close and Cheryl exclaim breathlessly, then a thud, similar to the noises Billy had been making while he fine-tuned his upstairs hidey-hole, but this noise came from the hallway on the ground floor and Teresa suddenly felt the urge to get downstairs as quick as she could, taking the stairs in a rush, her hand running down the bannister, the Celebrations tub falling out of her left hand and rolling ahead of her.

'Cheryl,' she yelled, hearing Billy thumping down the stairs behind her.

134

She rushed through the kitchen, dropping the flashlight onto the table, seeing in the corner of her eye it tip over and start to roll off the edge, and she rounded the corner into the hallway, skidded on the cold hard floor and shouldered the wall. She fell to her knees and raised a hand to her mouth, gasping.

Billy stumbled in behind her and gave a hideous, inhuman scream that Teresa would never forget.

CHAPTER 25

The main police station servicing the New Forest area was situated in Lyndhurst, part of the Hampshire and Isle of Wight Constabulary. A brown brick building built in the seventies, the station was spread over two storeys and connected with the Magistrates Court. Chief Inspector Arne Cristian managed the station from a small office at the back of the building, a short walk down a corridor from the bullpen where the detectives and police officers worked. He'd been in the role for almost five years now, moving quickly up through the ranks from when he started off as a police constable in Southampton.

The New Forest area, encompassing the national forest, was his father's old stomping ground, and no one could be prouder of his son than that old war horse. Now retired, Dane Cristian, who reached the same position as Arne in his thirty years on the job, never stopped talking about his son. Anyone who spent an afternoon with him, either his fellow retirees from the Constabulary down at the pub, the volunteer group he worked for in the New Forest forestry team while they were out clearing trees or, just some unfortunate passer-by, would have their ear chewed off about his son's achievements, sometimes when Arne was in the same room as him. Even at forty-seven, his father embarrassed Arne with his gushing praise and one-eyed support.

But he loved his father as much as his father loved him and the old copper had taught Arne everything he knew. Including what to expect on the job and what to prepare yourself for. The horrible things you may have to face.

Even though the story was never mentioned again, Arne always remembered his father recounting the case that had troubled him the most. A story his father felt needed to be told to forewarn his son about what he may come across on the job. A story that Dane, and now Arne, never repeated. A story that took place at a remote property on the outskirts of the New Forest National Park.

A story about the presence of evil.

That was why, when any report concerning that address came across Arne's desk, he took notice.

An elderly couple lived out there, Mr and Mrs Irvine. They had lived there for going on three years now. The property was quite remote, at the top of a bluff with the valley dropping down below them on one side. Hidden amongst the forest, it wasn't necessarily an easy address to access in an emergency, the access road winding up through the fields for about a quarter of a mile before reaching the house itself. When Arne had been informed about the new owners of the property, he'd made sure that each of his officers had their contact details and that regular visits were made, once or twice a month. Mr and Mrs Irvine welcomed the attention. It made them feel safe out there, they said.

The last three weeks they'd been on vacation, on a cruise in the Med somewhere. They'd left a note at the station to let Arne know. That wasn't something they'd usually do, inform the police of their movements, but they said they'd be gone for over a month and they wanted to let the station know just in case an officer turned up to the property and found it empty.

"Don't want to cause any concern" the note had read. They said a family member would pop in on the odd occasion to check on the property.

That was all fine, but now a note from the desk sergeant had been passed to Arne this morning, a call from the local church group who said that the Irvine's hadn't turned up to the past three services, which was very unlike them. They were also not answering their mobile phones.

Mr and Mrs Irvine were big contributors to the local Protestant church, were very active, and the leader of the congregation was a little concerned. The desk sergeant who took the call down in reception knew about the note given to the station by the Irvine's, in fact he had received it at the front desk, and the sergeant had informed the Church group that they were on holiday. As requested, even though that enquiry was satisfactorily closed, it related to a property Arne kept an eye on so the desk sergeant passed the query on.

It was strange, Arne thought, rubbing the one-day stubble on his chin as he read the query from the church again. Arne knew Mr Irvine to be quite pedantic and organised, so to not mention his month long holiday to his church group was a little odd, especially as he had been organised enough to mention it to the police.

Still, Arne didn't know the ins and outs of Mr Irvine's relationship with the church group. There may have been several reasons why he didn't tell them about his trip. The other possibility was that they had cancelled their trip or come back early and failed to inform the station and that they would be turning up to the next Sunday service, everything back to normal.

Arne knew this was a minor issue in an otherwise busy day of meetings, reports, and recruitment drives, but one of the things his father always stressed to Arne was to trust his instincts, trust that feeling in his gut, and Arne never ignored his father's advice. He never forgot anything his father told him about the job.

Chief Inspector Arne Cristian picked up his phone to the desk sergeant and asked that he send a unit around to the Irvine property, just to see if everything was in order. He then returned to the mountain of emails building up in his inbox.

***

Detective Constable Knight sat at her desk, head down, headphones in, watching something on her phone. She'd been on it for the past fifteen minutes and Roark wondered what she was looking at. Roark trusted Knight not to be wasting time, she was too professional for that, and she knew the young detective was taking this current case seriously, so it must have been something quite important to keep her attention for so long. Knight would tell her in due course, she always did, so Roark paid it no further attention.

Roark returned to her computer screen; she had an update with DCI Rawlins in thirty minutes, ahead of his daily press briefing. The case was gaining national attention, all the programmes were leading with it, social media was abuzz with commentary and would-be sleuths. Everyone was looking for Aaron Sparger and Jaime Collander.

Over two days since Jaime Collander had disappeared, it was decided to bring the press and public into the case in the larger sense. The key driver for the move was confirmation that the two abduction cases were linked. DNA analysis, fast-tracked due to the urgency around the missing person cases, confirmed that the samples from the Amazon delivery van used to kidnap Miss Collander matched those taken from Roark's crime scenes, including the van used to take Aaron Sparger. It was clear cut: they were dealing with the same person.

Problem was, they did not who that person was. The DNA profiles from the scenes did not match anyone in the National DNA Database. They now had significant evidence to convict the killer, but they were no closer to finding him.

In addition, the team members working the stolen car angles were coming up against dead ends. The car stolen from around Basingstoke was found, left on the side of the road near Newbury. DNA and blood traces taken from the car matched with the samples taken from the other Aaron Sparger crime scenes, confirming that Aaron Sparger was lying down in the back seat of the vehicle, bleeding, while his captor transported him from the van. However, there were no cameras capturing the dumping of the vehicle and there were no leads as to what had happened to Aaron Sparger next. The team working the Jaime Collander case were in the same boat: stolen vehicles found but no lead to what happened next. And no visuals on the driver.

Facing multiple dead ends, the decision was made: use the press to tap into the resources of the public. Someone had to have seen Aaron Sparger or Jaime Collander or the vehicles in question and it was felt that opening up to the public about the key points of the case, including the connection between the two, could yield some positive results. There was a risk of timewasters calling in to gain police attention, but it was worth the possibility of unearthing public provided information that could lead the police to the abducted victims. Roark supported the decision, but now wondered whether they'd left it too late.

As she worked on Rawlins's press briefing notes, using the Crime Database to summarise the latest information, she wondered how the press and public would react to the news that the two abductions were linked. For Roark, the connection worried her. One killer working in two different cities abducting two unrelated victims in a short period of time was cause for considerable concern. The escalation of the cases made it hard to have much hope for the survival of Aaron and Jaime, despite Roark's insistence to the team to remain positive.

Work had to continue. They could not give up now.

Roark read through the list of outstanding items on her case file. As Senior Investigating Officer on the Corey Whitman homicide and Aaron Sparger kidnapping, she was co-ordinating all facets of that investigation, even those elements she wasn't sure would yield anything. In particular, she had Behavioural Sciences building up a profile. This was something she never gave much weight to in an investigation, but she had to cover all bases, do everything humanly possible.

Her other role as SIO was the dissemination of all information. Everything she got, all the evidence, she passed on to the Anti-Kidnapping and Extortion Unit who were actively out there searching for Aaron and Jaime, and anything relevant also went to DI Moody in Bristol.

As if on cue, an email flashed up on her screen from Moody, the subject heading dropping further discouraging news.

'The Amazon driver didn't make it,' Roark said aloud. 'That's two homicides now. Jesus.'

'I can't stop watching it,' Knight said, possibly not hearing Roark's announcement.

Roark turned in her chair.

'What is it?'

Knight flipped her phone around to show Roark a BBC website video of a woman being interviewed by a throng of reporters outside the Bristol police station. The woman was speaking with tears running down her cheeks.

'Jaime Collander's mum,' Knight said. 'She's so distraught.'

'As you would be.'

'She keeps going on and on about how she'd raised Jaime right, did her best as a mum, that this shouldn't have happened.'

'Her daughter is missing. Understandable behaviour.'

Knight stared at her phone screen.

'It's not that.'

Roark moved her chair around, so she faced the detective.

'What is it?'

Knight shook her head and switched off her phone.

'It's nothing. What's next? I'm coming up with a lot of blanks and dead ends. I've got a lot of other leads but they're all a little woolly.'

Roark knew something was bothering Knight, but she let it go.

'Anything new on Aaron Sparger?'

'Nope,' Knight said, sighing loudly. 'Parents live out in Acton Town. The guy's mid-thirties, doesn't appear to have a current partner, slips under the radar for the most part. No one has any ideas about why Aaron would be targeted or who would do it.'

'Where does that leave us?'

Knight sighed again.

'Looking at a ten-foot brick wall with no way forward, but I'll keep digging. We have his banking transactions, social media accounts, a few friends to catch up with. Might get a lead from them.'

'We also need to identify any link between Aaron Sparger and Jaime Collander,' Roark said, tapping the screen with her pen. 'I've got a debrief with Rawlins in fifteen. Can you pick up on that too? I've got a working file in the database, looking into similarities between the crimes and the victims. There must be something linking these two.'

'Unless,' Knight said, 'it's all totally random.'

Roark scratched her head, winced.

'I don't even what to think about that.'

'Okay, I'm on it,' Knight said, emerging from her funk as quickly as she'd slipped into it, and she moved her mouse, activating her monitor and started typing on her keyboard.

Roark said thanks and tapped the screen again. She took a few more notes for Rawlins, keeping any talk of random killings out of her summary. That possibility was something that they would not be telling the press.

CHAPTER 26

Chief Inspector Arne Cristian walked past reception and told the desk sergeant that he was heading down the road to grab a late lunch. The desk sergeant, who was talking to two uniformed constables, held him up.

'These are the two I sent over to the Irvine property this morning,' he said.

'Oh yeah, how'd you go?' Arne said.

The two police officers faced their superior and recounted their visit. Arne knew them both quite well; good hard-working constables.

'It all looks fine, sir,' PC Roberts, the taller of the two constables, said. 'We drove up the drive and parked up near the house. Knocked on the door and there was no answer. We went around the whole property, place was deserted, but it looked tidy.'

'Apparently Mr Irvine has family checking in on the place,' Arne said. 'Goes in once a week, makes sure it's all looked after.'

The other officer, Dooley, frowned.

'That tracks,' Roberts said. 'Looked like someone had put out the rubbish, collected the mail.'

'Vehicles?'

'None, except that old campervan up on blocks. Not sure they'll ever get rid of that.'

Arne slapped Roberts on the shoulder.

'Good work, you two. I appreciate you checking up on that.'

'Our pleasure, sir,' Roberts said and made to turn away.

Arne caught Dooley's face.

'Something up, Constable?'

'Yeah,' Dooley said cautiously. 'You said the Irvines had family looking after the place while they were away?'

'That's correct.'

'I'd have to check with my mother, but I'm sure the Irvines don't have any family nearby. They're all up in Scotland. Maybe a niece in Snowdonia, but the rest are definitely based in the Highlands somewhere.'

'Over six hours away,' Arne said. 'You sure on that?'

'Pretty sure,' Dooley said, confidence in his voice.

'Roberts?'

'I wouldn't know, sir,' Roberts said.

'Stanley?' Arne said, turning to the desk sergeant.

'The note said family, sir. Could mean friends, possibly.'

'Possibly. Did Mr Irvine leave a contact number?'

'Yes, he did, but said it might be difficult to catch hold of him as they'll be on a cruise ship.'

'Stanley, find that number for me if you could. I'll see if I can get through to Mr Irvine, just to make sure. Dooley, Roberts, do me a favour and keep an eye on the place for us? Daily check-in will be fine.'

'We'll pop around there tomorrow, around lunch time. Check it out.'

'Perfect. Thank you, Constables.'

PC Dooley and Roberts turned and walked down the corridor, talking to each other as they went.

'Here's the number, sir,' the desk sergeant said, passing over a yellow Post-it note.

'Cheers, Stanley. I'll see if I can get hold of them.'

Arne stepped out of the station on a bright, sunny day. He pulled out his mobile phone and, referring to the note, he called the number for Mr Irvine. As he stood on the steps, the sun warm on his skin, he listened as the phone rang out.

No response.

They were on a cruise ship, possibly with no reception.

Arne rubbed the stubble on his chin and pocketed his phone. He wasn't sure why he couldn't let this go, other than the strange feeling in his gut. Something wasn't right.

It was probably nothing, the Irvine's making a few silly mistakes in their old age, forgetting to tell the Church group, misstating family when they meant friends.

Still, it didn't sit right. The Irvine's were in their seventies, but they weren't senile, for Christ's sake.

Arne couldn't let it go and he blamed his father. Not just because he'd inherited from him the need to trust his gut until confirmed otherwise, but because of the story Dane had told him so many years ago. Ever since his father had recounted that story from thirty years ago, there was something about that property that always bugged Arne. He just couldn't ignore it.

He promised himself he'd call the number again later that evening.

***

Sharp pain woke Teresa and she groaned loudly, grasping at her stomach. Before she opened her eyes, she could feel the hot blood soaking her hands, trickling out of the stab wound in her lower abdomen. The flash of the knife appeared in her mind and she opened her eyes wide, started to push back with her legs, trying to escape an unknown force but only managing to topple over on her side.

Head on the cold floor, panting, Teresa stared into darkness. It was all around her, clouding her vision, making it difficult to focus. She shivered and the pain in her stomach gripped her again with an intensity that was audible in her ears, a screeching in her head. She gritted her teeth and tried not to vocalise the pain.

Flashes of memory between the sharp stabs of pain. First and foremost, the knife in his hand, jutting forward, twice into her stomach, sending her to the floor. Another penetration to her flesh as she lay there, back against the wall, and then Billy kept screaming and Cheryl started yelling, trying to get up from where she had been pushed, yelling and screaming, not seeing anything but hearing her son wailing.

The dark figure walking away from her, towards them, in the hallway.

Teresa had blacked out. That had to be it because she could not remember anything else.

She suddenly felt pain, from deep within her stomach, as if the knife was going in again.

Teresa kept her mouth shut, breathing through her nose, until even that seemed too loud in the darkness.

She didn't know where she was, who was with her, what was going on. He could be right in front of her and she wouldn't know, the pain clouding her sight, drowning out all noises.

Her right hand was under her, still held stiffly against her stomach, and she felt the warmth of her life seeping out.

The knife went in again, or so it felt, and the pain was so intense that Teresa arched her back, gritted her teeth, and screamed.

The sound reverberated off the walls around her, filling her head, making her so scared that she felt like vomiting. Sharp daggers of lightning flashed behind her eyes and she opened them wide, suddenly with a burst of clarity that brought all the shapes into focus, bright and defined, before the darkness returned, dull, blurred.

In that brief moment, like in a flash from a camera, she saw the entrance to Cheryl's kitchen right in front of her, the bright interior, the flashlight on the floor, the Celebration tub and its contents strewn across the linoleum surface, and a telephone on the bench next to a bowl of decaying onions.

Her eyesight was returning, her vision sharpening, a resolve deep within her coming into sharp focus.

Slowly bending forward, she strained her head down past her body, the blood pooling around her stomach. Down the hallway, the front door was closed tight but the light in the front room was still on, splaying across the floor. Cheryl's cane lay on its side on the floor, dropped and discarded.

No sign of Cheryl. No sign of Billy. No sign of the man who'd launched himself at her with his knife.

The phone. She had to focus on the telephone.

Teresa took a moment, thought of who she would call – her father, her sister, the police – then stopped, chastised herself for losing focus.

The phone.

It wasn't far, the doorway to the kitchen almost within reach. All she needed to do was roll onto her stomach, no matter how much that would hurt, get up on her hands and knees, and crawl to the kitchen.

That's all she had to do.

Gritting her teeth, she brought her left hand flat onto the floor so that she could leverage herself up. She managed to lift herself up a centimetre from the floor and tried to push herself along towards the kitchen, but one hand wasn't enough. She needed both, and that would mean taking her right hand off her stomach, from the wound, and letting the blood flow.

There was no other option. If she didn't get to the telephone, she would bleed out there and then. A slow, painful death.

She thought of her family, her grandparents in Spain, her friends, dear, dear, Miguel, the man she desperately wanted to see again, and she pushed her left hand down and brought her right hand out from under her stomach. The pain flushed her, blood spilling from her wound, blood rushing to her head, and with both hands flat on the floor, she collapsed, face first, and blacked out.

CHAPTER 27

The shift was finishing, detectives and administration staff tidying up desks, grabbing coats and heading to the pub. Roark and Knight didn't make a move, glued to their screens, reading and writing notes, not making much progress. They hadn't been outside today other than for lunch and that was a sign that the case was not going well at all. No new leads. Nothing to follow up. No witnesses to interview.

Roark had considered taking a trip to Bristol to see first-hand what DI Clarice Moody had on her case, but Rawlins wanted Roark close by, just in case something broke and another press conference was needed. Heading off across the country just to discuss information that was already readily available on the online system or via email would not be approved. Roark knew it and hadn't even tried.

The press conference earlier in the day had gone well, according to Rawlins, and all the major TV channels – BBC, Sky and other national stations – had picked up the story about how the two cases were connected and had bumped up the photos of Aaron Sparger and Jaime Callander to the top of the news pile, above international news, current wars and elections. That would help, get the faces out in the public space, get millions of eyes on the ground looking for the two victims, but the news cycle was unforgiving, and the exposure wouldn't last long unless new information came to hand.

'Damn it,' Knight said, slamming her desk, frustration overflowing. She'd been working on connecting the two crimes for the best part of the day and was getting nowhere. 'There's nothing here, Kris. Nothing to connect the two.'

'There has to be something,' Roark said, a little too forcefully, unable to help herself. Her frustration was brimming too, and she was struggling to keep a lid on it. They really should take a break, finish up for the day, pass it on to fresh eyes, DI Lucas and the overnight team. Burnout was a real possibility if they didn't look after themselves.

'Nothing, I'm telling you. Family, friends, work colleagues, holiday trips, there's nothing but the most trivial of links and those amount to nothing.'

'Social media accounts, online connections, same interest groups?'

'Working through all of those. TikTok, Insta, fuck, I'm even resorting to Facebook, even though Jaime closed her account a year or two ago.'

'Any indication as to why she did that?'

'No, nothing.'

Roark rubbed her eyes. A headache was brewing.

'I think we have to start again,' Knight said. 'Interview the Sparger family a second time, ask Moody to do the same with Collander. We missed something first time around.'

'How about Corey Whitman?' Roark said, leaning back in her chair and turning to Knight. 'Maybe there's a connection there we're missing.'

'To Jaime Collander?'

'Maybe Corey did know Aaron Sparger. Maybe he knew Jaime too.'

Knight picked up her phone and swiped.

'Did that, or at least started on the obvious places to look. Nothing so far. I can't imagine Jaime having anything to do with lowlife scum like Corey.'

'Agreed,' Roark said, rubbing her temple. 'It's a stretch at best. I think we were right the first time. Corey was just in the wrong place at the wrong time.'

'Possibly. Don't worry, I'll keep on it. It's just pissing me off.'

DI Lucas walked onto the floor with a bag of MacDonald's in one hand. He was heading to the kitchen where he had been consigned to eat, the majority of the floor not appreciating the smell of a Big Mac wafting through the corridors and desks.

'Lucas is in. We need to get home soon,' Roark said. 'We'll burn out otherwise.'

'Another hour or two,' Knight said, matter-of-factly as if there was no debate. 'At the very least, we need to list possibilities and avenues of investigation for Lucas and his team to start on.'

'Got it. One hour max. Then we need to get out of here.'

It ended up as two hours, including a fifteen minute debrief with DI Lucas, a session Roark found particularly uncomfortable as he kept burping up the smell of McDonald's special sauce every other minute. Lucas was helpful though and said that he'd revisit some of Knight's interviews and keep working on possible connections between the London and Bristol cases.

Knight was still despondent when they left the station, downtrodden with the workload, disappointed with the lack of success. The Jaime Collander disappearance was hitting her hard even though they weren't directly involved in that case. They had a quick chat about it and Roark managed to convince her that it wasn't their fault Jaime was taken, they had worked as hard as they could with what they had, time was against them from the beginning. They shouldn't beat themselves up about the fact that they couldn't find Aaron Sparger's abductor before he struck again. Knight reluctantly agreed but her mood didn't change.

As they walked towards the station exit, Roark offered for them to have a quick drink at The Disgruntled Goat, but Knight declined. Roark understood and she welcomed the early night too. They both agreed that they'd get in early tomorrow after a good night's sleep.

After negotiating the press outside the station, Roark walked to the bus stop. A few of the reporters followed her but thankfully the bus arrived soon after and she managed to escape without having to conduct any semblance of an interview.

The bus trip from Camberwell to Vauxhall went by quickly, Roark lost in her thoughts on the case. She had to admit, she was feeling the pressure. Sparger was taken five days ago, Collander almost three days now. Time ticking on and the likelihood of the two victims surviving was decreasing every hour. DCI Rawlins was feeling the heat from the press and the bosses too, and he was funnelling it down to her. Rawlins knew that they were doing all that they could, but he was on her at any given moment, asking her anyway: were they doing everything they could? Roark was honest to herself, she wasn't sure, but she told Rawlins that they were.

The bus pulled into Vauxhall Bus Station and Roark stepped off into a coolish night. She walked through the station towards Kennington Lane. She saw one person littering, another pissing up against a wall in the underpass, and some seedy dealings on the fringes of Vauxhall Pleasure Gardens but she ignored it all. A group of three youths gave her an up and down look from in front of a fried chicken shop and she got a few glances outside of Tesco's, but she had long passed being self-conscious about her height, and she had bigger fish to fry.

Aaron Sparger and Jaime Collander.

Their faces were etched to the back of her eye lids when she closed them at night, haunted her waking hours whether she was engaged with work or not, but she had a job to do, and the faces of the victims were more than enough incentive to keep her at it.

Roark stepped up to her front door, fitted the key in the lock and pushed through into her sanctuary. Closing the door behind her, she leaned back on it, closed her eyes, and released out a long sigh. She let the back of her head tap the door, left it there, her shoulders dropping.

Finally, knowing she couldn't stand there forever, she pushed off the door and shuffled her coat off her shoulders, let it fall to the carpeted floor. She didn't turn any lights on, walked down the hallway and one floor up to the kitchen. She left the kitchen light off and opened the fridge, the interior light and coolness of refrigeration bathing her. Dinner was leftover butternut squash and lentil curry in a plastic container. She pulled it out and tossed it on the bench.

Switching on the light, she transferred her dinner to a bowl and popped it in the microwave. As she leaned against the bench, rubbing her eyes, she thought about a bath, wanting to start the process of washing the day away. She knew it was going to be harder than usual to do that, the case permeating every hour of her day, awake or asleep, but she had to try. The process of trying was therapeutic enough.

The NHS letter stared at her from the fridge door.

When the microwave announced the heating of her meal was complete, she took it out, burning her fingers on the bottom of the bowl, grabbed a spoon and sat down at the table. After five minutes of waiting for the meal to cool and trying to ignore the letter, she stood up and took it off the fridge, the magnet holding it up falling to the floor.

Roark laid the letter flat out on the table next to her bowl of curry. She took a mouthful and a spot of curry dropped on the letter, right in the middle of the page, and she absentmindedly wiped it away and took another bite. She read the letter over twice, the middle section a third time, and decided to open a bottle of Albarino she'd bought two days ago from the corner Tesco store. It was in the fridge and after pouring it out into a large wine glass, she sipped it, and the wine was delicious, cold in her mouth and throat. She closed her eyes, took another sip.

Lovely. Refreshing with the promise of numbness and oblivion.

Putting the letter aside, she finished up her bowl of curry and dropped it in the sink with a clatter. She took the tall thin bottle and her glass up with her to the bathroom, sat on the toilet with the seat cover down while she ran the bath and had her second glass. She had splashed out and bought a miniature fridge and, with the assistance of an extension cord, she had it permanently set up in the bathroom, tucked between the bath and the sink, for easy access. She placed the Spanish white on its side next to a bottle of Pommery, which she was keeping for either a celebration or a commiseration, she didn't particularly care which, whatever came first.

The water was hot, one or two degrees below scolding, and as she lowered her naked body in, she felt and thought nothing else but the invigorating feeling, followed minutes later by the relaxing soothing sensation of her body adapting to the temperature.

Roark leaned her head back on the waterproof pillow resting on the end of the bath and placed a hot face towel over her eyes. The bath wasn't large enough for her long legs, so her knees protruded out of the water, but the heat rising up countered any sense of coolness on her skin.

For a moment, she thought of nothing. As thoughts of the day, the case and the letter, started to circle around her mind, looking for a way in, she took off the face towel and reached over for her glass of wine, which she'd refilled before stepping into the bath. A sip of wine, still cool from the mini bar, made her smile and the thoughts drifted out of reach again. It was a process she followed for almost twenty minutes and when she decided to get out, she found the bottle of Albarino had half a glass left in it and discovered herself a little light-headed.

The half-glass didn't go to waste and, when swallowed, she was tempted to open the Pommery, but decided to get dressed for bed first, give her time to reconsider that particularly slippery slope. There was still work facing her tomorrow, and she best have her wits about her.

Roark towelled off, let her short blonde hair dry naturally, and put on silk pyjamas that felt smooth on her skin. The pyjamas were expensive, a treat she'd bought herself when she'd divorced Brandon. She rubbed night lotion into her face and neck and padded off to bed.

Immediately after lying on the bed, her head soft on the pillow, she felt intensely relaxed and sleepy, but she undid all that by picking up her phone and checking her messages. There were none, but she opened up her contact list and her finger hovered over Julia's phone number.

Before pressing it, she wondered what she was thinking. It was common for her to consider calling Julia when she'd had a few drinks. Very often she'd never go through with it at all, and after the last discussion, she knew it wasn't welcome and would be a colossal mistake that she would always regret, so she wondered why she was convinced she'd make the call, that she needed to make the call. She wasn't horny, she wasn't emotional, so why?

It had to be the letter. She needed to speak to her about the letter. It was time to decide, make her choice, and she still didn't feel one hundred percent certain she was going to make the correct one on her own.

Roark, now fully awake, but still slightly groggy from the booze, puffed up her pillow and sat up in the bed. She activated her phone again and was about to press Julia's number when the phone started to ring in her hand. Roark blinked twice at the name of the incoming caller and suddenly had a clear premonition through the haze of alcohol that this was going to be bad news.

CHAPTER 28

'Gale?' Roark said, the phone to her ear. 'Everything okay?'

'Uh, hi Kris,' Knight said, her voice quivering. 'I'm so sorry for calling.'

'It's okay, Gale, what's wrong?'

It sounded like she'd been crying.

'I shouldn't have called, sorry, but I just needed to talk to someone.'

'Of course.'

'I think I had a little bit too much to drink,' she said, and gave a small laugh. 'Numbing the pain of the day, right?'

'I'm right there with you, love. One bottle of wine under the belt.'

'Albarino, I bet.'

Roark laughed.

'How did you know?'

'You've told me loads of times. One of those with your bath when you're seeking a particular brand of unconsciousness.'

'You know me too well. How about you?'

'English Spiced Rum. Plenty of it.' Knight sniffed. 'Too much of it.'

'What's upset you?'

The phone went silent for a moment, save for one or two more sniffs down the line.

'I've been watching that poor mother being interviewed outside that station in Bristol.'

'Jaime Collander's mum.'

'Yeah. It's really upsetting me.'

'Still blaming yourself?'

'A little. But it's more than that. I really feel her loss, y'know?'

Roark heard the tinkling of ice and a short gulp.

'It's just, that, y'know, having children, getting pregnant, starting a family. I really want it, Kris, I really do, but then I see the anguish on this woman's face, and I'm not sure I could handle it.'

'Hey,' Roark said softly, 'listen, you could handle it. You're strong-willed, tough, and you're compassionate. You'd make a great mother.'

'But the *grief* the poor woman is going through. Jesus, it's heart-breaking.'

'Look, I know I've spoken about my opinion on starting a family, reasons why I didn't do it. Most of that was down to that prick Brandon, but I also held similar reservations like you have. Not only dealing with loss,

152

but thinking about what would be the point? Would it be irresponsible? What we see every day in our jobs, what's happening in the world on our news feeds, it's horrible. Why would we even consider bringing a child into this world? But I can imagine that having children, creating a family, is one of the most special things we can do, and I know, that when you have your own family, you'll be making the world a better place.'

'That's just the Albarino talking.'

'No, it's not, Gale. It's not.'

'How about you?' Knight said. 'Has your view changed? On having children?'

'Why, because I'm a barren fifty-two-year-old?'

'There are options, but you must feel some regret?'

Knight was being a little forward, and deep down in her stomach, Roark felt it, but the wine made her push that away and see that the moment required some truth.

'If you'd asked me six months ago, I would've said there was a little bit of regret but that I stood by my decisions.'

'And now?'

Roark moved the phone to her other ear, rubbed the back of her neck.

'I received a letter,' she said.

She searched her feelings, thinking she'd immediately regret saying the words out loud, but there was none of that, genuinely none that were strong enough to burst through the effects of the alcohol she had drunk.

'What type of letter?' Knight said, her voice steady, thoughtful.

'A letter from the NHS. I have had an operation approved. A hysterectomy. They've found early stages of cancer.'

'Fuck,' Knight whispered. 'I'm so sorry, Kris.'

'It's okay,' she said, downplaying it now. 'They've got it very early, which is good. The operation should fix it as it hasn't spread yet.'

'When are you getting it done?'

'I haven't agreed to it yet. They've given me two choices with a recommendation. The recommendation is surgery; a Lap BSO like your mother had. The other choice is to try radiation and chemo. They said the latter isn't advised at this early stage as it may not be successful, that they may have to do a hysterectomy later anyway, and the more they wait, the more likely it will spread.'

Roark heard Knight put her glass down on a nearby table.

'I have to make a decision soon.'

She expected to feel tears reach her eyes, describing what was in the letter, the decision she had to make, emotions mixed in with the alcohol, but she didn't cry. Just saying it out loud, to Knight in particular, who was a friend, a close colleague, but also a subordinate, she found she could hold it together, be focused on the facts, like if it was a case and they were discussing evidence.

'What are you going to do?' Knight said, her voice quivering again. If Knight started crying, Roark wasn't so sure she *would* be able to keep it together after all.

'I'm pretty sure I'll have the operation.'

'Good,' Knight said immediately. 'I agree with that.'

'It's just so final.'

Roark paused, stared across her room.

'I feel regrets I didn't know I had. Stronger regrets.'

Knight was quiet for a short time, and then she said, her voice sobering up, holding steady, 'I understand that, Kris, I really do. We haven't talked about it a lot, but your marriage, that relationship, there's regret about that mistake, that with the right person, you may have wanted children from the very beginning, but with him, it didn't feel right.'

'Yeah,' Roark said quietly, 'and I know I'm too old for starting a family. Christ.'

'It's not that at all. This is your health, Kris. First and foremost, you must consider your health, and if the doctors are saying that this is the recommended choice, I think you must listen to them. Get a second opinion if you need to, but it sounds to me that they know what they are talking about.'

Roark nodded in the darkness of her bedroom. She understood where Gale was coming from. It all made sense. But still . . .

'Thank you, Gale,' she said, her voice breaking a little. 'I really needed to hear that.'

'Of course, Kris. And listen to me, I'm here for you through this, okay? You may have others to support you through this whole thing, but I'm here with you too, okay?'

'I appreciate that,' Roark said, the tears threatening to spill now, thinking about those she didn't have to support her, but appreciating that Knight would be there for her now anyway, in whatever capacity.

'And we just don't know what's ahead of us, do we? Find the right guy and anything is possible,' Knight said.

Roark didn't like to think about that. The possibilities ahead that would fall flat up against the likelihood. Gale was right, this was her health she was procrastinating over, so why was she delaying making the damn decision? Why did she insist on kidding herself that there was a choice?

It had helped, talking to Gale, particularly given her Mum's experience, but now she wanted to talk about something else.

'You'll find someone, too,' Roark said, seizing the moment. 'Find Mr Right and it will all become clear to you. Starting a family will just feel right, regardless of your fears and concerns. It will just feel right, and you'll go through it together.'

'I walked into that one, didn't I?' Knight said, and Roark sensed her smiling at the other end of the phone. 'Just got to find this elusive Mr Right. He's out there somewhere.'

'And he's not on *Tinder* for Christ's sake,' Roark said, laughing.

'No, no, no, not doing those fucking apps anymore. Purely in the market for some grieving widower at a crime scene.'

'There you go.'

'One without his own kids, of course.'

'Of course.'

Knight went quiet on the other end of the line.

'You okay?'

'Yeah,' Knight said, paused. 'You?'

'Better,' she said, meaning it even if she was no clearer in her mind on what to do.

'I'm heading to bed now,' Knight said. 'You've sobered me up. Take care of yourself and remember, I'm there for you every step of the way.'

'Thanks, sweetheart. I'm going to sleep now too. Busy day tomorrow.'

'Don't I know it.'

They said their goodbyes and switched off. Roark leaned over and connected her phone to the charger on the bedside table. The phone's display came on and by the time it switched off and her bedroom was steeped in darkness, Roark was lying back, head on her pillow, and she felt the tears start to come.

Before they took hold, the phone's screen lit up again, illuminating the entire bedroom, and it began to vibrate on the nightstand. Roark shuffled across and picked it up.

'Gale, you okay?'

'I'm sorry to call again.'

'It's okay, love, what is it?'

'I just thought,' Knight started, then trailed off for a moment before coming back. 'I just thought, y'know, after what we were talking about, with your situation and everything. I don't know, this is silly, but I've only told a handful of people this.'

'It's okay, Gale, it's okay. Whatever you tell me, it's in the vault, right?' Roark said.

'That's what I thought. Like your news, in the vault. It's just, all my talk about having kids, how I'd handle it, I thought it might be worth giving you context on my headspace right now.'

'Sure. If you're comfortable with talking, I'm here,' Roark said. 'But, before you say anything, I just want to say I'll support you on this too, okay, and you don't have to justify anything to me. We're friends, Gale, not just colleagues, and I've got your back.'

'Thanks for saying that, Kris,' Knight said, and the line went quiet for a moment, Knight considering what she should do and what she should say. 'I think I need to tell you this. In this day and age, it's not such a big thing, but, y'know, fuck it, I'll just say it. I'm adopted.'

'Okay,' Roark said, nodding even though Knight couldn't see her. Not a major bombshell, but Roark sensed there was more, so she kept quiet.

Knight gave a short laugh and said, 'Like I said, not a major revelation, I guess, but, I'm a bit sensitive to the whole parent thing given what happened with me, if you know what I mean.'

'I think I do, yes,' Roark said.

'My mother gave me away when I was born,' Knight said. 'Just a baby, so I don't remember any of it, but it's had an impact on me.'

'I see.'

'To give a child away at such an early age, I just can't understand it.'

'No, that's a tough one.'

'That's why I'm so close to my mother, Alice, my adoptive mother, who is my real mother, to me anyway. Real close.'

Roark said nothing, could feel that Knight was purging this information, a discussion it sounded like she didn't have with too many people.

'It took me a few attempts,' Knight continued, 'but I am in touch with my biological mother now. We write each other letters. Haven't met her yet. Still working towards that. Maybe. It's been a rocky road. Took me a while to forgive her. Shit, I won't go into now, but I think I'm starting to have a good relationship with her. But Alice is my focus right now.'

'I understand.'

'Sorry, Kris, I'm oversharing.'

'It's okay, it really is.'

'It's just, after my biological mother did that to me, and she's tried to explain it, and I do understand her point of view and why she did it, what with my father being what he was. Fuck, no, I can't go there. Look I see where she's coming from but I still can't understand it, if you know what I mean, and then I start to worry, if I was in the same dire situation she was in when I was born, and I mean off the scale dire situation – I can't talk about it to you but it was real bad – then what would I do? Would I do the same thing?'

'Well,' Roark said, 'I think you know yourself well enough to know how you'd react. Look at Alice, your mum, and what she did, adopting a baby, raising her into a fine woman, a professional with a successful career and a good heart. That's what you're used to. That's your role model. On that basis, I think you'd know what you would do.'

'Yeah, I guess you're right,' Knight said but Roark could tell she wasn't entirely convinced.

'I am right,' Roark said, ploughing on, 'and I know you well enough to know that you'd be a great mother and you would put your child first in any circumstance. That's just your nature, Gale.'

'I guess so.'

'And your mum, Alice, is such a lovely person. That's who you'll emulate. She's your role model.'

'Yeah, you're right,' Knight said, her voice holding a moment of levity. 'That makes sense.'

'Fuck yes, it does. You're a fucking star, Gale.'

'Shut it, you. You're making me blush.'

'And Gale? Thank you for sharing this with me. I've learnt tonight that it's important to have someone you can talk to about certain things, and I know I can do that with you, and I hope you think you can do the same with me.'

'Definitely. I mean that. Thank you.'

'Okay. Well, you have a good sleep, and we'll have a big hug tomorrow morning, alright?'

'Got it, you too, Kris. Thank you. I really mean that.'

'I do too.'

'And make that call, Kris. Promise me.'

Roark swallowed, couldn't bring herself to lie.

'I'll give it some more thought.'

'Do that, and if you want to talk more, let's find the time.'

'Thanks love.'

They finished the call and Roark placed her phone back on the charger. She turned on the volume at its lowest setting just in case Knight wanted to call back at any stage during the night. She wanted to be there for her, with whatever was bothering her. She also wouldn't mind the interruption, the chance to flesh things out a little more.

Roark fell asleep thinking about their conversation, how supported she felt from Gale, how she still wasn't sure about what to do but at least didn't feel entirely alone with it anymore. As she drifted off, her final thoughts were of a small baby, handed over from mother to a stranger, alone in the world, and then not alone, the stranger not a stranger anymore but a beautiful adoptive mother called Alice Knight.

CHAPTER 29

Despite nursing a light hangover that even a bacon buttie from the corner café couldn't cure, Roark was at her desk a couple of hours earlier than the start of her shift. A constable using her desk was kind enough to move without Roark having to pull rank, and she was in front of her computer around quarter past six.

She'd had a solid six hours sleep before she'd woken up around five in the morning, groggy, a light headache behind her eyes, but awake. A quick shower and a coffee and she was up and decided that she needed to be in the office as soon as she could. The case required her attention, regardless of the lack of leads. There were two people out there and, assuming they were still alive, their sleep last night would be nowhere near as comfortable as hers was. She owed them to be awake and working on this as much as possible.

Over breakfast, she read the NHS letter again and put it aside. She couldn't deal with that right now, even after what she felt was a positive conversation with Knight. She still didn't know what to do and still didn't know why she was procrastinating, so the best approach was to procrastinate a little more. Another week wouldn't hurt, and she really needed to focus on the case right now.

DI Lucas debriefed her after she settled in and, unfortunately, there wasn't much to report on. No new leads, nothing more to investigate. There were still a few loose ends to follow up, and Lucas went through those, but otherwise, the case wasn't looking healthy. When Lucas finished his sparse report, she thanked him, and said she'd get Knight back on it when she came in.

Around half past seven Roark's mobile rang. It was Knight. Roark answered the call. Knight sounded flustered, rushed.

'What's wrong?'

'Mum's had another fall, real bad. The paramedics are over there now. They just called.'

'Go,' Roark said, without hesitation. 'I'll hold the fort. Just go to her.'

'Thank you, Kris,' Knight said and finished the call.

Roark put her phone down on the desk and looked at it. She hoped Alice was alright. She always thought Knight's mum was a good sort, given what she'd gone through recently, with her divorce and the cancer and her previous fall, and after Roark received the news about her own cancer and

159

particularly after the discussion Roark and Knight had last night, she felt closer to the woman, even though they'd only met once or twice.

Roark also spared a thought for Knight. Alice's previous fall had shaken them both and now, with another fall, depending on how bad it was, there would be the need for care and rehabilitation. Roark would do her best to support Knight on this, whatever she could do. It was obvious how important Knight's adoptive mother was to her.

For now, regardless of how bad the fall was, Knight would be out for most of the day. Her mother lived in Maidstone, somewhere near the River Medway, south-east from London. It would take Knight an hour to get to Alice's home or to the hospital if she was moved there, so Roark started to plan the day without her.

First thing she did was call the parents of Aaron Sparger. Knight made a good point yesterday afternoon when she was trying, unsuccessfully, to connect Sparger to Collander. Maybe the parents might be able to assist on that front.

The parents were understandably distraught, and Roark had to manage their emotions for the first part of the call. They were expecting news and Roark had none for them. When they calmed down, they said it was okay for Roark to talk to them again. Roark didn't want to do it over the phone, so they agreed to meet at the Sparger's residence in Acton Town within the next couple of hours.

Across the floor, Roark could see DI Lucas getting ready to leave, his shift over and done with. A call came through to him on his desk phone and he sat back down. He pulled his chair up to his computer screen and Roark saw that he was going through the Crime Database. Thinking that he may have a lead, she got up and walked over to his desk, but stopped when she saw his screen clearer and could see that he was working a different case. Despite the urgency of her case, she had to remember that there were other crimes to be investigated and Lucas would have his own caseload. Roark had a few ongoing cases too, some she couldn't offload to other detectives, and Lucas was in the same boat. Roark retreated to her desk.

Next call she made was to DI Clarice Moody in Bristol.

'Any news?' she said after introductions.

'Nothing. I've got a full team on it, mind, but we're chasing dead ends. You?'

'Same,' Roark said, 'nothing. Usual prank calls and loonies, of course, and they take time to follow up, but that's the only thing that's really keeping us busy. Necessary evil when we go public, unfortunately. Any luck on linking Collander to our case?'

'No, nothing on that so far. Thanks for sending that through but it's coming up a blank. No evidence Sparger's even been to Bristol, let alone to see Jaime Collander.'

Roark sighed down the line, sharing their frustrations.

'I'm seeing Sparger's parents again later this morning, see if they know anything more. Possibly they know of a trip to Bristol recently or something else that may tie them together.'

'I'll do the same with Jaime's parents,' Moody said before Roark needed to ask her. 'I've already asked them once, but they said they'd have a further think about it. The mother's a mess, so I haven't had much from her, only the father. She's gone through a lot, mind, but hopefully she might have something new for me.'

'Keep in touch on that and I'll do the same,' Roark said as an email from the desk sergeant pinged in her inbox, subject heading, "Message Received".

'Will do. Speak soon,' Moody said and rung off.

Roark opened the email and read the brief note. She picked up her desk phone again and gave the desk sergeant a call.

'Hey, Jill.'

'Hello, ma'am,' the desk sergeant said.

'What's this cryptic message you've given me?'

'Call came into the front desk, some guy, sounded a bit dodgy. Probably another prank.'

'And he gave you this address?'

'Yep, but that's all. Said it was for the police investigating the kidnappings. Nothing more. Hung up.'

'Just now?'

'Yep, five minutes ago.'

'Okay, thanks Jill.'

Roark put the phone down and read the message on the screen.

14 Ravenscourt Road, Newtown, New Forest. 1pm.

She picked up the phone again and made a call.

***

Chief Inspector Arne Cristian pulled up into the New Forest station carpark, turned the engine off and picked his thermos out of the cup holder in between the front seats. It was filled with his favourite coffee, a Norwegian brand that his father had gotten him onto recently. It was healthier than most, using natural ingredients, and his father shipped the coffee tins in from Selfridges in London, one of the many luxuries his father indulged in during his retirement. It was a strong blend, and Arne needed the caffeine to face a day of administrative meetings. Back-to-back meetings with Legal, the Media team and some governance matters he could do without.

The morning was fresh and cool, and the surrounding trees waved slightly in a light breeze. Arne took a deep breath in, let the fresh air fill his lungs, and then let it out. He knew he'd not see outside for a good few hours, so he savoured the moment.

Another thing he knew he'd struggle to do this morning was fit in a call to Mr and Mrs Irvine. He'd tried their number last night as he'd left the station and then again around dinner time with no luck. He didn't know much about cruises, had never travelled on one, but he knew that there were days, sometimes as long as three in a row, when the ship had no connection to the outside world. These sea days were one of the attractions to some passengers, a chance to switch off and be uncontactable. It was likely he couldn't reach the Irvines because they were on one of these sea days, but doubt still niggled at him, so he took a moment before heading into the station to try again.

After two failed attempts, receiving nothing but a strange dial tone that he'd come to expect, he took his coffee into the station, greeted the desk sergeant, and walked down to his office. His desk was tidy and clear, a ritual he ensured he completed at the end of every day. He made sure by the end of each day that he had addressed every email that came into his inbox, every document sitting in his in-tray and put away all the items on his desk into their designated spaces. This didn't mean he was on top of his workload, far from it, but facing a nice, clean desk at the start of each day gave him a feeling of control, whether that was true or not.

He placed his thermos on the desk and sat down in his large comfortable chair. He turned on his computer, typed in his password and, while the system loaded, he poured himself a nice steaming plastic cup of coffee. The smell filled the room and already he felt better.

His inbox had a dozen unread emails, which wasn't too bad, and three meeting reminders for the day, the first in fifteen minutes. As he opened the first email, his phone rang. It was the desk sergeant.

'Call from London for you, sir. A Detective Inspector Krystal Roark.'

'London?' Arne said, frowning. 'Okay, put her through.'

Arne took a sip of his coffee, closed his eyes against the taste and smell.

'Chief Inspector Cristian,' he said when he heard the click of a connecting call.

'Good morning, sir. My name is Detective Inspector Krystal Roark calling from Camberwell station in South London.'

Her voice was serious, professional, commanded his attention, but there was a pleasantness to it that he immediately found engaging.

'Good morning, Detective Inspector,' Arne said. He leaned back in his chair. 'What can I do for you?'

'I'm currently investigating the kidnapping of Aaron Sparger who was taken a few days ago in London. Are you aware of the case?'

'Yes, I've seen the APBs. There's another one in Bristol too, I believe.'

'That's right, two connected cases,' the detective inspector said. Something in the tone of her voice made Arne sit up.

Please, no, he thought. *Not here too.*

'This may be a wild goose chase,' Detective Inspector Roark continued, 'but I've received an anonymous message about an address in New Forest that I want to follow up on. The message is just an address and a time, one o'clock this afternoon. I was wondering if I could request one of your constables to go around and check the address, even just to dismiss it as the prank I suspect it is. I thought I'd ask you directly as a matter of professional courtesy.'

'Of course,' Arne said, putting his coffee cup down and picking up a pen. He moved a notepad across from where it was stationed near the computer keyboard. 'What's the address?'

'It's 14 Ravenscourt Road, Newtown. I don't have a postcode.'

Arne's pen hovered over the notepad. He didn't need to write it down. He knew that address. The Irvine's residence.

'Sorry, Detective, but what is this in relation to?'

'Just following up a lead, that's all. I have no idea what it could mean, if it means anything. Like I said, it's probably a prank.'

'This in relation to your case?'

'Possibly,' she said.

Arne pushed his notepad away and placed the pen on the desk. He glanced across at his computer screen as a meeting reminder flashed up. He'd have to cancel that. He'd have to cancel all his meetings.

'I don't believe it is a prank, Detective.'

CHAPTER 30

After talking with Chief Inspector Cristian for a further ten minutes and agreeing on the next steps to take, Roark put her phone down and stood up. DI Lucas was still at his computer even though his shift had ended thirty minutes ago. Roark had considered calling DC Knight to assist but thought better of it. She needed the time to attend to her mother, so she looked elsewhere for a partner.

'Lucas,' she called.

He slowly turned around in his chair to face her. His face was blank.

'Up for some overtime?'

He nodded without hesitation.

'We're going to New Forest.'

Lucas closed his mouth and nodded again.

'I'll get the car,' he mumbled.

'No,' Roark almost yelled across the office. 'We're taking mine and I'm driving. Just let me make this one call and I need to see Rawlins too. Then we'll go.'

Lucas said nothing and started to shut down his computer.

Roark scrolled quickly down a contact list on the Crime Database case file she was working on. She picked up the phone and, reading off the screen with her heart thumping away in her chest, she dialled the number for the lead of the Anti-Kidnapping and Extortion Unit team searching for Aaron Sparger and Jaime Collander.

'AKEU,' came the immediate reply.

Roark took a deep breath.

'I think we have something.'

***

Detective Inspector Lucas snored in the passenger seat. Roark didn't mind. The trip from the station to New Forest would take about two and a half hours and she hadn't been looking forward to spending all of that sitting in awkward silence. Lucas's shift had ended a few hours ago, so he was doing the smart thing, taking a short nap. Lucas was a strange one, distant, grumpy, not one for conversation, disgusting eating habits, but he was good at his job and Roark was glad he'd agreed to work this with her.

Roark merged the Hyundai that she'd picked up from the station carpark onto the M3 and moved into the central lane, ticking just over the speed limit towards Southampton. It was her usual car, the one with the extra legroom and space for her tall frame. She'd requested that it was put aside for her when the case started to pick up earlier in the week, but that didn't always mean it would be available when she wanted it, and she was lucky to find it waiting for her underneath the station and not pilfered by one of the other Detective Inspectors. The two-hour-plus drive would have been hell in one of the smaller cars.

Lucas moved around in his seat, his head resting on the passenger window, and farted. Roark almost gagged. She put on the air-conditioner, tried to move the smell out of the car. Lucas really needed to attend to his diet.

Her thoughts moved to Knight. It was a shame she wasn't in the car with her; she'd take Gale over this lump sitting next to her any day of the week, despite Lucas's experience. Her connection to Gale as friends over the past six months aside, Knight was young, skilled, and keen to learn, and they worked so well together. She was a great detective and Roark could not think of anyone else as her partner. Particularly on this case.

Roark just hoped Knight's mother was okay. She hadn't heard from Gale since she'd called earlier in the day, so it didn't sound good. Knight would be gutted that she was missing this, whatever *this* turned out to be, but she knew that she would prioritise her mother over anything, especially work, particularly after what she'd shared in their conversation last night.

Roark looked at her phone sitting in the cradle on the dash, considered sending a quick message of support, and decided against it. Let her focus on her mother. That was more important just now.

A sleek black Mercedes passed her on the right-hand side, doing about fifteen klicks above the speed limit. Most days she wouldn't pull this guy over, that wasn't her job, and right now, she didn't have time anyway. Instead, she edged the speedometer up a few notches.

One o'clock. That was the time on the note. It felt like a deadline, rather than an appointment, but Roark had decided the intention was the latter. She hadn't entirely ruled out the possibility that this was just a wild goose chase, that this could be a waste of time, but the Chief Inspector from New Forest didn't seem to think so.

'I've been concerned about that place,' he'd said, an intonation in his voice that was pleasant to listen to. Roark guessed him to be of European descent, possibly Scandinavian.

'How so, sir?' she'd said.

'A few irregularities. The elderly couple that lives there are on holiday, but something isn't sitting right, and now, you said you received this note? With their address on it?'

'Yes. It was a phone call into the station. Said it was to do with our case. We've had a lot of idiots calling in, wasting our time since we went public, but I thought this was specific enough for us to follow it up.'

'And you want me to send a car out?'

'Well, I was leaning towards this being a prank of sorts, but I'm not so sure now that I've spoken to you. It sounds like we should be taking this seriously. Let me call Anti-Kidnapping, see what they think. This man has killed two people so far, kidnapped two. If this note is from him, we must consider all possibilities. It could be a hostage situation and tipping our hand before the time given could be disastrous. We should approach this carefully.'

'So, we'll hold fire on the car,' he said. 'We've got over five hours until one o'clock. I'd suggest we all meet at my station here, in New Forest. Discuss what to do next.'

'Got it. I'm on my way.'

Plans had changed since that call. After filling in DCI Rawlins on the latest development, he had decided that MO19, the Specialist Firearms Command, should take point given the possibility of a hostage situation. That was beyond the capabilities of Anti-Kidnapping; this required the firearms unit of the Metropolitan police.

Roark hadn't questioned her boss. In fact, she supported the decision. They didn't know what they were dealing with yet, but if this was the man who had kidnapped two people and killed two others, having specialist armed officers on the scene made complete sense.

The only downside was that Sergeant Thomas Hoover, the lead officer in the Counter Terrorist Specialist Firearms team tasked out of MO19, demanded he'd lead the situation from the outset. He was to be in charge as soon as the team reached New Forest, and he requested that Chief Inspector Cristian suggest a meeting place near the Irvine residence that was hidden from any traffic on the approach. Somewhere closer than the New Forest police station where they would discuss tactics before approaching the property.

Chief Inspector Cristian gave everyone the spot to meet, and all parties headed there as fast as they could. Hoover and his team would take a couple of hours, and so would Roark, so in the meantime, Hoover asked for one of Cristian's constables to join one of the local Firearms Command officers out of Southampton to find a concealed location to observe the house, and for Cristian to have a full team of officers ready and waiting nearby just in case there were developments. Hoover would prefer to be there if any action was taken, but time could well be crucial and they needed eyes on the location to act immediately, if necessary.

As Roark left London, driving in the Hyundai with Lucas riding the passenger seat, she felt uneasy. Chief Inspector Cristian had convinced her that they had to take this seriously, based, if Roark had to be honest, on a feeling in his gut. That was fine. At worst, they'd waste time and resources on a hoax; at best, this was their chance to find the killer and save Aaron Sparger and Jaime Collander.

It was the deadline that worried her. One o'clock. What did it mean?

As Roark exited the M3 and joined the M27, avoiding Southampton city centre, she remembered the meeting she had arranged with the parents of Aaron Sparger. Using the hands-free controls on the car's steering wheel, she called them and apologised. She'd have to cancel their interview, move it to tomorrow. They said that was okay, their voices quiet and numb.

Lucas stirred at the sound of Roark's voice, and he rubbed his eyes, sat up straight. He stared out his window, looking at the passing trees and rolling hills.

'We're almost there,' she said.

Lucas nodded and grunted at the same time.

Her phone was set to Maps and instructed her to turn off at a narrow road cutting through the trees. Apparently this road ran parallel to the one that led to the Irvine property and would mask their approach.

Just before a T-section in the road, there was a secluded car park and camping area off to the right, currently blocked off by a two-man construction crew digging a hole. Placed there by the MO19 and Hampshire and Isle of Wight Constabulary teams to avoid unwanted interruptions, it restricted access to the area where Hoover and his men had set up their "base of operations."

Roark pulled up and one of the men wearing a yellow hardhat stepped up. Roark showed him her warrant card and he slid a lightweight barrier across. Roark thanked him and drove through, past the other construction worker and the small hole they'd begun to dig next to the heavy machinery, all of which sat just off the access road, out of the way to allow any quick exit by the MO19 team. In the rearview mirror, Roark watched them replace the barrier, blocking off the road.

Along the short access road, behind thick forest, Roark drove her car towards the car park and campsite area, which had been commandeered by Hoover and his team. Two black vans, three unmarked cars and two white police cars from the Hampshire Constabulary were parked in a line, pointing towards the access road exit. Roark negotiated a few potholes in the dirt road around the campsite and parked in behind the last car.

As Roark and Lucas stepped out of the Hyundai, she could see both black vans up ahead with their rear doors open. Inside each van was half a dozen Counter Terrorist Specialist Firearms Officers, decked out in black uniforms, black helmets and bulletproof vests, armed with Glock pistols and SIG Sauer assault rifles, most of them fidgeting as they waited on instructions.

The campsite was in a clearing amongst the forest. A toilet block was off to one side and the area next to the parking spaces was peppered with wooden tables and seats and cooking facilities. There were no tents or campervans set up today. Apparently only two groups of campers had to be moved along to other areas, undercover police officers citing "scheduled campsite improvements" as the reason, attempting to keep the privacy of this meeting intact. Without any campers, there were plenty of spaces amongst the trees and bushes, an oasis in the middle of thick forest and perfect for a central meeting place away from prying eyes.

Roark and Lucas approached a group of men standing around one of the larger picnic tables, a mixture of uniforms, shapes and sizes. A thin, medium height man with a white moustache strikingly contrasting his black outfit waved them over. It was Sergeant Hoover, head of the MO19 operation. He stood holding court, a large piece of paper laid out in front of him, held down with rocks sourced from the surrounding grounds.

'Detective Inspector Roark?' Hoover said.

'Yes,' she said, and those not facing her turned around. Some eyebrows involuntarily jumped up, one police officer could not help run his eyes up and down. She was the tallest there and, like in most circumstances, she stood out. She made an impression, one that she didn't always feel comfortable with, but had learned to live with.

'This is Detective Inspector Lucas,' Roark said, gesturing towards her partner. 'We're down from London.'

'Roark and Lucas are the homicide team on the Aaron Sparger case,' Hoover said. 'DI Moody is on her way from Bristol. She's covering the Jaime Collander disappearance.'

Roark was glad to hear Clarice Moody would be joining them. She wanted to meet her, but she also recognised that Moody had as much skin in this game as Roark did. She should be here.

'We're going to crack on without her for now,' Hoover said. 'Come on, guys, make some room for the detectives.'

The group shuffled along, creating two spaces for Roark and Lucas. Roark fitted in next to a man in his mid-forties with hard lines defining his jaw, a flock of fair hair, almost blond, and a stubble which was speckled with white. He was shorter than Roark, but over six foot and taller than the others, and his eyes were crystal clear blue. He wore a black uniform, white shirt and black tie and on his epaulette there were three white diamonds, the insignia of a Chief Inspector.

'Hi,' he said, offering a hand. 'I'm Chief Inspector Arne Cristian. We spoke on the phone.'

'Of course,' Roark said, taking his hand and shaking it. It was warm and dry. 'Pleasure to meet you.'

Hoover, who watched the two of them introduce each other, vocally stepped in.

'We also have Inspector Ahmed Khalili out of New Forest station and two of his men. I also have my second in charge, Constable Connors, who will be leading the team in, once we decide our plan of attack, and two of his team leaders.'

Roark nodded to each in turn.

'Okay,' Hoover said, 'now that the pleasantries are out of the way, let's get started. We're against the clock here people and there's potential lives at stake.'

CHAPTER 31

Sergeant Hoover turned to the map on the table, smoothing it out with his large wrinkling hands. Roark studied it. Although upside down to her, she could see that it was an aerial map of a property, including access roads and approaches. The property was reasonably big as designated on the map with the house in the middle.

'As you can see, the approach will be difficult,' Hoover said. 'The access road is long, about half a kilometre from the main road and snakes through some thick forest before cutting through an open area in front of the house. The property is dissected by a row of trees on this side of the driveway, about six or seven deep, reaching out from the nearby forest across here and up to the access road here. On the east side of this tree line, we have the driveway leading up to the garage and next to that, a large open area, the front yard, extending towards this long front section of the house.'

'Is this our preferred direction of approach?' Inspector Khalili asked as he rubbed his lips.

'At this stage, yes,' Hoover said. 'The approaches from the sides of the house are not ideal, too much open space, and the rear of the property drops off a little bit into what has been described by our eyes on the ground as too dense to traverse. Our best bet is using the access road and then approaching under the cover of this line of trees that intersect the property. We can then have the rest of the team join up with the officers already there. Sun will be behind us too, which is ideal for the approach.'

'Where are they?' Roark asked.

'We have one of my marksmen and a sergeant from Chief Inspector Cristian's team in these trees,' Hoover said, pointing out the row of trees on the map. 'It's dense enough to keep them concealed but gives a good view of the front of the house.'

'My constable is a local and knows the property well,' Cristian said, speaking to Roark. 'He checks up on the elderly couple there once a month and knows the best ways to get in and out. They were extremely confident of setting up in this position without being spotted.'

'Have they reported anything?' Roark enquired.

'No movement so far,' Sergeant Hoover said. 'Not in or out of the house. There are two vehicles, one parked in the driveway near the garage, a white utility van.'

'A van?' Roark interrupted.

'That's correct.'

'We ran the plates,' Inspector Khalili said, 'and it was stolen yesterday lunchtime in Manchester.'

'Jesus,' Roark said, feeling a mix of anxiety and excitement fluttering in her stomach. 'This is our man.'

'It appears so,' Hoover said, 'although, as I said, we have no confirmation of anyone in the property yet.'

'Any reports of missing people in the area? He may have abducted another,' Roark said.

'No, nothing has come through to us. Chief Inspector, you have concerns about the property owners, though, don't you?'

'Yes,' Cristian said, his voice light but clear. 'We did receive a note that they were on a cruise but that was only given over the phone, and not to me personally. I have not been able to contact them since. I am hoping that they are just out of network reach, on their cruise ship, but I have contemplated the worst.'

'You said two vehicles?' Roark said to Hoover.

'It's a campervan Mr Irvine has been working on,' Cristian said. 'It's up on blocks and not going anywhere.'

'Right,' Hoover said, slapping his hands flat on the table, 'we must confirm the best approach. We must assume that we have live hostages in this property, those that were taken recently from London and Bristol and possibly the Irvine couple. Maybe others. Time is critical.'

'What are our options?' Roark asked.

'Full tactical infiltration. Hit the property with our two teams, covering all exits, hit them hard and quickly. My only concern here is that our lookout has spotted no one in the property at this time. They could be hidden deep inside, which means it will take time to reach them.'

'During which time he could kill the hostages,' Roark said.

'Precisely.'

'There's a cellar,' Cristian said. 'In the kitchen, big enough to hold all the hostages.'

'A cellar? That's unusual.'

'Believe me, it's there.'

'Where's the kitchen?'

'Here,' Cristian said, pointing to the front of the property on the map. 'There's also an attic running along the length of the house, closest access is from the rear of the house. My officers have been inside the property several times over the years. We have a good relationship with the Irvines.'

'That's good,' Hoover said. 'I'd rather have blueprints of the house before we take the property, but we may not have a choice.'

'What other options are there? Besides a raid, I mean,' Roark asked.

'Well,' Hoover said, standing up straight, scanning the map on the picnic table, 'there's not a lot, if I was honest. As the time ticks on, our chances of success reduce. We have the element of surprise right now and we should use it.'

'I'm not sure that's the case, Sergeant,' Roark said. 'I've been thinking about the call that came into the station. An address and a time. Now, he may think we wouldn't take it seriously, that we may even ignore it, but I don't think so. I think he is expecting full attention on this. I don't think we have any element of surprise. I think he knows we're coming. All of us. At one o'clock.'

'Why would he send the note in the first place?' Inspector Khalili said.

'That's the big question, isn't it?' Roark said. 'He's set up the time and place, but for what?'

'To go out in a blaze of glory,' someone said.

'Possibly. Or to negotiate. He hasn't given us demands or ultimatums, just a time and place. There's a possibility he just wants to talk, but on his terms.'

'Or he could be a fucking psycho,' one of the MO19 officers said.

Hoover considered what Roark had said for a moment, rubbing his chin.

'It's quite a risky assumption to make,' he said. 'We're possibly dealing with up to four or five people's lives here.'

'I agree, and I'm just as anxious to ensure their safety as you are,' Roark said calmly. 'I just don't think we have any element of surprise right now and if we storm the place, all we are going to do is make him panic. And that's not good. Particularly as we don't have eyes on where they are. If they are all holed up in the cellar, as Chief Inspector Cristian suggests, we'll never get to them in time. If we approach this on his terms, it may play out differently. We may be able to draw him out and away from the hostages. Give us an opportunity to capture him.'

'Or put a bullet in him,' the same man clad in black said.

Hoover studied the map, playing out the scenario in his mind.

'What do you think, Chief Inspector?' Hoover said, looking across the table.

'I'm siding with Detective Inspector Roark,' Cristian said without missing a beat. 'The safety of the hostages is paramount, and we just don't have enough information to know how to conduct a raid successfully without risking their lives. It's a tough call, but I agree we should try to meet his demands.'

Roark nodded, thanking the Chief Inspector in her mind.

'The one o'clock deadline worries me,' Hoover said, not entirely convinced. 'You say it's a meeting time, but it could be a countdown. One o'clock could be time's up and we'd be too late.'

'Could all be bullshit too,' someone said.

'We can't make that assumption,' Hoover said, chastising the speaker with a look.

Roark checked her watch and considered a plan that was forming in her head.

'Let's hedge our bets,' she said. 'The note came into my station in London. Essentially, it's for the head of the Aaron Sparger case, and that's me. Let me go to the property, say around quarter to, a little bit earlier than expected, gives us a chance to react before one, if necessary.'

'And do what? Knock on the front door?'

'No, I think we need to take it carefully. We should try and establish communications with him, like we would with any hostage situation.'

'That makes sense,' Hoover said. 'I agree with that.'

'And it should be me who shows up, me who communicates with him. Me, and if she gets here in time, DI Moody. If not, Lucas here. Our killer needs to see that we're who he is expecting to see, who he wants.'

'I'm not sure I'm comfortable with that,' Hoover said. 'If we've lost the element of surprise, we should make it clear to him that this is a tactical situation run by experts, no offence. He should see that he must play ball or risk retribution.'

'I think that will just spook him, even if he is expecting you guys to turn up. Look, Sergeant, he made the call to my station, asked that the message be given to the lead on the Aaron Sparger case, and that's me. We should give him what he wants.'

Hoover's mouth closed tightly, and he looked out at the surrounding forest, eyes moving around, breathing through his nose, thinking.

'Okay,' he finally said. 'This is how we are going to do it.'

At that moment an unmarked car came billowing into the clearing, trailing dust into the air. It drove up towards the picnic table where they were all standing, watched by the eyes of everyone at the campsite. The car pulled up a few metres away, skidding to a halt, dust drifting around it and onto the onlookers.

A short, petite woman emerged, slamming the car door and hurrying up to the table. She had black hair down to her shoulders, curled and bouncing, and immaculate makeup, bright reds, deep blues. Her teeth shined as she smiled, her navy suit jacket and trousers gleamed.

'Sorry, I'm late,' she said. 'DI Clarice Moody. What did I miss?'

CHAPTER 32

In any other circumstance, Roark would find it comical. For some present, there was no denying the humour, and a few suppressed grins could be spotted amongst the remaining MO19 team officers who had been left behind and were prepping over the other side of the campsite. Another member of that team was ensuring both Roark and Moody's bulletproof vest was on properly, secured on both sides, covering as much as it could. He was focussed as Roark and Moody stood side by side, but Roark swore she could see a laugh just behind his eyes.

Roark looked down at Detective Inspector Moody. Moody looked up.

'We'd make a great comedy duo, mind,' Moody said.

Roark laughed, her nerves releasing for a moment.

'One of the greats,' she said.

'How tall are you?' Moody said. 'Six-six?'

'Six-four.'

'Five-five, down here. Nice symmetry there. I'm not sure either of us appreciate me having an eyeline at your tits, mind.'

'Probably the only thing that would work for us,' Roark said, smiling.

Clarice Moody gave a short laugh, cut off by the MO19 officer tightening the strap around her back, cinching the vest closer to her chest.

'Watch it, buddy. Careful with the merchandise.'

Sergeant Hoover and Chief Inspector Cristian approached. Their faces were serious, no suppressed smiles here.

'You've got your mobile phone,' Hoover said.

'Right here,' Roark said, raising it. 'Phone number is programmed in.'

'Here's the bull horn,' he said and handed over a megaphone. 'If he doesn't pick up, try that. The earpieces you both have are connected to my headpiece, so you'll hear everything I'm saying to the team and I'll hear everything you say. I'll turn it on once you've reached the property.'

'Got it.'

'We have people already in position around the house, concealed in the trees. Unfortunately, only our spotters on the tree line in front of the house have clear sight. The others will move up into better positions at the appropriate time. We don't want to let him know where they are until we need them.'

'Only if we go inside,' Roark said. 'One marksman is enough, and I don't want him spooked by the sight of anyone moving around in the bushes.'

Hoover nodded but didn't say anything.

'The cellar and the attic,' Chief Inspector Cristian said. 'That's my best guess as to where the hostages are. This type of thing has happened before.'

'I'm sure it has.'

'No, at this property. Over thirty years ago now.'

'Really?' Moody said, surprised. 'How did that turn out?'

'As best as you could expect. Only casualty was the man who'd taken the hostages.'

Roark studied Cristian's face. She didn't know him very well, but it felt like he had more to tell. Maybe now wasn't the time.

'Okay, let's roll on this,' Hoover said. 'You'll take your car Roark, with Moody riding shotgun. Drive all the way up but pull off and stop just past the treeline, off the driveway. That way he won't feel like he's boxed in. Like you said, we don't want to spook him.'

'Thank you, Sergeant,' Roark said, noting his tone. She knew he'd prefer to be running point on this, not two city pencil pushers. Not two women, Roark hastened to suggest. She had experienced enough old school police perceptions to know that she wouldn't be too far from the truth.

As Roark and Moody walked to her waiting car, she wasn't sure she was thrilled with what they were doing either. She felt less sure of herself now than when she was laying out her views at the picnic table. Talking the talk was one thing.

DI Lucas stood to one side and gave her a nod as the two female detectives walked past.

'Who's the chatterbox?' Moody whispered.

'What? Lucas?' Roark said, looking down at Moody. 'Detective Inspector out of my station.'

'Bit scruffy looking, mind,' Moody said smiling. Roark felt she'd missed a joke but didn't pursue it. 'He a bit miffed at being dropped from the team? I swear he was giving me the evil eye.'

'I doubt it. I'd say he's probably miffed that he has nowhere to sleep now I'm taking the car. He's good police though.'

They jumped in Roark's car. Moody clipped on her seatbelt and sniffed the air.

'What is that amazing aroma?'

'Lucas's diet could do with a review,' Roark said, strapping on her seatbelt.

'It's ripe.'

'Glovebox,' Roark said and turned on the ignition. The car roared to life. 'You'll find some perfume in there.'

Roark backed up a little and then drove forward, past the line of vehicles, minus one of the MO19 vans which had driven off fifteen minutes ago, carrying a team of six black-clad officers sent to set up a concealed perimeter around the property.

Moody adjusted her seat, bringing it forward as far as it could go, and opened the glovebox. She pulled out a small vial of perfume, a sampler of Versace.

'Classy.'

'Most expensive sampler from the duty free at Gatwick. I get a batch every time I fly.'

'I like your style, DI Roark,' she said as she sprayed the perfume around the interior and then on her wrist before rubbing it on her neck, just above the bulletproof vest.

'Call me Kris.'

'Clarice,' she said. Moody returned the perfume to the glovebox and snapped it shut. She was quiet for a second or two. 'So what do you think Kris? What are we heading into?'

Roark drove along the dirt track between the trees, glanced up at the rear view, through the rising dust, to see all the other remaining players filing into their cars, including Lucas who seemed to be joining Chief Inspector Cristian. The train of cars would follow Roark but with some distance between them. Hoover wouldn't be able to see what was going on first hand, he'd get an update from his man in the trees and from Roark over the radio, but he wanted to be as close as possible to the action if everything went south.

'Not entirely sure,' Roark said. 'I've gone beyond thinking that this is a hoax. We are definitely dealing with our man here.'

'But does it feel right to you?'

Roark knew what Moody was getting at. A gut feeling that all coppers had in certain situations. When something is a little off, not one hundred percent right, there was a twinge in the stomach, a knot of anxiety that didn't go away. Chief Inspector Cristian had it when talking about the Irvines. Roark had it now.

'Not at all,' she said. 'I hope he's organised this meet to talk, negotiate, but I'm not sure. I don't know enough about him other than he's killed two people and kidnapped another two.'

'Doesn't sound like the type for a chinwag over a cup of Tetley's.'

'No, I guess not. We have no choice though. We must assume he has two, possibly four, hostages in there, and that he is looking to negotiate.'

'Or looking to add two female coppers to his party.'

They reached the mock-up of the construction site near the exit of the campsite and the two men in hardhats moved the barriers aside. They walked away and left them parted, heading to the digger which would remain there until everything was over. Roark struggled to imagine that moment, when everything was over. It felt like it was still a long way off.

Using the directions Hoover had given her, Roark drove the car slowly along the paved road cutting through the forest. On any other day, she'd take in the surrounding scenery, the tall trees, the wildlife and sounds, the sweet clear air. Right now, she could only smell her anxiety, hear her heavy breathing, see the road ahead of her.

'How we going to play this?' Moody asked. 'I know what Hoover wants us to do, but do you have any other ideas?'

'Nothing useful, no. We'll stick to the plan. Call the phone or call him out. Try and get contact and draw him out of the house. The further he is away from the hostages, the better. I've got a signal to use, both physically and over the mike, for when Hoover's men need to act.'

'And if that moment doesn't come? If he isn't drawn away from the hostages?'

'We take it slow. We listen to him. We hear what he has to say. We don't be heroes. Once he's done, we come back out and reassess with Hoover and his team. The hostages' safety is paramount.'

Moody looked out the window at the passing trees.

'I'm usually a good reader of situations involving unhinged men, mind, but this one's baffling me. I have no idea why he's doing what he's doing.'

Roark nodded.

'Me neither. I hate dissecting motive, but he's kidnapped Aaron and Jaime for a reason, and if I knew what that was, we'd know what we're walking into. But I have no idea.'

'Well, we'll know soon enough.'

'We're here,' Roark said and pulled into a dirt road cut into the forest line, not unlike the one that led to the campsite where Hoover and his team had debriefed them. The car initially bounced along through a series of potholes in the dirt and then smoothed out. She drove at a steady pace, keeping the noise of the grit and stones underneath and the dust cloud behind the car to a minimum.

As soon as they left the main road behind them, the forest around them darkened, the tall trees blocking out most of the light of the day. Only the gap in the trees directly above the road offered any sunlight and it had turned into an overcast and dull day. Roark resisted the urge to put her headlights on.

'How long you've been in the police?' Moody asked.

'Over thirty years,' she said. 'Joined up in the early nineties.'

'Oh wow, a lifer.'

'Feels that way. You?'

'Coming up to twenty at the end of the year. Hard slog, I'll tell you that. Being a short-arsed woman in the police hasn't been easy.'

'Tell me about it. Standing out for all the wrong reasons. You married?'

'Sure, ten years. Not sure how we've managed to keep it together, but we have. Two kids too. They keep me sane, mind. You?'

'Free and easy,' Roark said, trying to make light of her answer.

'I hear that.'

'Here we are,' Roark said before Moody asked any other personal questions.

Both of their headsets crackled, and Hoover's voice, quiet but clear, spoke in their ears.

'*We've pulled into the drive, about a minute or two behind you. We'll stop as soon as we reach the clearing and stay out of sight. Keep me posted.*'

'Will do,' Moody replied for them both.

The trees parted before them and the sun peeked through the overhead clouds, bathing them in light.

They had arrived.

CHAPTER 33

The dirt driveway continued into a large clearing, extending upwards on a slight elevation towards a plateau of short grass. One or two trees sprung up in the clearing, birchwood, tall and elegant sentinels. Beyond to the left and right, the thick forest converged, ringfencing the property. The road stretched up before reaching the plateau and hooking around a row of trees which extended out from the forest on the left and ended next to the driveway.

Roark couldn't help but search the line of trees to see if she could see the two spotters, the local man from Chief Inspector Cristian's station and the sniper from the MO19 team. She hoped they were on their game when they were needed. *If* they were needed.

'What the fuck is that?' Moody asked, pointing over the dashboard.

Roark followed her finger and saw the camper van that Hoover had mentioned. It was a large white vehicle, a little dirty and rusted, sitting up on blocks, its wheels removed.

'Belongs to the people that live here,' Roark explained. 'Apparently the husband was working on it before they went on their cruise.'

'You think that's where they are?' Moody said. 'On a cruise?'

'I hope so.'

'Me too. I could do with a cruise myself, mind.'

'*Everything okay?*' Hoover crackled over the radio.

'Oh sorry,' Roark said, realising she hadn't given him an update. 'We've reached the clearing leading to the house. Can't see the house yet but we see the row of trees where your man is, and we can see the parked campervan. House coming into view now.'

'*Roger.*'

The house appeared like an abandoned ship emerging through the mist. The treeline on their left pulled back as Roark followed the driveway, revealing the garage with the white van parked in front of it. The garage seemed to be pushed aside as the remainder of the house came into view, a single storey brick building stretching out across six windows and a door, with an expansive lawn stretching out in front of it towards the tree line. As explained by Hoover during their planning session, there was significant clear space around the entire house, making it difficult to approach undetected.

'Nice place,' Roark said.

'Yeah, real homey,' Moody replied.

The attempts at levity fell flat. Roark scanned the façade of the house, the windows and the corners, expecting to see something or someone appear. Despite its lived-in look, the threat of what was behind closed doors and draped windows made her shiver.

'Shit,' Moody said, jumping in her seat. She was leaning back from her passenger side window.

'What is it?' Roark said, tapping the brakes.

'Nothing,' Moody croaked. 'A fox under the campervan.'

'We're passing the tree line,' Roark said for the benefit of Hoover and everyone else listening.

'Got it. We can see you.'

'Tell them about the fox,' Moody said.

Roark gave her a look.

'I'm not going to mention the fox.'

'Why not?'

'We can hear you both. Fox noted. Please proceed.'

'See? The fox was important.'

Roark smiled. She glanced in her rear-view mirror, thought she could see the second MO19 van and two cars from Hampshire Constabulary just back from the edge of the clearing, parked and waiting, but wasn't sure. They were well concealed.

'Our spotters are deep in that tree line,' Hoover said, 'so don't go searching for them. We don't want their position revealed.'

'No problem. We're looking straight ahead. I'm going to pull in around behind the trees and park.'

'When you get out of the car, move to the driveway, about five or so metres from the van. We'll be able to see you from there.'

'Will do.'

Roark passed the treeline on her left and, as planned, slowly drove the vehicle up onto the lawn, close to the trees but between the forest and the house. She parked the car, turned the engine off, keeping her eye on the house the entire time.

'Nice view down there,' Moody said.

Roark glanced briefly through the windscreen, saw the lawn drop away, the tops of trees lining the drop off and beyond that, the rolling hills of New Forest. The clouds filled most of the sky but dissipated closer to the horizon.

'It's quarter to,' Moody said.

'Okay, let's do this.'

Roark unclipped her seatbelt and opened the car door. She leaned forward and pushed up, standing to her full height. The front of the house didn't leave her sight. She left the car door open, and Moody did the same after she emerged. Moody walked around the rear of the car, holding the bullhorn she'd retrieved from the back seat.

'This way,' Roark said, and she led them towards the driveway and van a few metres away.

Nothing moved. No lights flicked on; no curtains twitched. The place looked deserted.

The thought that this was all a hoax returned briefly but then she saw the van, the stolen white van with dust on its tyres and the double doors at the back and none of it felt like a hoax at all.

'Okay, we're at the driveway,' she said, keeping her voice quiet. 'No movement yet.'

'*Right, we can see you,*' Hoover said.

'Calling the house phone now.'

Roark glanced down at her mobile, selected the number for the Irvine residence that Chief Inspector Cristian had given her, and pressed the button. She raised the phone to her ear, watching the front of the house as she waited. Moody stood beside her on her left, doing the same.

The call connected and she heard the phone ringing in her ear.

'I can hear it,' Moody said. 'The phone ringing. Coming from the house.'

It rang and rang and rang. No one picked up. After over a minute, Roark thumbed her phone, ending the call.

'No answer,' she said for everyone's benefit.

'*Try again,*' Hoover said in their earpieces.

Roark hit the number again and waited. After a few rings, she took the phone from her ear and listened. She too could hear the house phone ringing out from somewhere inside. There was no movement behind the drawn curtains.

'*Adil?*' Hoover said.

'*No movement, sir,*' replied a voice Roark had not heard before. The spotter in the tree line, the one with the long-range rifle trained at the house.

'*Okay, Roark, please try the bullhorn.*'

Moody passed over the voice receiver of the bullhorn, its coiled cord still connected to the speaker she held. Moody pointed the speaker out towards the house and nodded.

Roark turned her left hand towards her to read her watch.

12:50.

'Here it goes,' she said.

Roark held the receiver to her mouth and switched it on. The bullhorn hummed in Moody's hands.

'This is Detective Inspector Roark,' she said into the receiver and her voice echoed around them, eerie in the quietness amongst the trees and open grounds. 'With me is Detective Inspector Moody. We are the lead detectives on the disappearances of Aaron Sparger and Jaime Collander. We received your message and are here to speak with you. Please indicate your understanding and inform us of our next steps.'

She clicked off the voice receiver and studied the house, waiting for a response.

'That was good, Roark. Adil, any movement?'

'Nothing, sir.'

'Roark, try again. Ask him to reveal himself or come outside.'

'Okay,' Roark said, but waited another minute. She wanted to give as much time as possible to allow a response to her first announcement. She didn't know much about the killer but rushing him did not feel like the right move.

'I repeat, my name is Detective Inspector Roark and this is Detective Inspector Moody, and we are here in accordance with the instructions you provided to the station earlier this morning. Please let us know that you understand and that you wish to speak with us outside.'

Roark clicked off and lowered the voice receiver from her face. They heard birds launching out of the brush from somewhere beyond the treeline. The fox from the campervan padded passed them on the other side of the driveway, heading behind the house.

'It's one o'clock,' Moody said.

Roark said nothing, waiting, watching the house in an unwinnable staring competition. After another minute, she tried again, keeping to the same script, attempting to entice a reaction from the killer.

'What now, Hoover?' she said after turning off the megaphone.

'Adil?'

'I see no movement from inside the house, Sergeant.'

'Maybe he can't hear us,' Roark suggested.

There was a moment of silence on the line and then Hoover came back.

'Chief Inspector Cristian said it's possible they may be in the cellar or the attic and unable to hear.'

'Jesus,' Moody said, 'he's obsessed with the cellar, isn't he?'

Roark nodded, thinking that there was probably a reason for that.

'There is a doorbell near the door in front of you. The door leads to the kitchen where the cellar is situated. Please proceed and ring the bell. Adil, keep on them.'

'Got it, sir.'

'Okay,' Roark said, and she handed the voice receiver to Moody. Moody collected it and placed the bullhorn at her feet, stepping over it as they approached the house.

'This reminds me of a recurring dream I have,' Moody whispered as they walked together.

Roark could barely hear her, their height differential and the thumping of her heart in her ears making it difficult.

'Naked in front of a classroom, attempting to deliver a speech needed to pass the course. Butt naked, mind. Exposed. Open to ridicule. That's what this feels like.'

Roark shifted the Kevlar vest around so it didn't dig into her armpits.

'I hear you,' she said.

'Let's just hope he's either a crack shot and aims for our chest or a rubbish shot and aims for our heads.'

CHAPTER 34

Roark and Moody walked toward the house, through the grass that appeared to have been recently cut, possibly a week or so ago. Roark drew a blank on the timing of when the Chief Inspector had said when the Irvines had supposedly taken their cruise. Moot point now. They were either safe and sound on the Mediterranean or trapped in their own home with a madman.

As they approached the house, Roark kept her eyes on every window and the front door, shifting from each in turn, looking for signs of movement. As she got closer to the house and its façade filled their view, this action was more difficult to do surreptitiously, moving her head from left to right as she kept an eye out. She watched the corners at either side too, the far one at the left-hand side of the house, near where the grounds dropped away, and to their right towards the corner of the garage.

'Wait,' Roark whispered, two steps away from the concrete pathway that separated the lawn from the front of the house. 'The van.'

'I'll check it,' Moody said.

'Be careful,' Roark said softly, hardly loud enough for Moody to hear.

They were only a metre or two away from the van and garage and Roark watched as Moody carefully approached.

'*Adil*,' Hoover said, '*keep your sights on the house. Ulright, follow Moody.*'

Roark momentarily bristled. Ulright was a second marksmen, one of the six MO19 officers who had driven ahead in the first black van. Contrary to the plan, Hoover had moved his men in closer to the house, risking being seen within the tree line, close enough to take a shot if need be. For a moment she felt annoyed that he'd changed the plan, but it dissipated when she saw how exposed Moody was, stepping towards the parked van, and Roark was thankful for the extra protection.

Moody had to get up on her tip toes to look in the cab of the van. She shook her head without turning around and then preceded to move around to the rear of the vehicle.

'*Be careful, Detective,*' Hoover said, echoing Roark's earlier warning.

Moody replied but Roark didn't hear it, only saw her lips move and a quiet murmur. Both Moody and Roark's responses over the radio were muted to each other's earpiece to avoid feedback, something that now felt like a mistake as Roark would not be able to talk to Moody unless she shouted out to her.

Moody opened the rear of the van and disappeared from view.

Roark turned back to the house, studied the door in front of her. Curtains drawn on the window set in the upper half of the wooden door. No movement. The doorbell was set in the top right of the door frame.

'*Received*,' Hoover said and Roark turned back to see Moody returning to her, having left the van doors open.

'Nothing,' Moody said quietly when she returned. 'Didn't get a good look but there may have been some bloodstains in the back.'

'Okay,' Roark said, and she now felt a sense of urgency. In a whisper into her microphone, she said, 'I am now ringing the doorbell.'

Roark stepped off the lawn onto the concrete pathway lining the front of the house, the solid sensation of a hard surface under her feet feeling strangely reassuring. She reached across, and after one last glance up and down the length of the house, she pressed the button.

From within, she could hear the bell ring, a shrill two-tone sound echoing through the house. She pressed it again to make sure that the inhabitants of the house would not be mistaken about what they had just heard.

She stepped back on to the lawn next to Moody and waited.

No one answered. No one opened the door. From what they could see, there was no movement from within the house.

After a few minutes of silence, Hoover spoke softly over the radio.

'*Perimeter? Any movement from what you can see?*'

There was a series of replies from five new voices plus Ulright, the six MO19 team members who had driven ahead and set up a perimeter deep in the surrounding forests. As agreed, they would not move forward during the initial approach by Roark and Moody, but it was obvious that, like with Ulright, all the team members were close enough to the tree line surrounding the property to have a clear view and shot at the house. Hoover had moved them closer to the house and Roark had to admit, they had significantly passed the point of the "initial approach".

All responses from the perimeter teams were in the negative. No movement. Nothing spotted.

Time check: almost one fifteen.

'This is not right,' Roark whispered, and she saw Moody nod in agreement.

'*Please proceed.*'

Roark took a deep breath and said for all of those listening in: 'I'm trying the door.'

She reached out, long arm stretching across what felt like an impossibly great distance and gripped the door handle. Before turning it, a long list of scenarios flashed through her head – explosive rigged handle, shotgun blast through the window, even an electric shock – but when she twisted her wrist to the right, the door clicked open.

Moody let out a gasp from next to her, the same list of scenarios running through her head.

'Door is unlocked. I am now pushing it open,' Roark said quietly.

There was no response from Hoover and Roark felt that, collectively, everyone was holding their breath.

The door slowly swung inwards. Roark expected a creak or squeak from the hinges, but it was silent. Roark gave the door a nudge so that it would open all the way without her having to step inside. It opened and rested quietly, not swinging back, opening the way in, showing Roark and Moody everything inside.

The overhead kitchen light was off and no other light could be seen from within, but the sun had broken through the clouds outside and even with the curtains drawn on all the windows and the door, the kitchen was illuminated enough for Roark to see.

Only one section of the kitchen was visible through the door. There was one third of a wooden polished kitchen table to the left, completely clear of any ornaments, cutlery or centre piece, with, from what Roark could see, two chairs surrounding it. Next to it, up against the wall and to the left of a closed door, there was a wooden cupboard full of ceramic bowls and other crockery, all lined up in a tidy fashion. On the other side of the door, up against the wall that extended towards the front of the house, constituting the far-right wall of the kitchen, there was another wooden cupboard, this one full of books, large thick cookery books, small fat travel books and several hardbacks with frayed dust covers.

Everything was tidy, clean. No signs of a struggle. No sign of anyone having been here at all.

Next to the kitchen table, in front of the cupboard holding the crockery, was the cellar door, closed and firmly in place.

Moody, standing to Roark's right, leaned forward, head almost touching the door frame, and peered into the house, looking to see if there was anyone further down in the kitchen. She shook her head.

'Looks clear,' Roark whispered into her mike. 'I'm going to announce ourselves, see if anyone responds. The cellar door is right in front of us.'

***

Chief Inspector Arne Cristian took a deep breath at the mention of the cellar door. He sat in his car, parked next to the large MO19 van, with a restricted view of the house, not enough to see the detectives and what they were doing. Inspector Khalili sat next to him, breathing heavily. Detective Inspector Lucas was leaning forward in the back seat, looking between them through the window. They had said nothing between them since arriving at the house.

Arne took another deep breath as he listened to DI Roark announce herself to the empty kitchen and all he could think about was the cellar. That's where they were, he had no doubt. He felt it in his gut, just like he had held concerns over the Irvines and the inconsistencies surrounding their cruise trip. Deep seeded in his stomach, based on very little fact, a feeling that he couldn't shake but knew to be true.

His trepidation over what was in the cellar was based on very little, but what it was based on was compelling. His father's story, from thirty years ago, the same property, the cellar. And the attic.

The story had stayed with Arne from the moment his father had described it to him, which, Arne knew, was the whole point. This was what could happen on the job. This could be what you are faced with on any given day. Something that would live with you forever. Something you could never unsee.

Although Arne was not a superstitious type, he could not shake the feeling that the walls of the house that they were now looking at had seen so much thirty years ago, that it was always destined to be repeated, somehow, sometime; that the very grounds that the house was built on were cursed forever.

He pulled his mobile phone from his inside pocket and activated the screen. Before he was able to bring up his father's number in his contacts list, Roark said over the radio: 'I'm going in.'

Arne dropped his phone, fumbled for his mouthpiece, clicked it on and said, 'Wait.'

***

Roark paused at the door, one foot on the threshold. Moody had already gripped her arm even though both had heard Chief Inspector Cristian on the radio.

'*What is it Chief Inspector?*' Hoover asked, a note of impatience in his voice.

'*They're in the cellar,*' the Chief Inspector said.

'*How can you be sure?*'

'*I'm not, but trust me, you need to check the cellar first.*'

'Okay,' Roark said, 'happy to do that.'

The Chief Inspector cut in again: '*Not alone. Hoover, you need your men in there.*'

That wasn't the plan, Roark thought. Sending in Hoover's men could spook the killer into harming the hostages, they had discussed that, but there was something in Cristian's voice that suddenly made her think that opening the cellar door on their own was a big mistake. She turned to Moody who was nodding in agreement.

Hoover agreed too, with no argument.

'*Connors, Ulright, move in. Adil, cover their approach. Roark, Moody, step back towards the van.*'

Roark and Moody obliged, taking several steps back onto the lawn and towards the van, ensuring they were not in Adil's line of sight from the treeline in front of the house.

Two MO19 officers ran past them along the concrete pathway, Glock pistols out in front of them, high beam flashlights affixed to their helmets, already on. Roark pressed her back up against the van, wondered whether they should get as clear as possible from the house, but Hoover had not given that instruction and she had to trust that he knew what he was doing.

One of the black clad men crossed in front of the open door and stood on the opposite side. They nodded to each other and the man closest to Roark and Moody went in, closely followed by the second man. They were out of sight, but Roark could hear their voices over the radio.

'*Kitchen is clear. Constance, Taylor, move in.*'

Two more MO19 team members appeared at the far end of the front of the house, moving swiftly along, led by their weapons. They moved into the open door quickly without a sound. Roark realised she was holding her breath and let it out slowly. She could see Moody down to her right, back flat against the van.

'*Constance, take that far door; Taylor cover this one.*'

Shadows moved behind the curtained windows but not a sound was made.

'Sergeant, I am checking the cellar door.'

'Roger that, Connors.'

'The door is unlocked.'

'Use thermal imaging.'

'Roger that.'

Roark and Moody waited for what felt like hours, standing up against the van, so close to the action but ineffectual, nothing more than a bystander. The scenario list ran through her head again, knowing that Hoover's MO19 team knew what they were doing but worrying about the hostages, nonetheless.

Assuming they were even here. Roark and Moody hadn't looked in every room yet, just the kitchen, but the house looked empty, and not just because there had been no response from inside. It just *felt* empty.

Roark imagined whoever had sent them the note, the killer or otherwise, was now sitting back in the safety of their own home, laughing at the police, proud of how they'd wasted the coppers time on a wild goose chase.

'Thermal imaging coming up blank. No sound registration either, other than what sounds like rodents. Too small for the imaging to pick up. Cellar door not rigged, all clear.'

'Roger that,' Hoover said. 'Constance, take Taylor to the attic. Through the door beyond the cellar. Proceed with caution, Super says they could be up there. Connors, Ulright, enter the cellar to visibly confirm. Remaining team, stay on station.'

'Received.'

More movement in the kitchen, shadows across the windows, soft padding of feet on the kitchen floor. Roark thought she heard another noise, but it was so soft, she couldn't be sure. Moody took a deep breath beside her, clear as day.

'Opening cellar door.'

This time there was a creak, audible through the open kitchen door.

'Kris,' she heard Moody say, concern in her voice. Roark had stepped away from the van without thinking.

'Proceeding down.'

Roark paused, waited. She anticipated something happening. The cellar. Something was in there, she knew it. Chief Inspector Cristian was sure, a feeling in his gut, and Roark believed him. Hoax or not, Roark felt certain that there was something down in that cellar.

There was a sound over the radio, a gasp, a cough, possibly a retch.

A moment later: '*We have bodies down here.*'

A wave of anxiety rushed up from Roark's stomach and she felt a numbness clench her throat.

'*Repeat that, Connors.*'

'*Bodies, sir. Six of them. Checking for vitals.*'

'*Get the paramedics ready,*' Hoover said, professional and calm. '*Rest of the team, move in, secure the property.*'

The radio burst with noise and static as several voices spoke over each other. Roark caught a snippet of someone, either Constance or Taylor, stating that the attic was clear. Another burst of noise and within it, she heard Connors confirm the first body as deceased and Hoover shouting for everyone to clear the line.

Roark was already moving forward, Moody's hand on her arm but not holding her back. They moved together towards the open kitchen door. Across the threshold, in the kitchen, the cellar door yawned open, initially pitch blackness welcoming them, then a strong beam of light moving across as the two MO19 officers used their flashlights to check the vital signs of the bodies inside.

Roark put her hand over her microphone and called down to them.

'We're coming down. Roark and Moody.'

She had to go down. She had to see.

Moody's grip on her arm tightened. Roark reached across and put her own hand over Moody's and the detective from Bristol released her grip. Roark bent down and put one hand on the opening of the cellar and extended her left foot down to the first step. Right hand on the other side of the kitchen floor and she stepped down to the second step. Ahead of her, all she could see was a flashlight scanning across the interior, flashing quickly across surfaces, not lingering long enough for Roark to make anything out, only the darkness surrounding the edges of the light staying firm and consistent.

Roark took another step, bracing herself for what she was about to see, and a light shone in her face and a black clad figure emerged, ascending the stairs, hand outstretched towards her, warning her off, the eyes emerging from behind the black helmet, wide, alert, bloodshot, a wavering voice, dry lips, spittle on the chin.

'Sorry, ma'am, please stop there, you don't want to see this.'

The look in the man's eyes made her stop and slowly retreat.

CHAPTER 35

There was an eerie silence when Roark and Moody emerged from the house on the instruction of the MO19 officer. They stepped onto the lawn of the Irvine's property, stood in a small group of two about three metres from the van and stared off towards the tree line, the house to their backs.

It was a moment of silence, a moment of shock. Roark raised her hand to her eyes to shield them from the sun that blazed above the trees, and she spotted a bird, a kestrel, dip and dive out of sight. DI Moody was pulling her dark hair back in a ponytail, hair tie in her mouth, staring straight ahead at the van. Roark dropped her hand, cleared her throat.

The moment passed.

'*Property is clear and secure,*' someone said over the radio, and it was like a call to arms, officers in black emerging from the trees from all angles, the backup team descending on the house.

One man in black and another man in casual clothes stepped out of the line of trees in front of the house, Adil from MO19 and one of Chief Inspector Cristian's men from Hampshire Constabulary. Adil held his high-powered rifle down to one side and they were casually walking towards the driveway and exit. They'd been watching the house for almost four hours and looked beat.

Before they reached the point where the treeline met the driveway, dust billowed up, blown east across the open grounds by the wind, a prologue to three vehicles speeding towards the house: the first MO19 van with Hoover inside and two Hampshire police cars. They skidded to a halt in a cloud of dirt.

Hoover stepped out of the van, a black figure with a white moustache, and hurried forward. Roark saw Chief Inspector Cristian, Inspector Khalili, and DI Lucas step out of the second car. Only Lucas headed directly towards Roark and Moody.

Before Hoover or Lucas reached them, there was a squawk over the radio.

'*We have a live one,*' came the exasperated voice.

Hoover stopped and spoke into his mike.

'*Get paramedics in here now.*'

Lucas, who didn't have a microphone or radio, kept walking and joined his colleagues on the lawn. As he started to speak, Roark turned back to the house and the open door and focused in on the open cellar and the darkness within.

A live one.

Her next thought was: *and five dead ones.* A thought that sickened her stomach. One alive, five dead. Depending on how they looked at it, they were either early enough to save one life or too late to save five.

The ambulance sped up behind them, sirens off, having been parked on the approach to the property, out of sight but nearby on the off chance they would be needed. Indeed, they were now. With pure efficiency, three green clad paramedics rushed towards the house, two with a long stretcher to bring the survivor up out of the cellar in a supine position. They would fuck up the crime scene, but the life of the remaining person down there was of greater importance.

Chatter on the radio was kept to a minimum. The MO19 team had done their job and would be returning to their vans. Roark wasn't sure how it worked in Hoover's team, but she imagined that Ulright and Connors would need some counselling. The look on Connors's face as he emerged from the cellar would haunt Roark for many nights.

Roark heard Chief Inspector Cristian report that the Scene of Crime Officers were on their way, the Medical Examiner out of Southampton close behind. They had not been informed of this operation, five dead bodies not having been part of the scenario building over the picnic table earlier in the day.

As they waited, the man who had previously assisted Roark and Moody into their vests helped take them off and retrieved the microphones, earpieces and bullhorn before disappearing back to his team. The three detectives, foreign to this county, stood and waited, feeling next to useless despite everything they had done.

Without the earpieces, they were not forewarned that the paramedics were coming out of the cellar. They saw them, suddenly, as if they'd materialised out of thin air, backing quickly, but carefully, two paramedics on either end of the stretcher. They could see a figure laid out, arms by its side, oxygen mask over its face.

'God, I hope it's not him,' Moody said.

Roark looked across at Moody. She hadn't even considered that. Murder-suicide was common, the assailant unable to deal with what they had done, the lives that they had taken, and seeing the only way out was by their own hand. Failed suicide was less likely, especially if guns were involved, which wasn't yet clear in this case. Either way, it hadn't crossed her mind that the killer could be one of the bodies, alive or dead, in the cellar.

Roark didn't know what she'd do if the killer was now getting a high level of care to keep him alive, but now that Moody had put the thought in her head, she knew that the way of the world, the lack of justice in it, the cruelty of violence and loss, meant that it was one hundred percent likely that the survivor of the horror in the cellar of the New Forest house would be the man who had perpetrated it.

But it wasn't.

The figure was female, short, elderly, possibly late sixties or older. Varicose veins and wrinkled skin gave her away first, then the head behind the mask with grey thinning hair.

'Mrs Irvine?' Moody said.

'No,' came a voice close by and Roark looked across and saw Chief Inspector Arne Cristian standing next to them, leaning forward so that he could see the figure more closely. 'It's not Mrs Irvine. I've met her numerous times. That's not her.'

'Who then?' Moody said but no one had an answer.

Chief Inspector Cristian turned to the detectives and looked over at Roark.

'Are you going in?'

Despite the MO19 officer warning them off, both Roark and Moody would take the stairs down to the cellar to see the bodies in due course. This was a crime scene, and they would need to see it all in order to help with the case.

'We'll wait for SOCO and the ME to show first,' Roark said. 'The scene is contaminated enough as it is, but I'd rather give them as much chance at extracting evidence as possible.'

'Makes sense. I'll go down too. When you're ready.'

'The Irvines?' Roark said.

'I think so,' Cristian said and his eyes, although a bright icy blue, were dull with the inevitable.

'I need a smoke,' Moody said.

'Me too,' Lucas said, and they departed together in search of someone to bum a cigarette off.

Cristian filled the gap left by the two detectives, stood close to Roark.

'I'm sorry,' he said. 'You did all you could.'

'Thanks,' Roark said, 'I appreciate that. Normally I'd think there was more I could do in a situation like this, but I really do believe there was nothing that could be done. I suspect these poor people have been dead for some time. We were late by his design.'

'Yes,' Cristian said and looked down at his large hands. 'All we can hope is that the killer is one of the deceased and that this is all over.'

Roark rubbed the back of her neck.

'I don't think we're going to be that lucky.'

Cristian turned to face her, moving in closer.

'There's someone I would like you to meet. My father. I called him and he's coming over.'

'Okay,' Roark said hesitantly.

'He's ex-police. Was Chief Inspector like me, retired about fifteen years ago. I told him what was happening here. He has a story that I think is worth listening to.'

'About what?'

'Something similar happened here about thirty years ago.'

'Yes, you mentioned that before.'

Cristian rubbed the four-day growth on his chin, addressed her with his striking blue eyes.

'Look, it could be irrelevant, but I think it's worth a listen. I'm not a big believer in coincidences and what's happened here today echoes too closely to what has happened before. In my opinion. Call it a gut reaction.'

'Well, Chief Inspector,' Roark smiled thinly, 'for better or worse, I've come to trust your gut reactions.'

Cristian nodded sagely and gestured to his car.

'My father will have arrived by now. He lives close by. I asked him to meet us at the campsite. We can drive in my car.'

Roark looked behind her.

'What about Moody and Lucas?'

'Ah, I think it's best if it was just you. My father is a little reticent at the best of times and these days, he doesn't like talking to groups greater than one. His story,' Cristian said, then paused. 'He has only told it once before, to me. I don't want to put him off by turning up with an entourage, if you know what I mean.'

'Understood.'

Roark spotted Moody and Lucas over by a MO19 van that had not yet departed. Sergeant Hoover was sharing his cigarettes with the two detectives.

'Detective Inspector,' Hoover said when they approached. He puffed out smoke into the clean air. Moody was smoking like a chimney, looking like a natural. Lucas drew on his cigarette as if it was something he shouldn't be doing.

'Thanks for your help, Sergeant,' Roark said.

'Thank you, too. I wish there had been a better outcome, but the odds were against us today.'

'Yes, they were.'

'They your people?' he said, gesturing with his head towards the house.

Roark turned around, looked back.

'No positive identification yet, but we'll get down there soon. I want SOCO to get as much as they can.'

'Makes sense. Look,' Hoover said, dropping his cigarette and stamping it out on the dirt driveway, 'I'll get a full report to you by the end of the day. Let me know if there's anything to be done here, if we still have any missing folks. If the fucker that did this isn't down there in the cellar, let me know as soon as you get a lead on him, and we'll make it a priority. Other than that, I'm afraid there's nothing more to do here.'

'Thank you, Sergeant.'

Hoover ran a finger under his nose and along his white moustache and nodded to his cigarette partners. He shook Chief Inspector Cristian's hand and jumped in the cab of the MO19 van, next to the driver. They reversed out and in moments, disappeared into the forest, a billow of dust following them.

Moody flicked her finished cigarette down the road.

'What's next?' she said.

'Chief Inspector Cristian here has someone he wants me to talk to. Might be relevant. Do you two mind babysitting the SOCO and ME when they arrive?'

'Shouldn't be long,' Cristian said, checking his watch.

'Definitely,' Moody said without hesitation. 'Let us know if you find anything.'

'Thanks, Clarice. It didn't work out well today, but we did what we could.'

Moody flicked cigarette ash off her jacket sleeve.

'Until we find the fucker, I won't be sleeping. Between all of us, we'll get him.'

Roark nodded, not necessarily feeling her enthusiasm but appreciating it all the same.

'Let us know when SOCO are okay for us to go down. We'll want to see the scene before the ME takes the bodies away.'

'You got it.'

Roark looked to Lucas who gave her a nod. Fair play to him, he didn't look like he was on a double shift, but Roark suspected he was starting to flag nonetheless.

'If you want to take the car back to London, get some rest, I'm okay with that.'

'I'm good,' Lucas said, dragging the last inch out of his cigarette. 'I'll stick around.'

Chief Inspector Cristian and Roark walked back to his car. She got in the passenger seat and watched through the windscreen while Cristian conferred with his second in charge, Inspector Khalili. A few more officers had arrived and were securing the site. The crime scene was now owned by Hampshire Constabulary, and they'd make sure it was secured and that the SOCOs and ME got what they wanted when they arrived.

'Khalili will make sure things run smoothly while we're away,' Cristian said as he sat in his seat and closed the driver's side door. 'I also have a few plain clothes officers keeping an eye on the approaches, just in case our man decides to have a look at what's going on. This is his doing and if he is like any other psychopath, he'll want to see the fruits of his labour.'

'Assuming, of course,' Roark said, 'that he's not one of the dead down in that cellar.'

'Of course,' Cristian said and started up the car. 'Let's go and see what my father has to say.'

Cristian turned, put one hand behind Roark's seat and used the rear windscreen to reverse off the driveway and onto the lawn. For the brief moment before the car lurched forward onto the driveway and drove towards the exit through the forest, Roark turned and stared out the passenger side window, through the open kitchen door, into the open cellar and down the stairs into the darkness where five bodies waited their recognition.

CHAPTER 36

Returning to the campsite set back in the New Forest was surreal. The construction crew were gone, the partial hole in the ground that they had made to complete the cover story was filled in, the barriers taken away. As they entered the clearing amongst the tall trees, all the cars that had been parked there only hours before were gone. It was like the whole planning session they had performed, before they knew of the five bodies in the cellar of the Irvine property, had never happened.

There was one car in the campsite, however. One car and an old man sitting at the picnic table, shoulders hunched, hands clenched together. He looked up as Cristian drove his car into the clearing, his flock of white hair blowing in the light breeze that made its way between the surrounding trees.

'That's him,' Cristian said, and as he drove closer and parked next to his father's car, near the picnic table, Roark could see the family resemblance. Hair was whiter, skin weathered, but the tall stature, the four-day growth, and, as Roark exited the car and approached, the striking blue eyes, all were indications of an older version of Chief Inspector Arne Cristian.

Cristian's father stood as Roark approached.

'Dad,' Cristian said, 'this is Detective Inspector Roark from London. She's the lead on the case I told you about. Detective Roark, this is Dane Cristian, my father.'

'Please to meet you, Mr Cristian,' Roark said, offering her hand.

'Call me Dane, Detective,' the old man said as he took Roark's hand in a cool vice-like grip and shook it. His voice was gruff but clear and pleasant, a voice that had spoken many a word worth listening to. As he shook her hand, he looked directly at her, his eyes more striking than his son's, the white-blue of a glacier from the Arctic.

'Kris,' Roark said when her hand was released.

'Please, sit,' Dane said, gesturing to the picnic table.

Roark sat down on the picnic table bench opposite Dane Cristian. Chief Inspector Cristian sat on the same bench as his father but on the end, a few seats away. He was part of the conversation but deferred to his father.

'Arne informs me that there's been some problems out at the Irvine house,' Dane said.

'Yes,' Roark said, nodding. 'Five deaths.'

Dane turned to his son. 'The Irvines?'

'We're not sure,' Cristian said, 'but it's likely.'

Dane looked down at his hands.

'Shame. Lovely couple. They had a campervan, didn't they? Used to drive up to Scotland quite a bit.'

'That's right,' Cristian said. He didn't bother informing his father that the campervan was now up on blocks and had been for some time.

Dane looked up at Roark.

'Tell me about your case,' he said.

Roark looked across at Cristian and he nodded imperceptibly. No preamble, no explanation, no request for authority to discuss details. Roark had trusted Cristian when he said she should speak with his father, trusted his gut instinct, but now, sitting across from the ex-policeman, looking into Dane Cristian's eyes as they studied her, she knew that it was imperative that they talk and that she listen to what he had to say.

'We had two kidnappings, one in London, one in Bristol,' she said. 'Young victims, early to mid-thirties, taken off the streets in stolen vans. There were also murders at the scenes, one in London, one in Bristol, but we believe they were purely innocent bystanders. The kidnapped victims were the true targets.

'The killer was very careful. We have no witnesses and no descriptions to go on. He ditched the vans, switched to stolen cars, until the leads went cold. We have no fingerprints and only trace DNA samples, none of which has led us to identifying the killer.

'This morning, I received a message that gave the Irvine's home address and a time. I called Arne and he indicated that he had concerns over the Irvines, having not heard from them. He was quite adamant that this was not a hoax or a dead-end lead, and he was right.'

Dane turned to look at his son and Cristian breathed through his nose.

'We arrived at the designated time but there was no response to our attempts to open the lines of communication. Eventually, we entered the house and found six bodies in the cellar.'

'The cellar,' Dane said, raising a bushy white eyebrow.

'Yes. They are all down in the cellar, deceased. Except one, an elderly woman, who is in a critical condition and has been taken to hospital.'

Dane drummed his fingers on the wooden picnic table.

'Six you say. Your two kidnapped victims?'

'We haven't been able to verify the identity of anyone yet. The scene is currently secured and being processed by the SOCO teams. All I can confirm is that an elderly woman was removed and taken to hospital. Identity unknown.'

'Mrs Irvine?'

'No,' Cristian said.

'So,' Dane said, closing his left hand and sticking out a wrinkled thumb, 'elderly woman, survivor, so far.' He counted off the rest with his remaining fingers: 'Your two kidnap victims, plus Mr and Mrs Irvine.' On his other hand, he stuck out his thumb. 'The killer?' he asked, looking at Roark.

'Unknown. We can only hope.'

'Unknown,' Dane repeated, staring at the thumb on his right hand. He wiggled it and said, 'You may find that this isn't the killer, but another kidnapped male, possibly late thirties. Anyone missing from the Liverpool area?'

'Not that I know of,' Roark said, looking across at Cristian.

'Hmm,' Dane said and steepled his hands on the table. 'The elderly woman is an interesting addition. I wonder.'

Dane said nothing for a moment.

'Dad?' Cristian said.

When Dane didn't respond, Roark said, 'Is there anything you can help me with, Mr Cristian?'

Dane extended his two forefingers in the steeple and tapped either side of his nose. He then straightened and looked out over at the trees behind Roark.

'Dad?' Cristian repeated.

'Okay, son, hold your horses. I'm thinking this through. There are a lot of similarities here.'

'To your case?' Roark asked.

Dane didn't respond directly. He rubbed his stubble and nodded, to himself more than anyone else.

'I can't be certain,' he said to Roark, 'but I believe the man you are looking for was once called James Stern.'

'James Stern,' Roark said as she reached into her jacket pocket and pulled out a small notepad and pencil. She did not recognise the name.

'It's unlikely he's going by that name today. When I stopped keeping tabs on him, his name had been changed to Howard Bloch. Adopted you see, after what happened.'

'Howard Bloch,' Roark said as she wrote down both names. 'Neither of those names rings a bell, if I'm honest.'

'I would be surprised if they did,' Dane said, his blue eyes sparkling.

'Who is Howard Bloch?'

Dane leaned forward on the picnic table and arched his back. Roark heard a slight crack. He stretched his neck and then relaxed.

'Sorry, the old bones are not as good as they used to be. I'm sure my son would've mentioned I used to work for Hampshire Constabulary, reached the heady heights of Chief Inspector, like my son here,' he said, reaching over and tapping Cristian on the arm affectionately.

'Most days in New Forest are quite serene, not a lot to deal with. That said, I have my fair share of stories that stick with me, even to this day. Working in London, I'm sure you already have enough stories to dwarf my own. However, there was one day, about twenty-eight years ago, that I will never forget.'

Roark placed her pencil down on her notepad, wanted to listen intently, pick up what she needed, but also to give Dane Cristian respect, show that he had her full attention.

'This particular day I've recounted only once, to my son here. Never before, never again. It's not a fond memory, and even when I get together with those who were there on the day, we don't mention it. I can't forget that day, but I do not enjoy remembering it.'

'I understand,' Roark said. She wondered if he had made the decision to tell her or was still debating it. Cristian had said this might not be useful at all, but now, Roark needed to hear Dane Cristian's story. She felt the weight of it in every word spoken by Dane, spoken as prelude, as prologue. If he decided not to talk, she would now have to insist.

'Nineteen-ninety-three,' Dane said, studying his clenched hands on the picnic table. 'A mother and child went missing out on the Yorkshire Dales. Every station in the country received notice of it. They'd left their father in London, a trip for mother and son alone. Car was found near Hawes a day later, abandoned on the side of the road. Mother and child nowhere to be seen.

'Just over a month went by with no sign and then they were found in a national park somewhere in Wales. They were in shock, suffering from malnutrition, a few cuts and bruises but otherwise alive and well.'

'What happened to them?'

Dane drummed the picnic table.

'The woman, her name was Wendy Cooper, was kept in a cellar for the entire time. Fed and watered but she never saw the face of the man who had taken her and her son off the Dales, never saw the light of day for the whole month. The boy, six-year-old, Ryan was his name, was also kept in the cellar, but she said their captor would take Ryan out of the cellar most days. When they questioned the boy about that, all they could get out of him was that the man wanted to play with him.'

'Sexual abuse?' Roark said.

'No, nothing like that. Play with toys, read books, teach him things. Like a father or an older brother.'

'Did Ryan give a description of the man?'

'Ryan was only six at the time, so no, he was unable to give any worthwhile information.'

Roark picked up her pencil and wrote a few notes in her notebook, particularly the names of the victims. She tapped the notepad twice before saying, 'So the cellar was the one in the Irvine property?'

'Correct, but the police didn't know that at the time. Neither the mother nor the son could provide any information that would help in locating the place they were held. They were blindfolded or incapacitated when transported, unable to identify any landmarks or indications of location. The child, like I said, was too young, too traumatised, to take in anything.'

'But they were okay. They were released unharmed?'

'More or less.'

Dane pulled out a red handkerchief and sneezed aggressively. Birds flew from branches and small animals stopped and looked.

'Sorry,' he said. 'Pollen gets to me sometimes.'

Roark caught Cristian in a brief smile, affection there for his father.

'Where was I?' Dane continued after wiping his nose and returning the handkerchief to his pocket. 'Ah, yes, so, six months later it happens all over again. A mother and child, this time a four-year-old girl, disappeared out in the Lake District somewhere. Gone without a trace. Their disappearance was alerted nationally and the team working the Cooper case picked up on it, saw the similarities and started to coordinate the search. No use though, they had nothing to go on.'

'What were their names? The mother and daughter?'

'Iona and Laura Kilpatrick. I remember the details quite clearly. I did a lot of my own research, after what happened here a year later. They would've changed their names since though. Everyone went into Witness Protection. Their identities and lives were in all the tabloids when the search was on; made sense they'd want a new start.'

'They were released by the kidnapper?'

'That's right. Only a week or two after disappearing. Half the time of the Coopers, but it had all the trademarks of the same perpetrator. Cellar, mother kept in the dark, child taken upstairs on a daily basis, read to, played with toys, etc.'

'Strange,' Roark said.

'The only difference was that the mother heard a lot more shouting, a lot more noise, and even though the daughter was never abused, she was often very upset. Cried a lot. So he ditched them, alive and well, in the Cotswolds somewhere.'

'He likes to travel.'

'Indeed, he did.'

Roark referred to her notes quickly and asked, 'Sorry, where were the Kilpatrick's from? London?'

'No,' Dane said. 'Bristol.'

Roark looked up and both father and son were watching her for a reaction. London and Bristol. The same as her case, the same locations.

'I can see what you mean now,' she said to Cristian. 'There's an obvious link.'

'Or a coincidence,' Cristian said, 'but we don't always believe in those.'

'No,' Roark said slowly, 'no we don't.'

'It doesn't end there,' Dane said, rubbing his stubble. 'There was another disappearance, the one that broke the case. The one that led us here,' he pointed in the direction of the Irvine property.

'Single mother and eleven-year-old son. The Davies.'

Roark scribbled down the details.

'Cheryl and William Davies.'

CHAPTER 37

'Cheryl and William. That's what their names were. The next mother and child kidnapped by your father. The third kidnapping after the Cooper's and Kilpatrick's. Cheryl and William Davies, but you knew that, didn't you, Howard?'

He ignores the question and slowly takes his seat. The male detective waits, standing there, staring, until he eventually lowers himself into his chair, resumes his slouched position, eyes watching without interest. The shadows around the man with the moustache are deep, inches away from wrapping themselves around his ample frame. The dark spaces in the corners of the room are growing, stretching out towards the centre, towards where he sits on the dirty orange chair, wringing his hands, his eyes wet.

'Abducted in late-1994 from a weekend away in north Wales, about six months after the Kilpatricks. The boy was eleven years old. A lot older than the other two. Same age as you at the time right, Howard?'

He closes his eyes.

'Your father held them for over a year.'

She holds her pen above her notepad and looks at him. The folder of files and photos is open on her lap.

'What happened in that year, Howard?'

The boy hears angry noises, grunting, not his father. He scuttles quickly off his mattress towards the gap in the floor and peers down into the kitchen, cautiously.

His heart sinks.

Not again.

A woman over his father's shoulder, and a child, another boy, watching on, distraught. This boy is bigger than the other two, older, but from this angle, from what can be seen of this boy's face, it is contorted, strange, more childlike than the other two. And the boy is angry, throwing punches that miss, spit flying from his mouth as he tries to protest what is happening to his mother.

The boy in the attic watches and thinks that this boy looks like him.

'I know this is difficult, Howard, but it is important.'

'How?' he says, and his voice sounds foreign to him, almost animalistic.

'That's what I'm trying to find out. Unless I have all the details, I don't know exactly. What I do know is that it's relevant. What your father did thirty years ago is relevant.'

He rubs his eyes with his right hand, takes longer than is necessary to clear them.

'Howard, what was your father doing with this mother and son? Did he play with the boy like he did with the others? What was it that he wanted from them?'

Every day the boy stares down into the kitchen and sees the other boy.

Billy. That's his name. He heard his father say it many times as he sat with the boy at the kitchen table, food, toys, books, in front of them. His father tried to connect with Billy, but it was impossible. Billy would not talk often, and when he did, if it wasn't grunting, it was baby speak, as if he was a lot younger than he looked.

Baby speak was more than what he could do, the boy thought, squatting above the gap in the floor. The boy tries to remember: has he ever spoken a word? A proper word?

'Howard?'

'I don't remember.'

'No? They were in your house for over a year and you didn't know what was happening?'

'My father never told me.'

'But surely you could see what was going on with your own eyes?'

'Father kept me away from them.'

'For nearly fourteen months? How did he manage that?'

He places his elbows on the table and buries his head in his hands.

'I don't understand why we are talking about this,' he mumbles.

'How did your father treat you, Howard?'

The boy tries to remember: was he ever happy? Was his father ever happy?

Did his father ever love him?

The boy can't remember. All he knows is what is happening now. His father ignores him every day, doesn't seem to realise he exists up here in the attic. His father wakes, eats breakfast, goes to work, comes home, drinks, watches television, drinks more and goes to sleep.

Not once speaking to him. Not once seeing if he is okay. Not once looking up to the attic where he lives.

And now, with Billy, he is still ignored but his father's routine is different. He eats with Billy at the kitchen table. He reads Billy stories, plays games, holds conversations. Or he tries. It is obvious after a week or so, that his father is giving up on Billy.

No connection to Billy. No reaction from Billy. No love.

Just like the others.

Father, the boy thinks, I can give love. I have love to give. Please let me try.

The boy cries.

Behind his closed eyes, he can hear the detectives looking at each other. The silence, the small sound of movement; he can picture them, heads shaking, eyebrows raised, mocking him.

'I think I'd like to leave now,' he says into his hands.

'Tell me about Billy,' the female detectives says, changing the topic, pretending that she didn't hear him speak. 'What was he like?'

Father gives up. Billy is left in the cellar with his mother. No more books, no more toys.

The boy starts to feel better. In weeks, maybe days, Father will take this mother and child out of the house and not bring them back, just like the others. And maybe, just maybe, his father will never do this again, that this will be the last time. Maybe, just maybe, he will give this up. Maybe he will come up to the attic and hug is son.

Maybe he will let the boy love his father again.

After a week or two, this does not happen. Each day brings new despair. Each day the woman and Billy remain in the cellar. Each day the boy remains in the attic.

Each night, the boy cries himself to sleep.

One day, something changes. The boy hears crying and the sounds of a struggle. He peers down the gap and sees his father tying up Billy to the kitchen radiator, near the door that leads out of the house. Tied up with rope from the garage. Around the hands and ankles. Silver masking tape across his mouth.

Billy's eyes are red with tears and wild with fear.

The boy almost smiles at Billy's pain and suffering, happy that it is directed at this child and not himself, although part of him feels that this type of attention from his father, any form of attention, would be better than being ignored.

The boy looks on, worried, as he sees his father pick up a large white plastic container off the kitchen bench, heavy with a clear liquid, and leaves Billy tied up in the kitchen and walks down into the cellar.

'Did you like Billy? Feel sorry for him? Or did you hate him?'

He clenches his fists and slams them on the table. Thoughts of Billy infuriate him.

'I would like to leave. Right now,' he says, his voice cracking, betraying his frustration, reducing the impact he wants.

'Calm down, Howard,' she says. There is a note of accusation in her voice. 'Just calm down. We're almost done.'

'I don't want to talk about him,' he says and returns his head into his sweaty, stingy hands.

'I'm sorry, Howard, but we need to.'

The boy hears screaming, loud painful screaming. Billy contorts and struggles against the rope at the sound of his mother. Soon, Father returns, up the stairs into the kitchen, and throws the white container across the floor. It bounces against the kitchen cupboards and walls before rolling to a stop, empty of its contents except for a small trickle that spills onto the floor.

The boy doesn't understand.

The boy also doesn't understand the new routine that starts the following day. Every two or three days it happens: Billy is tied up, Father descends into the cellar, emerging after a short period of time, the woman whimpering in his wake, and Billy is returned to the cellar. The boy doesn't know how long this goes on for, but it feels like an eternity.

Then the routine stops. He is not sure after how long, but one day it just stops.

Billy is no longer tied up. Father no longer goes down into the cellar.

The book reading, games and attempts at conversation with Billy do not resume.

Everything is at a standstill.

The boy experiences hope again but this only lasts one night. One night when his father does not take the woman and Billy out of their home. One night is all it takes for the boy to lose hope. He no longer believes that anything will change. Not with Billy in the house.

No, the only chance that the boy believes anything will change will be the day when his father takes the mother and Billy out of the house.

That day never comes. Billy remains in the house and the boy remains in the attic.

And it takes almost a year before the boy realises what he must do.

'Tell me, Howard. What did you do to Billy?'

CHAPTER 38

Dane Cristian cracked his wrinkled knuckles, audible in the stillness of the forest. He sniffed and leaned back a little on the picnic table bench. Roark underlined the two names in her notepad: Cheryl and William Davies. The names meant nothing to her, just like the others, but she noted them down anyway.

There was a connection here. She felt it. She felt like she was finally getting somewhere. It took a lot of willpower to allow Dane to take his time.

'They disappeared in late ninety-four,' he continued, 'not long after the Kilpatricks were found. Cheryl was a single mother, raising her son, William, in the Liverpool area. They disappeared not too far from home, if I recall. Somewhere in North Wales, in one of those national parks. Car found, no sign of the mother and son. Immediately, the consensus was that this was the same perpetrator, and another national alert went out.

'Expectations were that it wouldn't be long before the two turned up somewhere unharmed, just like the others, but months went by and there was no sign. For me, out here in the New Forest, it was another one of those open missing persons cases that you get used to seeing stuck up on the noticeboard every morning you come into the station, until, at some point, someone takes it down, most often because the person has been found, but not always. Working in this area, around the forest, you'd be amazed how many disappear.'

Roark nodded, believing it.

'Anyway,' Dane said, sniffing, wiping his nose with a finger instead of a handkerchief, 'we did find them. Just over a year later. Not through good police work, mind you, but through sheer luck.'

***

'Howard? Please answer the question. What did you do to Billy?'

He feels tears at the edge of his eyes, a cry trembling on his lips.

How can he make her stop? How can he make her let him go?

'I just wanted it to stop,' he says, barely above a whisper.

'Sorry, Howard, I didn't catch that. Can you say it again? Louder, for the recording if you can.'

He clears his throat, wipes his eyes, and repeats himself.

'What did you want to stop? What your father was doing, with these children?'

'Yes.'

'Did it make you angry?'

He doesn't reply.

'Were you angry at Billy for what your father saw in him? For spending time with him?'

'No.'

'No? Who were you angry with then, Howard?'

'No one. I wasn't angry.'

The boy watches his father tie up Billy to the kitchen radiator.

The cycle is happening again.

It is happening for a second time and the boy can't let that happen.

'So how did you feel, Howard?'

He stares at the table, his eyes blurred.

'Sad.'

The boy watches his father descend the cellar stairs, his head disappearing into the kitchen floor, into the darkness down there, and the boy now knows what is happening, the same thing that happened what feels like a year ago, the thing that happened the first time.

He knows now why his father went down into the cellar, why Billy was tied up in the kitchen, why it happened over and over until it stopped.

He knows what it all means now and he can't let it happen again.

Billy struggles with his ropes, eyes wide open above the tape across his mouth, always struggling, never resigned to just waiting. He knows what is happening too.

Billy. It's all his fault. If Billy wasn't here, this would not be happening.

The boy moves without thinking, running along the floorboards of the attic, his bare feet slapping on the wood. He trips over his weakened legs, picks himself up, rips open the door that leads to the stairwell that takes him down to the kitchen.

'Why were you sad, Howard?'

He sniffs, his nose starting to run.

'For the boy. For Billy.'

The boy reaches the kitchen door and opens it slowly. He squints at the overhead lights, cannot remember the last time he was in the kitchen with the lights on, blinks, concentrates. It takes him a moment and when his eyes adjust, he can see Billy looking over at him from near the door that leads outside, on the floor at the end of the kitchen counter, tied to the radiator, his eyes, somehow, growing wider when he sees what has entered.

The boy takes a kitchen knife from the bench.

'How so?'

He wipes clear liquid from his nose with the back of his hand. He takes a moment to pull a handkerchief out of his trouser pocket and uses it to dry his nostrils. He tumbles the handkerchief into a tight ball in his right hand and stares at it.

'He was scared. He didn't want to be there,' he says.

'So what did you do?'

The boy steps slowly towards Billy. He keeps the knife by his side, the edge pointing down toward the floor.

A quick glance at the open cellar door.

He can hear a struggle, a scuffle, down there, and he knows he must be quick.

Billy starts to panic, wrestling with the rope that binds his hands to the radiator and his feet together, crying wildly under the tape across his mouth.

The boy reaches the end of the kitchen counter, across from the open cellar door, and stands above Billy, looking down at him.

'I helped him.'

He tightly clenches the handkerchief in his hand.

The boy raises the knife and brings it down, once, twice, a third time.

'You helped him? How? What did you do?'

'I set him free.'

The boy sees red at the corners of his vision and steps back, startled.

What did he just do?

He looks at the knife in his hand and sees a small trace of blood, dripping off the edge. A small trace, nothing significant.

What happened?

His arm hurts as if he has strained it, his slender arm, devoid of muscle, devoid of strength, so weak. Surely he is unable to cause anyone any harm.

He looks towards the kitchen radiator.

Billy is gone, nothing left behind but the ropes that had bound him – loose but still tied to the radiator, untied in a fit of panic – and a few small drops of blood on the floor where Billy had sat.

The kitchen door, leading outside into a blustering night full of rain, is open.

The noises behind him, down in the cellar, stop.

The boy runs, quickly putting the knife back where he had taken it from the kitchen bench, slinging the kitchen door open and rushing through, stumbling through the house until he reaches the foot of the stairwell. He scrambles up towards the attic door, tumbles through, closes it behind him and scurries to the far corner, the darkest corner of the attic, with the cobwebs and the rats, and pulls his knees up to his chest and buries his head in his hands and tries to block out the sound of his father screaming.

Chapter 39

'He was found not far from here actually,' Dane said, gesturing back to the entrance to the campsite. 'Running alongside the road, in pouring rain. A trucker saw him, picked him up and brought him into the station.'

'Jesus,' Roark said. 'Was the boy okay?'

'Not great. I was called in, being head of the station. He was traumatised beyond belief, drenched from the rain of course, but weak, suffering from malnutrition, a few cuts and bruises, marks on his wrists and ankles suggesting he'd been tied up, but nothing significant. He couldn't take the bright lights in the station, and when we turned them down, his eyes grew wild, darting left and right. We couldn't get much out of him. He was unable to speak, and when he did, he cried for his mother.

'It was William Davies, the missing kid. We didn't know that at first, but it didn't take long for someone to bring in the missing person leaflet from the noticeboard and make the identification. We'd found the son, but his mother, Cheryl, was nowhere to be seen.

'Billy kept on crying for her, but we couldn't get much out of him until he suddenly calmed down, went quiet. I thought he'd gone into shock until he spoke. He formed words slowly, like a child just learning how to read. I thought it was only shock that caused him to speak like that, but the child was a bit slow. On the spectrum, I think they say these days. It took a while, but finally he said that his mother was still out there, out there with the dangerous man, out there in the dark place.

'One of my officers at the time said that the closest property to where the boy was picked up was the Stern house. I knew of Richard Stern and his son but hadn't thought of them in a long time. Not since the mother had died about three or four years earlier. Stern had kept well off the radar and I couldn't remember much of the boy and that, in itself, suddenly didn't sit right.

'So, I sent a car out there to check it out.'

***

'You let him escape?'

'He escaped.'

'How did your father react?'

The screaming stops. The boy raises his head, listens for the loud footsteps up the stairs to the attic.

Nothing.

He notices, for the first time tonight, the sound of the rain on the roof.

He hears, faintly, the sound of his father's truck engine starting up, revving.

The boy rushes to the gap in the floorboards and looks down into the kitchen.

The cellar door is closed. The kitchen door, leading outside, is closed. The rope where Billy was tied up is gone. The kitchen is empty.

The boy listens and waits.

'Howard? How did your father react?'

Howard shrugs his shoulders.

'Is it correct that the day you let Billy free was the day your father died?'

His father, lying on the floor, on his side, a red pool of blood around his head, growing, expanding, covering the kitchen floor.

He feels his breathing heavy in his chest, rising, quickening.

'Howard?'

The boy awakens to the sound of a door slamming. He looks down into the kitchen and sees his father, standing by the door, looking at the cellar, rainwater dripping from his head, his clothes, the axe in his left hand, the rifle in his right.

Billy is not with him and for a moment, the boy rejoices.

Billy is no longer in the house.

The way the father is looking at the cellar door, the boy believes it won't be long until it will only be him and his father in the house again, just like it was in the days after his mother had died, and that they would have a chance this time to set things right between them, make a family again, a loving family, father and son.

The boy rejoices, and in an overwhelming moment of hope, lets out a small giddy laugh.

His father looks up. He glimpses the boy's eyes in the gap of the attic floorboards and puts the rifle on the kitchen table. He transfers the axe into his right hand and starts to walk out of the kitchen, towards the stairwell that leads to the attic, to where the filthy animal up there who had let Billy go will now have to pay with its life.

The boy screeches.

His father stops, turns sharply around, and stares out the kitchen window above the sink.

He drops the axe, grabs the rifle off the kitchen table and rushes up to the door that leads outside. He uses the butt of the gun to smash the small window set in the top half of the door and clears away the glass.

He trains the rifle out of the window and starts firing.

***

'We got a call in about shots fired at police. They'd arrived at the Stern property and before they could even stop the car, Stern started firing at them. He had a hunting rifle and had smashed through the window in his kitchen door, firing at the officers. Themselves unarmed, they retreated, and I called in backup, called in the Firearms Command team out of Southampton. This had quickly become a hostile situation and we had to assume that Stern had at least two hostages with him: Billy's mother, Cheryl, and his own son, James Stern.'

**

The boy cannot stand the noise. The loud report as his father fires his rifle makes him jump and scutter away, back into the dark corner. Hands over his ears, he can still hear the gun firing.

'Howard?'

He realises he has covered his ears with his hands.

The sound of gunfire stops. The silence is just as loud.

The boy slowly takes his hands away from his ears.

'Who was your father firing at, Howard?'

He takes his hands away from his ears.

'Did you hear the question?'

He nods.

'It was the police.'

'Okay,' she says, 'and his first reaction was to fire at them?'

He shrugs his shoulders again and he can see that the gesture is frustrating her.

'Where were you when all of this was happening?'

'Safe.'

'Safe? How so?'

'I was in the attic.'

He grimaces as if struck by a sharp pain in his stomach.

Why did he say that? Why did he mention that place?

'Did he send you up there before he started firing?'

'Yes, he did.'

'Do you remember what happened next?'

Nothing happens for what feels like forever. The boy, shaking uncontrollably with fear, eventually peers back down into the kitchen. His father is shifting frantically through the kitchen drawers and cupboards, moving in and out of the boy's eye line, cursing.

Finally, the boy hears something fall to the floor and at the edge of his vision, a handful of bullets roll. They are gathered up and his father shuffles into view, staying low to the kitchen floor, heading to the door again, a box of bullets in his hand.

In the blink of an eye, the boy is blinded.

***

'It took about an hour to set up around the property. Firearms Command were very efficient. They set up a perimeter as best they could, given the surrounding forests, but they were able to move in stealthily given the time of night and the intermittent rain. They were able to set up vehicles just beyond the tree line in front of the house and had snipers in the surrounding forest. It was decided that given we suspected possible hostages in the house, we would open up communications first.'

'We did exactly the same thing,' Roark said. A pointless remark but one she had to say out loud to remind her that it had actually happened, only thirty or so minutes ago. That it hadn't gone so well at all.

'Best approach given the risk to human life,' Dane said, nodding. 'I stood with the Sergeant of Firearms Command, just on the perimeter we'd set up, could hear everything that was going on, could see the front of the house clearly. We lit up that place with these large portable lights, hoping to disorientate Stern and give us a clear view, a clear line of sight. We felt it was enough to give him a message as to our intentions, but we quickly followed up with open communications on the bullhorn.'

'What was the plan?'

Dane sniffed and rubbed the back of his head.

'Completely out of my control. This was the Firearms Command's play, but I agreed with it. We'd try and talk Stern down, but ultimately, their snipers would come into play at the first opportunity.'

***

'Howard,' she said, voice rising, 'do you remember what happened next?'

Loud, distorted voices, reached his ears. He kept his eyes closed, colourful splashes of light behind his eyelids. He wanted to cover his ears again, but he didn't want to miss what happened next. He didn't want to miss what the voices were saying.

He heard his father crying and he opened his eyes, squinting.

His father sat up against the door, back to it, rifle in his lap, head up, looking up at the ceiling, looking up, tears falling from his eyes, his mouth open in anguish.

Looking up at him.

In that moment, staring down into his father's red rimmed eyes, the boy sees that his father wishes none of this had ever happened, that he is so sorry for what he'd put his son through, that he wished he'd never set eyes on Ryan or Laura or Billy.

Wished he'd never gone down in that cellar and did what he had done.

'I'm sorry,' his father says just before he stands up and starts firing wildly through the kitchen door.

Stay down, the boy wants to say. Be careful, he wants to shout.

The words don't come as he does not know them.

The kitchen window over the sink explodes, glass spraying everywhere.

The boy ducks instinctively, shouts out in shock.

His father stops firing and the boy looks back down the gap in the attic floor, tears dropping through into the kitchen below.

He sees him. He sees his father on the kitchen floor.

His father lies on his side, blood pooling around his head, his rifle just out of reach.

His father.

'They killed him.'

***

'The lead hostage negotiator was talking through the bullhorn when Stern started firing again. We were sure he couldn't see his targets, the lights we'd set up were too bright, but he fired anyway, unrelentless.'

Dane opened his hands on the picnic table, an act of supplication.

'From that point, it was inevitable. Firearms Command had no choice. Stern was dangerous. Not just to us, but to those inside. The Sergeant gave the order and a sniper took Stern out. One clean shot, through the open window, a shot to the head.

'Just like that, it was done.'

CHAPTER 40

A moment of silence and he thinks that maybe that is it, no more questioning, they have extracted the death of his father out of him, and that is that. No more questions.

'Howard, why did it take you so long?'

The question takes him by surprise.

'What?'

'Why did it take you so long to let Billy go? It was over a year, wasn't it? Before you helped Billy escape.'

Watching his father tie Billy up to the kitchen radiator and descend into the cellar, the boy knows what is happening this time, and he knows he can't let it happen again. When it happened the first time, everything changed. If it happens again, for a second time, there is no hope for the boy, no hope for him and his father, no hope for his family.

His life would be over.

'Late-1994 they were taken,' she says, 'and it was almost the end of 1995 when your father was shot and killed by police at the New Forest house. Letting Billy go led the police to your home. You said you were sad for Billy, that you wanted to set him free. Why didn't you do it earlier?'

He shrugs his shoulders.

'Okay, let me put it this way: what changed to make you want to help Billy? What happened to make you act?'

He cannot let it happen again.

His life would be over.

'What happened, Howard? What happened in that cellar?'

He looks up at her quickly as if she has slapped him across the face.

'What happened in that cellar in that year between when your father abducted Cheryl and William Davies and when you let the boy escape?'

His father lies on his side, blood pooling around his head, his rifle just out of reach.

The boy wants to crawl through the gap in the floorboards to crouch by his father's side and hug him with all his strength. Hug him and whisper to him. Tell his father he forgives him for what he did the first time, what he had planned to do again. Forgives him for everything.

He makes to leave the attic but stops when the cellar door opens.

'What did your father do, Howard? What did he do to make you betray him?'

'I loved my father,' he cries out suddenly.

A panic.

One night, long after that first time his father tied up Billy and went down into the attic, long after that horrendous cycle stopped, there is a panic. The boy hears it. His father shouting and swearing, a woman screaming, Billy yelling.

Billy runs out of the cellar, hides near the kitchen radiator, hands over his eyes. He isn't tied up with rope and the boy wonders why he doesn't just run.

Father goes up and down the cellar stairs like he's dealing with a burst water main, taking piles and piles of towels down there, bandages, and tubs of water and other things the boy can't identify.

The woman's screaming intensifies and the boy wonders if she is dying.

'What did he do, Howard?'

The cellar door opens and the boy looks to his father through the gap in the floorboards, but his father has not moved, and the pool of blood around his head is growing larger.

The cellar door slams on the kitchen floor and someone emerges from the darkness, walking cautiously, one hand tight against her chest, the other feeling around at the kitchen floor where the cellar entrance is.

It is the woman. The mother. Billy's mother.

She stops for a moment, listens, looking into the kitchen but with no real direction, bathed in the bright light but not raising her hand against it, staring at the floor as if she doesn't notice the boy's father, lying there, his head leaking.

She hesitates a moment longer, wraps the shawl that is over her shoulders tighter into her chest and steps out of the cellar, still feeling around as if she is walking in the dark and not in the stark whiteness that has drained the colour out of everything.

She reaches forward, feels the corner of the kitchen bench with her one outstretched hand, moves across, finds the door handle, and turns it.

***

'Sniper was pretty sure he'd connected, but the extraction team took it carefully, approaching the house from all sides. I moved up with the Sergeant, a little bit closer, and we could see the front of the house clearly.'

'The front door opened. It was from there that Stern had been firing, so all the Firearms Command team stopped in their tracks and trained their weapons at the door, cautious that Stern may have survived. They lowered them almost immediately. In the stark light, we could clearly see who was coming out of that house, holding something in her arms.'

***

'Okay, Howard, if you can't answer the question. Let me.'

The dark spaces of the interview room reach the table and pool around his legs.

The boy watches as Billy's mother steps out of the house.

'Let me tell you why you felt compelled to let Billy go.'

The boy watches as the woman's screaming stops and his father carefully emerges from the cellar, looking down at something in his arms.

'Your father raped Cheryl Davies, didn't he, Howard? Raped her until she gave him what he had wanted all along: a baby he could call his own. A baby that would love him from its very first moment, not one he had to convince, or trick into loving him. A baby that would love him unconditionally.'

The dark spaces curl up the legs of the table and his chair and he stands up abruptly, the chair falling over behind him.

'But that wasn't enough, was it, Howard? No, one child was not enough. He wanted a family, not just a child. So, after the baby was born, he tried for another.'

The boy watches his father tie up Billy to the kitchen radiator.

It is happening again.

He hears the baby crying in the cellar and it continues to cry while his father descends the stairs. The baby stops crying and the boy sees his father emerge from the cellar, carrying the baby, soothing it as he takes it into another room.

He returns without the baby.

The baby cries again, somewhere distant inside the house.

His father checks Billy's ropes are tied tightly.

He descends the cellar stairs.

The boy knows what is happening and he can't let it happen again.

'He starts to rape her again, doesn't he? He wants another child.'

A second child.

The boy can't let that happen. If him and his father are ever going to have a family again together, he can't let that happen.

'And that's when you decided to let Billy escape, right, Howard? You let him escape and the police found Billy and led them back to your father. Isn't that right?'

The boy decides he can't let that happen. He must make it stop and he now knows how.

He must kill them. He must go down there now and kill Billy and then find the baby and kill it too. Kill them both to stop this ever happening again.

'I need to leave.'

She doesn't let him.

'Sit down, Howard. Right. Now.'

***

Dane shook his head at the memory.

'She was thin, real thin, as if she was suffering from malnutrition. A skeleton of a woman despite obviously being pregnant only a few months ago. We didn't know it then, but she'd spent over a year in Stern's cellar, never seeing daylight. Her clothes were tattered, but clean, her hair long and stringy, falling limp along her shoulders. She walked slowly, tentatively, uncertain. She did not raise her arm against the light, did not cover her eyes, and she did not yell or scream. She just walked, slowly forward. As she walked closer, we could see that she was crying. Streams of tears down her cheeks, but she didn't make a sound.

'A female police officer approached, talking to her quietly, calming her, and the woman, Cheryl Davies, finally stopped walking and dropped to her knees. She held both arms out in front of her, held out the bundle of blankets in her hands. Held out the baby. The baby she'd given birth to in that cellar. The baby conceived with Richard Stern.'

Dane looked out into the forest that surrounded them.

'I can't tell you what the other police officers were thinking when they saw Cheryl Davies offering up that baby as if it was for sacrifice, but my mind went into dark places, thinking about what she had endured in that house. Billy had mentioned the cellar when he'd finally spoken back at the station and I immediately surmised that she'd been kept down in that cellar for the entire time, since she'd disappeared almost fourteen months prior. It would take a few days until we knew that for sure, but at that moment, I knew in my heart of hearts that it was true. She'd been kept in darkness for fourteen months, and during that period she'd been raped countless times and ultimately fell pregnant to a madman named Richard Stern. She'd been pregnant for a full term, kept in darkness, kept in sordid conditions, with her life and her son's under constant threat. Forced to give birth in poor conditions to a child conceived with her abductor.

'Without hesitation, she gave that baby to the police officer, gave her baby away, and at the time, I fully understood. The pain across her face, the dullness of her eyes, seeing her kneeling there and breaking down made me feel sick to my stomach and there is not a single day that I don't think about what it must have been like for her.'

'Jesus,' Roark said, thinking about what the woman had gone through, in that dark cellar for over a year. 'Did she survive?'

'Yes, she did. All things said, her condition wasn't too bad. Stern obviously had kept her healthy enough during her pregnancy. Cheryl Davies didn't talk a lot about what had happened in that cellar, not the details, but she gave the impression Stern had kept her healthy enough so he could try for a second child. Hence, her physical health was borderline, but she recovered. Mentally, she'd suffered, but her reunion with her son, Billy, helped a lot with that.'

Dane sniffed.

'Of course, later, it was determined that the poor woman was blind. Hydrofluoric acid. The bastard had blinded her with rust remover.'

'Jesus. What the fuck for?'

Dane just shook his head slowly.

They said nothing for a while. Roark tried to comprehend what it must have felt like for Cheryl Davies, and struggled.

'What happened to the baby?' she asked.

Dane ran a hand along his stubble. Roark noticed Cristian do the same, realising it, and dropping his hand.

'I don't know a lot about that,' Dane said. 'I didn't keep track. She disowned it there and then, on the front lawn of the Stern property. I'm not sure, but I think she may have put it up for adoption. She was a single parent, she was blind, and this was Stern's baby. I can't judge her for that.'

'It's possible,' Cristian said, speaking for the first time since Dane had started his story, 'that the elderly woman taken from the cellar in the Irvine house is Cheryl Davies. Age is about right.'

'And Billy would be the fifth body in that cellar,' Roark said.

'Could be,' Dane replied. 'Could be. But this harrowing tale doesn't finish here. There's still one person we haven't mentioned yet.'

'James Stern,' Roark said.

'That's right,' Dane said, nodding slowly. 'James Stern.'

CHAPTER 41

Dark figures move into the house, into the kitchen. One squats by his father's body, puts his fingers to his throat. Another descends into the cellar.

The boy stares at his father as they roll him over. His dead eyes stare blankly up at the boy, speckled with blood.

The man dressed in black holds his hand flat out as if to check for rain.

The boy realises his tears are dripping through the gap in the attic.

The man looks up.

'I won't repeat myself, Mr Bloch. Please sit down.'

He sits down.

They said that he could leave at any time but the look on her face says that this is not an option anymore.

He places his arms on the table and stares at his hands.

'How did that make you feel, Howard? When your father had another child? Did you feel threatened? Were you worried he would replace you?'

The boy scuttles back, his bare skin scraping across the wood. He doesn't stop until his back hits the inward slope of the attic roof. A beam bangs into him, bruising the skin.

There are sounds below, scuffling, static, voices. The boy can sense where the movement is, throughout the house, looking for a way up.

Up into the attic.

'That's why he kept you in the attic, wasn't it? That he had grown to hate you? That for some reason, he wished you hadn't existed?'

The boy hears footsteps on the stairs. On all fours, he scurries towards the far corner of the attic, the corner with the cobwebs and the rats and the deep dark spaces.

'You say that you helped Billy escape and that you felt sad for him. Is that true? Or were you angry at Billy? At Billy and the others. Did you blame them, perhaps, for what was happening to you? For what your father did to you?'

The steps on the stairs stop. There is shouting, one or two yelling out words the boy can't understand through the closed door.

The boy pulls his knees up, drops his head down and interlocks his hands on the back of his head. Tries to make himself as small as possible.

He holds his breath.

The door to the attic opens.

'Howard?'

He keeps his mouth tightly closed.

'The house has an attic,' Dane said. 'I'm not sure if you saw that or not.'

'Yes, we did.'

'That's where Firearms Command found him. Up in the attic. The Sergeant and I were heading towards the house when they found him. They secured the house, and we went inside. They took us upstairs to the attic immediately.

'I walked up those stairs, still a little shaken after seeing the state of Cheryl Davies. My legs were unsteady on the wooden steps. Armoured police stood aside to let us through. As soon as I walked through that door into the attic, the smell hit me. A horrid smell that I'll never forget.'

Dane took out his handkerchief and wiped his eyes with it. They'd turned red while he had recounted the story. Pollen in the air possibly. The formation of tears, Roark thought.

'I kept my composure, but it was a foul smell. An animalistic smell, although there was something distinctly human about it. I'd cleared squatters, moved the homeless along, discovered dead bodies out in the forest, and that's what this smelled like. Death, despair, desperation.

'The place was a tip, food scraps, dried faeces, obviously human. Rats and mice had fed off both. A thin mattress in the middle of the floor, dark, damp pillows, a hole ridden blanket. Blood in some areas of the mattress, dark and caked on. What really hit me were the toys strewn around the place. Stuffed toys with limbs ripped away in anger, board games warped with damp, several picture books with pages torn out. Remnants of a childhood under duress.

'He was hiding in the corner of the attic, deep in darkness, keeping quiet, reduced to a small bundle. I stepped closer and one of the officers shone a flashlight. The hair was long, ragged, hanging low over his face. The skin was black with dirt and exposed, uncovered, naked. Scratches and bruises covered the areas of the body the dirt hadn't reached.

'A female officer was brought forward. She tried to communicate, to coax him out, but the figure kept still, shrinking into the shadows. Eventually, they were able to grab the child. He fought like a feral beast, and I felt afterwards that's exactly what he was. Neglected, mistreated, starved of emotional connection, the boy was caged like an animal. He smelled like one too. Dirty. Hair long and uncut. Fingernails chewed away. Toenails torn.

'I tried to gauge his age from what I could see. I knew what to expect, an eleven-year-old boy, but this child looked younger, smaller. Shrunken. Growth stunted. Physically beaten, transformed through months, maybe years, of depravation and poor living conditions. Transformed from the child I remembered seeing at Stern's wife's funeral. James Stern.'

Even now, at the memory, Dane shook his head and pinched the bridge of his nose.

'They gave him a sedative to calm him down. They took him to Southampton Hospital for a full check-up. The house was cleaned up, evidence collected. Richard Stern was pronounced dead at the scene. The coverage of his crimes went international. Evidence linked him to the two previous abductions, one of the mothers even revisited the scene to confirm that this was where she was kept, down in the cellar. Case was closed and the story dropped out of the press.

'I spent my spare time taking an interest in the case. There were a lot of theories while the story was still reported. They all agreed Richard Stern was crazy. I agreed with them. Crazy for what, that was debated. To me it was clear. I'd spoken to Billy, with Cheryl, looked over the police reports of the other abductions. Information that the press didn't necessarily have. I formed my own conclusions.'

'Which were?' Roark asked quietly.

'Stern wanted a family. Not the one he had. Not his dead wife, not the surviving child. Maybe his wife's death was too painful, and James reminded him of that. Or maybe he was always an abusive father, but his wife had kept him in check, protected the boy. I don't know, but it was clear that Richard Stern did not want James anymore, and he wanted to start anew.

'First, he tried to connect to the children he abducted. Then he chose Cheryl Davies to give him the child he wanted.'

Dane dropped his head and shook it again, slowly. Cristian reached across, put a hand on his father's shoulder. When Dane looked up, the tears had come, wetting the edges of his eyes.

'What happened to that boy,' he said, his voice breaking up, 'happened on my watch. His mother died when he was eight years old and from that point on, his father kept him locked away. He didn't go to school, he didn't have medical check-ups, and he wasn't seen in public. How was that missed? How did no one notice? How did I not notice? That still bugs me after all these years.'

Several platitudes danced on her lips, but Roark said nothing. Dane wiped his tears away and lightly tapped his son's hand. Cristian slowly removed it from Dane's shoulder.

'I'm okay,' Dane said. 'I guess what I'm trying to say is I felt a responsibility to this child and that's why I kept an eye on him, after that horrible day.'

'What did happen to him?' Roark asked.

'He went into Witness Protection immediately, as to be expected, but I had contacts there who kept me informed. He was adopted, enrolled in a special school, saw a psychologist. It didn't go so well at the start, got into a few fights, went through a few families over a short period of time, but eventually he settled down with the Bloch family. They lived a simple life on the Isle of Wight which seemed to do wonders for James. A simple family, two hard working parents, but loving, and they gave him a lot of support.

'It was when he was sixteen or seventeen and had been settled with the Bloch family for some time, I started to relax. I stopped worrying about him, about how he'd turn out. He was looked after, he seemed to be making progress, so I left him alone. For my own benefit more than his. I never forgot James Stern, not after what I saw that day, but I decided it was time to let him be.'

There was a silence, not just at the table, but in the surrounding woods, as if every living creature had decided to stop and listen.

Dane gave an unconvincing laugh.

'Looks like I was wrong about that.'

Roark took a deep breath.

'Before you told me your story,' she said, 'you believed the person we should be looking for is James Stern.'

'That's right,' Dane said.

'Why?'

'Well, when Arne told me what was happening at the Irvine house, I couldn't help but think about what happened all those years ago. Arne thought it too, right?'

Cristian nodded.

'I understand you made the connection, that the situation has clear similarities,' Roark said, 'but what makes you think James Stern is behind this? From what you've told me, James Stern had recovered from the ordeal and appeared to be a normal teenager living in a loving home, yet you believe he's behind this, these killings.'

Dane looked above and to the left at the forest behind Roark. His eyes were still red-rimmed. Dredging up the memories had been harder than Roark could imagine.

'I said I felt a responsibility for him, given this had all happened on my watch.'

'Yes.'

'It wasn't just that. When I was in that attic, when we found that child, the first thing I noticed about James Stern was the look in his eyes. It disturbed me. It wasn't just the eyes of an abused child or the feral eyes of an animal. There was something more there, something evil, something that scared me. I was worried from that point about what this child would become, how the impact of what he'd been through would manifest itself in later life. I was certain that this child was dangerous. Stupidly, I convinced myself that the danger had passed, and I left James Stern alone.'

Dane opened his arms out towards the surrounding forest.

'And here we are.'

'Dad,' Cristian said, 'you're too hard on yourself.'

'No, I'm not, son.'

Dane dropped his arms and stared at the wooden picnic table. There was an awkward moment of silence and Roark knew it was time to finish. Dane had said all that he could.

'Thanks so much for your time, Mr Cristian. Dane. I really appreciate it.'

'We should have some of the old files back at the station,' Cristian said, shifting forward in his seat. 'You may be able to gather some more information to help you.'

'Thank you, Chief Inspector.'

'Dad,' Cristian said, his hand returning to Dane's shoulder, 'are you okay to drive home?'

'Of course,' he said, and he stood up slowly, stretching his back muscles.

Roark and Cristian stood up from the picnic benches.

'Just one more question,' Roark said. 'If you didn't mind?'

'Of course,' Dane said.

'If James Stern has done this, what's his motive? Why did he kill all these people? Is he just insane? Mentally unstable?'

'No, I don't think that's the case. He's doing this for a reason.'

'And what do you think that is?'

Dane took out his handkerchief, wiped his eyes, his nose, and pocketed it back in his trouser pocket.

'What else?' he said. 'That age old motive: revenge.'

***

She keeps asking questions. Painful questions. Insinuating questions. He can't take it anymore, so he places his hands over his ears and his head on the table. He feels the dark spaces crawling up his legs towards him, gripping him around the stomach.

The legs of a chair screech on the floor. Heavy footsteps thump forward. A presence stands nearby, the smell of something rotten drifting into his nose.

He closes his eyes tightly.

'Mr Bloch, will you please answer my questions? This is very important.'

He shakes his head in his hands, left and right, left and right.

There is silence in the room, deafening him.

He feels the shadows slide up his chest towards his neck.

'Howard? You need to answer my questions.'

Left and right, left and right.

'Howard, please account for your movements between yesterday morning and the moment the officers picked you up today.'

The darkness seeps into his nostrils, ears, eyes, mouth.

Left and right, left and right.

'Where were you, Howard?'

She slams her hand hard on the table.

'Why did you kill them, Howard?' she shouts. 'Why did you do it?'

The shadows cover the top of his head and the boy is lost in the dark spaces.

CHAPTER 42

While Chief Inspector Cristian spoke with his father alone, heads close together, talking softly to one another while they stood next to Dane's car, Roark received a call from Detective Inspector Moody.

'They're ready for us,' Moody said, meaning the Medical Examiner and Crime Scene team. 'We can go down.'

'We'll be there in five minutes,' Roark said and turned off her phone.

After a few more minutes, Cristian walked over to where Roark was standing by his car.

'Is he okay?' Roark asked.

Cristian nodded solemnly.

'He held himself well while discussing this, but I know it still hurts him. I'll go see him tonight, once we're done here. He hasn't revisited the case in that much detail for some time.'

'I can imagine it was difficult. What do you make of it?'

'Like you said, it's worth looking into further. The case files we have on the system should be detailed enough to pull any more information out. Names, addresses, ages.'

'Let's get back to the Irvine house. We can see the bodies now. We can talk a little more on the way over.'

They sat in silence while Cristian manoeuvred the car out of the campsite. Roark looked at Dane as they left. He stood by his car, staring up at the forest surrounding him.

'Your father is feeling a lot of guilt right now.'

'Yes, I guess so,' Cristian said as he waited for two cars to pass before pulling out onto the main road. 'There's nothing he could do for that boy at the time, though. He's too hard on himself.'

'Sure,' Roark said, tapping the dashboard, 'but it's hard to convince yourself of that sometimes.'

They drove in silence for a few minutes, Roark staring out the window as the trees flashed by.

'It's a tantalising proposition,' she said. 'James Stern, I mean. There's a lot pointing to him as a suspect. A lot.'

Cristian nodded without saying anything.

'Between you and me,' Roark found herself saying, 'I feel myself being led by motive here and I don't necessarily like it. It's not something I do, but to be honest, I'm desperate.'

'Like you said,' Cristian said without missing a beat, 'it's worth looking into.'

Roark stared ahead as they approached the turn-off to the Stern property. She couldn't see it as belonging to the Irvines anymore. Not after what she'd learned had happened here thirty years ago.

'This job never fails to both surprise and disgust me,' she said. 'The things we do to each other. I can see why your father can't shake the memories.'

'I suspect we'll have the same problem.'

Cristian reached the turn-off and slowed down. There was already a police car out the front and officers manning a checkpoint. It would be difficult to cordon off the whole property, but key access points would need to be covered initially. There was no need to show his badge; the local officers recognised their Chief Inspector immediately and waved him through.

They drove through the darkness of the forest.

'What your father said about the boy,' Roark said, staring ahead, 'about seeing evil in him. Do you think that's possible? I mean, I've seen evil acts by evil people, but to identify it in a traumatised boy like that...'

Roark didn't finish. She didn't know what else to say, what to think. There was a compelling case against James Stern, the circumstances, the similarities, the connections, but Dane Cristian was led by something else, by the presence of evil that he said he saw in the eyes of an eleven-year-old boy.

'I don't know either,' Cristian said softly, 'but I've always believed him.'

Roark nodded silently and said nothing more as they emerged into the clearing that was the forefront of the property. It appeared almost identical to when they had first arrived an hour or so ago, Roark and Moody in her car, approaching a situation they had no idea was going to play out as it did.

As Cristian drove the car closer, along the driveway, they could see six vehicles parked up near the house and on the front lawn, including Roark's car, and officers running police tape around the surrounding forest edge. Other than that, the scene was no different.

It wasn't the same, though, was it, Roark thought. The five bodies in the cellar and a sordid history retold by Dane Cristian gave the house an almost malevolent presence, a watcher of horrendous deeds, a catcher of horrific acts, a harbourer of pain and death.

Moody, Lucas, and Cristian's second in command, Inspector Khalili, stood in a circle near the Medical Examiner's car talking to a man dressed in a dark blue suit. The ME looked out of place, like a lost businessman stopping for directions. Only the light blue gloves he wore provided a hint to his authority at the scene.

Two men in light blue paramedic suits, leaning against a van belonging to the Coroner's office, waited for the signal to remove the bodies and take them to Southampton for their autopsies. They were waiting on the Chief Inspector and the London detectives to take a look at the crime scene and the bodies before they could do what they were paid for: protect the body of evidence.

'Let's make this quick,' Roark said, looking at the paramedics standing with hands in their pockets.

They stepped out and the ME, Moody, Lucas and Inspector Khalili turned towards them.

'Sorry about that,' Roark said, directing her apology to the ME.

'It's fine,' Moody replied on everyone's behalf. 'They've only just finished, mind. Crime scene team are still working the house, but we can go downstairs. How did it go with you?'

'Very interesting,' Roark said. 'We'll need to go to the station to pull a couple of files, so I'll fill you in on the way. Let's get down there, see what we've got.'

No one was looking forward to it, but they knew they had to do it. It was a crime scene, and the bodies were *in situ*; they would be remiss not to see that for themselves. There was also the hope that one of the bodies in the cellar could be their killer and that was something they needed to know immediately.

'ME Clayton,' the Medical Examiner said, raising his blue clad hands. 'Sorry, I haven't washed them. Come this way.'

They followed him towards the house, everyone keeping in step, no one in a rush. At Cristian's instruction, only Khalili stayed behind to continue the securing of the crime scene. Roark was right in behind the ME and could smell vapour rub, something the doctor put under his nose to decrease the odour of the dead bodies. She hoped he would offer some up to the team, but nothing was forthcoming. Only more blue gloves and blue booties for their shoes, which they all took a moment to put on before stepping into the house.

'SOCO's are pretty much done down here, but just in case,' ME Clayton said in reference to the precautions.

Through the front door into the kitchen, Roark could not help but look down at the area on the floor where Dane had said Richard Stern had been shot and bled out, thirty years ago. She looked up at Cristian behind her and found he was doing the same.

'Okay,' Clayton said at the top of the cellar stairs, 'as you can see, we've set up lights around the scene to assist us. Please be careful of them. They are free-standing and prone to toppling over if knocked. The cellar is large enough for all of us but just be mindful of feet and elbows. You two,' he said pointing at Roark and Cristian, 'mind your heads.'

Everyone murmured their understanding.

'The bodies are *in situ*, although I had moved them for my examination, before putting them back in position. Many photos and videos have been taken, so if you're feeling a bit squeamish, you can retreat and review those once I've uploaded them to the system. Just don't vomit down there, please.'

Roark sensed the tension in the people around her and swallowed.

'Okay,' ME Clayton said, 'let's go.'

CHAPTER 43

ME Clayton descended slowly, using the kitchen floor on either side of the opening as support. Roark followed, keeping one step behind, keeping her head down. Cristian was next, Moody and Lucas taking up the rear.

At the bottom step, Clayton stepped aside to give all of them room to reach the bottom of the stairs. Roark did the same and looked at the scene before her.

The bodies grabbed her attention immediately, five dead human beings laid out around the cellar floor, up against the walls, on display in the sharp, bright lights. Whether deliberately positioned or falling naturally, they were all in different positions, predominantly supine, with one body immediately in front of them, sitting with its back to the wall, two bodies either side of it. Even in the stark light of the lamps, it was difficult to identify the sex of each victim without closer scrutiny.

It wasn't just the sight that grabbed her attention; the smell, entombed in the cold, damp cellar, was overpowering, and everyone, other than the ME, covered their mouth when they stepped onto the cellar floor. Moody gasped when she joined Roark; Lucas only grunted.

'Okay, counterclockwise direction,' Clayton said, pointing across the group to their right-hand side. 'Over in the corner there, we have two bodies dumped on top of each other, as you see them. Late sixties, early seventies, male and female. No identification on them, but I suspect they are the owners of the property.'

'The Irvines,' Roark said.

'Excuse me, may I?' Chief Inspector Cristian said.

'Go ahead.'

Cristian moved closer to the bodies and squatted down, blocking their view.

'You won't be able to identify them, sir,' the ME called after him. 'By my estimations, they've been dead more than two weeks. You'll see the early signs of advanced decomposition. Taking into account the conditions of this cellar, their deaths did not occur recently.'

Cristian stood up and returned to the group. His facial features were severe in the bright lights.

'We received a note three weeks ago that they were taking a cruise,' he said to the group. 'I have my doubts that they sent it.'

'Three weeks would be consistent with their condition, maybe less, so I'd say you're right. Quite a large grumble of *lucilia sericata* larvae down in this cellar, which screws up the estimations a bit.'

No one asked what he was referring to.

'Maggots,' Clayton clarified. He cleared his throat when no one responded. 'Rats had a field day too. It will take a while to identify those two, unfortunately.'

'How were they killed?' Cristian asked.

'They appear to have cuts to the throat, possibly inflicted with a knife, but it's difficult to say given the flesh deterioration and what the maggots and rats have done to them. I'll need to examine the hyoid bone and larynx to be one hundred percent certain. All the knives in the kitchen and property have been taken by SOCOs for examination. Cause of death on preliminary examination is exsanguination from these wounds.'

Clayton gestured to the body propped up against the cellar wall, head lolled forward. It wore a dark-coloured business shirt with cufflinks.

'Next, we have a male, mid-thirties, in the early stages of decomposition, so I'd say possibly a week old or thereabouts. He's still a little bloated, which usually subsides by the end of week two, and the discolouration suggests he's entered his second week post-mortem. With so many bodies in such an enclosed space, it's a little difficult to be any more precise. The cellar is cool which will slow down the rate of decomposition but, as I said, we have a lot of critters down here, feeding away, although most of the rats seem to have concentrated on the Irvines over there.'

'Would I be able to identify this one?' Roark said.

'Yes, you should be able to,' Clayton said. 'He's lost some hair and looks a little green, but you should be able to see his features. Hold your nose though, this one is particularly ripe.'

Clayton stepped over to the body and squatted down. He leaned over and carefully lifted the head of the victim so that Roark could see. Roark was right behind Clayton and leaned in to examine the face. Clayton was right, she was able to identify the body, despite the discolouration and the sagging of the skin around the face.

'Aaron Sparger,' Roark said and quickly covered her mouth against the stench.

Clayton slowly lowered the head, so its chin rested on the chest.

'This victim was taken upon with an axe, I believe,' he said. 'There are numerous cuts to his stomach but a clear deformation on the top of his head, here, at the parietal bones,' he continued, pointing to the skull with one glove covered finger. 'More than likely the killer blow. I suspect death was caused by an extensive brain contusion following fragmentation of the neurocranium, but I'll need to confirm with an autopsy. He has a broken nose too, but I'm not sure when that happened.'

Roark considered the broken nose may have been administered when the killer had abducted Aaron Sparger near Waterloo station. She also remembered Sparger's blood in the rear of the van found in the Chiltern Hills. That could've been due to a crack across the face. Hard to know, and she wasn't sure it mattered anymore.

Clayton swivelled on his feet to the body on his right.

Before he could speak, Moody said behind her hand, 'That's mine. Jaime Collander.'

The female body laid on its side, knees pulled up to her chest, blond hair obscuring some of her face. She wore dirtied clothes, a once white shirt with a frilly collar, dark jeans. Her feet were bare, muddied, bloodied.

Clayton leaned over and curled Jaime's hair behind her ear. The almost gentle gesture hit Roark hard in her chest. Roark's mind immediately turned to Jaime's distraught mother.

'Yes, that's her,' Moody confirmed, a quiver in her voice.

'She's a few days fresher than Mr Sparger,' Clayton said, 'but it's hard to tell how many. She has more bloating but less discolouration.'

'She disappeared four days ago,' Moody said.

'That would be about right.'

'And the last one?' Roark said, hurrying it along.

'Sorry,' Moody said, interrupting. 'How did Jaime die?'

'Hard to say,' Clayton said. 'She has several bruises and possible fractures around her face and the back of her head, blunt force trauma, but she also has knife wounds to the abdomen, enough to suggest severe blood loss. Defence wounds on her hands suggests she fought back.'

Moody nodded and took a short step back.

'So, our final victim,' Clayton said after a moment's pause, swivelling back to the last body in the cellar, 'is our freshest. Early to mid-forties, heavy-set male. Less than twenty-four hours old as we still have full rigor mortis.'

Roark studied the body from afar. A tall, slightly overweight man, wearing a light blue pyjama top and bottoms with red fluffy socks over his feet, lying flat on his back. His complexion was white, skin dirty, hair unkempt. She didn't recognise the face.

'Multiple stab wounds on this one, I mean dozens, and what also appears to be strangulation. There are blunt force injuries to the neck, here and here, and we can see signs of facial petechial haemorrhages, suggesting strangulation was the method of death, rather than the knife wounds, but I'll need to do a full autopsy to confirm that.'

'This is going to sound stupid, but there's no chance it was self-inflicted, right?' Moody said, hope in her voice.

'No,' Clayton said. 'No way. I know what you're thinking, but my bet is that this is not your killer. This was not a suicide. This man was murdered. Viciously.'

Roark was listening and doing the maths at the same time, looking at the body before her. Early to mid-forties. Twenty-eight years ago, he'd be around twelve to fifteen years old. Considering that the man appeared to not have cared for his physical well-being and therefore looked older than he actually was, that would make him about the right age.

'Billy Davies,' Cristian whispered next to her.

'I was thinking the same,' she said.

'Any more questions?' Clayton said, standing up.

'I think we're done, Doctor, thank you,' Roark said. 'We'll look forward to the full report.'

'My pleasure.'

The group moved as one towards the bottom of the stairs.

'I'll stay,' the Medical Examiner said, 'but on your way out, can you send the coroner boys down here? We need to get these bodies to General so I can get the autopsies started.'

'Of course. Thank you again, Doctor,' Roark said. She stopped at the foot of the stairs as the others ascended. 'Oh, any word on the sixth victim? The elderly lady?'

'Not yet,' Clayton said. 'She had multiple stab wounds and there appears to have been an attempted strangulation there too. Critical condition. Not going to make it, if I was a betting man.'

'Okay, thanks. Let me know if there is any change in her condition.'

'Will do.'

They emerged from the cellar trying hard not to gasp for fresh air, trying to keep their professionalism in the face of the horrors they'd just witnessed. Moving out of the kitchen and outside onto the lawn, they started pulling off gloves and booties, throwing them aside, staying close to each other but allowing each individual distance and time to process and recover.

Chief Inspector Cristian motioned to the two men over near the coroner's van and they moved swiftly, taking a body bag and a metal stretcher into the house. The bodies would be removed carefully, one at a time.

'Let's go back to the station,' Cristian said to Roark. 'We can have a look at those files. I think one of the detectives might also have a bottle of something stashed away somewhere. I think we could all do with a stiff drink.'

'And more than one, mind,' Moody said, walking off towards her car, which had been driven to the scene from the campsite by one of the other officers.

'Lucas and I will follow you,' Roark said to Cristian, motioning to her own car.

'Okay,' he said and Roark thought she noted a hint of disappointment. Roark felt it too.

Lucas stepped up next to her, said, 'You okay?'

'Sure,' she said. 'Always hard to see that kind of thing.'

'Worst I've ever seen,' Lucas said.

Roark put a hand on his shoulder.

'Sorry you had to.'

She felt Lucas shrug his shoulders and she dropped her hand.

As they walked towards her car, her thoughts shifted to Detective Constable Knight and she considered texting her an update. Maybe later, she decided. It was not necessarily the time to share this news, not until Knight contacted her first with news of her own. As Roark sat behind the wheel and stared out of her front windscreen, she knew that despite whatever had happened to Gale's mother, there was a part of Roark that was glad Knight had been spared the gruesome scene down in the cellar of Richard Stern's house.

CHAPTER 44

Twenty minutes later Roark, Cristian and Moody were set up in a meeting room in the New Forest police station. Lucas had hit the wall and was currently lying on a sofa in Cristian's office, catching some hours before they left. They would have to leave soon, Roark thought. It was nearing four o'clock and she still had a three-hour drive to London ahead of her.

Cristian had provided them with computers and monitors to allow them access to the old files of the Richard Stern case from 1993 to 1995. Notepads, pens, and a tumbler of Irish whiskey were handed out. Moody had necked hers and asked for another. Roark had given hers a sip and savoured the warm liquid moving through her body.

Cristian confirmed that he would be able to email through the complete files to Roark and Moody's teams in the next few hours. There was a little bit of red tape to go through to allow him to distribute the files, but he didn't see it as a problem. They could access the files on the network computers for the time being.

Everyone sat at a computer, but Roark asked the two of them for their attention before they started.

'Chief Inspector Cristian,' Roark said and after a look from the tall policeman, corrected herself. 'My apologies, *Arne* kindly introduced me to his father this afternoon. Dane Cristian. He used to run this station. Thirty years ago, he was lead at an incident at the Irvine property. That's right, thirty years ago, but back then, the house and land were owned by Richard Stern.'

With assistance from Cristian, Roark went through the key details of the case of Richard Stern for the benefit of Moody, covering the two initial abductions, finishing with the siege at the property which saw Stern shot dead and four survivors recovered: Cheryl and William Davies, James Stern and a new-born baby.

'After hearing about our current missing person cases, Dane voiced a theory that the man we may be looking for is James Stern.'

'The kid in the attic?' Moody said. 'Why?'

'His theory is that Richard Stern wanted a new family, excluding his son, James. He kept him in the attic, neglected him, and abducted these children to try and connect with them, to try and establish a parental bond with them.'

'Fucking psycho,' Moody said.

'Dane believes that James may blame the children for what his father was trying to do. Easier for him to believe the children were manipulating his father's emotions than to accept that his father didn't want him anymore. He could also, through some twisted logic, blame those children for his father's ultimate death.'

Moody blew out a long, exasperated sigh.

'No offence to your dad, Arne, but that's a bit of a stretch.'

'Maybe,' Roark said, stepping in, 'but there is something there.'

'Okay,' Moody said, catching up quickly, 'he thinks this James Stern is killing the kids that were abducted. That those kids are our victims, all grown up.'

'I mentioned to Dane that our victims were abducted from London and Bristol. He confirmed that the first two abductees taken by Richard Stern back in 1993 were also from London and Bristol.'

'Oh wow,' Moody said.

'Same order too: London, then Bristol.'

'He's recreating history,' Moody said. 'Abducting the same victims but instead of trying to connect to them, like his father did, he's killing them.'

'Revenge,' Roark said. 'Anyway, it's a possibility I want to pursue a little further. That's why I wanted to check the case files from 1993.'

'I've got them in front of me,' Cristian said. 'What do you want to know?'

Roark leaned forward in her chair.

'What was the address in London of the mother and son who were abducted in 1993? Wendy and Ryan Cooper?'

Cristian scanned the screen in front of him, scrolled down with the mouse.

'Found it. 126A Lille Street, Elephant and Castle, London.'

Roark clicked her fingers.

'That's the same address. Aaron Sparger's residence in London.'

'No fucking way,' Moody said.

'And Iona and Laura Kilpatrick from Bristol?'

Cristian closed and opened folders, clicked on menus, moved his mouse around efficiently until he found the case file information pertaining to the second abduction from 1993.

'Flat 11, 73 Gas Street, Bristol,' he said, and they both looked at Moody.

Her bottom jaw dropped, and she nodded.

'Different flat number, but that's Jaime Collander's address,' she said quietly.

Roark leaned back, stared at the ceiling.

'We've got two sets of abductions from the same locations, thirty years apart.'

'One by Richard Stern,' Moody said, 'and one by his son, James Stern. Jesus, your Dad's right, Arne.'

'Hold up for a minute,' Roark said, trying to keep all their emotions in check. 'We don't know that for sure. We need confirmation of the two victims' identities, that they are the same children, before we can go down that road.'

'Wait,' Moody said, typing on her computer, 'let's see if the ages match up.'

Roark did the same on her screen, scrolling through the old files from 1993, searching for the details on the victims.

'Here it is,' Moody said first, 'Laura Kilpatrick was four years old in 1993, which makes her, what, thirty-five today. Ah shit, Jaime Collander's thirty-one.'

'Same here: Ryan Cooper would be thirty-seven today and Aaron Sparger is thirty-five.'

'Birth dates are completely different,' Cristian said.

'There goes that theory,' Moody said, slouching in her chair.

'Not necessarily,' Roark said. 'These matching addresses can't be a coincidence, and given what we found in Irvine's cellar, the link to James Stern is very strong.'

'That's what we should focus on,' Cristian said. 'That's all we have to work on.'

Roark looked across at Cristian and recognised herself in his approach to the case. Stick to the facts, forget about the motive.

Forget about the why until you arrest the guy.

It was true, but the why was so compelling. She had a feeling about James Stern, and she couldn't ignore it. Still, she had to be careful.

'You're right,' Roark said, looking at Cristian. 'That's all we have, so we need to dig further. What we have is purely circumstantial, so it needs work.'

Cristan nodded but Moody cut in.

'Didn't your father say that these abduction victims went into Witness Protection? Back in 1993?' she said.

'Yes, that's right,' Cristian said, cautiously. 'The cases had so much publicity at the time, they all requested it, every single one of them.'

'And what happens under that program? Change of names, right?'

'Normally.'

'Change in ages? Like, fake birth certificates?'

'I'm not sure.'

Roark suddenly felt a buzz at the nape of her neck and along her arms.

'Shit,' Moody said, leaning back in her chair. 'It still could be them. They go into protection and have their names and ages changed.'

'I don't know,' Cristian said.

'Why?' Moody said.

Roark studied him, saw that he was cautious about something, and that calmed the buzz she'd felt inside her stomach. Even though she'd only known him for less than a day, she knew she could trust his opinion, trust his gut feeling.

'What do you think, Arne?' she said.

'The addresses,' Cristian said. 'One of the key aspects of Witness Protection is relocation. They would not have remained at the same addresses. They would move to a new city, maybe even another country. They would not stay at the same house.'

'Cristian's right,' Roark said, a little deflated. 'The addresses would change.'

'I'm not saying there's not something here,' Cristian said. 'The addresses are exactly the same as those in 1993. That cannot be a coincidence, but I think the stronger link is the fact the bodies were left at the Irvine house, Richard Stern's old property. I would build a case against James Stern around that for now.'

'Makes sense,' Roark said.

'That doesn't leave us with much,' Moody said. 'If we could confirm we're talking about the same people, it could be the difference in the case. Like, couldn't we get a court order to open the Witness Protection files on the 1993 victims, confirm where and who they are now?'

'Good luck with that,' Cristian said. 'I'm not an expert, but I don't think that will be easy.'

'We could just ask the parents,' Roark said. 'The mothers in particular.'

'That could be tricky,' Moody said.

She had been dealing with the significantly distraught mother of Jaime Collander and this line of questioning may not be welcomed. Roark thought the same of Aaron Sparger's parents.

'It's worth us trying. There's definitely something here,' Roark said. 'Question is, is it enough to bring James Stern in?'

'Dane thinks James Stern is capable of doing this, doesn't he?' Moody asked.

Roark remembered Dane Cristian's comments about the boy he found in the attic.

There was something more there, something evil, something that scared me.

'Based on what he saw back then, yes, he thinks it's possible.'

'Then we need to bring him in,' Moody said. 'Have an initial chat with him.'

'What do you think, Arne?' Roark said.

Cristian was nodding his head.

'Given the urgency around this case, and the possibility that there may be more victims, I think a careful conversation with James Stern is in order.'

'Great,' Moody said.

'Okay,' Roark said, glad they were acting on something. 'Let's get the feelers out there looking for men in their late thirties, early forties, named James Stern or Howard Bloch, see if we can narrow it down to our man. Once we've done that, I'll start some interviews, see if we can shake something loose.'

'We need to be careful, though,' Cristian said, standing up to make his point. 'I feel we're close, but we need to build the case further for any charges to stick.'

'Agreed,' Roark said.

'How about our unidentified victims?' Moody said. 'The deceased male and the elderly woman in the hospital. They could be the third abduction victims, right?'

'Right, they could be. We need to identify them to try and confirm that. It can only help our case if we link them back to James Stern. Get your teams to look for any recent MisPers.'

'We should start in Liverpool,' Cristian said, pointing at his computer screen. 'My father suggested that could be where the third victim would be taken from. Liverpool was the hometown of Cheryl and William Davies when they were abducted in 1994. If the pattern continues, whoever lived at their address could well be our two unidentified victims.'

Roark agreed and felt another buzz of electricity along her forearms and at the base of her neck. She knew she shouldn't jump to conclusions or use motive as a crutch to make a case, but she couldn't help but feel that they had their man.

They just had to find him.

CHAPTER 45

Roark broke several road rules on their way back to London. Speeding for one; she hovered just over the limit for most of the journey, occasionally neglecting to notice when the speed limit dropped for some sections of the M3, powering through at seventy miles per hour. Driving while on the phone was the other rule she took apart, on several occasions. As Lucas took a kip in the back seat, Roark fielded calls on her mobile phone, sometimes using the speaker option, sometimes holding the phone up to her ear as she drove with one hand. She didn't care; she had a job to do and a killer to find.

James Stern.

He was now suspect number one, their main focus, their main person of interest.

It wasn't perfect, it rarely was, and it troubled Roark how she was now running her investigation on a series of circumstantial evidence, but something about it felt right, that gut feeling that had served Chief Inspector Arne Cristian so well.

A gut feel or a feeling of desperation. Either way, it was the only lead she had.

Her phone buzzed and she picked it up.

'I've found them,' Detective Sergeant Thompson said with his usual annoying confidence. She had loathed to give him work on the case but despite his huge ego and annoying chauvinism, he was good at grunt work, and she had to admit, if he'd not picked up the Aaron Sparger missing person case and linked it back to her murder, they'd be nowhere.

'Tell me,' she said, keeping her eyes on the road, if not the speedometer.

'Yesterday, in Manchester. Young woman by the name of Teresa García was attacked in a home. I say a home, as opposed to her home, as the flat she was found in belongs to an old lady. Miss García was visiting her as part of some support group for old farts. She was stabbed multiple times but managed to call it in. They traced the call and found her. Didn't make it, unfortunately, died at the scene.'

'Okay, but how does this link to my case?'

'Another call came into the station this morning, a woman from the same support group, worried about one of her workers who hadn't checked in.'

'The worker being Teresa García.'

'Correct. The woman was also concerned about the old lady who Teresa was visiting at the time. She hadn't been answering her home phone. She wasn't there when the paramedics arrived for Teresa.'

'What's the old lady's name?'

'The old dear is Cheryl Palmer and her son, who is also missing, is William Palmer. She's late sixties, he's late thirties.'

Roark almost drifted into the middle lane, pulled it back in time before rear-ending a blue Chevrolet, momentarily fumbling the phone against her ear.

'Fuck, that's them,' she said. 'Cheryl and Billy.'

'Sorry?'

'I'll tell you later. Great work, Thompson.'

'That's what Thommo's here for,' Thompson said with a hint of bravado in his voice.

'Give me the details.'

Thompson provided the name of the support group, Home Assist, and the lady who called it in, Pamela Goldenberry.

'And Cheryl Palmer's home address?'

Thompson read it out and said he'd text it to her too. He'd also update the criminal database with the report.

'Thanks, Thompson, I owe you one.'

'That you do indeed.'

Thompson hung up and Roark dropped her phone into the compartment between the front seats.

Cheryl and Billy Davies. Cheryl and William Palmer.

It had to be the same mother and son abducted in 1994, the woman who ended up giving birth to Richard Stern's baby before they were rescued by Dane Cristian and his team.

'It has to be,' she said aloud.

Same first names, twenty-eight years apart. Names likely changed under Witness Protection.

The only inconsistency was that Cheryl and William Palmer lived in Manchester, not Liverpool, the city where Cheryl and Billy Davies had been living when they were abducted in 1994. That made sense given relocation was a major part of Witness Protection; it just wasn't consistent with their other findings, where the addresses of each victim, thirty years apart, were the same. This was compounded by the fact that the people living at the old Davies's address in Liverpool were alive and well and had not been targeted for murder.

Inconsistencies, but there was no denying the connections. Everything she now knew tied back, directly and indirectly, to James Stern, but she wasn't sure it was enough to pin him to the wall for seven murders.

It almost hung together. *Almost.*

Roark made a call to the station head in Manchester and said she'd send through the headshots the ME had taken of the unidentified deceased male in the cellar and the elderly woman taken to hospital. If he could contact the lady at Home Assist to help with a positive identification, that would be very helpful. When the station head agreed, Roark called ME Clayton, updated him and made the request for the photos. He said he'd do it immediately.

She called her team, asked for updates on the hunt for a man in his early forties going by the name of James Stern or Howard Bloch. They said they were making the enquiries and would get back to her ASAP.

Roark hung up, thought about calling Knight to give her an update, decided against it.

Eyes back on the road, hands on the steering wheel, she considered what she could do to firm up the case against James Stern. She had significant links tying back to him – his family home from 1995 where the bodies were found and the same addresses for the first two victims – but it didn't feel enough to put James in the frame for homicide beyond reasonable doubt.

If she could prove that Aaron Sparger and Jaime Collander were indeed the two young children who had been abducted in 1993, that could nail it down, provide a stronger connection, possibly be enough to allow James Stern to be charged for the murders. Roark could then obtain DNA samples and put him at the scene, case closed. However, there were only two ways to make that stronger connection: court order to open up the Witness Protection files for Ryan Cooper and Laura Kilpatrick or talk to the parents of Aaron and Jaime.

Roark tapped the steering wheel, wondering if even that connection, if established, would be enough.

She grimaced. There was one person she could call that would know the answers immediately, but it was both tricky and awkward, particularly after the disastrous call Roark had made to Julia last week.

Roark chastised herself. This was professional and they were adults. For an important case like this, surely they could put all that aside. Julia was a High Court judicial assistant; she would know the answer or have the means to find one.

Roark called, her heart beating heavily in her chest, but Julia did not answer. Roark left a voicemail that sounded both unprofessional and desperate. After hanging up, she beat herself up over it and then eventually shrugged it off. The message was clear enough; hopefully Julia would respond.

Next, she decided to call Detective Constable Knight. It was time to fill Gale in on what had been going on, which was a lot within the past twelve hours. Roark was also desperate to get an update on Knight's mother after her fall. It hadn't sounded good.

As with Julia, Knight's phone went to voicemail. Roark left a message, a brief update on the case and a heartfelt expression of best wishes for her and her mother.

Not her real mother, Roark thought as she hung up. Her adoptive mother.

Thoughts of Knight's adoption led to images of James Stern. Roark considered the different outcomes despite similar stories. Knight was adopted and turned out as an amazing individual – trustworthy, compassionate, smart and great at her job – whereas, if her current theory was correct, James Stern, also adopted, was now meting out a twisted sense of revenge.

Knight hadn't been kept in an attic for three years, Roark reminded herself.

As the image of the young boy in the attic came to mind, as recounted by Dane Cristian, wild-eyed and feral, Roark's phone rang.

'Yes,' Roark said.

'I think we've found him, ma'am.'

***

If Detective Inspector Krystal Roark held any spiritual beliefs or suppositions of any kind, she may have taken the fact that Howard Bloch lived in Basingstoke as a sign. When the call came through from Camberwell station that they had found only one Howard Bloch matching the age of Roark's suspect, she had just passed the turnoff for the southern England town.

A sign or not, she was grateful that the search had been quick and decisive. The James Stern search was taking a little longer and the names on the list reaching close to half a dozen, but this one felt right.

Howard Bloch, the name taken by James Stern when he settled in with his adopted family. It wasn't a common name and the description fit. It had to be him.

The town of Basingstoke also fit in with the profile she had built up based on the evidence. It was close to several key locations. The first car that had been stolen, the one that had been used to transfer Aaron Sparger from the van, was taken in Basingstoke. The Irvine residence in New Forest where the bodies had been found was only forty minutes away. It was also central as a base of operations, close enough to Bristol and London, the cities where the victims were abducted. Only Manchester was out of the way, four hours up the M5, but if he planned it perfectly, he'd have the time to travel back and forth, no problem.

It all seemed to hang together.

The town centre was busy with small pockets of built-up traffic. It was closing in on six o'clock and many commuters were making their way home. Roark negotiated traffic lights and roundabouts before she turned into a business park and found the blue and white building of Basingstoke Hampshire Constabulary.

In the car park, Roark found a space near the front of the station and switched off the engine. Lucas murmured something but settled back into low snoring in the rear seat. Roark would wake him in a minute.

First, she called Moody to let her know where she was and what she was doing. Moody's phone rang out – three for three – and Roark left a message. No doubt she was halfway to Bristol by now.

Roark made a second call, this one to New Forest station.

'Chief Inspector Cristian speaking.'

'Arne, it's me, Krystal Roark.'

'Krystal, is everything okay?'

'We've found him. Well, I'm hoping that's the case. Howard Bloch, forty years old, lives in Basingstoke. I'm at the station now.'

'You're bringing him in?'

'Yes, that's the plan,' she said. 'I won't charge him yet, I don't have enough to do that, but I can probe him a little.'

'Take it carefully,' Cristian said. 'There's a fine line that you'll have to negotiate around.'

'Got it,' she said. 'I can't wait anymore though.'

'Agreed.'

'I was wondering,' she said, 'if you could pave the way a little bit with the local Super. I'm not sure how helpful they'll be if I come in shouting out orders. I'd like them to pick Stern up, but I also need time to review his file before the interview.'

'Let me speak to him,' Cristian said. 'He'll be fine if he's given enough background. I'll get a room for you and a desk so you can review the file. I've sent your complete copy through.'

'That's great, Arne, I really appreciate it.'

'What's your approach?' he asked.

'I'm working on it, but key for me to begin with is establishing that he is the James Stern we are looking for. Once that's clear, I can zero in on the case.'

'I won't tell you how to do your job, Krystal, but can I offer some advice?'

'Yes, Arne, please. I value your input.'

'It's unlikely he'll be forthcoming with what he's done. You may get lucky, that he wants to confess his crimes, but again, unlikely. I do think he has something to say though. In my opinion, the note he gave you to come to New Forest could be more than just to show off his work. It could be he wanted you to see his father's house, make a connection, find out what had happened to him thirty years ago. The house holds a special meaning for him. The cellar where his father kept his victims; that's where James displayed the bodies. He may want to tell you his story, about that time in his life, for sympathy, understanding, justification, I don't know, but let him talk. If you get him talking, he may incriminate himself in the process.'

'Thank you, Arne. I agree that's a sound approach.'

'Okay,' Cristian said, 'I'll give Bob a call, see if he can show you some good old Basingstoke hospitality.'

'Appreciated.'

'No problem and good luck. Let me know how it goes.'

'Thank you,' Roark said and finished the call.

She briefly reflected on Arne Cristian. Smart, experienced, helpful. It had been interesting working with him, even for such a short time.

'What's happening?' Lucas said from the back seat, suddenly sitting bolt upright. His eyes were bloodshot.

'We're interviewing James Stern shortly. Get some more kip. I'll need you riding shotgun.'

Lucas said nothing and dropped back down onto the seat, his head up against his jacket rolled up into a makeshift pillow.

She'd rather Knight or Moody but for now, Lucas would do.

A text message came through on her phone. Arne Cristian.

You're all set. Robert McCallish is your man. Good luck.

Roark clicked off her phone and stepped out of the car.

CHAPTER 46

Fifteen minutes later, Roark was set up in a small office with a computer, working through the file on the Richard Stern case that Cristian had sent by email. A weak cup of coffee was half-drunk next to her keyboard and a new page open in her notebook.

Superintendent Robert McCallish was accommodating beyond what she was expecting but he had a look in his eye that held suspicion. Cristian may have given him some background, but McCallish would, ultimately, know nothing about what was going on once James Stern was brought into his station. That would make him nervous, but his friendship with Cristian paved the way for full cooperation. McCallish gave her an interview room and this desk and computer and agreed to have his officers pick up Stern for questioning.

Roark checked her phone. No messages, no missed calls. Nothing from Julia, Moody or Knight.

Lucas was due to join her from his sleep in the car. She hoped he was refreshed enough to help her out with the interview. She would need someone in there with her, as a wing man, and, if needed, as an unsettling, brooding presence to put Stern off his game. If Moody ever returned her message and made it here in time, he would sub out. For now, Lucas was her partner and she allowed him as much sleep as possible ahead of the interview.

McCallish's police had left the station to get Stern five minutes ago. That gave Roark about fifteen minutes before the Basingstoke police officers walked him into the station. She could keep him waiting a little longer, make him sweat in the interview room, but she needed as much time as possible with him, so she wouldn't delay for too long.

Roark opened the James Stern file on the computer screen and reviewed what she had, including what Dane had told her about the night they found Cheryl and William Davies. Overall, what Roark had in her armoury for the interview with James Stern was minimal. Ideally, she'd have more to work with, but there was an air of urgency now that she had identified her key suspect. She had to speak to him, find out what she could, get him talking about what happened with his father back in the mid-nineties, add more fuel to the fire. If she felt confident, she would take a step further and draw out what happened to Aaron Sparger, Jaime Collander and Cheryl and William Palmer. She would work him until she felt confident enough to charge the son of a bitch for multiple homicides.

As simple as that, Roark said, smiling wryly to herself.

ME Clayton called on her mobile just after she came back from refilling her coffee.

'Manchester police came back to me. Positive identification of Cheryl and William Palmer. They are already searching out relatives to inform them of the news.'

'Okay, that's great Clayton, thank you. Any update on Mrs Palmer?'

'She's still in critical condition at General. Doctors believe she is slowly slipping into a coma, body shutting down. At her age, I don't hold out much hope for her.'

'Right. Okay, give me an update if I need to add an eighth murder charge to this.'

'You getting anywhere?'

'Maybe.'

'Okay, good luck. I'll keep you posted.'

'Thank you.'

Roark placed her phone on the table. She hoped Cheryl pulled through, not just for the sake of the sixty-six-year-old victim, but for the case. She could be an eyewitness to the attack on her and her son. That would trump all other evidence that they had, enough to arrest James Stern on the spot, even if for just one crime, and then Roark could make the case, get DNA samples, link him to the murders, put him away for good. As it was, it was going to be a struggle to establish enough reasonableness to arrest him for the crimes committed based on what she had to hand.

Less groundbreaking but just as important, Cheryl Palmer in recovery could also confirm that she was indeed Cheryl Davies, that her and her now deceased son had been abducted by Richard Stern back in 1994. That would set out a clear motive for James Stern, a solid connection that, along with the weaker connections they had made to the other two abductions and murders, could prove enough to charge James Stern and arrest him for the homicides he had committed.

Unfortunately, Roark couldn't wait. Cheryl Palmer may not pull through. ME Clayton wasn't positive that she would. She couldn't rely on her recovery. Roark had to act now.

Roark took a sip of her coffee and grimaced at the taste.

Thinking of Cheryl Palmer, something Dane Cristian had said over the picnic table in New Forest suddenly popped in her head and Roark knew she had a way of confirming, just short of for certain, whether the Cheryl Palmer identified as the elderly lady taken from the cellar in New Forest was Cheryl Davies, the woman abducted by Richard Stern.

She called the Manchester police and asked for the number of Pamela Goldenberry, the supervisor who worked at Home Assist, the charity that had supported Cheryl Palmer with home care. They gave her the number and Roark called it immediately. This time, the call was answered.

After a quick introduction, and a thank-you for identifying the bodies, Roark cut to the chase.

'Mrs Goldenberry, are you able to divulge the reason why Cheryl Palmer required the help of Home Assist?'

'I guess so,' Pamela said, uncertainty in her voice. 'She had her son there, of course, but he is on the spectrum. I mean, he was.'

Her voice quivered and it took a moment for her to continue.

'He couldn't help her much, with looking after the home, looking after herself, so we sent Teresa there, a lovely girl. They really got along. It's such a shame what happened to Teresa. Do you know what this is all about? Did you catch the killer?'

'Pamela, does Mrs Palmer have any physical disabilities?'

'I'm sorry, yes, she does. She's blind.'

Pamela Goldenberry continued to talk, asking how Mrs Palmer was, if she was okay, but Roark wasn't listening. Instead, she was hearing Dane in her head, describing the moment when Cheryl Davies walked out of Richard Stern's house, in the rain and wind, holding a baby to her chest, eyes straight ahead, tears running down her face.

The poor woman was blind. Hydrofluoric acid. The bastard had blinded her with rust remover.

Fumbling while she typed in the number, she called ME Clayton back.

'Mrs Palmer's blind,' she said abruptly.

'Okay,' Clayton said hesitantly.

'Does she have any signs of scarring or burns around her face, around her eyes?'

'Indeed she does. Significant scarring. Quite old wounds, I'd say. What's this about?'

Lucas opened the door to the office and poked his head in.

Roark ignored Clayton on the phone and looked up at him.

'It's him,' she said. 'I'm fucking certain of it. It's him.'

'Well,' Lucas said, rubbing sleep out of his left eye, 'he's here.'

Chapter 47

He resists them, flays at their outreached hands, bites at their outstretched fingers. They want to take him away, but he does not want to go. He does not want to leave here. He does not want to leave his father.

His father is dead.

'Howard, did you kill William Davies?'

The other children, the women, that baby, they are no longer in his home. For so long, that was all he ever wanted, and now he has it.

But his father is dead.

'I don't buy this tortured and tormented soul routine, Howard, not one bit. Your silence tells me more than you know. It tells me it's all bullshit, this whole act.'

A hand grips his arm, cool and tight. He tries to claw it away, scrape at it, bite it, but another arm is around his stomach, one around his mouth.

'But if that's the way you are going to play it, that's fine. Let me talk to the real person in this room. Let me talk to James Stern, the boy from the attic.'

He struggles but they are too strong. A man with kind blue eyes squats near him, talks to him, cares for him, but the boy closes his eyes.

'Why did you kill them, James? Why did you kill the children? Was it because your father loved them more than you? Was that it? Were you jealous?'

He keeps his eyes closed shut and goes limp. He has no choice now. As he is lifted, he wonders why he feels sad. Not just because of his father. No, it's something else.

'Ryan Cooper, Laura Kilpatrick, William Davies. Why did you kill them, James? Why?'

He opens his eyes and stares at the ceiling of the attic, sees the beams and wood, cobwebs and spiders. He watches the attic pass above him and he realises why he is sad.

'Mr Stern? Answer my questions.'

'Detective.'

'No, Lucas, I'm sick of this. It's time for James Stern to talk to us about what he has done. It's time we got to the truth. Isn't that right, James? That's what you want, isn't it? To tell us why you did it?'

As they carry him across the threshold, he wriggles around and stares over the shoulder of the policeman carrying him and looks back into his home.

'James?'

He stares back into the attic and understands.

'James?'

He says nothing. He keeps his eyes closed. He keeps the shadows over him like a cloak.

He doesn't want to leave. He wants to stay in the dark spaces.

***

Roark stormed out of the interview room and slammed the opposite wall. Lucas followed, closing the door behind him.

'Fucking hell,' Roark said, wringing her left hand. She dropped her pen, notepad, and audio recorder on a small table sitting out of place in the corridor.

'That could've gone better,' Lucas said, his voice deadpan.

'Fuck off, Lucas. You saw what went on in there,' she said, pointing at the closed door. She wiped her forehead, removing a thin film of sweat. She felt out of breath and her heart was racing.

Lucas said nothing. He had picked up the files off the interview desk when Roark had left abruptly and now put them on the table.

Roark took a moment, studied him, turned away as he backed up against the opposite wall in the corridor.

Lucas was right; it could've gone better. She had to admit that she lost it a little bit at the end, and if she was honest with herself, she knew why. Over the entire hour or so they had spoken, she had been given very little by James Stern, insights here and there, but nothing of weight, not the full confession or gloating grandstanding she had hoped for, and when he'd clammed up at the end, her temper got the better of her.

It was the unspoken words, the hesitations, the moments of silence between answers, that told her, without a doubt, that James Stern was the murderer, and there was now a real chance he was going to get away with it.

'I'm going to arrest him,' she said suddenly, standing up straight. 'Right now.'

Lucas scratched the back of his neck.

'Do you think that's wise?'

'You were there, Lucas, you saw it. The photo of Sparger, Corey Whitman.' She clicked her fingers and pointed again. 'Jaime Collander. He hesitated each time. I could see it in his eyes, he knew those people.'

'He's unhinged, I'll give you that. You would be too, if that happened to you as a kid.'

'That's the point, Lucas. He was abused as a child. His father locked him up in an attic and tried to start a family with other kids. He fucking hates those kids for what happened to him. There's your motive.'

Lucas cringed, his moustache dancing above his upper lip.

'Come on, Lucas. You saw his reactions when I mentioned those kids, when I spoke about his father.'

'I just don't see it.'

Roark shook her head and let out a short breath.

'I'm going to arrest him,' she said again.

'Review the audio, Roark,' Lucas said. 'I don't think it is as clear cut as you think. He doesn't incriminate himself in the slightest.'

'No alibi for Sparger and Collander,' she said, counting them off on her fingers. 'He drives the same type of van used in the crimes, he hasn't been working lately due to having some bullshit sickness, which gives him freedom and time to move around. It's him.'

'Listen to the tape.'

'And he knew the names of those kids. All of them. Ryan Cooper, Laura Kilpatrick, William Davies. Why would he still remember those names unless he had been planning something against them?'

'He knew first names. Not unreasonable for him to remember those.'

'Bullshit.'

'You're forgetting the evidence, Roark.'

She waved him away, part of her knowing his argument was logical, but not giving in to it. Motive was leading the case right now, but she didn't have anything else.

'Anyway,' Lucas said, 'we don't even know if our victims are these people, these kids. You said it yourself, the connections are not enough.'

Roark gathered up her things off the table.

'I'm going to arrest him,' she said, her back to Lucas. 'I'm going to arrest him, take a DNA sample, and match it to all those trace samples we have from the crime scenes. Then you'll see.'

She moved to the interview room door.

'I think that's a bad idea.'

She stopped across from him.

'Based on what I heard,' Lucas continued, 'those DNA samples would be thrown out of court on the basis that you did not have enough evidence to arrest him in the first place. They'd be inadmissible, and you'd lose your one chance.'

Roark was about to respond when she saw DI Clarice Moody bustling down the corridor towards them, visibly exasperated.

'I'm so sorry I'm late,' she said, out of breath. 'I was almost back at the station when I got your message. Had to do an about turn and hightail it down the M4. What's going on here?'

'She's about to make a mistake,' Lucas said.

Roark gave him a look, but he had her worried now. Lucas hardly uttered a sound unless he was passing wind. When he was this talkative it meant he was certain what he was saying was right.

'Did you get my text?' Moody said, replacing a lock of hair behind her ear. Her cheeks were flushed with exertion.

'No,' Roark said and rummaged in her jacket pocket for her phone.

'Jaime Collander wasn't in the Witness Protection programme.'

'What?'

'I spoke with her mother. I had to arrange a viewing of the body, so Jaime could be identified. I had to ask her, whether they'd been in the programme, whether she knew Richard Stern. She didn't. She was upset obviously. Looked at me like I was crazy.'

Roark stared at Moody for a moment, letting that sink in. Jaime Collander wasn't in a Witness Protection programme. She never changed her name. She was never Laura Kilpatrick.

'Doesn't matter,' Roark said, dismissively. 'Her address in Bristol is still the same as Laura Kilpatrick. That's enough to link it back to James Stern even if he didn't get his intended victim.'

Lucas scoffed, a strange sound coming from him.

'Have you spoken to Aaron Sparger's parents?' Moody asked.

'Not yet. Doesn't matter. Cheryl and William Palmer, that's the link. They are the same two who were abducted by Richard Stern back in 1994. One hundred percent certain.'

'Listen to yourself,' Lucas said. 'You're jumping to conclusions.'

'Is that him in there? James Stern?' Moody said, pointing to the interview room.

'Yes,' Roark said, out of breath.

'Has he given you anything?'

'No,' Lucas said.

'That's not entirely true,' Roark said. 'He has no alibi and he is clearly shaken up by the questioning.'

'Doesn't mean anything,' Lucas piped up.

'Can I go in? Meet our friend?' Moody asked, already moving towards the door.

'Be my guest,' Roark said.

As Moody opened the door and slipped in, Roark looked at Lucas. He shook his head and moved into the room behind Moody.

'Fuck,' Roark said after the door closed. 'Fuck, fuck, fuck.'

She looked at her mobile, saw the network bars in the top right of the screen were non-existent. There was no network down this corridor, none in the interview room. Otherwise, she would've heard Moody's text come through.

'Damn it,' she said and stuffed her things into her jacket while she headed down the corridor.

As she pushed through the door into the reception area, she saw Superintendent Robert McCallish talking to the desk sergeant.

'You done?' he asked.

'Not yet,' she replied. 'Excuse me.'

She stepped out of the station into the cool night. There had been rain while she'd been inside interviewing Stern, the roads dark and wet. The handrails along the ramp leading down to the carpark held droplets of water. Overhead clouds rolled, dark in the night, threatening more.

As soon as the four bars on her network appeared on her phone, Roark received Moody's text and several other messages, including notification of a voicemail. The number for the voicemail was Julia's. Roark quickly pressed the notification on her screen and listened to the message.

'Krystal, it's Julia. I received your message. Sorry I'm only just replying, I was in court. If I heard you correctly, you are asking whether it's possible to obtain a court order to reveal the identity of a witness under protection. Not easy. We take protecting witnesses very seriously and there must be a strong reason to reveal their identity, even in a closed court.

'I'd say the likelihood of using someone in Witness Protection to make a conviction is very low. You'd only be given this option if there is substantial evidence to suggest that revealing their identity will help stop a crime from occurring, and there will always be an argument to say that if you have that substantial evidence, you probably don't need to reveal the witness.

'Based on your message, you are well short of going down this route, and for what it's worth, you don't have enough evidence right now to have a conviction hold up in court. I'd suggest asking the parents of the victims or, if your one surviving victim pulls through, ask her. Even if you get something from that, you need to work this one a bit harder, Kris.

'Sorry, I couldn't be of more help. Good luck.'

The message ended with a resounding click.

'Fuck,' she said. The news wasn't good, and Julia's deadpan delivery made it worse.

It started to rain. Roark retreated into the station. The desk sergeant looked up when she walked in, nodded. McCallish was nowhere to be seen. She passed the desk and pushed through the door to the interview rooms.

Moody and Lucas were standing at the end of the corridor, talking quietly. As Roark strode down towards them, Julia's message echoing in her ears, she felt her chances of arresting Stern slipping away. She knew in the pit of her stomach that James Stern was the man she was after, but could she make the charges stick? Doubt was starting to creep in, and she wondered whether she could, objectively, arrest this bastard on the evidence she had and the interview she'd just conducted.

They both looked at her as she reached them.

'What do you think?' she asked Moody.

'He's a bit of a mess, right? Disturbed to say the least. He didn't respond to me at all. I assume he hasn't had anyone with him during the interview?'

'No,' Roark said, 'he denied legal representation.'

'I was thinking more of his mental state. He probably should have someone with him.'

Roark scoffed, mimicking Lucas.

'He's not that bad,' she said.

'He's not great.'

'So, you're with Lucas. You don't think I should arrest him either?' Roark said, trying not to sound confrontational.

Moody kept eye contact and said, 'I'd have to listen to the tape of your interview but from what Lucas has said, I think you need a warrant. Just to be sure.'

'I think we may have moved too early,' Lucas added.

'Well, thanks for that timely advice, Graham,' Roark said. She pulled out her phone again to make a call, saw the poor network coverage again, swore. 'Look, this guy has killed seven people in the past three weeks. Who knows what will happen if we don't arrest him now. In my book, that's enough justification.'

Moody didn't like it; it was written all over her face.

'I'm not sure about that,' Moody said. 'I know our theory about Stern killing those kids is hanging by a thread, but it if is true, there's no one left for him to kill, right? They're all dead. He's done what he set out to do. Whether he's killed the right people or not, it's over. There is no urgency other than to make sure we catch the guy and put him away.'

'There's still the baby,' Roark said.

'What baby?'

'Cheryl Davies's child, conceived with her rapist, Richard Stern.'

'Come on, you don't think—'

'I don't know, Clarice,' Roark said, cutting Moody off. 'I don't know.'

As Roark turned away and walked back up the corridor, Moody shouted out after her.

'Where are you going?'

'To make a call,' she shouted back.

Chapter 48

By the time she was outside again, the rain was coming down in buckets. She found some shelter under a gutter along the side of the station's roof, one or two drops finding its way into her face as she dialled a number.

It's slipping away, she thought. He's going to get away with this, she could feel it.

But maybe not.

'Clayton.'

'Hi Doc, it's me again, Roark.'

'Good timing.'

'How so?' She felt her heart thrumming in her chest.

'I think our survivor may pull through.'

'She's awake?'

'Not yet, but her signs have suddenly stabilised. She's still in a prolonged loss of consciousness, but it's looking better.'

'That's great news, Doc. Thank you.'

'My pleasure. Anything else I can help you with?'

'It's not going so great here. I may have to let my suspect go.'

'Bugger.'

'Yeah. Could you arrange some protection for Mrs Palmer? Just in case. I don't know what this guy is capable of if he finds out she survived.'

'Sure, I'll do that.'

'And please keep me updated on her recovery.'

She hung up, pocketed her phone, and leaned up against the station wall.

She hated to admit it, Moody and Lucas were right. She didn't have enough to arrest Stern right now, not under her own authority. A court approved warrant, just like Moody said, would be the better option. If she could get it, of course, which said a lot. If she thought she couldn't get a warrant from a judge with what she had now, she shouldn't be arresting James Stern without it.

She had to remind herself, she went into the interview with little evidence that she could tie back to James Stern. Despite how certain she was after speaking with him, that hadn't changed. She was still short of key evidence, and the connections she thought she had to Aaron Sparger and Jaime Collander appeared to have been broken, all at least were barely hanging by a thread.

It was up to Cheryl Palmer. Speak with her and she could serve James Stern up on a platter. Palmer may be able to identify him as her attacker, if not by sight, but by other means. She could also confirm beyond any doubt she was Cheryl Davies, the woman kept in the cellar all those years ago, kept by Richard Stern and, after thirty years, targeted by his son.

That would be more than enough for a judge, Roark decided. She just needed to speak with Cheryl Palmer as soon as she woke. She just had to hope that would be soon.

Moody and Lucas were still standing outside the interview room when Roark returned.

'Cheryl Palmer is going to pull through,' she said.

'That's great,' Moody replied.

'She's still in a coma, but the Doc is positive that she will wake.'

Lucas nodded; Moody smiled.

'You are both right. I don't have enough to arrest him. I need to speak with Mrs Palmer. I need to speak with Aaron Sparger's parents. I need enough to convince a judge.'

'Excellent,' Moody said.

'But I'm not letting this bastard out of my sight.'

Roark put her phone away and opened the interview room door. She heard Moody's sharp intake of breath but ignored it. They obviously didn't trust she wouldn't do something rash, and that was fair enough. Roark felt ready to push boundaries, she knew Moody could see it in her eyes. This was Moody's case too, so she had a right to be nervous.

James Stern didn't move when Roark stepped into the room. He kept his head down on the table, hands clasped over his ears. His left foot was tapping furiously. Sweat matted his hair across his forehead.

Roark kept the door open, so Lucas and Moody could bear witness.

'You're free to go, Mr Bloch.'

He didn't move. His foot didn't miss a beat.

'Howard?' Roark said, forcefully raising her voice.

He lifted his head and dropped his hands in one quick motion. His eyes darted around, then squinted, as if he'd just awoken from a restless sleep. He rubbed each eye with his right hand in slow motion.

'You can go,' Roark repeated.

He flinched as comprehension seeped through.

'Oh, really?' he said, his voice croaking.

Roark stood aside and with a flamboyant wave of her arm, she proffered the open door to the corridor outside.

'Thank you for your time, Mr Bloch. I am sorry to have kept you.'

She could hear the sarcasm dripping from her words and wondered if anyone else could. She didn't care. She knew this was the right thing to do but she didn't have to like it.

He slowly stood up, pushing the chair back with his legs.

'That's okay,' he said softly, tentatively.

'A police officer will drive you home.'

He nodded and moved around the table. He kept close to the edge, staring at the far corner of the room to Roark's right with caution.

Part of the act, Roark thought. Afraid of his own shadows.

He stopped near where Roark stood, stared out into the corridor where he could see Lucas and Moody.

'I hope you got everything you wanted,' he said sincerely.

Roark wanted to punch him in the throat.

'Of course,' she said.

'I hope you find the man who did all of those things.'

'We'll do our best. I'd really appreciate it if you made yourself available for further discussions.'

He looked down at Roark's shoes and nodded. He waited for a moment, almost waiting for permission, before he exited the interview room.

'Oh, Mr Bloch, just one more thing,' she said.

He turned back, his hair covering his eyes.

'Just as a precaution, would you give me authority to take fingerprints and a DNA sample from you? Just so we can eliminate you as a suspect on this case?'

He looked at her feet again, seemingly considering the request, before he shook his head.

'I'd rather not.'

'It would mean a lot to our investigation, and I would see it as a personal favour to me. It would be greatly appreciated.'

He said, 'No, thank you,' and began walking down the corridor.

'Didn't think so,' she said, under her breath. 'Lucas, can you escort Mr Bloch out of the station and see that one of Superintendent McCallish's officers drives him home? Thank you.'

Lucas drudged off down the corridor behind James Stern, grumbling to himself.

Moody stepped up to the doorway.

'If he's the killer, we'll get him,' she said. 'We just need to bide our time.'

Roark looked back into the interview room to see if anything was left behind. Just the three cups Lucas had brought in during the interview, including the one Stern hadn't touched. He wouldn't handle the photos of the victims and the van either. Intentionally, Roark thought. Not giving us any physical evidence we can cross-check against the crime scene, even if it was admissible in court, which it wouldn't be. He's not stupid. Despite what Moody and Lucas said, Roark still thought it had all been an act.

'I'm going to follow him, stake out his flat tonight,' she said. 'He'll be confident he got away with it, so that may make him sloppy, make a mistake.'

Moody made a humming sound Roark hadn't heard from her before in their short time together, but she knew what it meant.

'I'll keep you up to date,' Roark said, and she moved past Moody and out of the interview room.

'I'm just picturing a basket overloaded with eggs,' Moody said as she fell in behind Roark. 'We haven't really considered other possibilities, have we?'

Roark stopped and put a hand on Moody's shoulder.

'I've still got you and Lucas, right? Pursuing all those *other* leads we have.'

'Your sarcasm is good, but it needs work, mind. I'm the queen of sarcasm, so I'll give you about a seven out of ten for that one.'

Roark smiled and patted her shoulder.

'I need to watch him, just for a bit,' she said.

'Understood,' Moody said. 'Go, before he disappears on you.'

They walked side by side down the corridor, the edge of tension that had developed easing.

'We did alright today,' Moody said.

'I guess,' Roark allowed.

'I mean us, working together. We'll obviously keep in touch on this, but if you're ever down in Bristol, come see me, we'll go out for a pint or two. When it's all over, of course.'

'I'd like that,' Roark said.

Roark pushed through the door, hoping to see that Stern was either still in reception or out in the car park. The desk sergeant was on the phone. Lucas was walking back in, his hair and moustache dripping wet, the shoulders of his jacket damp.

'Has he gone?' Roark asked, looking past Lucas.

'Just pulling out now.'

Roark could see through the rain-streaked window one of the blue and whites exiting the carpark. It paused at the street and then drove away. Roark could just make out a figure in the back seat.

'Okay,' Roark said.

'Detective Inspector,' the desk sergeant called.

They all turned. He was holding up the phone in his hand.

'It's for you,' he said, motioning towards Roark.

'Who is it?'

'A woman. Alice Knight? Says she knows you.'

Roark first felt relief. Alice Knight. If she was calling, her fall hadn't been too bad, and she had recovered. Then she thought it odd that Gale's mother would be calling her at all.

Roark stepped to the other side of the desk and took the phone.

'Hello, Mrs Knight?'

'Oh, Krystal, I'm so glad I caught you.'

Her voice quivered, shaken, weak.

'Is everything alright? I heard you had a fall,' Roark said, turning around to face Moody and Lucas. Moody motioned she'd follow Stern and ducked out of the station. Lucas followed forlornly like an old dog.

'No, no, I'm okay. I – I just haven't heard from Florence. Is she with you?'

Roark frowned.

'No, she's not.'

'The lady at the police station said she was with you.'

'She has been working a case with me, but she went to see you earlier this morning. I haven't heard from her since. When did she leave?'

'Sorry, I don't understand. I haven't seen her today.'

Roark swapped the phone to her other ear.

'I'm sorry, Mrs Knight, you haven't seen her today? She left this morning, after your fall.'

'Fall?' Alice said. 'I didn't have a fall. She was supposed to come to dinner tonight and she usually calls if she can't. I know she's working late on your case, but I haven't heard from her.'

Alice's voice was suddenly faint and distant as Roark stared out the police station window. Something wasn't right.

'Mrs Knight.'

'Alice, please.'

'I'm sorry, Alice, Florence didn't come into the station today. She called first thing this morning saying she'd received a call from your local paramedics. You'd taken a fall.'

'That didn't happen,' Alice said, concern in her voice. 'I didn't have a fall. Krystal? What's going on?'

'One moment, Alice,' Roark said.

Cradling the receiver in the crook of her neck, she pulled out her mobile phone and checked for messages. Nothing. She had full network coverage but there was no response to any of her texts during the day. No calls returned. She remembered making a call to Gale earlier and the phone had rung out.

'I'm worried,' Alice said when Roark came back on the call.

'It's okay, Alice, leave this with me. I'll find her.'

'Why would she not call me? She always calls me,' Alice said, her voice strained.

'This case,' Roark said, instinctively expressing a rational explanation without entirely believing it, 'has been quite difficult. She may have needed some time to herself.'

'But not call? Why wouldn't she call?'

Good question, Roark thought.

'Give me your number and I'll give you a call back in a few minutes.'

Roark handed the phone back to the desk sergeant with a thanks and tried Gale's number, walking to the station window. The phone rang out as Roark watched the rain come down outside. The call connected to Knight's voicemail, and she left a message for her to call either her mother or Roark immediately.

'We're worried about you,' she said, finishing the message.

Saying it out loud gave her a sick feeling in her stomach. She realised she'd been worrying about her for most of the day. All the events of the day – the siege on the Irvine house, Dane's story about Richard Stern and his son, the bodies in the cellar, the interview with James Stern – had monopolised her attention. She hadn't consciously noticed that there was something digging at her each time she sent a text to Gale and did not receive a reply. It was Roark's concern for Gale's mother that had given her that uneasiness, but she knew now that part of it was Knight's lack of response. She was on her phone so much, it was so unlike her not to return a message, whatever the situation.

Something was wrong.

Roark made a call to the front desk at Camberwell.

'Nope,' the desk sergeant said, 'she hasn't been in all day. Her mother called, looking for her.'

'Yes, I've spoken to her, thanks. Can you issue a message out to everyone, ask them if they've seen her and if they do, to call me? Tell them it's urgent.'

'Right on it.'

Roark's message via the desk sergeant to everyone working out of Camberwell station would let them know that Gale's disappearance was cause for concern. Knight would be royally pissed off, embarrassed and angry, if she was sitting in a café somewhere or skiving off at the local Picturehouse and the police jumped on her as if she was a suspect, but Roark didn't think that would happen. It was that feeling in her gut, that something was not right.

Roark called Alice Knight back, said, 'Are you at home?'

'Yes.'

'I'm coming over.'

'Did you hear from her? Is she okay?'

'No, I haven't been able to reach her. Please stay calm, Alice. I am sure there's an explanation for this.'

Roark checked the time on the clock above the Basingstoke station desk sergeant. Almost nine o'clock. Alice lived in Maidstone, an hour south-east of London. It would take time to get there, but there was no other option.

'Alice, I will be with you in a couple of hours. Keep the phone lines open just in case Florence calls. I'll send a car around to keep you company, okay?'

'She's been upset lately,' Alice said, on the verge of tears. 'Worried about me, worried about other things.'

Snippets of Roark's conversation with Gale only a few nights ago came to mind: her desire to have a family, her adoption, the impact on her of her biological mother giving her up at such an early age, that feeling of rejection. She'd fixated a little on the response of Jaime Collander's mother, how distraught she had been over her missing daughter, trying to understand how any mother could give up on a child like her mother had.

'I'm worried she's gone and done something silly,' Alice said.

'Florence is a strong woman,' Roark said. 'She can handle anything. They'll be an explanation for this, Alice, please don't worry.'

'Okay,' Alice said, quietly.

'Okay, I'll be there as fast as I can. I'll send a car over immediately.'

'Thank you, Krystal.'

'Let me know if you hear anything. I will do the same.'

'I will.'

'She'll be fine, Alice, I promise.'

Roark finished the call and felt sick at lying to Alice Knight.

Gale, where the fuck are you?

CHAPTER 49

The four-door Hyundai car taken from the Camberwell station that Roark had effectively commandeered on a permanent basis was perfect for her height. Comfortable and roomy, she didn't feel squeezed in, and with the seat all the way back, the leg room under the steering wheel and dash was the best she could hope for. The windscreen wipers, on the other hand, were shite, and struggled to give Roark a clear view through the tumultuous rain that lashed the car.

The steering could be better too. She felt the wheels slide on more than one occasion, not responding to her attempts to course correct the car into the far-right lane of the M3. When she passed long-haul trucks, the rain abated for a moment, but the wind picked up and she almost found herself ending up in the grassy embankment in the middle of the motorway.

Focussing more on her phone calls rather than the road didn't help.

'I'm heading back to London,' Roark said, finding herself shouting into the phone attached to the dash, fighting against the sound of the rain against her driver's side window. 'My colleague's in trouble.'

'*Trouble?*' Moody said, her voice tinny over the phone's speaker and riddled with static. '*Is everything alright?*'

'I hope so. I haven't heard from her all day which is unusual. I'll fill you in later. I know it's late, but can you watch Stern a bit longer?'

'*I can give you a couple more hours, then I must head back to Bristol. I'm sorry, but I've got to get home.*'

'I understand,' Roark said and jerked the steering wheel away from the centre lane and a cautious driver in a white Volkswagen. 'Has Stern done anything?'

'*Nothing. Officers dropped him off and not too long after, Stern turned his lights off. Calling it a day, I suspect. I've got the front entrance covered.*'

'Where's Lucas?'

'*Roaming the surrounding streets, drenched to the bone the last time I saw him walk past. He's pretty pissed off. His idea, mind. Worried about Stern sneaking out the back door.*'

That was Lucas for you. He was lazy, disgustingly unhygienic and could not be bothered most of the time, but he was loyal to the job and, even if he disagreed with Roark on this and saw a stakeout as pointless, he wasn't going to do it half-arsed.

'I'll talk to him later. I'm hoping to be back in a few hours.'

'I called McCallish. He's okayed a car for Lucas after I leave, on loan.'

'You're a star, Moody, thank you.'

'Drive safe out there, Roark, and I hope your partner is okay.'

'Thanks, Moody,' Roark said and reached over to end the call.

A spray from the eighteen-wheeler she was overtaking hit the Hyundai like a breaking wave. Roark gripped the steering wheel, her knuckles turning white.

'Jesus,' she said, tapping the brakes.

A sign for the M25 flashed above her, another for Thorpe Park Resort. She'd be off the M3 soon, but the M25 would be no better. Roark hoped the late hour would mean less traffic. She prayed for no delays caused by road accidents.

After joining the M25 heading south five minutes later, she made more calls. One to the desk sergeant in Camberwell to see if there had been any word, another to Knight's mobile. The desk sergeant had no updates and Knight's phone rang out again. Roark left another message, this time more frantic, desperate. The weather and treacherous driving conditions weren't helping, but Roark was on edge, eager to get to Maidstone, eager to find out what had happened to her partner.

Scenarios played out in her mind like a horror anthology show on Netflix. A car accident was a possibility, nothing more than a lost phone was a hopeful outcome. Roark had sent a car to Knight's flat in Denmark Hill just in case Gale was lying on the floor after an electric shock or a heart attack or something. The officer's had called to say her flat was empty. They'd broken in when there was no response, to find a relatively tidy home, no sign of a struggle, no sign of a panicked exit, no suicide note.

That last thought stuck in her head until she swore at herself to shut the fuck up. She didn't want to think about that. Surely there was nothing to put Gale in that frame of mind.

Unless, Roark thought, it was about her mother. Her biological mother.

Traffic built up just north of Leatherhead, slowing to a crawl. Roark slammed the steering wheel and shouted at the car in front of her. She was about to turn on the car's built-in sirens when the traffic picked up again and she was moving.

The rain reduced in intensity improving visibility. The headlights and rear lights of the surrounding cars were blurry and streaked across Roark's eyes. The wipers now seemed to be stuck on the one setting and the insistent rubbing on the drying windscreen was driving Roark nuts, but there were still showers around and Roark couldn't afford to turn them off.

Past Leatherhead and Roark entered the Surrey Hills. High trees and bushes surrounded the motorway, protecting the cars from the inclement weather. Driving was easier and the traffic moved quickly.

Roark called Alice to see if she was okay and if she'd had any word from Knight. There had been nothing, but having two officers with her, parked outside her home in Maidstone, had calmed her a little. Roark said she was not far off.

She made another call. Moody and Lucas were still outside Stern's house. It was dark and quiet, no sign of Roark's main suspect. Moody said she'd stay for another hour. Roark thanked her again, asked to pass on that same message to Lucas. The man was wet, tired and far from home, going beyond the call of duty today, not having a proper sleep in thirty-six hours. He'd be hungry, too, no doubt. She'd have to make it up to him somehow.

The motorway split between the M25 to Stansted Airport and the M26 to Maidstone. Roark stayed in the right lane and passed a turnoff to Sevenoaks before typing in Alice Knight's address into the Maps app on her phone. She didn't know this area very well and Gale's mother was in some hidden corner of the countryside between West and East Farleigh, not too far from the River Medway. It was out of the way, but idyllic and quiet for someone living alone. An hour out of London, it didn't stop Gale seeing her mother, staying over on weeknights when it was too late to return to her flat in Denmark Hill. They were close, mother and daughter, which made the current lack of communication between them more ominous.

The directions took her across the River Medway at Teston, the water on either side of a narrow single lane bridge pitched in darkness. It was past ten o'clock and Roark was in proper country now, only her lights and those of the occasional oncoming car, illuminating the way.

The rain had stopped and Roark turned off her annoying wipers. Her headlights flashed on a sign for West Farleigh. She wasn't far; seven minutes per her phone. She called Alice again to let her know she was moments away, but there was no answer. Roark felt anxiety spill over in her stomach and she stepped on the accelerator, almost taking out a fox dashing across the lane.

Roark pulled out into a two-lane blacktop and sped along the road, keeping an eye on the map on her phone, shining brightly in the car. A high hedge and the occasional house lined the road to her right, a low fence and open fields to her left.

Up ahead, blue and red lights flashing.

'Shit,' Roark said aloud and slowed down.

One officer stood next to the panda car, waving her past. She pulled up next to him, rolled down the window. The officer, who looked fresh out of the College of Policing, walked around to her side of the car with an air of authority. He paused when he saw her warrant card, held up above the open window.

'Ma'am,' the officer said, 'we thought you might come through here.'

'What is it?' Roark said.

'Call came into the local station, car found down near the Medway,' he said, pointing over Roark's bonnet. 'Detective Constable Knight's car, ma'am. The mother identified it.'

Roark reversed in a spray of mud, sending the officer back a step. She wrenched the car around into the narrow slip road and accelerated along the bumpy, mud-clogged surface. It was an access road, one car width across, her headlights illuminating open fields on either side. She had to slow down to avoid coming off the side, into a ditch. She gritted her teeth, negotiating a pothole filled with water.

The road sloped downwards and a hedge, about six feet tall, rose to her right. No streetlights, no houses, everywhere outside of her two beams of light was pitch black. Spots of rain peppered the windscreen, but she kept the wipers off.

Ahead, she could see the red lights of a parked car. The driver's side door was open, the interior lit up. She stood on the brakes, slid a little sideways, the front of the car scratching along the hedge, and came to a stop.

A gust of wind blew rain into her face as she stepped out of the car. She wiped it away and hurried towards the parked police car, trying to maintain her professionalism in the face of personal tragedy.

She wiped the thought from her mind like the rain from her face.

Alice Knight sat in the front seat of the police car, her feet out on the wet road, her head in her hands. A female police officer squatted in front of Alice as Roark approached, turned to look at the noise of her feet on the wet road, stood up straight.

'Ma'am.'

'Constable,' Roark nodded.

'We've found—' but she stopped when Roark held up her hand.

'One moment.'

The Detective Inspector took the police officer's place at Alice's feet. Alice looked across at her, face wet with rain, eyes red with tears, her face ashen. Her shoulders collapsed when she saw Roark. Roark caught her before she fell forward. Her frame was petite, and Roark could feel her shoulder blades through a thin woollen cardigan.

'Is it Florence?' Roark asked quietly.

Alice lifted her head, a pained expression across her face.

'There's no sign of her, ma'am,' the officer said behind Roark, her voice faint behind a gust of wind.

Heavy drops patted on Roark's jacket.

'What has she done?' Alice said, a sob stuck in her throat. 'Why?'

'It's okay, Alice. I'll take care of this. Please, you're catching a cold. Let me close the door.'

'Can you find her?' Alice said. 'Please find her.'

'The officer will join you in a minute, Alice,' Roark said. She softly squeezed Alice's shoulder. 'I'll find her.'

With Roark's assistance, Alice lifted her legs into the police car and Roark closed the door. She turned to the officer.

'What's happening?'

The constable wiped rain from her neck and looked out through a break in the hedge. Roark followed her gaze and could see that it wasn't a natural break. Something had forced its way through the brush.

'There's a car beyond this hedge, parked up near the edge of the river. A Toyota. Blue, two-door. Mrs Knight identified the vehicle as her daughter's.'

'Any sign of DC Knight?'

'No, ma'am. We have officers searching along the river, but it's dark out there.'

'Who called it in?'

'Nearby farmer, checking his property. I think he saw the headlights from his house.'

'Stay with her,' Roark said, motioning towards the car.

'Yes, ma'am.'

Roark ducked through the hole in the hedge, which was wide but not tall enough for her. About the size of a car, she thought. Gale's car.

Beyond the hedge was darkness and she pulled out her mobile phone, turned on its light. Muddy tracks from a motor vehicle stretched out into the darkness, across a field, narrowly missing a large oak tree which stood by like an ancient observer. Through the low branches of the tree, Roark could see twin headlights pointing to the left, towards the River Medway. Flashlights danced across the grounds.

As she walked towards the abandoned car, through mud and wet grass, rainwater seeping into her shoes, she felt the wind pick up again, bitingly cold. One of the flashlights was headed in her direction and before she could reach the blue Toyota, a male officer walked up to her.

'Detective Inspector Roark?' the officer said in a gruff voice.

'That's me,' she said.

'Sergeant Patel,' he said, swapping the flashlight to his left hand and reaching across.

Roark shook his offered hand, which was cold and wet. The police badge affixed to his navy blue turban shone brightly in Roark's phone light.

'What do you have?' Roark said, keeping her voice steady.

'I understand this car belongs to one of your detectives?' he said, motioning to the Toyota.

Roark nodded, looking at the open door on the other side of the car.

'My partner,' she said.

'Her mother is with one of my officers,' Patel said, dispensing with any platitudes.

'Yes, I have spoken to her.'

'Come around this side,' he said and walked around the front of the car, keeping his flashlight down and behind him so Roark could see where she was walking. 'After the call came in, the farmer showed us where he found the car. It was parked here, as you see it, driver's side door open. We put the headlights on, to help us.'

They reached the open door and Patel stepped aside.

'We didn't touch anything else.'

Roark squatted next to the open door, her feet sinking in the wet field. The driver's seat was empty, car keys still in the ignition, turned to auxiliary by the officers. The dashboard was lit up, indicators at zero. On the passenger seat was Knight's double-breasted woollen coat, half on the floor, the coat Alice had bought her recently, the one Roark had coveted. On top of it, her warrant card, purse, a purple and white handkerchief.

'Any sign of her?' Roark said standing up and looking back out towards the river.

'No, nothing. She drove the car through the hedge back there, as you saw, parked up here. I have officers along the river's edge. The farmer is out there too.'

'How deep's the river?'

'Farmer said it's usually no more than a metre, but the rain has raised it a bit. We've had drownings here before.'

Roark winced in the darkness, felt something rising in her throat. She swallowed.

'Can I see?'

'Of course.'

They walked together, lights shining in front of them. The short grass of the paddock owned by the farmer gave way to calf high grass that tried to scratch through Roark's trousers. The ground dipped slightly forward, and Patel stopped.

Roark looked to her right, saw the men with their flashlights, combing the banks, occasionally pointing their lights out towards the river. To her left was darkness that her weak phone light could not penetrate. Ahead of them, the river waited in the darkness.

'We have more officers coming. Coastguard out of Medway will be here soon. Hoping to get a helicopter out here too. They're currently assessing the weather.'

'Do you think she drowned?'

'We're focussing on that possibility first. She may have wandered off back towards the road, but we work from the worst-case scenario backwards.'

'There's none of her clothes about,' she said, scanning the embankment with her light.

'Most people don't go in undressed,' Sergeant Patel said.

Roark looked out at the darkness of the river again, pictured Gale walking out into it, fully clothed, until her head submerged down in the muddy, green water.

'A metre you said?' Roark said. 'She's about six feet tall. Too hard to drown when it's that shallow, right?'

'Accidentally, sure. Hard to do so intentionally, too. Body will go into survival mode, prevent yourself from drowning. People find a way, though. Weigh yourself down somehow; I've seen it all.'

'In this river?'

'No, haven't seen it in this river, but we've had our share of accidental drownings. Particularly if the water level is up, like tonight. River's quite rough now too, what with all this weather about.'

'Drowned in one metre?' Roark said, incredulously.

Sergeant Patel shrugged his shoulders.

Roark pictured Knight standing in the middle of the river, jacket and trouser pockets weighed down by heavy rocks, kneeling in the water, letting herself sink down.

She couldn't see it. It didn't make sense. She didn't believe Knight would do such a thing, but physically, it felt impossible.

'Ready to help?' Patel said, offering up his flashlight, which had more reach than her phone.

Roark breathed through her nose, looked up and down the river, silent in its slow currents.

Without uttering a word, she took the flashlight and joined in the search.

CHAPTER 50

The episode with the police upset him. He couldn't sleep last night, after they had dropped him back at his flat. Afterwards, he felt like he was in a state of shock. The way that tall female police officer had poked and prodded, made him relive some horrible memories, leaving him feeling insecure, afraid, the way she treated him and spoke to him, he felt like he'd be subjected to a physical attack. An assault, a rape.

He couldn't sleep, so he had sat in his living room and stared out at the rain that attacked his windows. Stared out and relived the horrid episode that, half an hour since they had let him go, felt like it had happened to someone else, something from one of the true crime documentaries he liked to watch, not something that had happened to him personally.

It had happened, though, he knows that. She had made him remember. She had made him think things he didn't want to think. Made him say things out loud that he didn't want anyone to hear.

At one point in the night, as the rain started to get a little heavier, he stood and stared down into the road just in front of the block of flats. He saw the other detective, the large grumpy one with the moustache, staring up at him, standing in the rain.

Stepping away from the window, he had decided he needed to hide for the rest of the night, so he returned to the attic, the confined space in the loft of his flat. Once up there, he slept soundly on a thin piece of mattress. Up there, he forgot about what he'd just gone through.

In the morning, he descended the step ladder, closed the hatch that led to the loft, and left the memories of that boy up in the attic, locked away. For now.

Looking out the window on a new day, one that appeared to have survived the torrid storm from the previous night, there was no man standing in the road staring up at him, forcing him to barricade himself in his own home. The street was empty. No people, no cars.

That had made him feel better. After the night in the attic, he felt a little more secure in himself, a little cleaner and in control, like he'd purged himself of what he'd been through the previous night. Thoughts of that time in the small interview room with the dark shadows reaching out to him only seeped in when his mind wandered away from what he was doing. It didn't take him much to shake the memories loose, refocus on the task at hand.

The task of disappearing.

He owns the flat that he lives in, so that is not a problem. He could leave it unoccupied for a year and if he paid the ground rent and service charges, kept on top of the utilities that he didn't disconnect, it would be fine sitting empty. He could return whenever he wanted to check on the place, he'd only be a few hours away at any time. It could sit here for a year, no problem, although he didn't plan on returning anyway.

He would have to let his job at the delivery company go, that was obvious. There was no way they'd keep the position open for a year, waiting on him to return. He could give notice, make it official, but he decides just to stop turning up for work. He hasn't been to the site for over a month now, due to sickness, so they aren't expecting him. Maybe they have already written him off. That was fine.

There was nothing else significant that had to be addressed. It surprises him how easily, and how quickly, he could just disappear. No family to inform, no friends to say goodbye to. Most of his important post was delivered by e-mails, bills and the like, so the mailbox wouldn't overflow with unopened mail. No one sent him letters anyway. Not anymore.

Earlier this morning, he made the decision, and now, only seven hours later, he drives down the M3, leaving Basingstoke behind, possibly for good. In the van he had taken from work, he has a few of his things packed up – clothes, books, paperwork he felt he couldn't leave behind – but there isn't much if he was honest. He leads a simple life, a non-materialistic life, one that could be picked up and dropped elsewhere in less than a day. He likes it like that.

Besides, where he is going, there are other clothes, other books. There are pots and pans, vacuum cleaners and mops, a fully stocked pantry and fridge, his own bedroom, his own bed. It is all set up for him already, has been for many years.

It has everything he needs.

As he leaves Basingstoke behind, he smiles at himself in the rear-view mirror.

It even has an attic.

***

Driving back to London, a few hours after dawn, having spent most of the night searching the area up and down the River Medway with no luck, then taking Alice Knight back to her home in West Farleigh for a few hours until the distraught mother fell asleep, Roark pulled over in an emergency refuge area on the M25, turned off the engine, leaned her head on her arms across the steering wheel and cried.

She was tired. Yesterday had taken a lot out of her, so she could raise her hand and admit to being emotional, but it wasn't that. It was her partner – Florence "Gale" Knight – who brought her to tears.

Roark didn't believe it at first, but now, it was hard to ignore the possibility. After discussing it with Alice back at her home, it seemed that their worst nightmare may have come true.

'It doesn't take a lot,' Alice said. 'You could be on the brink all your life and it just takes a moment in time. You never know, you just don't know when people are struggling, not even your own daughter. I just can't believe she'd do this.'

Alice broke down and cried, her small shoulders shuddering.

Roark had kept her emotions in check, stayed strong for Alice Knight, but now, in the car on the M25, it all came out and she cried, silently, shaking her head in the cradle of her arms.

After a while, she gathered herself. In the rear-view mirror, she could see her red eyes staring back at her, almost bringing her to tears again.

She had to pull herself together, but in that moment, she didn't think she could.

Her mobile phone rang.

Instinctively, she picked it up and answered it quickly.

'Roark,' her voice croaked.

'Krystal, is that you? It's Arne. Is everything okay?'

'Not really, no,' she said, almost losing it again, but swallowing the tears down.

'What happened?'

Chief Inspector Arne Cristian. She'd only met him yesterday. She hardly knew him.

'My partner,' she said. 'She's missing.'

More tears swallowed. She almost felt like she couldn't breathe, trying to keep it down.

'DC Knight?' Arne said, his voice steady, solid.

'Yes.'

'You were leaving messages with her yesterday, right?'

'That's right,' Roark said, wiping tears that threatened to fall from her eyes. 'She didn't answer any of them.'

'What happened? Tell me.'

His voice didn't sound like it was coming from miles away, down the end of a cheap mobile phone. It felt present, in the car with her.

'We don't know. Her car was found, near a river. Empty. She was nowhere to be found. They haven't found her.'

'Where?'

'South of Rochester, about an hour out of London. Her mother lives there.'

'When did you last speak to her? Did she respond to any of your texts during the day?'

'No, she didn't. I spoke to her in the morning, yesterday morning. She said the paramedics had called her, said that her mother had a fall and needed to go to the hospital, but Alice never had a fall, there were no paramedics. I don't know. I don't know what happened.'

'Where are you?'

Roark looked outside her car window as if she didn't know.

'In a layby, off the M25. I've just had a big cry.'

'That's good. Stay there for a while. Talk to me a bit more.'

And she did, for almost thirty minutes. Arne let her speak her mind, ramble on, and on a couple of occasions, cry a little bit more. He didn't ask about the Stern case, he didn't interrupt, he didn't cut the call short. He listened and Roark thanked him for that.

CHAPTER 51

Roark entered her flat just before five that afternoon. Dumped her bag in the hallway and closed the door behind her. The flat was quiet, untouched for almost thirty-six hours. Everything in here was the same as it was before the five bodies had been discovered in New Forest, before the frustrating interview with James Stern, before Detective Constable Florence Knight had disappeared.

The day at the station had been difficult. There was no one around to support her. Lucas had gone home to sleep, most of the other detectives were on other cases. She spent time with DCI Rawlins, discussing the Stern case, and talking about Knight's disappearance. She left his office feeling like it had been a pointless exercise.

Back at her desk, she made calls, asked for updates, made enquiries, and felt utterly useless. Around four thirty, she hit the wall and decided, if she was going to be of any use, she needed sleep. She left the station without telling anyone.

When her mobile phone rang, she was sitting at the kitchen table with a glass of white wine, the letter from the NHS about her appointment face down on the table. She'd started to read it, but had turned it over, unable to concentrate on it just now.

It was Arne Cristian calling. She pressed a button on the phone and left it on the table.

'I've got you on speaker,' she said, 'so I can keep filling up my glass.'

'*Fine by me. What are you on?*'

'Some white plonk from Tesco. Does the trick. Don't worry, I'm only on my first glass.'

'*How are you holding up?*'

Roark put her elbow on the table, rested her head in her hand.

'Not very well. Feeling useless. Feeling tired. I should be out there looking for her.'

'*I know what you mean. Unless you're out there with a flashlight, you feel a little useless.*'

'More than a little.'

'*I saw the bulletin from the ACEU. You've got the best looking out for her.*'

'I'm thankful for that. She's one of our own, so they fast-tracked the national search. River came up empty so far. They are working their way north towards Rochester, but even with the storms, they don't think she would've got that far. Unless she's snagged under somewhere, they say she should rise to the top, given she's wearing clothes. Air pockets or some shit, I don't know.'

'*That's a good sign, Krystal. If she's not in the river, she's somewhere else.*'

Roark looked at the glass of wine in her hand. She didn't feel like drinking right now.

'I guess. She could be in the river, and we never find her.'

'*I know, it's possible.*'

'I appreciate the lack of platitudes,' she said.

'*I'm not very good at those.*'

Roark sat up and sipped her wine. It didn't taste very good, so she pushed it aside. She ran a hand over her head, felt the grit in her hair.

'I don't understand any of it, Arne,' she said. 'You think you know someone, know where their head is at, and then they go and do something like this.'

'*I get it.*'

'I thought she had a strong personality, intelligent, had her shit together. She was young, for sure, and some of the cases, like this one, shook her up a little, but she seemed to cope.'

'*People have reasons. Sometimes it's just in a moment when they can't face it anymore.*'

Reasons, Roark thought. Did Knight have a reason? Wondering about starting a family. Concerns over her own family. Her real mother. Her adoption.

'We were close, we spoke about things,' she said. 'Closer than just colleagues. We were friends. It just doesn't seem believable.'

'*You thought you were there for her, that she would come to you before doing this,*' Arne said.

'Yeah, you're probably right. Don't want to make it all about me, though, right?'

'*I don't mean that. It's just, sometimes, people don't want to be saved. Not in that moment.*'

Roark ran her hand through her hair again.

'I need a shower.'

'*Go,*' Arne said. '*We'll speak tomorrow.*'

'Thanks, Arne.'

'*And don't be so hard on yourself, Krystal.*'

'Okay. And you can call me Kris. Only my mother ever called me Krystal.'

Arne laughed, a light, delightful sound and Roark smiled.

'*Speak tomorrow.*'

***

Arne Cristian called again the next day. Roark was walking out of the station to grab a bite to eat. She'd taken the rear exit. Reporters were hovering around the front, still trying to squeeze out headlines on the recent murders. The bodies found in New Forest had made the front news the day before and although she had no new leads, they were still seeking updates and new angles to report on. Roark didn't have time for them, not now.

Before emerging from the alleyway behind the station, her phone rang and she answered it, turning from the busy road a few metres away, finger in her ear.

'Hey,' she said, turning her back on the noisy traffic.

'Hi Kris,' Arne said, his voice clear. 'Any news?'

'No, nothing,' she said. 'I think they'll be stopping the river search today.'

Wind whipped down the alley and she backed into the small shielded rear entrance of a Lebanese restaurant. She could smell garlic, lemon and onions, wafting through the gaps around the door.

'What are you thinking?' Arne asked.

'I don't know anymore. I'm struggling to believe she's taken her own life. Not finding her in the water gives me hope, but I don't know.'

'What have you got so far on what happened?'

'Not a lot,' she said and sighed.

'Tell me,' Arne said.

'Well, Gale, I mean, DC Knight, informed me that she'd received a call from local paramedics that her mother had taken a bad fall. She was to come as soon as she could. I let her go, of course. I didn't hear from her after that.'

'What time was the call?'

'I don't know. She called me at half seven in the morning.'

'Her car was found near her mother's house,' Arne said.

'Close by, down by the river. That is strange to me. I would've thought she'd go to the hospital, but no, CCTV footage shows her passing near Teston around quarter to nine. She'd driven straight to her mum's village.'

'Any cameras on her after Teston?'

280

'No, nothing. Looks like she'd pulled off into that field at nine.'

'Parked her car and disappeared.'

'Walked into the river, apparently,' Roark said. The smell of onions suddenly felt overpowering. She felt like throwing up. She stepped back into the alleyway.

'Anything in the car?'

'Her jacket, warrant card, purse, a couple of other effects.'

'No mobile.'

'No,' Roark said, staring up at the clear blue sky above her. She started to pace around the alley. 'We haven't found it. There were several calls to it that morning, a lot of them blocked. Trying to trace them but not having much luck. Nothing from the paramedics.'

Roark stopped pacing.

'Arne, what's your gut feel?'

Roark heard him breathe in down the line.

'What's the relationship with her mother like?'

Her adopted mother, Roark thought.

'She spoke to her every day, visited her most weekends. They were close. Alice Knight is an amazing woman, has gone through a lot recently with a divorce, cancer. Gale's been by her side the whole time.'

'A strong relationship.'

'Yes,' Roark said, then blurted out, 'but Alice isn't her real mother. She was adopted when she was a baby.'

'Okay,' Arne said.

'That's in the vault, okay?' she said, suddenly feeling guilty.

'Sorry?'

'The vault. That information, locked away, not to be repeated.'

'Yes, yes, of course,' he said. 'In the vault. That might be a reason to do something rash. Maybe it was a sore point for her. Maybe something happened with her biological mother recently, tried to get in contact.'

'You might have something there,' Roark said.

'Do we know who the mother is?'

'No, she didn't say. Alice doesn't know much about it either. I know Gale was trying to connect with her recently. We could try to find out.'

'That could take some time,' Arne said. He didn't need to remind her of their conversation about identifying witnesses under a Witness Protection programme. Adoption records could be equally difficult to access without a warrant or permission.

'I'll be frank with you, Kris,' he said, 'I see this has gone one of two ways. She has taken her own life, or she wishes us to believe she has. She used the story about her mother and the fall to give her time and space. Whether it was to deal with something relating to her biological mother, or something else entirely, something more final, we may never know, but whatever she was planning to do, she's gone through with it.'

'Yeah,' Roark said, nodding, 'It does look that way. Still struggling to believe it, I guess. Of course, I'm hoping it's the latter, that she's just gone off to hide somewhere.'

'Yes, well, like I said yesterday, I'm not great with platitudes.'

'Fair enough, Arne,' she said, lightness in her voice.

A bus driver leaned on his horn only a few metres away on the nearby road.

'I should let you go,' he said.

'How about James Stern? We haven't spoken about him yet.'

'Call me tonight,' Arne said. 'We'll go through it over a glass of wine.'

'Okay . . . okay. Thank you, Arne. Thanks for listening. And helping.'

'Anytime,' he said.

Arne finished the call. Roark looked down at her phone, envisioned getting through the rest of the day so that she could sit down and have that glass of wine and talk more with Arne Cristian. She knew she'd feel better for it.

CHAPTER 52

That night, with her laptop set up on the kitchen table, Roark and Cristian spoke over a video call. It was close to nine by the time both were free. At this point, Roark had changed out of her work clothes and into black slacks and an old Radiohead t-shirt, her hair damp from her recent shower. Another bottle of Tesco's finest white wine sat on the table. She held a half-full glass, swirling it as Arne Cristian logged on.

His face, even over her dodgy internet connection, was a sight for sore eyes. She couldn't help but smile when she saw him, and he smiled back. She also felt like crying, but she kept that at bay.

The healthy shock of blond hair, the square jawline, the kind blue eyes, and a blue and green plaid shirt.

'What's that you're wearing?'

He looked down at his chest, picked at it, said, 'What, this old thing?'

'You look like a lumberjack.'

'It's my casual wear,' he said. 'Look, I didn't know how formal we'd be.'

Roark laughed.

'I'm practically in my gym gear,' she said.

'Radiohead, nice. Actually, wait,' he said and stood up and left the table he was sitting at.

Behind where he had been sitting was a room with a sofa to one side, another long table and a fireplace, a recently stoked fire crackling away. It looked homely and Roark suddenly wished she was there.

He came back on, sat down, and stretched his t-shirt down so she could see.

'Foo Fighters,' she said. 'I like it.'

The t-shirt, a little too tight, accentuated a broad chest, rounded shoulders and biceps that still held form, despite him pushing fifty. The stomach held a little bit of weight, but hardly noticeable.

Roark cleared her throat and asked what he was drinking, and he showed her a bottle of golden-coloured liquid. It was mead, a popular drink from his home country. His heritage was Norwegian, his grandfather emigrating when he was in his twenties, also a police officer on transfer from the Politi. They spoke about his upbringing, particularly about his father, Dane, for about two more glasses and then Roark said, 'Let's talk about James Stern.'

She recounted the highlights of the interview she had with Stern. Or, more aptly put, the lowlights of the interview. The more she thought about it, the more she knew she could've handled it much better.

'Sounds like you did a very good job,' he said.

'And I thought you didn't do platitudes.'

'It's the truth, but what's important now is what you do next. You need to build up your case against him, so you can arrest him.'

'So,' she said, taking a sip of her wine, 'you're with me. You think he's our man.'

Arne nodded, placing his glass to one side.

'I spoke to my father again, after we had spoken in the forest. He's adamant that James Stern needs to be looked at for this. Sounds like your interview only supports this approach.'

'Lucas doesn't think so.'

'What's he say?'

'He's just not convinced, and he thinks our evidence is weak.'

'He's probably right there.'

'He just sees the boy from the attic, all grown up, fragile, challenged, confused. Not capable. I see all of that, but I think he is more than capable. I think he was pulling our chain the whole time in there.'

'What are you planning to do next?' he asked, leaning in.

'I'm working on an arrest warrant for the judge. Hope to be done in the next couple of days. She'll reject it, but I'll know where I stand and what I need to do.'

'I'll send you a statement from my perspective, my father too. I'm sure Moody will weigh in.'

'That would be very helpful, thank you.'

Roark finished her glass of wine and saw that the bottle was empty. She knew she had another bottle of Alberino in the fridge, but that was probably a slippery slope she didn't need to go down right now.

'I was informed yesterday that two of the bodies were positively identified as Mr and Mrs Irvine,' he said.

'Yes, I have those identifications. Aaron Sparger, Jaime Collander, William Palmer, all identified. I also asked Aaron Sparger's parents about Witness Protection, Richard Stern, all of that. They had no idea what I was talking about. Just like Jaime Collander's parents.'

Arne rolled a sliver of ice in the bottom of his glass of gold.

'It'd be nice,' Roark said, 'if the real Ryan Cooper and Laura Kilpatrick stepped forward, but I guess that wouldn't be smart.'

'Our theory that Stern was targeting the children that his father had abducted doesn't ring true now, does it?' Arne said.

'Except for Cheryl and William Palmer. Not confirmed yet, but I'm sure they are the same mother and son abducted in '94. If I could make that connection, we could get a warrant on Stern, but I'm struggling to access those protection records. If I could ask her, get her account of everything that's happened,' she started but trailed off.

'How she doing?'

Roark shook her head.

'Still unconscious. Stable, but no sign of recovery. Feels like she's my last hope.'

'Maybe,' Arne said and downed the last of his mead. 'Where's James Stern now?'

'Moody and Lucas watched him for most of that first night. He didn't leave the house. Since then, I don't know. I put in a request for surveillance, but it wasn't approved. I need that warrant before I can do anything.'

'Agreed,' he said. 'I'll get those statements over to you tomorrow morning.'

'Thank you, Arne.'

'I'll call McCallish too, see if he can spare a car to drive by a few times a day, see if we can get eyes on Stern.'

'That would be brilliant.'

There was a silence between them for a moment. Arne was studying his empty glass; Roark watched him.

'Looks like your fire is dying,' she said.

Arne turned around in his chair to look at his fireplace. The fire had reduced to embers.

'I'll let you go,' she said.

He turned back, looked directly at her, his eyes sharp on her screen.

'Keep your head up, Kris. Keep on top of it, stay ready. Something will happen and you need to be there for it.'

'I will,' she said with a certainty that surprised her.

'I'll speak to you tomorrow,' he said, and she already knew she was looking forward to it.

***

They spoke most days over the next two weeks, either on the phone at lunch or Zoom calls after hours, depending on evening plans. Roark had no plans, didn't feel like going out with friends or even leaving her home in Vauxhall. She felt flat and only her calls with Arne kept her spirits up.

More than two weeks since Gale had disappeared with no sign. More than two weeks since the James Stern interview and no progress.

Roark worked hard on both cases, as hard as she could. Some days, there was nothing she could do. National teams were still searching, Gale's face distributed throughout the country and to all ports of exit. No one had seen her. One or two false sightings a day but even those had begun to taper off. There was no sign of her anywhere.

All evidence pointed towards what now felt inevitable.

In the first week, Roark had dealt with this the only way she knew worked, at least temporarily. At the end of each day, she would go home and drink. A bottle usually, sometimes more. Drink to forget, that was the plan, but each time she'd end up in floods of tears, more upset than before. It had been a bad cycle, working hard, drinking hard, unable to make any progress in her life, including making an important decision about her own health. Another NHS letter had arrived, a reminder, and it was all she could do to keep herself from crawling up into a ball in the corner of the kitchen and wishing for oblivion.

Her regular calls with Arne pulled her out of it. Daily calls that grounded her, supported her, reduced her need to dull the thoughts and the feelings of regret and guilt. Enough so that the only time she drank was one small glass of wine when they video called every other night. Just enough to calm her nerves and help her sleep.

On more than one occasion, Roark had considered telling Arne about the NHS letters, see what he thought, even though she knew by now what he'd likely say. Each time, she found herself closer and closer to confiding in him about it, like she had on so many other things, but she always held back, felt it was inappropriate, selfish. That couldn't be the focus right now. She had other priorities. The last two Saturdays, Roark had driven down to West Farleigh to see Alice Knight. The poor woman was a mess. She was distraught each time Roark visited, her eyes widening when she saw Roark, hope that she had good news, and when Roark said that she didn't, Alice would crumble in a heap. She'd stopped eating, even the small amount that she could stomach since her chemotherapy, and her tiny frame was at risk of wasting away.

Roark did her best, kept her spirits up, talked to her about her daughter and some of the fun times they'd had on the job. When Alice was at her most settled, Roark even talked about Gale's adoption, her concerns over raising her own family, any other issues she may have had to help them both understand what had happened, why it had happened. None of it helped.

Roark stayed over on those Saturday nights, left the next day after cooking lunch for Alice, trying to keep her healthy in her time of despair. On the drive out of West Farleigh, Roark always took the turnoff that led towards the river and the field where Knight's car had been found.

She'd stand there, at the water's edge, looking at the calm green surface as it slowly passed her by.

She still couldn't picture it, but she was starting to accept what she couldn't see.

Two weeks.

Sitting at her desk, a few hours before she signed off for the day, she shuffled scraps of paper around. Scraps where she'd written theories, plans, ideas, regarding both Gale's disappearance and the James Stern case.

The families of the deceased were becoming disgruntled and angry at the lack of progress. All Roark could tell them was that she was working on it, priority number one. A murderer of seven people was still out there, and Roark was not going to stop until she arrested him.

Thankfully, there had been no new murders considered related to her case. It seemed that the killings had stopped. The downside, if you could call it that, was that the press had stopped leading with the case, and the story was slowly drifting out of the public eye. As was the disappearance of Detective Constable Florence Knight.

Roark left her desk and poured a coffee from the machine down the hall. She came back sipping the tepid drink and dropped in her chair. Next to her computer, on top of a pile of papers, was the physical copy of her submission to the judge, the one requesting an arrest warrant for Howard Bloch. She pulled it out, leafed through it.

It was a solid report. The statements and information provided by Arne, his father and DI Moody were invaluable. The judge had denied the warrant, as expected, as she was not convinced by Roark's arguments against Bloch. She agreed that Bloch, previously James Stern, was a person of interest, but she didn't like the circumstantial evidence that supposedly tied him to the crimes. No physical evidence, just theories. Not good enough to hold up in court.

Get more evidence, the judge had said.

Just like that, Roark thought.

It seemed to be a familiar tune. All her requests for adoption or Witness Protection records seemed to be blocked, either straight out denied or taking an unnecessarily long time to be approved. Even her request for information on Gale's biological mother seemed to be stuck in an administrative cycle.

Didn't she have a right to know that her daughter was potentially dead? Roark thought so, but one possibility Arne had suggested was probably right, that Gale didn't want to be found, and that accessing her adoption records would be a violation of her privacy.

Was two weeks too soon to presume otherwise? It was seven years before anyone missing was declared legally dead.

Roark shook her head, closed the Bloch warrant file and dropped it on her desk.

Her mobile phone, sitting next to her computer keyboard, connected to the charger, vibrated. She ignored it until it vibrated again. A call, not a text. Roark glanced at it.

ME Clayton.

She detached the phone from its charger and answered it.

'Charlie?'

'She's awake.'

Roark stood up, her chair rolling away.

'When?'

'A few hours ago. The hospital called me. I didn't tell you immediately until I saw her, but she's awake. A little fragile, but you can come and talk to her if you like. I'm here too. General Hospital in Southampton.'

'I'm on my way.'

She finished the call and made another one immediately.

'Arne, she's awake. Cheryl Palmer's awake.'

'I'll meet you there,' he said without hesitation.

Roark finished the call, grabbed the Howard Bloch arrest warrant file, and rushed out of the station, knocking over her half-drunk cup of coffee in the process.

CHAPTER 53

Roark had never felt so impatient in her life.

Cheryl Palmer was awake, and Roark needed to talk to her, ask important questions that could turn the James Stern case on its head. She wanted to be at her bedside now, but the drive was over three hours: Camberwell police station to General Hospital in Southampton. Thankfully she escaped the London traffic before rush hour started and was making a good run on the M3, but her car didn't go fast enough to calm her nerves.

She was desperate to find out what happened to Cheryl Palmer, what she could remember, what evidence she could provide. A positive identification of James Stern as her attacker would be amazing, but she knew that Mrs Palmer was blind, thus making that possibility more complicated.

Blind or not, she was still a witness to her own abduction, maybe even her son's murder, Roark thought, but was it enough? She just wanted to get to the hospital and find out.

Arne had arrived before her but did not go in, respecting that Roark was lead on the case. When she pulled into the hospital car park after a harrowing and snail-paced three hours on the road, she saw him standing next to his car, a free space right next to him. She pulled in, turned off the engine and stepped out into the beginning of a breezy, overcast evening.

There was no hesitation. They hugged. Roark was slightly taller than Arne, but his arms and shoulders were strong, his chest solid, and his embrace was comforting.

'We're close to finishing this,' he said when they parted.

'I feel it too.'

'McCallish is waiting on our word to move on Stern,' Arne said.

Despite Roark not impressing the Superintendent of the Basingstoke police station when she'd last been there, conducting her interview, Arne had managed to use his friendship with the burly Scotsman to co-ordinate the instant arrest of James Stern by Hampshire police, if Cheryl was able to provide enough evidence for the judge to approve the warrant. Two police cars were currently parked down the street from Stern's apartment, ready for the call.

'I appreciate that,' she said.

They walked side by side towards the hospital entrance. Roark felt an urge to grip his hand, a feeling that threw her off her step momentarily. She stuffed her hands into her jacket pockets.

'ME Clayton,' Arne pointed, seeing the doctor on the other side of sliding doors, waiting for them in the hospital reception.

The doors slid open and they shook hands. They turned and walked towards a wide corridor, Clayton leading.

'I'll introduce you to the doctor later, he can fill you in on how she's faring, but I've seen her and she's doing quite well. Recovering from the stab wounds and the strangulation. When she woke, her confusion was quite severe, her blindness not helping, but over the past few hours, she's calmed. Does get upset easily, so I've held off telling her about her son, but she's asking for him a lot now.'

'We'll handle that,' Roark said.

Cheryl Palmer's room was a five-minute walk from reception. They passed quiet rooms with sleeping patients, let one gurney go by with a young male blankly staring up at the ceiling as they rolled him to the surgical wing. Roark had been in many hospitals, and this was like all the others she'd seen: quiet, organised, and reassuring, but with a reminder of her own mortality.

There were no other patients in Cheryl's room, the other three beds empty. There was no police officer out the front, as the one that Roark had requested two weeks ago was pulled after five nights. Resources stretched, it was decreed that any threat to her life had passed, and the officer was returned to normal duties. Roark kicked up a stink at the time but to no avail.

A nurse stood by Cheryl's bed, leaning over, helping the patient with a glass of water which she was drinking through a straw. Roark, Arne, and Clayton stopped a few feet away and waited for the nurse to finish. It gave Roark a chance to have a look at Cheryl Palmer.

She appeared frail, although it was difficult to know how much was due to her recent ordeal, as Roark was seeing the woman in her mid-sixties for the first time. Her hair was grey and rested on her shoulders, messy and dishevelled. Her face was wrinkled, one or two red marks across her forehead, and the skin around her throat was lightly bruised, still healing from the attempted strangulation two weeks ago. Wrinkles, bruises and varicose veins lined her chest above the paper-thin nightgown she wore and her skin clung onto her left arm when she returned her glass to the nurse. The dressings over her knife wounds could be seen through the nightgown, wrapped tight around her stomach.

Her head turned towards the nurse, slightly left of her shoulder, as if she was staring out at the darkening sky through the window. When she thanked the nurse, blinked, and stared straight ahead, Roark could see the light bluish-grey marble opaqueness of her eyes. She also saw the scarring too, the old burns, around her eyes and across the bridge of her nose.

Hydrofluoric acid.

'You have some visitors, Cheryl,' the nurse said, stepping away.

'It's Doctor Clayton,' the ME said quickly, 'we spoke earlier.'

Cheryl turned her head towards his voice and nodded.

'I have two detectives here that would like to talk to you. Detective Inspector Krystal Roark from London and Chief Inspector Arne Cristian from New Forest.'

She pushed herself up slowly in her bed.

'Is it about Billy?' she said, her voice as thin as her night-gown.

'Mrs Palmer, can we sit with you?'

'What happened to my boy? Is he okay?'

Roark and Cristian pulled two chairs closer to Cheryl's bed and sat down. ME Clayton left them to it, said he'd find Mrs Palmer's doctor.

'Mrs Palmer,' Roark said, keeping her voice steady, 'I am sorry to say that your son did not make it. He passed away from his injuries.'

'No,' Cheryl said, her hand, the one with a catheter plugged into a vein, rose to cover her mouth. Tears immediately formed in her eyes, and she dropped back onto her pillow.

'I am so sorry,' Roark repeated, but then kept quiet, allowing Mrs Palmer as much time as she needed to take in the news.

Cheryl's mouth opened and shut a few times before she could say anything, and then all she could manage was a weak whimper. The tears dripped off her chin. She clasped her hands together and closed her eyes.

'How?' she finally managed, opening her eyes again, her pupils turning a slightly darker shade of grey. 'How did he die?'

'We believe he was strangled, just like you were, but he did not survive.'

Her head dropped to her chest, then back up again, anguish across her face.

'My poor Billy,' she said. 'My poor boy.'

'Do you know who did this?' Roark asked tentatively.

'No,' Cheryl said, shaking her head. 'Who would do such a thing?'

'I know your grief is raw right now, Mrs Palmer, but we want to arrest the man who did this. Are you able to recall anything about what happened?'

Cheryl did not reply for almost five minutes. Roark didn't press. Cheryl tried to speak but could only cry out in silent anguish, unable to keep her head up off the pillow as if it was twice its weight, wringing her hands incessantly, threatening to dislodge the catheter.

'Take your time,' Roark said and touched her arm.

'I'll get some more water,' Arne said and left to find a nurse.

'I know this is hard right now, Mrs Palmer, but I need to ask you some questions about the day you were attacked.'

Cheryl slowly wiped tears from her chin and taking a deep breath, nodded.

'Do you remember what happened?'

Cheryl touched the area around her left eye, her fingers running slowly along one of the red marks there.

'It's difficult,' she said, softly. 'Everything is so hazy.'

'I understand. Please, take your time. Anything that comes to mind will be helpful.'

Roark took her phone out and placed it on the small table next to Cheryl's bed.

'I am going to record our conversation if that is okay,' she said. When Cheryl didn't respond, she pressed play on the device. 'You can take your time, start wherever you want to.'

Cheryl dropped her hand and sunk further into her bed. She stared up at the ceiling.

'I don't know where to start.'

'Let me help,' Roark said, touching Cheryl's arm again. 'This is probably the most important thing, so if you have anything you can tell me, it would be much appreciated. Can you identify who did this to you and your son? Do you know the person who attacked you?'

'No,' she said, confidently, initially relieved that she could answer something definitively, but when she realised what her answer meant, her bottom lip trembled. 'I'm sorry, I don't.'

'That is okay, Mrs Palmer. Tell me what you can remember, what happened that day?'

'I can't really think,' she said, shifting in her bed restlessly.

'It's okay. Let me help. Were you in your home?'

'Yes, yes, I was.'

'Before the attack, who was with you?'

'My son, Billy. And, and Teresa, the lovely girl who came to visit. That's right, she brought me chocolates and fried chicken. We were having such a good time.'

'Okay, that is good. Now, do you remember how the attack happened? Where were you?'

She rubbed her left eyebrow and frowned.

'I was in the front room, yes, I was in my chair, eating a chocolate or two. Teresa was upstairs. That's right, there were noises upstairs. She asked if it was Billy, but I thought Billy was still at work. It was confusing, but we could hear someone up there.'

'Is that where the attacker was? Upstairs?'

'No, no, it was Billy. He had been upstairs all along.'

'Where were you?'

'I was at the front door. That's right. The doorbell rang and I asked who it was. The voice said it was a delivery for me. I thought maybe Teresa had organised something more; she was so generous. I opened the door, and I was knocked to the floor. The door hit me, I think. I fell. This,' she said, touching the mark on her forehead, 'this is where it hit me, I guess.'

'What happened next?'

'Billy was screaming and yelling. They had both come down the stairs. I could hear Teresa gasping. The front door closed. I was picked up off the floor, I remember that. There was an arm around my throat. I was finding it hard to breathe. I was so scared.'

'I am so sorry this happened, Mrs Palmer.'

'Please call me Cheryl,' she said. She was calmer now, despite what she was recounting, as if she was gaining solace from being useful. Suddenly, she grimaced and her eyes watered. 'Oh, my poor Billy, he was so upset. I could hear him calling for me. I sensed him wanting to help, but the arm would tighten whenever he tried.'

'Did the man speak? Did you recognise his voice?'

'No, no, he didn't. He never spoke a word. I could just hear him breathing, steady, calm, in control. That breathing scared me so much.'

'Was there anything else you could remember about him? Did he smell of anything?'

'No, nothing I could identify. He was taller than me, a lot taller. I could feel his breath on my head. Strong too.'

Vague as it was, the description did not conflict with that of James Stern.

'What happened next Cheryl?'

Cheryl closed her eyes, tried to think. She flinched.

'He hurt Billy. I remember that. I don't know how, but Billy cried out and was silent. The man then dropped me to the floor, and I could hear a tussle, a struggle, and oh dear, I could hear Teresa crying out.'

Cheryl turned to Roark, her eyes darting around, her hand flashing out and gripping Roark's wrist.

'What happened to Teresa? Is that poor girl okay?'

'I'm not sure,' Roark said, knowing full well that the young woman who worked at the home care agency had died from blood loss on the floor of Cheryl Palmer's kitchen, loss from multiple stab wounds. She decided that she would withhold that information just in case Cheryl became upset again, possibly too upset to continue.

'I hope she is okay,' Cheryl said, removing her hand from Roark's wrist, 'it sounded horrible, what he was doing to her.'

Cheryl shifted in her bed and Roark could see her chest rising and falling.

'Why would he do that?'

'We are trying to work that out,' Roark said, quietly.

'After he struggled with Teresa, everything went quiet. I laid on the floor and couldn't hear anything. I was more scared at that point than at any other time, waiting for what would come next. After a while, I think I heard him go into my front room, rummaging around in there, I don't know what for. I just kept thinking, who is this man, what does he want from us?'

'I know you haven't had a lot of time to think about it,' Roark said, 'but do you have any ideas about why this happened? Anyone you think may act like this towards you and Billy?'

'No, I don't,' Cheryl said, shaking her head. 'What would he want? We have no money in the house.'

Cheryl grimaced again and fresh tears brimmed. Roark felt like she was about to lose her. She had to be careful. The poor woman could get upset again, too upset to continue, and then Roark would have to wait, come back later, take more time. Roark didn't think she could wait any longer.

'Cheryl, you were taken from your home to another location.'

She looked confused for a moment, then nodded, 'Yes, in the back of some large vehicle. A van maybe. He tied us up. I tried to wake Billy, but he wouldn't answer me. There was blood on him, I could feel it.'

Her bottom lip trembled again.

'Cheryl,' Roark quickly said, 'do you know where you were taken? In the van?'

'No,' she said, 'I – I don't remember leaving the van.'

'You didn't leave the van?'

'No, the van stopped and the rear doors opened. I was so afraid. He came into the van with us, not saying a word. I could hear him close the doors. It was quiet and then I felt his hands, oh God, I felt his hands.'

She raised both hands to her throat, started to breathe heavily.

Roark swallowed. She would have to be careful on the next part. If what she suspected was true, what she said next would upset Cheryl Palmer. In a moment of selfishness, she could only hope it did, as that would mean a positive result for her case, but she felt for the woman too and didn't want to cause her too much more stress.

But she had to have the answer.

'Cheryl, I need you to listen to me carefully.'

Cheryl sucked in her breath, she tensed, and her hands went to her mouth.

'You were found at a remote property in New Forest, a house that once belonged to a man called Richard Stern.'

Roark watched Cheryl as her hands dropped to her lap.

'Richard Stern?' she said quietly.

'Do you recognise that name?'

'Yes, yes, I do,' she said, her chest rising and falling quickly.

'Where do you recognise that name from?'

Cheryl gasped for air, turned to Roark, whispered, 'It wasn't him, it couldn't be. They told me he was *dead*.'

'Mrs Palmer,' Roark said, forcefully keeping her voice slow and steady, 'you are right, he is dead. Please, Mrs Palmer, please listen and answer my question: where do you recognise that name from?'

Her face dropped. Her shoulders dropped. Her mouth opened. Her eyes widen.

'It's James, isn't it? It was James.'

CHAPTER 54

The hospital around them seemed to hold its breath as Cheryl spoke the name, an eerie stillness descending on the corridors and rooms. Roark didn't answer her immediately. She was surprised Cheryl had made the connection so quickly, that she'd found her own path to James Stern. Still, Roark had to be careful not to lead her to the answer she desired so much.

'James who, Cheryl?'

'His son. Richard's son.'

'James Stern?'

'James Stern. Did he do this?' she said, and turned, her opaque eyes pleading. 'Did he kill my boy?'

'How do you know James Stern, Cheryl?'

'The letters.'

'Sorry?'

'The letters he sent me. To my house. He contacted me. Through the agency.'

'Cheryl, are you talking about James Stern? He sent you letters?'

'Through the agency, through the programme. He reached out to me. He sent me letters. He wanted to connect with me. Oh my God. Did I lead him to us? Did I do this?'

'Mrs Palmer, I don't understand.'

'The letters,' she said, her voice rising. She gripped Roark's wrist again. 'He sent them to my house. I gave him my address. He wanted to contact me. They passed on his information to me, gave me the option. He's not legally my stepson, so it was my choice. I refused at the beginning, but over the years, he kept trying and I couldn't think of a reason not to, so I agreed to write to him. I thought it was the right thing to do. We spoke. I told him everything. We met, he came to our house, oh God.'

Roark moved to the edge of her seat, took Cheryl's hand from her wrist and held it.

'Did you change your name, Cheryl? After it happened. After what happened at Richard Stern's house.'

She nodded.

'Cheryl Davies,' she said. 'It was Davies, my late husband's surname. I changed it after what happened. They said I should, when we went into the programme, to protect us. Change your last name, for protection, move cities, change everything. I let him into our home, didn't I? I did this. Oh God, I did this.'

Cheryl pulled her hand away, started to writhe in her bed as if she was trying to will the strength to get out. Her hand went to the catheter.

'Mrs Palmer, please calm down,' Roark said, standing up and lightly gripping the distraught woman's arm.

Arne appeared on the other side of the bed, taking Cheryl's other arm so that the catheter was not in reach. Cheryl started to wail, noises of a stricken soul, an animalistic noise, a noise of grief, remorse and guilt all rolled up in one continuous howl.

The nurse moved in, asking what had happened, pushing Roark aside gently as she reached over to calm Cheryl down. Another nurse joined her and entered a syringe of something into her saline bag. It took a few minutes, but Cheryl finally succumbed to the drug and sunk into her bed, eyes closing, limbs dropping harmlessly to her side.

'I'm sorry,' Roark said. 'I just had to speak with her.'

'She'll be fine now, but I think that's enough for today,' the nurse said.

'Please,' Roark said, handing over her business card, 'call me if she wakes again. I would like to apologise.'

The nurse took the card reluctantly and put it in her uniform pocket.

'I need you to leave now,' she said, ushering them out while the other nurse checked Cheryl Palmer's EKG reading.

Roark picked up her phone and stopped the recording, headed for the exit. Arne caught up.

'It's him,' she said. 'She confirmed it, she's Cheryl Davies.'

'I heard part of it, didn't want to interrupt. Did she identify him as her attacker?'

'No, but it's James Stern. They corresponded, they've met, he knows where she lives. He found her through the Witness Protection agency, gave her the choice to speak with him. She thought it was the right thing to do and he took advantage of that.'

'They met?'

'He's been to her house.'

She shook her head.

'I have other questions for her, but this is enough. He did this, Arne,' she said. 'He blamed them for what happened, to him, to his father. Killed Billy and tried to strangle Cheryl as retribution. I don't know what the others were about, Sparger and Collander, symbolism possibly, but it was Cheryl and Billy he was after. He blamed them the most.'

They stormed through the corridor of the hospital. Roark looked at her phone, made sure the recording had saved. She listened to the part where Cheryl confirmed her identity, the phone held up to her ear.

'I'll call McCallish,' Arne said, his own phone in his hand, 'tell them to get ready to serve the warrant. Reception's not great in here.'

'Outside,' Roark said, pointing. 'I'll call the judge, get her approval on the warrant.'

'Then we'll arrest him.'

'It's him, isn't it, Arne?'

'I'm convinced,' he said without missing a beat, and she believed him.

Arne Cristian raised his phone, making the call to Superintendent McCallish as they stepped outside.

They walked to their respective cars, stood by them as they made their calls. As Roark dialled the judge, she looked up to the sky. The weather had turned inclement, dark clouds forming above in the early evening, rain threatening. There was a scent of electricity in the air. Roark didn't know whether it was the onset of a storm or the buzz she had for making the break.

The judge answered after the fourth ring. Roark filled her in on the conversation with Cheryl Palmer, said she'd send through the audio when she logged on to the network and could upload the file. The judge took a moment to consider the new testimony.

'I'm one hundred percent certain Howard Bloch did this,' Roark said when the silence stretched. 'I'm certain it's enough to justify arresting him, and when I do, the evidence we've found at the crime scenes will place him at the scene.'

'Okay,' the judge said. 'I'll approve. It's still hanging by a thread, Detective Inspector, but I think you are right. I'll message the approval and you can serve the warrant.'

'It's done,' Roark said after thanking the judge and ending the call. A message pinged on her phone, the judge's approval for the warrant.

Arne was still on the phone to McCallish and gave him the green light to arrest Howard Bloch, aka James Stern, for the murders of seven people and attempted murder of Cheryl Palmer.

The silence as Roark waited was painful. The more it went on, the more she became anxious. All they had to do was knock on Stern's apartment door and serve the warrant for his arrest, but it was taking forever.

'Are you sure?' Arne said.

'What is it?' Roark said, almost shouting across the roof of her car.

Arne lowered his phone and gave her a look that she immediately recognised.

'He's gone, isn't he?' she said.

'He's gone.'

CHAPTER 55

He sits on a kitchen chair listening to the local radio station. They are talking about the weather. It's going to be a rough one, they keep saying. He turns and looks out the kitchen window and sees dark clouds rolling low in the sky. The trees just outside the window are moving gracefully, balletic.

They say on the radio that the winds will reach almost thirty miles an hour. Rainfall anticipated to reach twenty millimetres. Not the worst they've had around these parts, he thinks, but still a lot more than usual.

He switches the radio off.

The property is on flat ground with trees surrounding it, close in, protecting the house from rain and wind. One of the older trees could topple, that was a risk, but he'd never seen it before and he'd lived here, on and off, for the past thirty years. The house is ancient but strong and any flooding will be limited to the driveway a hundred metres away. It's a safe a place as any to see out a storm.

Mother is worried though. He can hear her busying herself, going around to all the windows, making sure they are closed and secure. She keeps saying she's worried that the roof is going to fly away this time, but she says that every windy night. The roof on the small outhouse, sat near the front of the house, is usually the one that suffers the most. The number of times he's had to relay those tiles. He's lost count.

There is a sudden gust of wind and it shudders the walls.

He shivers, feeling more on edge than he usually is. He blames that blonde policewoman who verbally attacked and abused him at the Basingstoke police station.

He shakes his head. He thought he'd never think about her and that night in the police station again, but the memories always come back, especially when he's nervous about something. He shouldn't keep worrying about that, he knows this. That was almost three weeks ago now. A long time ago.

Still, his nerves are shot and he blames her.

He looks up to the kitchen ceiling. Like the rest of the house, it's old and worn away, threatening to disintegrate, but he knows its solid. There are holes in it, but not big enough to risk collapse. Big enough to peek through though.

After a moment's further contemplation, he pushes back his chair and leaves the kitchen.

Down the short hallway to a cupboard. He opens it and pulls out an old wooden step ladder. Positioning it on a specific spot in the middle of the hallway, he tests its sturdiness and then ascends. At the top, he pushes open a trapdoor in the ceiling. It slams open against the floorboards near his head.

He takes another step and raises his head into the attic.

It's far from a big space, bigger than the one in Basingstoke but nothing like the one in his old home in New Forest, but it serves its purpose, and when the trapdoor is closed, as it is now after he crawls up into the attic, it is dark and quiet; the sounds of the wind outside buffeting the roof dulled by the sturdy structure of the house. This old building will creak and moan but will never fall. Even with his nerves on edge, he knows that to be true.

It's smaller than his old house, but it still feels like home.

And it still serves his purpose.

***

The rain lashing the windscreen reminded her of the night she drove to West Farleigh, wondering frantically where Gale was. It was darker than that night, albeit at around the same time, but the weather was the same, possibly even worse, and it made her feel anxiety deep in her chest.

'What did they say? Thirty miles per hour?' she said, focusing on the stalled traffic ahead.

'Twenty-eight. Twenty-four knots. Ferries might not go out if it reaches that.'

'Christ,' she said, looking down and checking the weather app on her phone. It said the winds were currently twenty miles per hour. They were only five minutes from the Royal Pier in Southampton, but the traffic had not moved for about ten, the rain causing drivers to panic. Or maybe there was an accident up ahead. Or maybe this was the queue for the ferry after all, everyone rushing for that last boat before the winds shut it all down.

They were in Arne's car, deciding that one was enough. Arne's also had better windscreen wipers than Roark's and it was spacious enough to fit her tall frame. She kept moving in her seat as if it wasn't.

'Maybe I should get out and walk,' she said.

'And once you're off the ferry, then what?' Arne said, a note of impatience in his voice. It was the first time she had a sense that Arne didn't have it all together.

They were heading to the Isle of Wight on a long shot.

James Stern was nowhere to be found. His flat in Basingstoke was empty, Stern had left. This was confirmed when McCallish reported back that Stern hadn't shown up to his job at the delivery centre in the past two weeks, except for a few days ago, when he'd signed out one of the vans, a clueless attendant on the site not questioning where he'd been for the past month or so and letting him take the vehicle. An APB had been issued for the van immediately.

They'd stood in the General hospital car park staring at each other over the rooves of their cars. Roark had been swearing, Arne thinking.

'Where would he go?' he said aloud, and Roark answered that she didn't have a fucking clue.

She was livid; having finally obtained the arrest warrant, her suspect had disappeared. She cursed the Basingstoke police, she cursed the idiot at Stern's work who let him take the van two weeks ago, and she cursed herself for no other reason than it was easy to do.

While cursing, she had a thought.

'The letters.'

'Cheryl's letters?' Arne said.

'Yes, the ones Stern sent to her. They'd have his return address on the envelopes, right? Maybe he sent them from a different location, not Basingstoke.'

'Maybe,' he said. 'Worth a shot.'

Roark called her contact in Manchester and asked to check whether any letters had been found at the Palmer residence.

While she waited, Arne clicked his fingers and said, 'His adoptive parents,' and made a quick call.

Roark missed his conversation as the detective in Manchester had come on the line and started to run through items they'd found. No letters had been logged as evidence. Roark cut him off halfway through, apologised, and ended the call.

There were no letters. Roark wondered whether Stern had taken them when he'd ransacked Cheryl Palmer's home. Maybe that's what he was looking for in the front room. Evidence of his connection to Cheryl which he had to get rid of.

'Got it,' Arne said, finishing his call.

'What?'

'Just spoke to my dad. He pulled out his notes on the James Stern case. He took down the details of Stern's last adoption placement before he stopped keeping tabs. Mr and Mrs Bloch. Gerald and Nancy.'

'You think he's with them?' Roark said, not entirely convinced.

'Where else could he hide?' he said. 'One way to find out.'

Arne called his station, spoke to one of his officers and after ten minutes, obtained the current address of Mr and Mrs Bloch.

'An area near Newchurch,' Arne said, hanging up.

'Where's that?'

'Isle of Wight. The same address where Stern was placed with them thirty years ago. We can take the ferry from the pier, fifteen minutes away. Quick, jump in.'

Roark had not protested. Only when she was in the car, sitting next to Arne, did she have questions. One of them was why did the car smell like Norsca, but she kept that to herself.

'We don't know for sure that this was the last family he was placed with, right? He could've moved again after Dane stopped keeping tabs,' she said.

'And kept the Bloch surname?'

'That's true. That would be odd.'

'Anyway, it's the best we've got right now, and it's close. Fifteen minutes to the ferry, one hour on the water, thirty minutes tops from Cowes.'

'We'll be there quite late,' Roark said, checking her phone.

'All the better,' he replied.

'Okay, let's do it.'

They sped out of the carpark and right into Southampton traffic. A ferry was due to leave in fifteen minutes and they were going nowhere. Arne looked ready to lean on his horn. Roark hadn't been fully invested in this line of action at the beginning, but Arne had convinced her. Since the hospital carpark, as the prospect of not only missing a ferry, but ferries being cancelled due to the weather, she was as anxious to get to Newchurch as Arne appeared to be.

About five minutes later, the rain heavier and the wind picking up, they worked their way through a one-way traffic system that had been temporarily put in place for road resurfacing and had been the cause of the go-slow. Although the council workers had been tucked up in their warm, dry homes for more than a few hours, they'd left the job partially done and the one-way system in place.

They reached the terminal dock gate and using Arne's warrant card, they were given priority access to the waiting ferry. Roark checked the weather again, the winds now up to twenty miles per hour out on The Solent, the strait separating the Isle of Wight and mainland England.

It was touch and go. The ferry boarding time of nine o'clock came and went and Roark feared the worst, but eventually, all the waiting cars and trucks received the all-clear and they drove into the belly of a large white ferry, Arne and Roark first cab off the rank.

Arne parked the car right to the end of the boat facing the direction of travel and turned off the car's engine. They took a moment but then exited the car and sat upstairs in the passenger area. They went directly to the onboard café and chose a table near one of the windows on the starboard side. None of them had eaten dinner, so Arne picked up a couple of sandwiches, crisps, and soft drinks for them both.

'Romantic,' Roark said.

'What can I say, it's a classy establishment,' Arne said, looking around at people on nearby tables who were eating similar meals, staring aimlessly out at the water.

The ferry left port and headed across the Strait, chugging away with the fuel efficiency of a steam train. The trip began smooth enough, but by the time they reached the strait, the waves were choppy, and Roark could feel her chicken salad sandwich swilling around in her stomach with the can of Coke she'd drunk.

The hour took forever, but Roark was grateful the ferry was still running. The weather looked atrocious outside, and she suspected that they might end up having to spend the night in Cowes after they spoke with Mr and Mrs Bloch.

Romantic, she said again, but to herself this time.

The ferry docked and they rushed to their car. Arne resisted the urge to spin his wheels as they waited for what seemed an eternity for the gates to open. The approach to East Cowes, one of the northern ports of the Isle of Wight, was choppy to say the least. In better circumstances, Roark wouldn't have cursed the ferry operators for taking so much time over health and safety, but now that they were on the island, she was desperate to head towards Newchurch and the Bloch residence.

They drove out of East Cowes towards the middle of the island, passed residential houses on narrow two-lane roads, Arne keeping the car five miles over the speed limit, driving safely but with urgency. Now that they were on the isle, they weren't up against any deadline, other than their own eagerness to find James Stern.

Residential streets gave way to roads cutting through darkness. Either side were trees and bushes, pushed and pulled by the high winds that buffeted the land. Roark's phone was struggling to obtain a network signal, but at last she was able to check and announced that the winds on the Isle were up to thirty miles per hour.

'No turning back now,' Arne said when Roark told him that the ferries were likely to be all cancelled.

Fifteen minutes of driving, negotiating rain, wind and the occasional slow car, they turned left at a roundabout that seemed like it had been picked up and dropped from another part of the country, and headed east towards Newchurch. Arne had to slow down as the roads narrowed and the open fields on their left allowed the winds to attack the car. The rain had also intensified and when they reached the turnoff to Newchurch, according to Arne's Satnav, they almost missed it.

Even narrower than the other roads, it cut through high trees and gated fields and swerved this way and that. Arne had to drop into first gear on occasion, slowing down to avoid missing a corner and heading into a cluster of bushes.

When the navigation systems announced they had reached their destination, they looked at each other in disbelief. There was nothing here, except a small hidden road off to their right.

'Number six,' Arne said, checking his messages for the address.

They rolled down a slight decline and passed a metal gate with the number one on it.

'Looks like we're going in the right direction.'

Roark had looked up the area where the Bloch's lived on the web. The area was home to several farms that were now only used for residential purposes. Staring out her window, in the rain and darkness that surrounded them, she struggled to find any signs of life, besides gate number one.

Eventually, they passed more gates on either side of the car and then reached the end of the dirt road, facing an old wooden gate bordered by two large pillars. Metal-rusted fences leaned in from either side. Trees devoid of leaves swayed back and forth in the wind as if trying to reach out and scratch the roof of Arne's car. There was no light beyond the car's headlights.

'This is it,' Roark said. 'Stern's here.'

Chapter 56

Arne switched off the headlights and the surroundings disappeared into a black inky well. Only the sound of the wind and rain gave them any sense of direction. Roark leaned forward, peering through the windscreen as the wipers continued to do their job.

'There,' she said, pointing. 'Light. A house. About two hundred metres in.'

'Let's go.'

They used the lights on their phones to lead the way, keeping them pointed down on the ground in front of them, trying not to let anyone in the house see their approach. Roark lost her balance on more than one occasion, the wind funnelling through the surrounding trees and pummelling them from all quarters.

The light that Roark had seen grew stronger but still appeared broken up, intermittent, flickering. They passed a large tree standing stoic against the weather and saw why. The driveway snaked around a collection of trees. Through those trees, they could see the lights of a house, protected from the weather by dense foliage. Protected by the weather and hidden from view.

Instead of taking the driveway, they made their way through the treeline, slipping between thin trunks and low bushes, their feet wet underneath. It was Roark's idea, wanting to get a look at the house, and possibly James Stern, before they approached the house itself.

The Bloch's house was an old brick building that appeared to have seen better days. Single storey with a high roof, it had a thick chimney at its top, guttering that threatened to fall and dark coloured creepers covering most of the flat façade. Light came out from within the house, but only around the frames of the windows as the white panelled shutters covering them were shut against the weather. A small outhouse sat in front like a punished child and Roark swore she saw tiles shift on its roof, disturbed by what little wind made its way through the protection of the surrounding trees.

A one car garage sat separate, almost as an afterthought, and the overgrown driveway led past it towards the house's front door. Inside the garage, Roark could make out a blue, rusted pickup truck which had seen better days.

'No van,' Arne said.

'Probably ditched it,' Roark said.

She had a feeling deep in her gut that told her James Stern was here, hiding out at his adoptive parent's home, thinking he was safe from harm, and no evidence against this, other than an empty house, was going to dissuade her.

'I think he's here,' Arne said, feeling the same.

'Let's go see.'

They backtracked out of the trees and walked up the driveway, phones off, using the faint house lights as a guide. As they neared the front door, the smell coming from the outhouse reached their noses, a putrid, rotting smell.

'Christ,' Roark said, and wished for the wind to pick up to take the smell away.

Arne stepped up to the large brown door of the Bloch residence and knocked three times.

Despite the rain and wind, Roark heard noises from within. Not voices, but movement. Doors closing, furniture scraping along floorboards, what sounded like something breaking.

The door opened.

Standing in the front hallway of the house was a thin rake of a woman, grey stringy hair playing on her shoulders, wearing an open pink cardigan with holes in the elbows and buttons missing, what looked like a once white pain singlet underneath covering small breasts and a dour brown skirt that reached her ankles. She wore no shoes, revealing feet caked with dirt, her teeth were yellow and her eyes were wild. Roark put her at late sixties, but it was difficult to tell.

'Mrs Bloch?' Roark said.

'Yes,' she said, her voice rasping like a three pack a day smoker. Her right hand gripped the door handle with strength, but her other hand twirled the tail of her jumper nervously. Roark had to remind herself that she had cause to be nervous with two tall official looking individuals knocking on her door in the middle of a storm.

She's hiding James Stern, Roark thought, contradicting herself. That's why she's nervous.

'My name is Detective Inspector Krystal Roark, and this is Chief Inspector Arne Cristian,' she said and they both flashed their warrant cards. 'We'd like to talk to you for a moment if that was okay.'

'What about?'

'Could we come inside? It's miserable out here,' Roark said, gesturing to the rain coming down. Water trickled off her forehead to labour the point.

'Not 'til you tell me what this is about,' she said, gripping the door handle tighter, twisting it with a squeak.

'Howard Bloch,' Roark said, not seeing a reason to lie. Her reaction would give her the answer she needed.

'My Howard?' the old woman replied.

'Yes.'

'Is he okay?' she said, a worried look creasing her face.

'We were hoping you could tell us that.'

'Of course, yes, come in, come in,' and she ushered them in quickly, standing aside as Roark and Arne entered her home. 'It is horrible out there.'

'It sure is,' Arne said.

'You're both very tall, aren't you? Here, let me take your coats.'

'Thank you,' Roark said and took off her coat, pulling out her mobile phone before she did so. She checked the network coverage on it just in case she had to make a quick call. It appeared okay, given the weather outside and the remote location.

Nancy Bloch hung their coats up on a hook behind the front door and led them down a short hallway towards the kitchen which was lit brighter than the rest of the house. As they passed another hallway, Roark glanced down it and saw something lying on the floor in the darkness. She couldn't make it out.

'Oh, ignore that,' Mrs Bloch said, seeing Roark's line of sight. 'The place is a bit of a mess.'

The kitchen appeared to not only be the brightest room in the house, but the largest. It stretched out towards a rear door leading outside, a sink and counter lining the right-hand side, cabinets and shelves filling the walls. The kitchen table, which could hold at least six people, was in an odd position, in the far corner of the room, farthest from the sink, benches and oven. It blocked the fireplace, the chimney of which they had seen outside. It appeared disused, set aside, out of the way.

'I was just making tea,' Mrs Bloch said, slinking across to the kitchen bench. Her feet made sticky noises on the linoleum floor. 'Would you like some?'

'We're fine,' Roark said. 'We'll ask you a few questions and be on our way.'

'Are you sure?' she said, filling up the kettle. 'I hope you don't mind if I make one for myself. This cold weather chills my bones.'

'No, of course not,' Roark said, looking down at Nancy Bloch's bare feet again, thinking some woollen socks would help with that chill.

Just behind where Mrs Bloch stood at the kitchen table, Roark noticed scratch marks along the linoleum floor, a shallow groove in the flooring that led away towards the table and fireplace.

'Oh,' Mrs Bloch said in surprise and Roark looked up. She was holding a piece of porcelain and looking into her sink. 'I dropped it when I heard you knock. I've been expecting thunder all night and I thought it was the first of it, gave me a right old fright. I hate the thunder. Always have.'

'We're sorry to have startled you,' Roark said.

'Is Mr Bloch about?' Arne said.

'Oh, no, my poor Gerald passed.'

'I'm sorry to hear that,' Arne said.

'It's been ten years now,' she said. 'Silly sod had a heart attack.'

Nancy Bloch put the full kettle on the bench and flicked the switch to start the boil. She turned to face the two detectives.

'Biscuits?' she said, turning again to a cupboard above the kitchen bench.

'That's very kind of you, Mrs Bloch,' Roark said, 'but we're okay.'

'Please, call me Nancy.'

'Thank you, Nancy, but we'll be quick. Just a few questions.'

Taking his cue, Arne said, 'I'm really sorry, Nancy, I've been caught a bit short. It was a long journey out here. Do you mind?'

'Of course,' Nancy said, and Roark detected a slight change in her tone, a wariness creeping in. 'Down the hallway and to the right. First door. Sorry, it's a bit of a mess down there.'

'Thank you,' Arne said and left the kitchen.

'Mind that ladder,' Nancy called out, then smiled at Roark. 'So hard not having a man around the house.'

'I can imagine,' Roark said, sympathetically. 'Must be difficult out here on your own.'

'Oh, it's not too bad. I'm used to it, but I'm not getting any younger. My joints and bones start to play up, especially in this weather.'

Roark smiled back. Mrs Bloch was hiding something. Not since letting them in had she enquired about her son.

'Can I ask you a few questions about Howard?'

'Yes, yes, of course,' she said and turned her back to Roark as the kettle clicked off. She pulled three cups from the cabinet to her right and placed them in a row on the bench. 'Is he okay?'

'We are trying to locate him. We have some very important questions to ask him.'

'About what?'

'A crime that we believe he may be able to help us with.'

'Oh, he's such a good boy, I can't see him doing anything bad. Earl Grey, okay?'

'I'm fine, Mrs Bloch. Have you seen Howard recently?'

Nancy was silent as she opened a ceramic jar filled with tea bags and dropped one in each of the three mugs.

'Let me see,' she said as she poured the hot water. 'A few months ago now, I would say. He's very busy. Tries to come out as much as he can. I don't blame him, of course. He has his own life to live.'

'Have you spoken to him since then?' Roark asked and felt her phone vibrate in her hand.

She glanced at it, expecting to see Arne calling from elsewhere in the house, but the number was blocked.

'No, he doesn't like talking on the phone. I understand that. We do a good enough catch-up when he comes to visit.'

'Sorry, Nancy,' Roark said, holding up her phone, 'I have to take this.'

'Of course,' Nancy said, stepping away from the sink. 'I'll go get some biscuits from the pantry.'

Before Roark could say anything, Nancy left the three mugs on the counter and walked towards the rear door, her feet padding along the floor, skin sticking to the lino. She disappeared around a corner.

Roark stepped back against the kitchen wall behind her, looked down the hallway towards the front door, and took the call.

'Hello, Detective Inspector Roark speaking,' she said, searching the short hallway for signs of Arne. There was nothing but shadows.

'Hello, Inspector. It's Nurse Ecclestone from General.'

'Oh, hello,' Roark said, turning back to the kitchen. 'Is everything okay?'

'Yes, everything is fine. Cheryl is asleep just now, but she did wake a few minutes ago.'

'Oh?' Roark said.

'She was asking for you. She wanted to speak with you. Something was upsetting her, so I calmed her, but she kept referring to her daughter, that her daughter was in trouble.'

Roark frowned.

'Daughter?'

She tried to make sense of what the nurse was telling her. She stared down at the linoleum floor, seeing the scratch marks leading to the table.

'She kept asking for you to find her daughter,' the nurse said, confusion in her voice.

Roark stared at the scratches on the floor, followed them to the table, directly to the foot of one of the table legs.

She suddenly knew what had caused the scratch marks on the floor. The table had been moved.

'She kept saying that he has her letters. James Stern has her letters.'

The letters. Cheryl's letters.

'The ones he wrote to her?' Roark said, leaning forward a little so she could see under the table. A tablecloth blocked her view.

'No, the braille letters her daughter sent to her. That's what she said. She said her daughter's address is on the letters she sent to her and now James has them. He took them from her home.'

It clicked, almost audibly in her head.

Cheryl Palmer's daughter. She was talking about the baby she'd had in the cellar. The baby now grown up and sending Cheryl letters.

The baby she'd given away. Richard Stern's baby.

With horror, she realised one of her concerns, one of her fears, had been realised. Cheryl and Billy weren't the last targets. The killings hadn't stopped with them. In fact, it may have never truly been about them.

It was the baby Stern was after. The baby Cheryl had with his father, the baby that had loved his father unconditionally, knew nothing else. She was the one that his father had wanted as part of a new family, a family without James. She was the one that stole his father's heart.

She was the one that James blamed the most.

Roark dropped to her knees and looked under the low-hanging tablecloth.

Directly underneath the table was the outline of a cellar door.

'Oh shit, she's here,' she said and scrambled under the table.

CHAPTER 57

'Arne,' Roark yelled over her shoulder. 'Quick. She's here.'

Roark reached out under the kitchen table and found the latch on the cellar door. She pulled it up, but it only rattled, not budging. There was a bolt on the door, and she gripped it and tried to slide it across. It jammed once, then she moved it side to side, and it shuddered along and out of the groove. She unlatched it and pulled the cellar door up. It stuck in its frame for a moment, then dislodged and opened.

Roark banged her shoulders on the bottom of the table as she rose with the door and it slammed back down, almost taking the tips of her fingers. She moved out from underneath, stood up, and pulled the heavy table towards her, trying to move it back to its original position, out of the way so that the cellar door could open. The table legs groaned and screeched against the linoleum, making new scratches on the floor.

There was a noise above her head, a thumping, someone running along the boards, sounding like thunder. Roark instinctively looked up and saw the whites of someone's eye staring down at her through a gap in the ceiling.

A screech filled her ears and Roark stepped back.

Nancy Bloch stepped into the kitchen and screamed again, wielding a long-handled shovel, swinging it wildly at Roark, missing her and taking a piece out of the kitchen wall. Roark dragged the table with her as she moved backwards, right up against the kitchen bench, and Nancy Bloch fell into it as she ran forward, the table hitting her in the stomach. Still, she swung the shovel again, the rusted blade arcing towards Roark's head. Roark put her hand up instinctively and ducked. She felt the blade swing just above her outstretched hand. She landed on one knee, her heart hammering.

Nancy screamed manically across the table and started to climb over it, eyes bloodshot and glaring, spittle dripping from her stretched mouth.

Roark shuffled backwards, moving along the floor towards the kitchen door. She backed up against a wall, felt glass behind her, a sharp corner at the back of her head, part of her noting that she was up against Nancy Bloch's kitchen oven, another part of her yelling that she couldn't be backed into a corner like this, she had to move.

There was a loud crash from within the house, from behind Roark, followed by the sounds of a struggle in the hallway. Someone crashed against a wall.

'Arne,' Roark yelled over her shoulder.

'I'm going after him,' she heard him say, his voice faint.

She turned back and Nancy Bloch was over the table, standing on her kitchen floor in bare feet, raising the shovel over her head.

The lights in the house went out.

Roark moved quickly, rolling to her left towards the kitchen door. The sound of glass shattering and Nancy grunting with effort filled the darkness.

Roark didn't wait. She pushed up with one leg in a runner's stance and lurched forward out of the kitchen and into the hallway that led to the front door. Ahead of her, the door was wide open, heavy rain lashing the overgrown driveway, the surrounding trees bending in the wind, the weather darkening the night sky. The little light that was coming through the doorway was enough for Roark to find her way down the hallway and out of the house.

The rain was cold on her face as she stumbled out onto the driveway. She raised a hand to shield her eyes and looked around, searching the surrounding trees and yard for Arne. There was a crash behind her and she whipped around, seeing the roof of the small outhouse tear from the structure and flip onto the ground. The wind had picked up, the rain coming down harder, the trees surrounding the property unable to protect the house any longer.

The house.

Roark turned quickly, back towards the door to the Bloch house. The door stood open, darkness beyond the threshold, pitch black with no movement. Nancy Bloch was in there, armed with a shovel. Cheryl Davies's daughter was down in the cellar. Roark needed to go in there and save her, but the immediate threat was not in the house. It was out here, in the rain and wind.

He was out here.

She heard a faint voice above the rain and realised she was still holding her mobile phone. The nurse from Southampton was still on the line. With one more glance at the open darkness of the Bloch's front door, Roark started to move away, walking cautiously down the driveway, looking around her, trying to keep her eyes everywhere, scanning the area, looking for Arne, looking for James Stern.

She raised the phone to her ear, told the nurse to call the police, and hung up.

One of the garage doors was banging against the side, competing with the roar of the rain and wind. The battered car sat in there, its headlights staring out, darkness all around it, a place for someone to hide.

The trees lining the front of the property to her right swayed back and forth in competing winds, their leaves heavy and dark with rain. Between the thin trunks, shadows lurched back and forward, left and right.

Roark was halfway down the driveway, turning around in a circle, checking everything around her, the house, the garage, the treeline. Cold rain ran down her forehead and into her eyes.

She decided she would call the police too, just to be sure. She looked down the driveway, the phone halfway to her ear, and then she ran.

At the end of the driveway, there was a fallen figure, lying on its side. Roark skidded on the wet ground and fell to her knees.

'Arne,' she said, breathlessly, and gripped his shoulder.

There was pain etched across his face, his damp hair stuck to his skull, his blue eyes vivid in the light of Roark's phone. He grimaced and gripped his left leg.

'Let me look,' Roark said and slowly moved his hand away. In the darkness, the blood was black on his trouser leg. She pushed his hand back fast and he groaned.

'On your back,' she said, helping him move. 'Keep both of your hands on it. Let's get it elevated. I'm calling for help.'

'I'm,' Arne spluttered, 'okay.'

'You're not okay.'

'He's,' Arne began, then started coughing.

'I know,' Roark said, stabbing her phone with the number, raising it to her ear and scanning around them. 'He's here.'

'Go,' Arne managed.

'No. You've been stabbed.'

'Only . . . just,' he whispered coarsely. 'You came . . . before he could finish . . . me. He ran, around the house.'

Arne started coughing again.

Roark put a hand on his shoulder and turned back to the house.

'Emergency,' the operator said.

'This is Detective Inspector Roark. I need armed response and paramedics here immediately.'

'Where are you located, Detective?'

Roark stated the address as her eyes flitted back and forth between the treeline, the house, the garage. She turned once behind her, saw nothing but the surrounding grounds lashed with rain, then down at Arne.

'We have an officer down, stab wound to the leg, he's stable but bleeding. We need paramedics fast. We need Firearms Command out of Southampton.'

A gust of wind blew rain directly into her face and Roark blinked the water away, raised her free hand to rub her eyes, and turned back to the house.

She stopped. The operator asked if she was still there, that the paramedics were coming but she should stay on the line. Roark lowered the phone to her side, squinted against the wind and rain.

A ghostly figure, a white apparition, a thin streak of light against the enveloping dark, emerged from the house, drifting slowly out into the rain, confused, disoriented.

'Arne,' she whispered.

'Go,' he said.

Without looking at him, afraid that if she turned away the image would disappear, she gave him her phone and stood up. It took a moment before her legs obeyed her order to move, the image before her both joyful and disturbing, but then she was walking quickly up the driveway, breaking into a run, wanting to get to the house as quick as she could.

The figure saw her, took a step back as if scared, then saw who it was approaching and slowly lowered to the ground.

Roark caught her before she collapsed, grabbed her under the armpits to hold her up, slowly lowered her until they were both on their knees and she wrapped her arms tightly around her and squeezed.

'I thought you were gone,' Roark said, speaking through tangled and matted hair.

'Kris,' came a whisper and Roark hugged her tighter.

'It's okay Gale, it's okay, I've got you now.'

Roark moved her cheek and kissed Knight on the head.

'I've got you now.'

'It's Stern,' Knight whispered and Roark could barely hear her over the wind and rain. 'He took me. He kept me down there. He – .'

'Shhhh,' Roark said, rubbing Knight's back, 'it's okay now.'

'My mum.'

'She's okay.'

'A fall?'

'No, no, she's okay. It was all part of it, to lure you out.'

'Kris?'

Roark moved back, softly held Knight's shoulders and faced her.

There was little light and the rain washed across their faces, but it was clear that Knight looked different. She'd lost some weight around her face, her hair was frayed, and her eyes struggled to stay still. Her bottom lip began to quiver. The thin white nightgown she wore, soaking with rain, was not hers. The sight of her chilled Roark's heart and made her sick to her stomach, made the anxiety in her throat rise up, made her think about what she could've done to stop this from happening.

She wanted to say sorry, but instead she said, 'It's going to be okay,' and leant in again and hugged her as tight as she felt Knight could bear, closed her eyes and wanted to cry.

Roark heard movement above the noise of the rain and flashed her eyes open.

Nancy Bloch moved through the rain, swinging the shovel across and down.

Chapter 58

Roark instinctively rolled her shoulder and pushed Knight away. The blade of the shovel deflected off her shoulder, a sharp pain that made her yell out. Before she could move, a heavy body landed on her, forcing her face down into the gravel of the driveway. She felt Nancy Bloch straddling her, her light frame still enough to keep Roark down.

Gritting her teeth against the pain, Roark elbowed behind her, into Nancy's ribs, connecting with skin and bone, once, twice, a third time. Nancy yelled, lost balance, and Roark rolled over, pushing the mad woman off her. Roark landed on her back, rainwater peppering her face.

Nancy was on her before Roark had a chance to move, jumping onto her stomach, straddling her again, and this time she was grinning as she took the shovel by the handle and aimed the blade down at Roark's neck.

A flash of movement and Nancy was knocked off Roark, another body slamming into her and taking her to the ground. Roark didn't pause, getting to her knees quickly so that she could help her saviour, seeing immediately it was Arne, still bleeding from his cut leg, his clothes drenched in rain, his large body on top of the mad woman that was James Stern's adoptive mother.

With a burst of violence, he punched Nancy Bloch in the face twice, immediately wringing his hand, and her struggles ceased and she laid still.

'I've got her,' he said, exasperated. He threw the shovel out of arm's reach and pinned the unconscious woman down with his weight. 'He took her inside.'

Roark didn't know what he was talking about until she scanned the driveway where she'd pushed Knight and found it empty.

'Go,' Arne shouted over the wind and rain, tossing a mobile phone over to her. 'I have my phone. I'll call for help again. Be careful.'

Roark didn't stop to respond. She grabbed her mobile in one hand and the shovel in the other and launched towards the house, almost tripping over.

She had to move quickly. She couldn't let Stern harm Gale. That was not going to happen.

Roark ran into the frame of the open door, her shoulder hitting hard, the pain matching the throbbing in her other shoulder which had taken the brunt of Nancy Bloch's blow.

No time for that now.

Roark thumbed the screen of her phone and the light switched on, illuminating the hallway entrance to the house. There were drops of blood on the floor, maybe from when Arne and Stern had crashed into the wall in their initial struggles, maybe from Gale.

Stepping slowly inside, she followed the blood drops with her light as they trailed around into the other hallway, the one on her right before the kitchen door.

She took further steps into the house and out of the rain, the sound of the weather outside abating in the close confines of the hallway. She raised her phone towards the kitchen, making sure it was clear. There was shattered glass from the oven door everywhere. The table was where Roark had moved it. The cellar door was wide open, resting on the floor.

But they would not be in there.

It wasn't just the trail of blood that told her that. She just knew it.

They were in the attic.

Roark slowly moved up to the corner of the hallway that led deeper into the house. She hesitated, steeled herself, ignored the pain in her body and the fear in her heart, and turned the corner.

Ahead of her, shining in the light from her phone, was the back of a wooden ladder that had been placed under an open door in the ceiling. It was the shape she'd seen on the floor when they had first arrived, kicked aside after Stern had gone up into the attic. This time he hadn't kicked it away. This time he'd left it for her.

'James,' she called, knowing now that she did not have the upper hand. He knew she was coming. He wanted it. There was no point in pretending that she could catch him by surprise.

'I'm coming up,' she yelled.

There was no other choice. She just hoped that Gale was okay, and that, somehow, Roark would be able to talk some sense into Stern, or at least create a chance to hold him until the armed response team arrived, hold him before he did anything stupid.

Roark took a deep breath, hefted the shovel in her right hand, and moved down the hallway. Her breathing was loud in her ears, drowning out the sound of the rain and wind lashing the house. She shined the light down the hallway beyond the ladder, just in case this was a double bluff, but there was no one down there, at least not within the reach of the mobile's light.

She took a position at the base of the ladder and looked up. The darkness above her was complete. She raised her phone and pointed it up through the attic entrance, the light only just reaching the cross beams supporting the roof.

Roark looked back down at the shovel in her hand and tightened her grip on it.

Even with the weapon, she would be vulnerable at the top of the ladder. She didn't have a choice.

Gale was up there with a murderer.

Pocketing her mobile phone, she used one hand to steady herself on the ladder and ascended. The wood creaked under her feet with each step. It would only take a few rungs before she would be through the open attic door, so, balancing herself, she gripped the handle of the shovel closer to the blade and raised it above her head, an attempt at self-preservation.

Even in the dark, she knew when her head had entered the attic. The air changed and the sound of the rain was louder. It was cooler in the attic, the insulation not as good in this old house, but there was also a mustiness and a heavy smell that held the promise of claustrophobia. The rain hammered the roof with unrelenting intensity.

Leaning her back against the attic entrance, the top half of her body through, Roark steadied herself and pulled out her mobile phone, the shovel still raised in front of her.

'James?' she said, quieter this time, loud enough to be heard over the rain.

She switched on the mobile phone's light and he was there, at the other end of the attic floor, standing over ten metres away, too many metres away, a frame larger than she remembered, taller, broader, a short-handled axe held in one hand, the arm of a slouched, Florence Knight in the other, water still dripping from his overcoat onto the wooden floor at his feet.

His face was unrecognisable in the stark brightness of the light, shadows in the pits of his eyes, darkness enveloping around his neck, but it was him. There was no doubt. It was James Stern.

She kept the light on him and he didn't blink or raise his hand. Just stood there and stared.

Gale's eyes were closed, clearly unconscious. Her face from the nose down was covered in blood. Her lower body was on the floor, her upper body pulled up by Stern's grip on her arm.

'Okay, take it easy, James,' Roark said, holding the phone steady. 'I'm going to slowly stand up here, okay, but I'm not moving any closer.'

'Put the shovel down,' James Stern said, his voice steady, commanding, deep, nothing like what Roark had heard in the interview room.

'I can't do that,' Roark said as she took the next step up, the hand holding the shovel steadying her on the attic floor.

'Put it down,' he repeated, the volume of his voice the same, low but penetrating over the sound of the rain hammering the roof.

Roark entered the attic and stood at her full six foot four, her head almost touching the beams above. She stepped forward away from the entrance behind her, holding the phone steady so she always had James Stern in the spotlight.

'Let her go and I will, James.'

'That is not possible.'

Roark took a deep breath, her eyes flitting between Stern's face, the axe, and the bleeding figure of her colleague and friend, the one she thought she had lost.

'This will work out better for you, James, if the killing stops now.'

'It will stop,' he said. 'After you.'

'Okay, alright,' Roark said, ignoring the threat, focussing on what she had to do for Gale right now. 'Let her go and let's talk about that.'

Stern scoffed and grinned, the whites of his teeth shining in the light.

'Do you think I'm going to kill her?'

Roark gripped the shovel harder, bit her bottom lip.

'I'm not going to kill her. Not yet,' Stern said. For the first time, he looked away from Roark and down at Gale. 'She has a bigger purpose than that.'

Stall him, she thought. Keep him talking. Like in the interview room. Keep him talking and his mind distracted.

'And what would that be, James? What's her purpose?'

Stern looked up, across the attic towards Roark and smiled again.

'You'll never know.'

Not moving his eyes off Roark, Stern slowly placed the axe on the ground.

'What are you doing, James?' Roark said, feeling a wave of fear shudder through her.

He let go of Gale's arm, letting her flop to the attic floor without a glance, and pulled a rifle from behind his back, the strap suddenly visible across his chest, shifting around as he raised the gun in Roark's direction.

'Wait,' Roark said.

The report was like thunder inside the house. Roark was already diving to her right, dropping the shovel and her phone. She slammed the floor with her bruised shoulder and felt splinters of wood rain down upon her.

The attic descended into darkness.

Colours bloomed in front of Roark's vision and her ears were ringing with the gunshot. She had to ignore that, had to retreat down through the attic door, but it was behind her and doubling back had its risks. Instead, she moved quickly forward and further to her right, hoping he couldn't hear her over the rain.

'You no longer have purpose, DI Roark,' Stern said, his voice bouncing off the walls she could not see. 'Your usefulness is at an end.'

Roark stopped moving, stopped breathing, tried to calm her thrumming heart and racing mind enough to think clearly.

Back to the attic door. It was the only way out. Go down and wait for the armed police.

'Your role up until this moment has been of great importance, and I did enjoy our conversations.'

Roark, flat on the floor, moved slowly, trying to shuffle around, so that she faced the exit.

'The boy did not,' Stern said, his voice raised in anger and Roark froze, her hand in mid-air for a moment, before she slowly lowered it. As she put pressure on the floor, she touched something soft and slightly damp, a thin mattress laid out in front of her.

'But that,' Stern continued, the volume of his voice lowered, 'that was also useful. Helpful.'

Roark raised her hand again, paused in the blackness.

'You do not know what happens next, but the story is told, and now you know why it was all necessary.'

Her hand came down on a pile of papers that rustled under her fingers.

A flashlight shone in her face, metres away, Stern titling it in his left hand towards her, his arm across in front of him, the rifle resting on it, pointed at her, and Stern lined his eye up along the long barrel and said, 'And now your time has come.'

Roark didn't have time to move or blink or raise her arm. She didn't have time to flinch or close her eyes. She just stared at the light and watched as Stern aimed and prepared to fire.

Nothing happened.

Roark blinked and watched Stern shudder, grunt and pitch slowly forward, the rifle dropping to the ground in front of him as he let go and sunk to his knees. His face contorted in pain, staring straight ahead at Roark, before he slumped onto the floor.

His flashlight rolled away, illuminating the darkness of the attic in a lazy circle, the sloping roof, the dark square hole where Roark had emerged from only moments ago, the discarded shovel, her phone, and finally, the image of Florence Knight, blood smeared across a tight grimace, her nightgown splashed in red, bringing the axe down for a second time into the back of James Stern.

Her eyes wild, Knight managed to bring the blade down two more times before Roark was at her side, staying her hand, holding her tight and telling her that everything was alright now, everything was alright.

CHAPTER 59

It wasn't until the next day, just before lunch, that Roark was allowed to see Gale again. Once the Isle of Wight police arrived, everyone, excluding James Stern, were hurried over to the hospital in Newport in the middle of the island. Roark and Gale were looked after by local doctors, attending to their wounds and overall health, while Arne was stabilised, the gash in his left leg stitched up. He would be fine, the doctors said. It could've been a lot worse, but he would pull through.

Nancy Bloch was kept overnight and observed by doctors and police alike. She'd had a mild concussion from Arne's blows during the heat of battle, blows that Roark knew had saved her life. Nancy Bloch now lay with a sore head and her right wrist handcuffed to the hospital bed.

Gale was kept under closer watch than the rest of them, the extent of her injuries and ill health carefully diagnosed. She'd been kept in James Stern's cellar for over two weeks, ever since he abducted her from near the River Medway. He'd lured her there under the ruse that her mother, Alice Knight, required medical attention after a fall she'd never had. He'd roughed her up, overpowered her and taken her to the cellar in the Bloch house on the Isle of Wight while Roark and everyone else had been discovering the horrors at the Irvine residence in New Forest.

Your usefulness is at an end, Stern had said, and it pained Roark to realise that she had played a role in his mad scheme, distracted by the bodies in New Forest while her partner had been abducted by a madman.

'I'm so sorry,' Roark had said as they'd waited in Arne's car for the police to arrive, blankets over them both. 'I wasn't there for you.'

'It's not your fault, Kris,' Gale said quietly. 'You came for me. You found me.'

She said nothing more, the full impact of the last two weeks and what she had been through sinking in. Roark had put her arm around her shoulders, held her tight, but still, Gale could not stop shivering.

Suffering from malnutrition and some severe bruising and broken bones, it was decided that Gale would be transferred to Southampton hospital with Arne. The winds had not died down and, with the ferry crossings cancelled, they'd all been airlifted, including Roark, after it was decided that Southampton was better equipped to treat them all from this point on.

Roark stayed close to Knight for as long as she could before the doctors took over. She didn't want to let her out of her sight. She was relieved that they had found her but Roark was still worried. Two weeks locked in the cellar, in the dark, not knowing if anyone knew she was alive. Roark couldn't imagine what it was like, and she didn't press Gale to tell her.

Roark didn't ask Gale about what James Stern may have said to her during her time in captivity either. In time, the details of his plan, his motives, could come to light, but now was not the time to inquire as to whether it had been shared with her.

Roark could piece it together though. As she had realised way too late, the target of Stern's actions, his retribution, had been his father's newborn baby, the one forcibly conceived with Cheryl Davies, the one that Richard Stern had loved more than anything in the world, more than his own son, who had watched it all unfold through a hole in the attic floor where he had lived.

Gale had been his target all along.

***

Roark remained in the hospital overnight, tired, exhausted, yearning for bed, but staying so she could keep updated on Gale and Arne. She lay down across three chairs in the waiting room, occasionally drifting off, the dulled pain in her shoulder almost soothing her with its rhythmic throbbing, but waking up, with a start, with the image of James Stern standing over her burnt into her mind.

He was on the premises too, she knew, in the General hospital's coroner's wing, ready for transportation to the morgue. ME Clayton had spent several hours performing an autopsy to ascertain the cause of death.

'Four big fucking holes in his back,' was his medical conclusion.

Roark knew it would take some time, but the seven murders would be traced back to Howard Bloch, formerly James Stern, through DNA samples taken from his dead body and matched to those found at the numerous crime scenes of Roark's case. Even though it troubled her, motive, Roark decided, was irrelevant in the end. As she had always said, the evidence would make the case. Stern's reasons for doing what he did were enough to put the cherry on top – if they were ever truly known – but were not entirely important other than to support the arrest warrant that set the case in motion.

Forget about the why until you arrest the guy.

Evidence was paramount; motive was the sideshow.

Not for Gale it isn't, Roark thought.

One other person was still staying at the Southampton hospital when they had all arrived. She'd been there during the whole ordeal since the bodies were discovered in New Forest. After a restless sleep on the chairs, just before the hospital kitchen did the rounds for lunch on the following day, Roark decided to arrange a visit.

After several enquiries, she found her way to the hospital room of Florence Knight and walked in. The curtains were drawn around her bed, but Roark knew she could part them. She was expected, having sent a text to Gale early in the morning, letting her know she was coming to visit, no questions asked. She could hear quiet voices on the other side of the curtain, mindful of two other residents in the room, both who were elderly and fast asleep.

Roark moved the curtain aside and the two people behind them turned to her.

'Kris,' Alice Knight said, slowly getting up from her chair and coming around the end of the bed.

'You made it,' Roark said.

Alice hugged her as tight as she could, weak arms around Roark's waist. 'Thank you for finding my girl.'

'My pleasure, Alice,' Roark said.

Gale smiled at her from her bed, not a grin, but a tired parting of her lips, barely visible within the bruising around her nose, cheeks and mouth. She'd been through a lot, but thankfully, the initial screenings showed the only severe injuries had been to her face. Not all injuries were physical though, but Roark didn't want to think about that just now.

'How you going, partner?' Roark said, taking the chair on the other side of the bed to Alice.

'Hungry a lot of the time,' Gale said. 'It hurts to eat.'

'You've been through a lot,' she said.

'You could say that,' Gale said.

'We don't need to talk about it. I'm sure some local detectives will want to speak to you, of course.'

'It makes me sick to think about what he did,' Alice said, shaking her head.

'The detectives came earlier this morning, locals from Southampton,' Gale said. 'I spoke for a little bit. Will you be needing something from me, for the case, I mean?'

Roark nodded and said, 'Lucas will be here at some point. A detective from Bristol too, DI Moody. She's great, you'll love her. You can talk when you're ready.'

Gale's nod was almost imperceptible.

'Well,' Roark said, clearing her throat, 'you think you're up to visiting someone today?'

Gale pushed herself further in her bed and looked at her mother, before turning back to Roark.

'I guess so,' she said, tentatively, 'although my face may spook them.'

'I'm not sure that's going to be a problem.'

Realisation slowly dawned on Gale's face and she nodded while looking down at her hands.

'She's here,' she said.

'Yes, she is. She's been through a lot.'

'I know,' Gale said. 'Mum told me.'

Alice Knight turned to Roark apologetically.

'I know you told me in confidence, to protect me,' Alice said, 'but I thought she had a right to know.'

'Of course she does.'

'I also know,' Gale said, her voice quivering as she almost couldn't finish the sentence. 'I also know what she went through before. Truly know. For the first time.'

Roark touched her arm, so did Alice.

'We can do it another time,' Roark said. 'She would understand.'

'No.' Gale pulled back the cover of her hospital bed. 'I want to see her.'

Although she didn't really need the help, Roark and Alice guided her into a waiting wheelchair. Roark told the nurse that they would be back soon, they were just going for a brief visit to another patient.

They left the hospital room behind, Roark pushing Gale along, Alice by their side. They walked in silence for a moment, observing the doctors and nurses going about their business around them.

'It's just around this corner.'

'Can we wait for just a moment?' Gale said, looking up at Roark.

'Sure,' Roark said, slowing down.

'I want to tell you something.'

'Okay,' Roark said, and she stopped the wheelchair next to a bank of empty seats. She put the lock on and moved around in front of Gale before sitting down next to her.

'I'll wait over there,' Alice said, pointing ahead of them.

'Thanks, Mum,' Gale said.

Alice walked off and around the next corner, both of them watching her.

'I don't know if anyone told you,' Gale said.

'No,' Roark said, suddenly concerned. She touched her arm. Gale put her hand over Roark's.

'The doctor confirmed what I already know, but I thought they may have shared it with you.'

'No, they haven't Gale. Is everything okay?'

'This is in the vault, okay? Mum knows, but no one else, okay?'

'In the vault.'

Gale took a deep breath. Roark studied her bruised face, trying to read what may be coming. She had an idea and it sat heavy in her stomach.

She has a bigger purpose.

'He raped me,' Gale said.

Roark squeezed Gale's arm, held back tears that threatened to spill, kept quiet so Gale could say it all.

'Many times. He wanted me to give him a child,' Gale said. 'Just like his father wanted. Like his father got. With me.'

'I'm so sorry, Gale,' Roark said, not able to think of anything comforting to say.

'He said he was going to kill it as soon as it was born. To show me what his father should've done, what he should've done himself if he'd had the chance.'

Gale studied her own hands, her eyes unfocused, her face slack. Her voice was close to devoid of emotion, but it wavered a little and Roark could see tears begging to fall from her eyes.

'That didn't happen,' Roark said. 'I found you, so that didn't happen.'

'I know what my mother went through now, what Cheryl went through. I can't blame her for what she did, giving me away, given what happened to her. I don't know if I won't do the same thing.'

She dropped her head, her shoulders shuddering as the tears came.

'Hey,' Roark said, rubbing Gale's arm, 'this is different. Cheryl had nothing, no support. She had no choice. You have a choice, okay? And you have support.'

'I don't know if that's worse,' Gale said.

'Look,' Roark said. 'Gale, look at me.'

Gale raised her head, her eyes red amongst the dark bruising.

'It's too early to know, okay? We don't know if it's true or not.'

Gale turned away and shook her head.

'But,' Roark said, leaning forward so Gale could see her, 'but if it does happen, I'm here to help.'

Gale nodded and carefully wiped the tears from her eyes.

'More importantly, you have two women,' Roark said, pointing to where Alice Knight had walked, 'who love you very much and will do everything they can to support you. Okay?'

Gale nodded again, tears replacing the ones wiped away.

'Okay, let's clean you up and go say hello.'

Roark took out some tissues from her coat pocket and helped wipe Gale's face. She squeezed Gale's shoulder and took her position behind the wheelchair, unlocking the brake.

'Ready?'

Gale sniffed and said, 'Yeah, I'm ready.'

Alice Knight met them at the next corner, squeezing Gale's hand while speaking to Roark.

'She's in that room. I think she's just waking up.'

'I'll let you both speak with her,' Roark said, taking her hands off the wheelchair.

'Oh, it's okay,' Alice said. 'You're family, Kris.'

'Thank you for saying that, Alice,' Roark said and she gave Gale's mother a warm hug. 'But this is for you three, and I've got someone else to see.'

'Thank you, Kris,' Gale said, looking up from the wheelchair. 'For everything.'

'No, thank you, Gale,' she said. 'You saved my life remember.'

'Yeah,' Gale said, looking off down the corridor. 'I guess.'

'Hey, I almost forgot.'

Roark dug deep into her other jacket pocket and pulled out a pile of individually folded pieces of paper.

'Found these in the dark up there, in the attic,' she said. 'Your letters. Yours's and Cheryl's. She will be so pleased to see them.'

'Thank you,' Gale said, carefully taking them in her hands. She rested them on her lap.

'And she'll be glad to see you too,' Roark said.

She said her goodbyes and walked away before the tears spilled freely.

CHAPTER 60

Arne Cristian was sitting in the reception area of the hospital, his jacket folded on his lap, reading a magazine. His left leg was stretched out in front of him, bandages invisible under his trouser leg. He was wearing new clothes, not the ones covered in blood and rain from last night.

Roark walked up to him silently, studying the flock of blond hair on his head, his slightly pinkish ears, his strong hands leafing through the pages. She sat down next to him and he looked up, closed the magazine and put it aside.

'What's with the new suit?' she said.

'Dad brought it,' Arne said, shifting in his seat and wincing a little. 'Sorry, he didn't have anything for you.'

'You're not my size anyway. He's here?'

Roark looked around the reception area but couldn't see the rugged good looks of Dane Cristian. A face she suddenly missed.

'Gone to get some coffee. How's the shoulder?'

'Fine. How's your leg?'

'Sore, but I'll live.'

'So will I. Thanks to you.'

Arne closed his mouth and nodded.

'I mean it. Thank you.'

Arne reached across and squeezed her hand.

'You've been crying,' he said softly. 'Is everything okay?'

'Yes, it is,' Roark said. She looked across to the corridor of the hospital she'd just walked down. 'I think it is.'

'How is your partner? Detective Knight?'

'She seems okay, physically. She's keeping it together. There's a lot she'll need to work through.'

Roark stopped there, not unlocking the vault, not for Cristian, not yet.

They sat in silence, lost in their own thoughts, comfortably sharing the moment.

Cristian shifted in his seat again. Roark turned to him. He nodded towards the hospital exit.

'I'm staying at my father's house tonight,' he said. 'He's cooking an early dinner. He used to be a chef, before he joined the police.'

Roark raised an eyebrow.

'But he prefers the simple dishes. He's cooking Farikal.'

'I don't know what that is,' Roark said with a light laugh.

'Unless you're vegetarian, you'll love it.'

'Sounds tempting.'

'You can also have my home office for as long as you like, to make any calls.'

'Okay,' Roark said without hesitation. 'That sounds lovely. Thank you, Arne.'

'There's plenty of space too, if you want to crash. Norwegian coffee and fresh air in the morning. We could go for a walk in the woods if you'd like.'

'I would love that.'

They both stood, jackets in their hands, Arne taking a little longer, slowly bending his leg.

'Dane's driving?' Roark said.

'Yep. We'll pick up our cars later. Mine's still on the Isle of Wight.'

'Mine belongs to the station. Someone else can pick it up.'

'Good,' Arne said. 'Oh, here he is.'

Dane Cristian walked down the corridor of the hospital holding two small cardboard cups of coffee. He placed them on a table by the chairs and soundlessly gave Roark a warm hug. Her shoulder complained but Roark didn't.

'Let's go,' Dane said. 'We're leaving that swill behind and having some real coffee.'

'You know the way to a girl's heart,' Roark said, smiling.

They walked out of the hospital together, out through the sliding doors and into the car park.

Later that night, after Dane Cristian had fallen asleep in front of the fire, his belly full of mutton and cabbage and white wine, Roark and Arne talked into the night while the fire crackled, talked about a lot of things, some things that were hurtful, personal, and made Roark cry, but this time she had a shoulder to cry into and the crying felt good.

What they didn't talk about was what had walked out of the cellar and what she had found in the attic.

The End.

330

ACKNOWLEDGEMENTS

Thank you to James Shaw, Anthony Barlow and everyone at Matthew James Publishing for giving me the opportunity to share my novel with the world; to the subscribers of my monthly newsletter for their eagerness to know more about this novel and my writing process; to Christy and Paul, Joosje, and Heather D, who I can always count on for positivity, support and belief; and to my family, Mum and Dad, Narelle, Craig, Jade and Adam, Cathy and Ben, and all my extended family who have supported me from Day One, not just with my writing, but in everything.

Finally, much love to Kathy and Marcus, the loves of my life, who supported, encouraged and inspired me on my journey to becoming a published author.

www.ingramcontent.com/pod-product-compliance
Lightning Source LLC
Chambersburg PA
CBHW050549260626
47157CB00002B/492